David Docherty is an accomplished academic who has published several important books on the media. He is now the managing director of broadband content at Telewest. He was previously the Director of New Media and Deputy Director of Television at the BBC, London.

THE SPIRIT DEATH

David Docherty

POCKET
B O O K S

LONDON · SYDNEY · NEW YORK · TOKYO · SINGAPORE · TORONTO

First published in Great Britain by Simon & Schuster UK Ltd, 2000

This edition first published by Pocket Books, 2001

An imprint of Simon & Schuster UK Ltd
A Viacom Company

3 5 7 9 10 8 6 4 2

Simon & Schuster UK Ltd
Africa House
64–78 Kingsway
London WC2B 6AH

Simon & Schuster Australia
Sydney

A CIP catalogue record for this book is available from the British Library

ISBN 0-671-02945-2

Typeset in Garamond 3 by SX Composing DTP, Rayleigh, Essex
Printed and bound in Great Britain by
Omnia Books Limited, Glasgow

For Kate

ACKNOWLEDGEMENTS

I would like to thank Dr Sue Stuart-Smith, Serge Hill, and Dr Richard S.G. Knight of the CJD Surveillance Unit in Edinburgh for their invaluable comments on the medical elements of this story. All mistakes are of course down to me. My agents, Julian Friedmann, Conrad Williams and Carole Blake, have provided rock solid support over the years and know that I wouldn't have finished this without them. Anna Kiernan at Simon and Schuster has been a terrific editor. But this book would not have been written without the faith of Nick Webb.

'Each thing hostile to every other thing.'

Ovid: Metamorphoses

Part One

THE SECOND DEATH

CHAPTER ONE

Mike Davenport had been dead before. In a small dirt-poor Bolivian town his exhausted body, savaged by the Machupo virus, had crashed – blood seeping from his eyes, nose and anus.

He could remember nothing of his first death. But this time, two years on, he hovered above the hospital bed and looked down on his bloated face that had twisted until he was barely recognisable. His arms and legs were contorted like those of a beaten-up doll.

Mike watched Tess, his sister, sit ashen and silent by his bedside and his twelve-year-old twin daughters, Jo and Molly, cling to each other's hands and keen softly. Sucked prematurely from his body, his spirit sought peace. As he stared at the flat lines on the monitor that told him his physical heart had stopped beating, he was filled with overwhelming panic. He screamed silent encouragement at the doctors and nurses trying to revive him. And he howled for his sister; but Tess could not hear him: his words had no physical reality.

Then someone said: 'Darling.'

As the gentle voice summoned him, he turned, floating like an astronaut in space, and saw a light high and to his left. It broke open like a chrysalis and his wife, Anne, shone in the middle of the nimbus. The last time he had seen her body had been twenty months before in a morgue in Southampton – her short, blond hair a tangled mass of blood and brain after an articulated lorry jack-knifed into her Renault. But now she looked as she did on the day he met her. She wore a short, blue shift dress that clung to her small breasts and emphasised the elegance of her long, thin legs.

He wanted to say sorry for all the months they had spent apart; for all the times he did not or could not call because he was in a remote village; for missing a wedding anniversary when he was in South America dealing with another crisis. He was desperate to tell her she was unique and that on the day of her funeral he had sat on his bed with a bottle of Scotch and a handful of sleeping pills, longing to be with her.

Her elfin face was subtle. 'Make it up to me,' she said and held out her arms. The struggle in his soul between death and life was overwhelming. But as he moved towards her, desperate once again to smell the freshness of her body, Anne's skin began to bubble and melt and slip from her skull and drip from her arms and legs. He wanted to vomit again, as he had done so many times in the past year. Shaking and shivering, he turned back to his cadaver on the bed: it opened its eyes in a wild, abandoned stare and a single drop of blood leaked down its cheeks. Mike screamed into the void.

'Mike, Mike.' A soft, female voice, flat in its calculated monotony, edged through to his consciousness. 'I'm going to bring you down now. When I touch your hand you will acknowledge my presence.'

His body was hurtling to the ground like a pilot in an out-of-control helicopter. He was turning, crashing and screaming towards his grave.

'Mike.' The voice was more urgent now. 'C'mon, Mike.' He

heard the echo of flesh on flesh as someone clapped their hands. What was the sound? He recognised it. It was safety. He heard music. Warm washes of chords began to soothe him as the opening of Brahms's Fourth Symphony sought him out.

He opened his eyes wide, turned his shoulders, and threw up in the white plastic basin by the side of the sofa. As he retched, Dr Sheila Spielman said: 'Easy, Mike. Easy.' She rubbed his back gently. 'It'll take time.' He looked up at the soft, moon face of Sheila, his friend and a psychiatrist at King Henry's Hospital, where they both worked. Her eyes told him a truth he did not want to accept. The vomit welled up and he turned again to the basin. This time Brahms was no consolation.

CHAPTER TWO

The following day, Mike hauled himself out of bed at seven in the morning, pulled a pair of black shorts over his long legs, and a grubby, white running vest over his chest. His body had still not recovered entirely from the aftermath of the Machupo attack and he was trying to build up and retain some basic fitness.

He surveyed the debris on the floor of his bedroom: four empty, crushed Coke cans, the remains of a packet of Rolos, three coffee cups and a tangled blue tie he had worn the previous night to go out to dinner. A call from a doctor in Sierra Leone had come in just as he was about to have a meal with his girlfriend, Jane. Mike had been up from eleven until two in the morning on a conference call to give advice on the latest research on Lassa fever. He cursed the civil war that was creating the conditions for the rampant resurgence of a disease that had been kept under control for so long.

As he stepped from the door of his house, the low morning sun bounced from the windows of a grey Saab opposite and blinded him. He took a deep breath and coughed a little as the polluted grit of a city trapped in a month-long heatwave settled on his throat. He began a laboured jog, hating every second of it but forcing himself into the park on Primrose Hill and up the first gentle incline. Sweat immediately seeped down his chest and forehead as the oppressive heat took its toll; his luxuriant blond hair became quickly matted against his neck. When he reached the brow of the hill, he looked down on central London, trapped in the haze of noxious yellow smog that had settled across the city's skyline.

He turned right and took the path towards the lattice-work aviary of London Zoo while he considered his options. They did not seem to glitter. What does a retired virus cowboy do, he thought? Fifteen years of chasing the bloody things from Central America to Africa and now I'm tied to a desk for the rest of my life. When it gets out that I can't hack it any more, he thought grimly, I'll be given a nice, safe task handling nothing more threatening than a grant application form. He wondered whether he could take up a research job with Laura Holmes, a fellow WHO doctor, who had resuscitated him when he died in Bolivia. Laura was at the forefront of research into the new DNA vaccines. It had been a long time since they had last talked. Not since . . . No, the thoughts were too painful. He did not want to dwell on their parting. I was such a prat, he thought. But he was glad that Tess had brought about the beginnings of reconciliation. He planned to call Laura that night. Perhaps she had heard of something on the grapevine that he could do.

Mike could hear a fast padding sound behind him. A young man in his twenties wearing red shorts and no top sprinted past him, hardly blowing. Mike edged up on the other guy's shoulder, glad to be opening up his lungs. The young runner did not appear to notice his presence, but he, too, nudged up his speed and nosed ahead of Mike, who started to breathe harder. As they remained in step for a minute, Mike began to feel good, felt like he could still cut it.

The guy turned, smiled his contempt, and put five metres between them. Gritting his teeth, Mike lunged forward until again he was almost shoulder to shoulder with the other jogger, who turned and said, 'Bye,' then pinned back his shoulders and sprinted through the gate.

Mike collapsed against a thin Victorian lamp-post and almost fainted. As he struggled to catch his breath, he giggled about being a macho prick. But in his heart he was glad he was still challenging kids. It made him feel alive. Two years earlier Mike had been dead for no more than a few minutes. But dead was dead, as he constantly reminded himself these days when the darkling dreams shattered his sleep. The Orphic nightmares had begun when Anne died. First, they were infrequent; the product of long hours in the lab. Then, six months ago, he had accidentally speared himself with a needle containing a low-grade bacterium. Although he was only slightly ill for a few days, the incident shifted his psychological state from caution to fear. Now, Mike realised, his career was over and Sheila could do nothing about it. Her use of hypnosis was designed to help him confront his growing anguish; but it was no use. If anything, he was getting worse. He had made up his mind after the session with Sheila the previous day. It was time to move on.

He gathered himself for the jog home and began to compose his resignation letter in his head. It hurt like hell that he would have to leave. There had been a lot of begging phone calls and political compromises to raise the money from the WHO and the NHS for the London Centre for Infectious Diseases. He did not want to leave with the job half done, but he could see no alternative.

Labouring back towards home, he fantasised about the ice-cold Coke in the fridge. In a way, despite the feeling of loss that hovered around him like a swarm of flies, he was rather looking forward to telling his boss to take his job and shove it. He recalled his pain on the day that James Graham had been parachuted in as Head of the Centre. Graham, widely credited with helping the government in resolving the BSE crisis, was given the Centre as a reward. Mike had to settle for Deputy Head.

He turned up the volume on his Walkman and Springsteen's 'Born to Run' mocked his loping stride; then he headed out of the park, up his leafy street, and into the short drive towards his two-storey white Edwardian house with its Gothic windows and stained-glass door. He surveyed its neat, comfortable elegance and realised he wouldn't be able to afford the mortgage. What would he tell the girls? They would need a family conference that night.

CHAPTER THREE

In the early morning chaos of A & E at King Henry's Hospital, Staff Nurse Tess Davenport had spent the night dealing with the usual cases: breaks, burns and bile. Tall and slim like her brother Mike, she moved gracefully but firmly through a waiting room of people who looked tired and anxious. Her red hair was cropped into a short bob. She bent over a desk and wrote a quick note on a patient's file and then ushered an old woman towards a cubicle. Her hands were large for a woman, and strong from hours in the gym, but she was gentle with the brittle bones of the stooped, coughing figure she guided across to one of the other nurses. Tired though she was after a long night shift, Tess found herself looking forward to twenty minutes of back-chat with Mike's two daughters – who were closer to her heart than she could ever have imagined possible. At twenty-seven, Tess was acting as a surrogate mother. After the car accident, her brother was incapable of sorting himself out, let alone two eleven-year-olds, and she had transferred to Mike's hospital and moved in with them.

Out of the corner of her eye, she saw Bill Green, one of the ambulance drivers, holding up a handsome, well-built man in his mid-twenties and then heard the driver ask: 'What's wrong with you, sir?' The man staggered like a drunk and fell on the grimy off-white floor, where he shook as if having an epileptic fit. Tess was quickly by the driver's side, helping him to pick up the patient and take him into a cubicle, where they put him on a bed. She quizzed Bill as she triaged the patient: 'What's his name?'

'He won't or can't talk and the woman who dropped him off drove away before she could answer any questions,' the driver replied.

Tess searched in the pocket of the patient's leather jacket and found a wallet of credit cards made out to Peter Palowsky. 'Well, Mr Palowsky, you don't seem in the best of health, do you?' She checked the thermometer. 'Forty degrees. You are most definitely not a well boy.' Her voice was deep and throaty.

As she looked into Palowsky's jet-black pupils, Bill asked: 'Are you on for a drink tonight?'

Tess bent over and continued to chatter to the young man, who was sweating and staring into the middle distance. His body was shaking in a bizarre, random fashion. 'His pupils are unfocused,' Tess noted, and then added, 'I wouldn't go into a pub with you if it was the last place on earth that sold lager.' She looked up and her blue-grey eyes glinted mischievously. 'And you know how much I love lager.'

'What've you got against me?'

'You're fat, bald and married – not exactly a recipe to set a girl's heart racing. Do me a favour and find the SHO for me.' This was definitely one for the Senior House Officer, she thought as Bill's bleeper sounded.

He read the message. 'Sorry. Got to go,' he said. 'Car crash on the Euston Road.'

As Palowsky coughed up greenish mucus, Tess completed her preliminary examination. 'What've you got to say for yourself, Mr Palowsky? What's your story?'

The man stared back at her, a strange, fixed smile on his face; his head flopped to one side like a broken toy. She felt his arms and neck. He was burning and the heat was rising from his skin. This was a fever and a half. 'Straight to a ward for you, my boy.' Then he began retching a reddish-black bile through which Tess could see blood flowing slowly like a stream on the tiled floor. He was shaking and coughing violently – sending spumes of vomit from between his lips. Tess almost slipped on the floor as Palowsky's convulsions intensified and she shouted for help. Two nurses rushed in to give her support. 'He's going into shock. Prepare four units of blood and let's get him into Crash,' she shouted as she tried to restrain Palowsky and was rewarded with a faceful of bile.

Half an hour later, Palowsky was linked via a series of tubes and monitors to machines that were trying to save his life. His signs are all over the place, Tess thought. But at least the vomiting and shivering have stopped. The sedation had hit him and his blood pressure had stabilised.

Jack Lim – a wiry, forty-five-year-old Malaysian doctor who had been with the hospital's Centre for Infectious Diseases for a year – strode into the room. He was given immediate charge of the situation by those around him. 'What are we looking at here, Dr O'Mara?' he asked the Senior House Officer, who had been sufficiently concerned by the curious symptoms to summon Jack. The tone of his voice was a light baritone; his English accent was pure North Oxford, the consequence, Tess knew, of ten years as a perpetual university student in the 1970s.

'Fucked if I know,' Liz O'Mara whispered to Tess in her Dublin accent.

'What was that?' Jack's eyes did not leave the patient.

'I'm afraid it's out of my league, Dr Lim.' Liz sounded contrite.

'Good for you, Dr O'Mara. When you are in the realm of

abject ignorance, tell the truth. Otherwise you'll end up killing even more people than is your quota as an SHO.' Jack looked at Tess and her warm smile was quickly smothered under her serious professional face. It would not be a good idea for the whole of the unit to know that she had spent the best part of the previous evening making love to Jack in an expensive hotel in the West End.

Jack's face had an elegant structure – light skin stretched on a fine frame of cheekbones. She loved to stroke his arms and long, tapering fingers. Only she knew he chewed the edges of his right thumbnail when he was tense. Only she saw him drunk and roaring on the anniversary of the death of a young boy he had misdiagnosed and who died in agony. Jack had a reputation for being cool and self-contained, but she had seen him weep with pleasure, groan with lust and grin like a dope as they lay in bed.

'Nurse Davenport, will you take blood, urine, faeces and tissue samples, please?' His voice cut through her reverie.

'Why doesn't she just hand her uniform to Haematology?' Liz asked.

Jack looked startled as he turned again to Tess and this time noticed that she was covered in red and black stains and that her hair was matted with vomit. 'I take your point,' he said. 'I think it's best if you clean up, Nurse Davenport.' He turned to Palowsky and began to examine him. 'Now, Mr Palowsky, where have you been, my friend? Where have you been? And what has returned with you?'

CHAPTER FOUR

Louis Fernandez, tall, white-haired, smooth-faced and with the bearing of a soldier, nursed a cold cup of coffee in the staff cafeteria of King Henry's and wondered how to kidnap and kill Dragoslav Uzelac, also known as Peter Palowsky. Uzelac had been rushed to the hospital just as Fernandez was making his final preparations to assassinate him. Fernandez had tracked his man halfway across the world, using every means at the Company's disposal.

He was listening to the Northern tones of a young white woman who was taking care of Uzelac as she chatted to a black companion sucking smoke from a cigarette deep into her lungs. 'I've never seen anything like this Palowsky guy,' she said. 'One minute he's shaking like a leaf, and the next he's staring into space with this really spooky smile.' The nurse's white face was tired and as worn as a dish rag. 'Jack Lim said that it's eighty–twenty at best as to whether he'll survive the day.' She rubbed at her temples with hard fingers.

'Is Mike Davenport on the case?' asked the black woman,

who, Fernandez noted, looked African – possibly Kenyan.

'Jack's putting in a call later today. Mike's a real hound for this stuff; he'll find out what the guy's got.' She attacked an iced bun.

'I don't know how you can work for Davenport's Centre. I wish he'd never got started.' The Kenyan crunched her biscuit wrapper inside a chipped, white coffee cup. 'It gives me the creeps every time I hear of that Ebola virus and stuff. There's enough of that at home, without someone playing with fire here.'

'He's really driven and wants to make a difference,' the white nurse said. She grinned. 'And he's got a great bum.'

The Kenyan laughed. 'White women have no standards.'

Fernandez walked past the couple, stumbled on the leg of a chair and spilled some coffee on the Northern nurse's green uniform. As he apologised profusely, smiled winningly and offered to pay for the damage, he read her name tag: Gillian Trimble. That was all the information he needed to begin a computer search.

Outside, in the blazing sunshine, he put on a pair of dark glasses and headed up the hill to a pavement café where an Indian woman was cleaning a white, ironwork table with a large, yellow cloth. She turned, smiled, and offered him a seat. Fernandez nodded his head a little in acknowledgement and ordered a glass of iced water. Opening his palm-sized personal organiser, he e-mailed the Company's security force:

Find out details on:

Dr Jack Lim, Dr Mike Davenport. Both of King Henry's Hospital.
Find out condition of Uzelac/Palowsky.
Find out what they do with bodies.
What do they think Uzelac/Palowsky has? Do they have any understanding of what they are dealing with?

The Indian woman put the glass in front of him and he said, 'Thank you so much. You are very kind,' in an accent that would not have been out of place at Sandhurst, but would have surprised anyone who knew Fernandez from the Buenos Aires slum in which he was born.

Her melancholic brown eyes registered unexpected pleasure at his politeness. 'You're welcome,' she said. 'Very welcome.'

Fernandez sipped the water, grateful for its coolness, and looked around him. Londoners, he mused, wore a curious mix of clothing that betrayed people who could not trust that each day would be hotter than the next, and who therefore were hopelessly caught in a jumbled confusion of suits, ties, bare white legs, sweaty shirts and short tops. Some of the men even wore dark, heavy suits that made them look as if they had time-travelled in from a winter's day. Their faces were red and sweaty. If they can't cope with the sun, how would they deal with death?

CHAPTER FIVE

Wearing a loose-fitting pair of black trousers and a clean shirt, his hair dripping slightly at the ends, Mike spooned milk-sodden Sugar Puffs into his mouth and walked down the short, white hallway of his house looking for Molly and Jo. He put his head round the door of the curious little box room that was their private space and watched their blond heads staring into the computer. His girls' pert, inquisitive faces briefly acknowledged their father's existence before they were again absorbed in the screen.

Tess wandered in behind him, having just returned from her shift. 'They're too busy destroying the fourth zone of the dark planet to acknowledge that they are flesh and blood children of an ordinary man. Jo is the Grand Mistress Vulcana and Molly is, apparently, the Grand Vizier of Fang,' Tess said.

'I've just been promoted to Empress.' Molly beamed.

'She speaks. She speaks.' Tess smiled. 'It's a miracle. Call off the Child Psychology Unit.'

'Uh oh. It's Queen Sarcasm time again,' Jo said to Molly in a stage whisper.

'That's Aunt Queen Sarcasm to you, titch. Now be nice to your dad and make him think you love him. Otherwise, I'll turn your software into the electronic equivalent of confetti.'

'Dad,' they cried in unison. 'No one told us you were back from your jog.'

'Very funny,' Mike said, kissing each on the head in turn. 'Now, don't be any more precocious than you should.'

'What's precocious, Jo?' asked Molly.

Jo mugged a dumb double-take and said: 'Duh. I think it means he thinks we're kind of priceless.'

'Oh, that's all right then; for a second I thought he was accusing us of being unnecessarily well-developed intellectually for our age.' Molly's long legs and gangly, half-formed body emerged from behind the computer desk and she gave her father a hug.

'I don't know where you get this sarcasm from,' Mike said, casting sidelong glances at his sister.

'The dark side of your psyche, sweetheart,' Tess replied. 'They are what you, deep down, aspire to be.' She looked in the small, pine mirror beside a bookcase that contained a jumbled collection of tattered children's books and winced as she saw the mess the morning's events had made of her expensively cut thatch of hair.

'God preserve me from the consequences of my own genes.' Mike grinned.

Tess gathered together her Prada bag, black Comme Des Garçons jacket and skirt and presented them for inspection to the girls. They had cost a fortune, but it was worth it. 'What do you think?' she asked. 'This is what I'm going to wear tonight.'

Jo thought for a second and said: 'On a slightly older woman a black skirt that short might look out of place. And on a less confident person shocking-pink lipstick could be thought, what's the word, Molly?'

'Tarty?' Molly replied and then giggled — her face turning a light shade of beetroot.

'That's it, tarty. A great choice of words, Moll.'

Mike grinned again. 'You'll look fabulous. A real babe. Don't listen to those two fashion victims. I like the eccentric look.'

'Ahh.' Tess hissed and cast her eyes to heaven. 'Eccentric. Thanks a bundle.' A conspiratorial grin spread across the faces of the other three. 'Get ready for school, you two,' she ordered, then she took Mike by the arm, steered him outside and whispered: 'You look like shit. Did you get any sleep last night? Take the morning off; nothing's that important. If you push yourself too hard you'll collapse again. Think of the girls. It's been really tough on them since Anne's death.'

He nodded, wearily. But he knew he would go in. He could not stand being alone in the house. 'Am I on twin watch later?' he asked.

'No. I'll pick them up from school,' Tess replied. 'Just be back by six.'

'The mystery man?' he enquired.

'As I know exactly who he is, how can there be a mystery? And the answer's yes. Be home on time or I'll tell the girls that their father has sold them to a camel dealer.'

'And I'll tell them that their aunt bosses their father around as if he is four years old.'

'Are you trying to make a point, Davenport? Would you like me to move back to my own house?'

Mike hugged her. 'You know I'd be completely lost without you.'

'I know,' Tess said, her voice muffled by Mike's shirt. 'You think I'm a cross between Mother Teresa and Albert Schweitzer. Just don't be late tonight, or I'll turn into Margaret Thatcher.' She looked disapprovingly at her brother's thin arms. Despite the fact that he existed on crisps, chocolate and Coke, he was too skinny. His soft, blue eyes were red with lack of sleep and his strong face, with its slightly crooked nose — broken in the car crash that killed his wife — and high cheekbones, seemed paler to Tess than normal. 'How did your dinner go with the dragon queen last night?' She was referring to Mike's girlfriend, Jane Hume.

'Jane is not a dragon, Tess. Why can't you be nicer about her?'

'Because she patronises the girls.'

Mike's shoulders drooped a little and he grimaced. 'I kinda made a mess of it.'

'What do you mean "kinda"?'

'An urgent call came in from Sierra Leone. Jane hadn't turned up. She had phoned to say she would be five minutes late. I took the call and—'

Tess put her right hand to her mouth in amused horror. 'You didn't?'

'I did. I just kind of got into the car on auto-pilot and forgot to leave a message for her.'

'Have you spoken since?'

His eyes slid to one side. 'It was late when I finished the first call to Sierra Leone.'

'Coward.' Tess rubbed his arms. 'I'm glad I'm not going out with you. I'd have killed you by now.'

A voice came from the twins' study. 'Dad, Jo says that God's a woman. But can something that does not exist have a gender?'

'Good luck, genius.' Tess grinned and wandered upstairs to bed.

CHAPTER SIX

At lunchtime Fernandez was in the run-down beer garden of King Hal's Inn – a scruffy, working-man's pub at the corner of Primrose Hill and Regent's Park roads, whose only virtue was the view overlooking Primrose Hill Park. The April afternoon was hot and inviting and he was grateful that he was not in this country in the middle of one of its interminable dull seasons. In the distance, above the thin, dusty trees, he could see the satellite dishes crowning the British Telecom Tower – the visible sign of a world obsessed by information and communication. Well, this is one thing they do not want to know about, he thought.

He sipped tomato juice and waited patiently for the man who was vital to the success of his plan. As he watched a grey squirrel scuttle up a brown tree trunk, he reflected that England had once been filled with red squirrels, but the grey immigrant had denied them an ecological niche. Nature will not allow the weak to endure, he thought. Only the strong survive.

Through the double-doors that led into the dark guts of the pub, Fernandez watched Alan Wilkins waddle to the bar and order a pint of stout. How could anyone allow himself to go to seed like that? Eighteen stones of blubber. Perhaps he needed to indulge in the warm sins of the flesh to cope with his many hours among the dead. Who could take pleasure in handling cold skin?

Earlier, Fernandez had received e-mailed photographs and details of people working in Security and in the Morgue. Wilkins was the obvious candidate for the sting: ex-army, resigned the previous year, two warnings for drinking on the job. Armed with this information, Fernandez had phoned one of Wilkins's colleagues to say that he was an old army friend and was in town for only one day. Was there any chance that he could pay a surprise visit? He was told 'in the strictest confidence' that Alan always had a quick one at the King Hal before his afternoon and evening shift. Fernandez stepped into the muggy gloom of the bar, walked up to Wilkins and, in an English upper-class accent, enquired: 'Excuse me. Aren't you Alan Wilkins? Sergeant Wilkins, as was.'

The big man took a draught of his Guinness and quietly sized up Fernandez. 'Do I know you?' he asked.

'No. But I know you. Everyone who has been in the regiment knows about you. Your face is famous.'

'When were you in the Guards?' asked Wilkins.

'Oh, a long time ago. But I heard all about your rescue mission. How many of our boys did you pull from that burning car after the landmine?' asked Fernandez.

Wilkins looked grim and troubled at the memory of the event. He was glad to be out of the army and still shivered in his dreams at the sight of the melting face of a nineteen-year-old boy. He worked among the dead because he could no longer stand the fear of living.

'May I buy you a drink? As a kind of thank you. One of the people you pulled out was the son of a great friend.'

Looking at his watch, Wilkins shook his head and said: 'I've got to go to work.'

Fernandez turned to a bald, pallid barman wearing a frayed tartan waistcoat and said: 'May I have a double Scotch, for my friend here? You do drink Scotch, Sergeant Wilkins?'

It was obvious to Fernandez from the broken veins around Wilkins's nose that he was a spirit drinker. It is a short walk from war hero to loser – as I know only too well, he thought. He saw Wilkins eye the drink covetously and could sense the urging in the other man's mind. Fernandez, too, had been dependent on the welcome oblivion offered by alcohol after his military discharge. Now he was strong again.

'Well, thanks, yeah. Just the one then.'

'Have a seat.' Fernandez indicated an alcove cocooning a table with an overflowing ashtray and the remains of a reheated shepherd's pie. 'And I'll bring it over.' A few moments later, as Wilkins gulped his drink, Fernandez asked: 'So what are you doing these days?'

After three quick double Scotches, Fernandez could see that Wilkins was woozy and would sleep well in his warm little office beside the corpses; well enough not to notice the disappearance of Uzelac. When the third drink was drained, Wilkins shook Fernandez's hand, got up and marched towards the exit. Fernandez mentally reviewed the layout of the Morgue and the timing of the security guard's rounds. Wilkins had been very loquacious as the alcohol had worked its magic on his inhibitions.

Walking up the little path of cracked concrete into Primrose Hill Park, Fernandez enjoyed the chirping of birds as a sleepy, gentle, English afternoon settled on the red-bricked houses that fringed the side of the park. In a glass conservatory he could see a mother and her three young children laughing over some private family joke. If only you people knew the fate I will save you from tonight, he thought. You would erect a statue to me.

His electronic organiser told him there was a message from the Company and he punched it up on the screen.

Uzelac close to death. Blood, urine and skin cultures taken.

Must be returned urgently. Do not leave them in hospital's hands.

'Where are they?' he typed back.

Blood and urine in Haematology Lab on seventh floor. Room 739. Cultures are to be sent to the offices of Dr Mike Davenport.

'Is Dr Davenport aware of what he has in his possession?'

No. Davenport not yet in contact with patient. Keep it that way.

CHAPTER SEVEN

Mike was in a dark cubicle at the end of a long room with a view over the railway tracks. The humidity made it feel as if he was standing in a bowl of warm soup. The heat from the machines, coupled with the rising temperature outside, meant that the staff's clothes were sticking to their backs. The three other people working with him were stripped down to shorts and T-shirts. There was no sound other than the quiet hum of the machines as Mike's postgraduate students focused intently on cultures or sera.

Mike was peering over photographs and absent-mindedly humming the opening bars to the Rolling Stones' 'Brown Sugar'. He was doing research on an avian bacilli that was rampaging through Shanghai. He scanned a teeming world magnified 125,000 times, of aggressive, spiky, rod-shaped creatures bursting to escape the confines of their island. The phone beside him rang and he picked it up immediately.

'Mike?' a voice enquired.

'Oh, hi, Jack. How's things?'

'I've got something weird down here,' said Jack Lim. 'I want you to have a look.'

'How weird? Blood weird?'

'Don't know. No blood haemorrhaging to speak of; but a bunch of other stuff that I can't make sense of.'

'Viral or bacterial?' asked Mike.

'Don't know yet. I've sent the samples to your people to do some work on them. C'mon. Get down here. You'll be intrigued by this one.'

Mike sucked breath between his teeth, fidgeted and stared at a fly that was walking haphazardly up the wall. 'I don't know.' Mike prepared himself to say no. 'I'm pretty busy up here. I've got an urgent report for the WHO on a nasty avian bacilli that's killed thirty people in Shanghai.'

'C'mon, Mike. It'll take you five minutes. No more.' Jack sounded puzzled. It was unlike Mike to pass up an unusual virus case. 'I would really value your advice.' His voice was persistent, and Mike knew that Jack regarded any 'no' answer as simply an opening position from which to negotiate.

Mike blew out softly between his lips. He still had responsibilities. 'OK, I'll be there in a few minutes.' He left the lab and pushed open the door of the gents' loo. Inside, he headed for the washbasin and splashed cold water on his cheeks. He was shaking: the panic attacks and the flashbacks to the weeks he had been in a coma were becoming more intense. Every time he had to go into the Isolation Ward he wanted to vomit. He fought the bile rising up his throat, realised there was no point and entered a cubicle to throw up his breakfast. When he had finished, he washed his face and rinsed his mouth. Then he took the lift down to the hospital's foyer. The threadbare brown carpet that covered the old, Edwardian wooden floor was stickier than usual in the heat.

A large black woman was sorting out a box of greeting cards. She was wearing a bright green dress with red swirls that reminded Mike of designs from her Kenyan homeland. Her face was wide and flowing with emotion. Jill Obudo greeted him with a raised, open hand. 'Dr Mike Davenport. What is it today? Let me guess, let me guess.' She lifted a giant Mars bar from the box and proffered it; the black wrapper seemed an extension of her large hand.

'Got it in one, Jill.' He grinned at her and wolfed down the chocolate. It felt large, sweet and gloriously sticky in his mouth as he chewed and swallowed with the enthusiasm of the first child turning up at a birthday party.

'I don't know how you stay so skinny, Dr Davenport. The amount of sweets you eat. I wish I was on your diet.'

I don't think so, thought Mike. 'How's your boy? Is he home yet?' he asked, changing the subject. Jill's son, Victor, had just come out of prison, a fact Mike had dragged from her one day when she was looking uncharacteristically gloomy.

'He's fine, my Victor. Fine. He's a good boy really. Just hanging out with the wrong crowd.' Her lips drooped downwards and Mike could see the pain and confusion in her eyes. 'He didn't do it. He promised me. He's not that sort of boy, my Victor. Not violent.'

. Mike reached across and touched her shoulder. 'With you as a mother, how could he be? You look after yourself, Jill.'

'And you,' she replied as she took the empty wrapper from him and put it in the bin beside her.

Five minutes later Mike entered the eight-ward Isolation Unit. It was the only properly funded part of the Centre and was filled with gleaming machines, white walls, colour prints of seascapes and sad African faces — deposited there by Immigration whenever someone turned up from West Africa with so much as a cold.

Through the windows of Ward 4, Mike could see Jack examining the new patient. He paused, fighting the instinct to run, feeling hopeless, as if he could just sit on the floor and say, No more, please, no more. He breathed deeply. C'mon. C'mon, he urged himself. It won't happen again. Just be careful. After putting on a surgical mask and scrubs, he joined his colleague. 'How's he doing?'

'I've used antiemetics to control the vomiting and I've brought the blood flow under control; but this man has definitely fought ten rounds with something unpleasant.'

'Any test results yet?' asked Mike.

'No. We're running everything now. I'm expecting the first findings within a few hours.'

'Petechiae?' Mike searched for the tell-tale tiny red-blood spots on the skin that would reveal evidence of subcutaneous bleeding and a strong possibility of a haemorrhagic fever.

'Curiously, no. That was my first thought,' replied Jack, 'but his trunk and tongue show no signs.'

'Where's he been?' asked Mike.

'No one knows anything about him. Other than the fact that he was dropped outside A & E by a blonde woman who then took off without leaving her name or address.'

'Headache? Back pains?'

Jack explained that the ambulanceman who brought him in said the patient seemed confused and didn't know where or who he was, that he shivered and shook a great deal and had a weird smile on his face. He also seemed to have abdominal pain and paralysis. Showing Mike a computer printout, Jack said: 'And, on top of that, the poor bugger's got some kind of pneumonia.'

Mike looked at Palowsky's bluish lips and then examined the heart monitor: 'Bradycardia?'

'The heart rate is a little slow; but nothing disastrous.'

'So what are the worst symptoms so far?'

'Gastric haemorrhaging, severe – and I mean very severe – shaking and this weird stare,' replied Jack.

'So what's your guess?' asked Mike.

'You know I never guess, Mike. That's for you virus cowboys.'

'No bleeding around the irises,' Mike noted. 'No haemorrhaging spots. Certainly not one of our more obvious viral chums.' He looked at the man's flushed face.

Jack shook his head. 'Two and two don't make four on this one.'

Mike looked at the two nurses who were tending Palowsky. They were masked. 'Which nurse admitted him?' he enquired.

Jack did not look at him, but instead busied himself with writing up the notes and then replied: 'Tess.'

A silence fell between them.

'Was she masked?'

'No.'

Mike shuddered as he struggled to keep himself in check. Calm down, he thought, it's probably not haemorrhagic. 'Let's have a look at his tests,' he said.

In the Haematology Lab the atmosphere was lethargic as the warmth from the many computers and machines in the room reinforced the heat of the dry, windless evening. The three men and two women in the lab looked sweaty, dishevelled and desperate to go home. Four of them, dressed in light cotton clothes, were saying their goodnights and heading for the door. Terry Smith, the Head of the Unit, had a bright red nose from which the skin was flaking off in whitish slivers.

'Jesus, Terry,' said Mike. 'At a glance, I'd say you had leprosy.'

'Very funny, Davenport.' Terry grinned at his friend. 'Picked up a slight tan at the weekend. I had one beer too many and fell asleep on the lawn. When I woke up, I thought I had been barbecued.'

'This is some weather,' noted Jack. 'I wish to hell it would rain.'

'What's rain?' Terry raised his eyes to heaven.

'Have we got Palowsky's results yet?' asked Mike.

Terry nodded and handed Mike a buff folder. The tests showed that Palowsky had all the signs of infections in the kidneys and urinary tracts.

'What about the lymphocytosis?' Jack asked scanning the

results, looking for the increase in circling lymphocytes that would show evidence of acute inflammation.

Terry scrabbled around on his desk for another set of results. On the railway line outside, Mike caught a glimpse of the tops of two stalled commuter trains and felt sympathy for the poor buggers inside. At this time, during the middle of the rush hour, the trains would be heaving with over-heating bodies packed too tightly together. His time in Bolivia and Sierra Leone had acclimatised him to heat and crowds. But London was not built for this type of weather, or rather Londoners weren't: no patience.

'He's got viral pneumonia,' said Terry.

'That can't be all,' Mike responded. 'You don't get symptoms like that with pneumonia. There must be more.'

'Well, I can't find anything else.'

'Let's do some more tests. Christ,' continued Mike, catching a glimpse of the clock on the wall, 'look at the time. It's half-past six. Tess'll eat me alive. She's going out on the tiles tonight and I'm late.' He asked Terry to send the cultures and serum to his lab and promised to have a look in the morning. He didn't notice the flick of interest in Jack's eyes before they settled. 'In the meantime,' he said, 'I suggest that we ask the police to check on our man. We need to know if he's been abroad. And who he has been in contact with since coming to this country.' He looked at the chart again. 'Palowsky sounds Polish, doesn't it? See if anyone at Immigration has heard of him.' And with that, he set off at a rangy trot from the lab.

Mike was still mulling over the case when he walked down the patched-up stairs of the hospital's Administration Block and on to the street. As he headed up the hill, he did not notice a tall, soldierly, grey-haired man with brooding eyes and a handsome face leaning against the wall across the road.

CHAPTER EIGHT

Li Danping felt the sharp blade of an open razor on his throat and closed his eyes with pleasure: being shaved by a white man was a small packet of treasure stored and lovingly cherished.

'There you are, sir.' The man's clipped New York accent had the anxious, pleading quality of someone used to disapproval from this particular customer.

Li waited for ten seconds before opening his eyes. He wanted the person shaving him to realise that Li alone had the power to influence even the smallest of events. Then he looked in the simple, black-framed, square mirror held by the barber and examined his own face. Everyone told him he looked fifteen years younger than his sixty years. Although he refused to accept such compliments as anything other than fawning by subordinates skilled in fluent lick-spittle, he had to admit that the plastic surgery had been successful. He had not enjoyed the feeling of growing old, and liked even less the ravages on his face. Younger aspirants were circling his throne as they watched for any evidence that his power had waned or that the

Company was looking to replace the man who had run it for
twelve years.

He looked around his large, circular office and a feeling that
this was his natural home suffused him. On the wall were
signed, framed photographs taken with various governors and
mayors of New York. His honorary doctorate from Columbia
University sat proudly between simple oak bookshelves
containing first editions of P.G. Wodehouse, his favourite
English author. His wife Sarah, tall and exquisite, read Plum to
him in bed whilst he sipped Glenfarclas single malt whisky and
feasted on her skin.

On his large, simple ash-wood desk, designed in the high
days of fifties modernity by an architect long fallen from favour,
was a twelve-inch dagger that was created for a seventeenth-
century taipan. Li fingered the bejewelled hilt of the weapon
and looked at his chief assistant, Leonard Jacklin, whose
perfect, tall good looks, dark hair, hand-tailored London suits
and brogues gave him entry into any society. Those attributes
were helped by five generations of Jacklin money. As he often
did, Li wondered whether rich boys could imagine the kind of
real hunger that drove him from a Hong Kong slum to the top
of the Company. Did Jacklin have the vulpine stomach for the
job? Or was he another for whom death was a long-distance
affair orchestrated by computers? It is easy to kill electronically.

Li was cautious about what he told Jacklin: he was one of the
new breed of men in this section of the Company, one of the
first not to come from a military background. If he learned the
ways of the Company, he might go far. But not at my expense,
thought Li.

After the barber scraped his way from the room to receive one
hundred dollars from Li's personal assistant, Jacklin said:
'Fernandez has been in touch. The news from England is
positive.'

Li walked across to his fiftieth-floor window that offered him
a view of New York Harbor. Through powerful binoculars, he

scanned a long, sleek liner nudging her way towards Ellis Island and the Atlantic crossing. It was a miserable day – intermittent sheets of filthy rain clattered off the tall buildings and Li could feel his office swaying slightly as winds buffeted the skyscraper. 'Mr Fernandez is a professional. He will do what is necessary. Have we sent some friends to keep him company?' His voice was clipped and purposeful; his accent upper-class English.

Jacklin punched the keys on his personal organiser and said: 'Ren Benli and Wu Shuo arrived yesterday on the morning Concorde.'

'A good choice, Leonard. They are both strong men. Good Company men.' Li turned back towards his immaculate office. 'Are we sure we have protection? Is there evidence that this problem may visit us politically?' he asked.

'Once Fernandez has eliminated Uzelac and returned his blood to us, we'll be fine. Just fine.' Jacklin's face radiated the inner confidence of a man for whom few things had gone wrong in life.

'It's a pity it has gone this far, Leonard. A great pity. I'm not certain that you were at your very best on this project.'

Jacklin looked unconcerned, but Li noticed his tongue lick quickly on his lower lip, as it always did when the younger man was anxious. The phone on the desk buzzed and Jacklin picked it up. He listened for a second and then asked: 'Are you absolutely certain?' His face creased into a slight frown, no deeper than that on the elbow of his suit. 'Take care of it, please.' He rattled out the words like Morse code. 'Maximum impact.'

Li noted the decisiveness of his lieutenant as he issued an MI order without consulting his superior. He would have to go.

CHAPTER NINE

'So Ulysses was a coward.' Jo stated her view bluntly to her father.

'No,' Mike replied. His long, lean face turned to his daughter and looked at her in surprise. He could see in her clever, soft features the adult that his twelve-year-old would become.

He held his well-thumbed Penguin edition of Homer's *Iliad* open on his lap as he sat on a chair between the twins' single beds. Although his daughters could have a separate bedroom each, they insisted on sharing. 'He was wise and he didn't want to fight in a futile battle with the Trojans,' Mike said. As a teenager he had loved the *Iliad*'s mythical world of flawed heroes and capricious gods fighting over the golden Helen and he wanted to share it with the girls.

'But Ulysses pretended to be mad until someone threatened his son so he didn't have to keep his promise and fight for Menelaus,' Molly responded, backing up her sister as she always did.

'But Menelaus was vain and greedy and Helen was even

worse.' Jo scrunched down under a blue duvet, pulled it up to her chin and turned to the side. 'Ulysses should have kept his promises,' she muttered.

Mike replied gently: 'Ulysses didn't see why he should be asked to sacrifice his time with his beautiful wife and young son. And if you're a little patient, darling, you'll discover tomorrow night that he turns out to be a pretty interesting guy. Besides, his son was a teenager before his father came home again and that was a bitter price to pay. Just think if I didn't come home for fifteen years.'

Molly and Jo looked deeply incredulous that a bad man could turn out to be good. You've got a lot to learn, my girls, Mike thought. Long may you be sheltered.

As he walked to the door, Molly, in a small, sleepy voice asked: 'Dad, you're not going to marry Jane, are you?'

'Night girls. See you in the morning.'

He trudged down the stairs to the kitchen to grab a Coke. Truth is, he thought, no matter how passionate I am about Jane, I still miss Anne every day. I see her in the bedroom in the morning when I wake up, in the car when I'm driving to work, in pubs when I see anyone who looks remotely like her. I can't subject any woman to a constant drip of my memories.' And what if we have to move out of London now that I'm almost out of a job? I'd better talk to Jane.

Sipping his drink straight from the can, he dialled Jane's home number and got the answering machine; then he tried her mobile, which answered after three rings.

'Mike. How delightful to hear from you.' Jane Hume's Edinburgh accent was soft against his ear; he always loved the rounded, smooth manner with which her accent negotiated vowels.

'Sorry about last night,' he said sheepishly.

'I bet you have that look on your face,' she said in a voice that could have crushed a truck.

'What look?'

'Your crestfallen, "please don't criticise me too much, I'm really a good person" look. I can always tell it's coming: your bottom lip droops a little, your eyes widen and moisten with petulant innocence.'

Mike stared at himself in the 1930s art deco mirror above the fireplace. 'Bang on,' he admitted.

'I long to see your other look,' she responded, her anger lifting and being replaced with soft flirtation.

'Which one?'

'The one where your eyes roll up into the back of your head and you bark like a dog.' They joined in a conspiratorial erotic giggle and Mike tried to make up for his bad behaviour of the previous evening.

'Why not come over now and we'll have some supper?' He was sure he had a frozen pizza in the fridge.

'I'm just putting the finishing touches to a press release for the new AIDS clinic. The Trust is opening it tomorrow.'

'What's happening to the old one?'

'We've sold it to a property company. They're going to build some flats. It's falling apart anyway,' she said. 'I've done the briefing for the Director and the communication plan for the rest of the press office. I'm entitled to dinner with my boyfriend. See you in fifteen minutes.'

After he hung up, he put Marvin Gaye on the CD, shoved the pepperoni in the oven, and laid the table. He was wondering how to tell Jane about his intention to resign when the phone rang.

'It's Jack. This guy's getting worse. His temperature is through the roof and that damned shaking is intensifying.' There was a pause. 'Could you come back in tonight? I'm going to do the CAT scan and it'd be great if you could be here to go over the results with me.'

Mike thought about Jane. What would she say? Curtains, probably. 'I'll be there first thing, Jack. Whenever you want. Seven. But I've got personal stuff to do. Sorry.'

'That's OK.'

'You sound tired, Jack. Go home. You're no good to anyone knackered.'

'That's a bit much coming from you. I'll see you tomorrow.'

Two short rings on the doorbell told him that Jane had turned up. 'Bye, Jack. Talk later.'

After he opened the door, Jane poured through and entangled him in a kiss. She pushed him against the wall and pressed her lips against his. She giggled. 'Is that a corkscrew in your pocket or are you just glad to see me?' She handed him the bottle of Dom Perignon Champagne she had picked up from an off-licence on the way; the bottle felt pleasantly cold against his palm. 'I need to unwind,' she said, 'and, as you never have any decent wine in the house, I brought my own.' Kicking off her shoes, she collapsed on the sofa, let out a contented sigh, and swung her long, slender legs up on to the thick, white cushions of the sofa. Her short, bobbed, blond hair looked buttery against the whiteness of the upholstery. She eyed him greedily as he poured her a tall glass of Champagne. 'I hope you don't mind, darling.' Her voice sounded tired, and she stifled a yawn. 'I've booked next weekend for us in Prague.'

'I don't think—'

'No excuses, Mike. You promised. You said whenever, wherever.'

'It's just—'

'It's just that you are deeply in love with me and can't bear to spend a minute apart from me. Remember that speech? It wasn't that long ago. Or was that just to get me into your bed? Or, rather, my bed. Because, of course, we can't do it here; it might upset the girls.'

He sat beside her, enjoying the warmth of her body beside his. She placed her head on his shoulder.

'No,' he said, 'it's just that it's the twins' birthday on Sunday and I promised I'd do something special with them.'

Her emerald eyes looked pensive for a moment.

'I know.' Mike brightened. 'Why don't we take Jo and Molly to Prague with us?'

She sat up, sipped her Champagne and was silent for a second.

'I don't think that's a good idea.'

He caressed her hand. 'Think about it,' he gushed, 'It's a great opportunity for you to get to know each other.'

'Oh, I think the girls and I know each other pretty well, darling.' She smiled a little at a private joke. 'Very well indeed.'

Mike expressed surprise: after all, the four of them had only had a few dinners together and a short weekend at a friend's cottage in Cornwall.

'Let's compromise,' Jane replied, looping a long, elegant arm around his neck and pulling him in close to her until their lips touched. Then she outlined a plan that he spend Friday and Saturday with her in Prague and fly back on Sunday to be with the twins. Her warm tongue found his and locked him in a deep kiss.

He was desperately trying to find a solution. Would the twins understand? No, he didn't believe they would.

'I'd hate to upset the girls,' he said, pulling himself away slightly and then gently nuzzling her nose.

'But, darling, the girls would be bored in Prague. And, let's face it, they wouldn't be thrilled to see us disappearing at all hours of the day to thrash around. Be realistic.'

'C'mon,' she smiled, her eyes engorged with the idea, 'two days in bed.'

The smell of her expensive scent caressed his senses; it reminded him of a fantastic weekend they'd had the previous month – the first time she had worn it. She licked his ear and he felt the soft heat of her breath.

His bleeper went.

'Leave it,' she whispered.

In the background, Marvin Gaye was telling Tammi Terrell that she was all he needed to get by; Jane was touching her tongue against the tip of his; he caressed the moist warmth between her legs.

The phone rang. The answering machine clicked on, and Tess's voice told the caller that no one was at home and asked if they would leave a message. Liz O'Mara's voice cut through to Mike's lost, swimming senses: she sounded agitated and tense.

'Dr Davenport. Jack Lim asked me to call. He says he's sorry, but he thinks you should be here. Palowsky has crashed badly. Blood is leaching everywhere and it won't coagulate. Jack is using clotting agents, but we're getting nowhere.'

Jane's eyes were damp with a combination of anger and confusion as she watched him respond. 'Don't go, Mike. I need you tonight. Please. Other people are at the Centre, they don't need you. You're not a surgeon.'

'No. But I'm one of the few doctors in this country who have treated haemorrhagic fevers. Besides, you know what it's like in situations like this. All hands on deck.' He kissed her quickly. 'Sorry darling, I've got to go. You must see that.'

She sighed and got up from the sofa.

He reached over to pick up the phone. 'Liz, tell Jack and all the nursing staff to go into barrier mode. Don't go mad. Just make sure that everyone is gloved and has a bio-mask.'

Jane stood by the fireplace and gulped the remains of her Champagne. Her left foot tapped the rug to an imaginary tune and she pretended to be interested in the music. When Mike took her hand, she pulled it away and put a metre of space between them. He tried again; but she retreated to the sofa, sat and stared at the patterns on the rug.

'Darling, I must go. Will you do me a favour?' Silence. 'Will you please wait here and look after the girls until Tess comes home?'

'You are joking, aren't you?' Her eyes sparked.

'Please.' He got down on his knees and lifted her head to catch his gaze.

'I really want to be with you,' Mike whispered. 'Tomorrow

night. I promise. Kensington Place and then a night at the Halcyon. Just you and me. I'll ask Tess.'

She held his look and, with a resigned shrug, sighed: 'All right. I'll watch them.' She barely responded to his farewell kiss as she poured another drink.

Mike rushed out promising himself that he would look after Jane. She deserved better.

Twenty minutes later, he edged into the room they used to treat the most infectious patients. A half-dozen people were working on Palowsky. Their clothes were saturated in blood and Mike was glad to see that they were properly suited up. Mike's hands were shaking a little and he breathed deeply to control himself.

They had dispensed with the space suits that the Head of the Centre, James Graham, had forced them to wear at the beginning of the Centre's existence. Now, at Mike's insistence, they were using the simple barrier methods that he had perfected in the field – allowing them to act properly as doctors and nurses, without risk to themselves or the patient. In his lectures to the Centre's nursing staff Mike reiterated his mantra that they should protect their eyes and mouth, and prevent any virus entering an open wound. After that, it was counter-productive to attempt to treat patients in a suit more suitable to the moon than a hospital.

Around the bed was evidence of slippery brown-red blood. A horrified-looking nurse stared at Mike helplessly and he had every sympathy with her. He almost passed out the first time he saw someone crash with a haemorrhage virus, and he had his own reasons to avoid the blood on the floor. Gingerly, he edged around to Jack, who was working urgently and with great focus. One of the nurses was spreading foam on the blood seeping from Palowsky's gut.

'Won't coagulate. Nothing I can do,' said Jack. 'It's been like damming a flood with one bag of sand.'

Mike was puzzled. None of the tell-tale symptoms of an

impending haemorrhage crash had been present earlier. The high-pitched whine of the heart monitor told them that Palowsky's heart was no longer beating and his brain scan was flat-lining. Mike looked around the team and could see in their eyes that they thought he should let Palowsky go. There was nothing they could do for the guy. Even if he could be pulled round, his internal organs and his brain would never recover.

Mike whispered something to Jack, who shook his head in frustration.

'Enough, Jack,' Mike muttered quietly.

Jack turned and, without a word, left the room. After the chemicals washed the blood from his gloves, he snapped them off and put them and the rest of his clothes in a bag to be taken to the incinerator. He was standing naked, seemingly unable to move with exhaustion. 'What is this thing?' he snapped.

Mike took a few seconds to gather his thoughts. 'There are some really confusing symptoms,' he responded. 'I don't get the shaking or the rictus smile. And what about the lack of petechiae? It doesn't correspond to anything I've seen with Lassa or Bolivian haemorrhagic fever. Or even Ebola. We'd better find out where this guy has been, and fast. I'll call the police and Immigration in the morning. Let's hope to God that he's an isolated case.'

Looking at his friend, Mike thought that in the small, white changing room his pale face looked lined and strained. Despite being in his mid-forties, Jack was in great shape. He ran marathons and there was not an ounce of excess fat on his five-foot-eight frame. Mike was surprised to see him hit so badly by this. There was something personal in this for Jack; something related to the reason why he had left his well-paid consultancy in Kuala Lumpur and joined Mike's ropy marginal outfit in a run-down hospital in Chalk Farm. Jack would not explain his reasons and Mike had not pried.

'It's midnight, Jack. Get some sleep. You've been with this thing for twelve hours. You should've been out of here ages ago.

We'll know a lot more in the morning once we've done the post-mortem.'

Jack rubbed the side of his face. 'You're right. I'll see you in the morning. I'm sorry for dragging you in here. You're one of the few people who've seen stuff like this. And I just thought . . . you know—' He trailed off.

'That's all right, Jack. It was a good call.'

'Have you ever thought how London would respond to a haemorrhage virus?' Jack asked.

'You are joking, of course. This city wouldn't know how to cope with a bad outbreak of the flu,' responded Mike, aware of the fact that yet again, despite his efforts, the NHS Executive and the Home Office's Director of Emergency Planning had refused him funding to develop a proper model for a major viral outbreak in London. They were still too fixated on biological warfare to take true account of the natural dangers literally under their noses.

'True. Very true. You going home?' Jack asked as he screwed the back of his knuckles into his eyes, trying to relieve the pressure.

'Sure.' Mike replied.

'See you in the morning, then.' Jack pulled on an elegant white shirt.

Mike turned to the phone on the wall and told the Staff Nurse that Palowsky's body was to be double-bagged and placed overnight in an isolated part of the Morgue, ready for the post-mortem. Everyone was to treat it as a Level 3 fatality and take great care. 'And we'd better inform the WHO and the Department of Health,' he said. He waved goodbye to Jack and walked to his office to store the blood and urine samples, and make some notes.

CHAPTER TEN

Fernandez leaned on the steering wheel of his black Mercedes and watched through binoculars as two porters wearing bio-masks wheeled Uzelac's double-bagged body on a trolley into the Morgue. He had been informed by one of the Company's computer specialists that Uzelac was dead and that he would be moved at this time – all information hacked from the hospital's own computing system.

'Is this the man you were so careless about?' Ren Benli asked from the passenger seat beside him. Ren could pass for a dance teacher: light limbs, quick on his feet, small, delicate hands and a refined face. In the back sat Fernandez's other new companion: Wu Shuo – a tall, thickset man whose hands could span the neck of a grown man, and then break it in a second. Both men were former captains in the Chinese People's Liberation Army and were, in Li Danping's words, 'good Company men'. Fernandez had heard from a friend that a few years earlier Ren had taken the nails out of a girl's hands one at a time until she told him the hiding place of her brother, a financial journalist, who was writing investigative stories about the extensive links between the PLA and major industries in Hong Kong and Shanghai. The two men had been sent with the message that they were to help Fernandez all they could. Fernandez knew that if he failed, they would kill him.

'This is the man,' replied Fernandez.

'Well, then. Let us repair the damage you caused.' Ren pulled a revolver from the glove compartment and checked it.

'Before we go in,' Fernandez put his hand on Ren's arm, 'let me reiterate that we do not want to kill anyone. I want to close this operation down; not make the British police suspicious. Do you both understand?'

'Are you being racist, Fernandez?' asked Ren – who could not understand why a foreigner was running the security operation for the Company. Did Li not trust his own people? 'Do you think we thick Chinee?' Ren spat out his words; his American accent was the product of three years taking a degree in engineering at Stanford University.

'Of course not.' Fernandez was a little exasperated. 'I merely want to ensure that we share objectives on this mission. And that we take this calmly.'

'So,' Ren showed his teeth, 'we are blood-thirsty Chinee. No have foreign devil's ability to hold temper?'

'Stop playing with him, Ren.' Wu's Chinese accent was much thicker. Fernandez found him difficult to understand. 'Let's finish this.'

'Yeah. Ret's finish ris.' Ren imitated his colleague's voice, drummed on the leather seats and hummed to himself as Fernandez completed his instructions.

A minute later they stepped from the car and regrouped in the shadows of a large oak tree. The air was still warm after another day in the eighties and the chords of the last song from a free open-air rock concert on Primrose Hill drifted across to them.

'Can't you hear what they're playing, man?' Ren asked. 'It's the Clash. "Police and Thieves". I love that old punk stuff. I used to listen to it all the time at Stanford. A complete rush.'

'It's a decadent form of music,' responded Fernandez absent-mindedly.

'Rat's right. I forgot,' Ren made an exaggerated bowing gesture, 'you are a Christian intellectual who listens only to Beethoven.'

'Beethoven was a genius.'

'I'm told they used to play Mr Beethoven's Fifth Symphony in Auschwitz. Just before the gas.' Ren grinned.

Fernandez refused to rise to Ren's provocation. The three men walked down the hill and emerged behind a group of three filthy 1970s pre-fabs that housed the children's wards before dropping into a thin alley that twisted between the kitchens and the cancer wards. The smell of greasy bacon belched from the extractors.

'These Brits sure know how to look after the sick, don't they? And they call us savages.' Ren kept up his banter.

'Quiet, Ren.' Wu's gruff order silenced his colleague immediately and Fernandez knew then who was in charge and whom he should look out for.

The three of them were dressed in the black uniforms of the hospital's privatised security guards and had no fear of detection. The Morgue was housed in a one-storey, red-brick building, with a small incinerator attached.

Fernandez punched in the security numbers. They entered the blue double doors from which paint was peeling in large strips and walked into a cool, quiet, white-tiled ante-room that was cramped and functional. As Fernandez expected, Wilkins was asleep in a deep, black armchair, his head on top of his podgy hands, which were splayed on the desk in front of him. The bottle of Scotch I gave him as a leaving present is probably half empty by now, Fernandez thought.

'Where is Uzelac?' asked Wu quietly.

'In the room at the end. They have the body isolated.'

Fernandez led the way, following the directions that Wilkins had earlier described. When they reached the room, they discovered it was locked and a security pad required a combination. Fernandez entered the numbers hacked from the hospital's computer and waited for the click that told him he could enter. Nothing happened. 'They must've changed the numbers.'

'Well, well. Mr Fernandez fucks up again. You're slipping, old man,' Ren said. 'This calls for a bit of Oriental ingenuity.'

Before Fernandez could stop him, Ren doubled back to Wilkins's little reception room and was standing behind him with the snub of his .45 at the fat man's temple. Wilkins's head was being held up and his face pointed at the ceiling; but he was still asleep. Ren bent down and whispered, 'This is going to be a bad dream, fat man.'

'Don't do this, Ren,' Fernandez ordered. 'We cannot afford to leave a trail.'

'Do you have any other suggestions, Mr Fernandez?' enquired Wu.

When he received no response, Wu said: 'Carry on, Ren.'

'Your friend is a little drunk on duty, Mr Fernandez.' Ren tutted. 'That will never do. He needs a little wake-up call.'

Ren took Wilkins's right hand, opened the top drawer of the desk, and draped the little finger between the lip of the drawer and the desktop. He put his own hands across Wilkins's mouth and when he kicked the drawer shut the sound of cracking bone echoed off the walls.

Fernandez watched as the agony burst through Wilkins's booze-addled brain. Wilkins tried to scream but was prevented by Ren's barrier across his mouth. A combination of fear and his army training produced an unexpectedly fast response in someone so large and he broke Ren's grip and grabbed his hair. Ren grunted in surprise as Wilkins rose like a bear and head-butted him; this time the sound of broken bones came from Ren.

Fernandez stopped himself from grinning. Ren would be capable of killing his own child at a moment like this; he hated losing face.

'I'm gonna kill you, you fat fuck,' Ren hissed.

'No, you're not,' said Fernandez calmly and walked between the antagonists.

'Get out of the way or I'll shoot you first.'

'Speak to your colleague, Wu. I'm afraid he's not focusing hard enough on the long-term aspects of this mission. Our friends will be extremely unhappy if you return without a resolution.'

Ren looked at Wu, who nodded. Ren holstered his gun. The pain in his face must have been considerable: Fernandez enjoyed the thought as he watched the bruises begin to emerge.

'Now, Mr Wilkins.' Fernandez spoke to the startled man, whose own shooting pain was now beginning to manifest itself. Fernandez reached under the desk and took the half-drunk bottle of Famous Grouse from its hiding place. 'Please be seated.'

'What the fuck do you want?' Wilkins was belligerent and terrified in the same measure.

'I want what is best for you. Believe me, my friend. I would strongly advise you to sit while I speak to you, otherwise my colleague here will be forced to retaliate.' He handed Wilkins the bottle and watched as he took two large gulps. The whisky dribbled slightly down the fat man's chin as his hand shook with nerves. 'I can see why you won a bravery award, Sergeant Wilkins. But I would advise you not to be foolish.'

'Hang on. I know you. You're the guy from the pub.'

'I want the security code for the isolation room.'

'Why?'

'It's best you don't know.'

As Wilkins looked at them, his heart was thumping and he was finding it difficult to draw breath. He stared at the ground; his fighting days were left behind in a blown-up jeep in Kosovo.

All he wanted now was some peace. 'Four-nine-zero-seven-five.'

'Thank you. Now, one more thing. We are about to dispose of one of your clients. I have arranged for responsibility for this disappearance to be laid at the door of someone else at the hospital. I would advise you to go along with the story that Palowsky was given the wrong tag when brought here. And, therefore, his disappearance is another sad case of failed bureaucracy.'

Ren pushed the .45 under Wilkins's nose. 'If you don't, I'll make sure you won't be able to pour Scotch down that fat face of yours again.'

Whilst Wu stayed with Wilkins to emphasise the seriousness of the situation, and to guide in the ambulance that had been stolen by two of his colleagues earlier that day, Ren and Fernandez went to the isolation room. Ren was emphatic: 'I'm going to kill that guy. Slowly. I'm going to do it slowly.'

'Do it on your own time,' said Fernandez. 'And don't do it for at least a week. I don't want any link back to this operation.' He entered the security code and walked into the small, pitch-black room. In a cold half light he saw the refrigerator and, after pulling open the drawer, he stared at Uzelac's body-bag.

'Time for the second death, Uzelac.'

'What are you talking about, man? What second death?' Ren's eyes were menacing as the harsh light played on them.

' "And death and hell were cast into the lake of fire. This is the second death." Revelations chapter twenty, verse fourteen.'

They wheeled Uzelac's body out of the door and replaced it with one from the main section of the Morgue.

CHAPTER ELEVEN

Tess felt giddy and put her head against the door. 'That fourth vodka and tonic was a bad mistake, girl,' she muttered to herself. Why the hell am I going out with a bloody doctor? Why can't I fall in love with one of those nice guys that come home at night and cook me spaghetti carbonara? 'I miss you, Jack,' she mumbled. 'Miss you, miss you.' She looked at her watch: two o'clock. Should I phone him? No, no, girl. If you're drunk enough to think that's a good idea, you're way too drunk. Her head felt thick. God, I've got to be up in five hours' time. Bed, bed. Mmm. I want to be tucked beside you, Jack. Slipped into the crook of your arm.

She tiptoed into the house and was surprised by the sound of the TV. Who on earth is up? Rounding the corner into the sitting room, sobriety returned to her in a rush when she saw Jo sitting on the floor, cradling Molly in her arms and dully watching an old Tom Hanks movie. Tess knelt beside them. 'Hey? What's this? A pyjama party? What is Mike thinking about? You've got school in the morning.'

'Dad's had to go out,' Jo said, her eyes red with lack of sleep.

'An emergency at the Centre,' a voice behind Tess explained.

She turned and saw Jane walk into the room carrying two glasses of milk and some biscuits that she handed to Jo. 'Perhaps these will help you sleep,' said Jane.

'I don't think so,' Jo replied coldly. 'Not having nightmares about our mother's death might. C'mon, Moll,' she stood and lifted her sister to her feet, 'you can bunk up with me.'

As Molly followed her sister like an automaton, Tess scooped the girl up in her arms and spoke softly into her ear. After a second or so, Molly responded with a tight hug and kissed her aunt on the nape of the neck.

Tess took them up to her double bed. 'I'll sleep in your room,' she said to Jo. 'You two snuggle up here.'

'You know,' said Jo, with barely disguised scorn, 'when I went down to ask her to help me calm Molly down, all she knew how to do was to turn on the TV.'

'She was doing her best, Jo.'

'I know. That makes it worse.'

Out of the mouths of babes, thought Tess. Downstairs, she saw that Jane was standing with her coat on, ready to leave.

'Are they OK?' enquired Jane.

'Sure.' Tess paused, 'Thanks. I know it's tough when the kids aren't your own.'

Jane seemed to weigh up the compliment and decide that it didn't contain an insult. She picked her car keys from the table beside the sofa and replied: 'If only Mike didn't rush off like this, it'd be a lot better for the children. He wouldn't need to leave them in the hands of comparative—' She searched for a word.

'Strangers?' Tess offered.

'Newcomers,' countered Jane, her lips pursing into a disappointed bow.

Tess poured herself a glass of still water from a green bottle on the table. Her fuzzy, slightly drunken senses needed to be rehydrated. 'The kids understand their father. They know that he needs to feel involved. That he has a kind of calling. Anne knew that. They were a great team. He backed her up when she returned to the Bar, and she was there for him when he was needed abroad.'

Jane considered this information with her head cocked slightly to one side. 'Well, the good news is that the girls won't have to be so understanding in future. He's told me he's giving up fieldwork and detailed research and will try for Head of Centre when James Graham goes.'

Tess took a gulp, and then replied: 'He'd shrivel in a desk job. Just shrivel.'

'Everyone's got to grow up sometime,' said Jane. 'And Mike has made, it seems to me, a pretty shrewd career decision to take over from Graham. I can help rebrand him; take off a few of those rough edges and sharpen up his political senses. He can be a bit naïve, as you know.'

Tess looked at her for a long second. 'I'm not sure I do know. What I know is that when he was in the field everyone, but everyone, thought he had a gift – a kind of epidemiological sixth sense. He could smell the source of a problem. He'd admit himself that he's not the greatest doctor or biochemist or administrator. But put him in the field and he's one of the best virus cowboys you can find. You can't consign that kind of ability to a bloody office.'

Pulling her coat around her, Jane prepared to leave. Tess could see in her face that she thought this argument was futile. 'Mike and I have discussed this.' Jane's voice was firm. 'And he will not return to the field. Besides, he can teach and pass on his knowledge to others.'

'You can't pass on gut instinct.' Tess shook her head. 'You're born with it.'

'All a bit mystical for me, I'm afraid. I think Mike's pretty level-headed really. Bye.' She left.

Tess looked at the space where Jane had been, then down at the water in her hand. She sighed, put down the glass and headed off to the kitchen to open a bottle of wine.

CHAPTER TWELVE

Marie Kecman sat in the darkened room and watched her son's chest rise and fall. How could he be eight years old in a week's time? she wondered. It felt like he was born yesterday. He looks so like his dad, Marie reflected, and sadness fell across her soft face. She desperately missed her husband, who had been killed the day after Simi's birth, the victim of a sniper.

She was hot and sticky and wore a long cotton T-shirt that doubled as a night-dress. Her second husband, Martin, who was snoring loudly in the other bedroom, had stumbled home from the Serbian community centre, drunk on the money she had raised from her brother when she had travelled to Cologne a few weeks earlier. The bastard had forced his thing inside her. But she had said nothing; as she always said nothing. She had married him to get Simi out of Bosnia. And for that she had always been grateful; but no more.

Martin didn't know that she had kept five hundred pounds of her brother's money and she and Simi would leave the following week for somewhere safe; somewhere where men don't fuck you when you are having your period and feeling sick. The bastard would have to carry on with that tart on the next floor. She felt ill at the thought of Martin spending her scarce funds on a disgusting prostitute when Simi needed new shoes. His current pair were full of holes. She was glad that it had not rained in a long time.

Swaying back and forward in her chair, she hummed a rock song that the driver had played in the bus on the way back from Cologne. The song's lyrics spun gently in her head as she allowed her fingers softly to touch the top of her thighs and recall the intimate memories of the man's fingers inside her. Meeting him on the bus had been a surprise. He had such a beautiful face. She closed her eyes and remembered him whispering to her as they passed through the tunnel. Marie had parted her legs and he had burrowed his fingers tenderly inside her pants and then inside her. At first he was gentle and then, just as she was about to come, he had pushed a bit harder until . . . Marie could feel the muscles contract in her stomach and thighs as she recalled the waves of pleasure. It had been so difficult to stifle her cries. And then he had stroked her hair until she settled. Marie had surprised herself when she bent over, under the blanket they were sharing, and took him in her mouth. She had never been forward with men.

The red Manchester United clock on Simi's bedside cabinet glowed: two o'clock. She must go to bed. Marie leaned over her son and stroked his hand just above the bandage she had put on when he fell off his bike two weeks before. He had been so brave: the bleeding had lasted for ten minutes whilst she cleaned out the gravel. I'll take off the bandage tomorrow, she thought, and smiled.

Dots of lights danced before her eyes, she felt momentarily nauseous and her back ached as she stood. I wish I could shake off this cold, she thought. Now there's something I must remember. What is it?

I'll forget my own name next.

CHAPTER THIRTEEN

At 7.30 a.m., whilst Mike was on the phone to Jane in the kitchen, the twins were alternately spooning down cereal and making gagging gestures with their fingers as their father waved at them to shush. His face was tired and drawn. 'Darling, I'm extremely grateful to you for looking after the girls last night,' he said.

'Did your visit to the hospital make any difference?' asked Jane.

'No. The patient was pretty much dead by the time I got there.'

'I'm sorry,' she said.

'So am I. So, tonight?'

'Eight o'clock. Kensington Place. I've booked a table for two by the windows.'

'Great,' he replied, 'looking forward to it.'

'Mike?'

'Yes?'

'I do love you, you know.'

'Same here.'

'Is that it?'

'Is what it?'

'Why can't you tell me you love me in front of the girls?'

'I can.'

'C'mon then.'

'I will.'

'What's that sound?'

'What sound?'

'Hell freezing over.'

'What?'

'Hell will freeze over before you tell those two that you love me.'

'That's not fair.' He realised he was talking to the dialling tone and looked at his girls: their hair was white-blond like their mother's and their eyes, like his, were a translucent blue. They had weathered the twenty months since Anne's death as best they could. Could they accept Jane?

'Dad,' asked Jo, 'you won't let us down, will you?'

'What d'you mean, darling? Is everything all right? You don't really mind that I'm going out tonight?'

She looked at him full in the eyes. 'We didn't know you were going out tonight.'

'Ah, yes. With Jane. I had to run out on her last night. There was a patient I had to attend to.'

'Yes. Jane told me that when Molly started screaming in the middle of the night.'

'Moll, what was it?' Mike asked, looking worried.

Molly stole a sideways glance at her sister and said it was nothing, just a bad dream, 'about Mother'.

Mike hugged her close and said: 'I know, darling. I get them too. I'm sorry I had to go out.'

'That's cool, Dad,' she replied softly. 'Totally cool.'

'Tess came home and helped. Which was just as well, really, the state she was in.' Jo made glugging noises and mimed someone downing a drink.

'Jane's a good person, Jo. You'd like her if you gave her a chance.'

'She's not very . . . what's the word, Moll?'

'Tactile?'

'Yeah. That's it. Tactile.' Jo nodded to herself.

'Does Tess like her?' enquired Molly, her open face turned to her father.

'We haven't really discussed it much but I—'

'Don't speak for me.' Tess emerged red-eyed into the room; she was wearing a wrap, her hair looked raggle-taggle and the remains of the previous night's make-up hovered around her eyes. 'I don't know the woman – only her reputation.'

'What reputation?' Jo's face brightened.

'You look terrible, Tess. Can I get you some aspirin?' Molly charged to the kitchen cupboard.

'She'd defend the management if it sold the hospital to McDonald's for a new chain of McDrug,' said Tess.

'That's unfair and you know it, Tess,' snapped Mike.

'Thank you, sweetheart.' Tess gratefully accepted two pills from her niece and swallowed them with a glass of water. 'Don't jump down my throat, Mike. Not this morning.'

A silence fell on them: Molly chewed silently on a piece of toast; Tess had her eyes closed and was sipping water; and Jo had her head buried in a magazine called *MORE!* with a young, male pop star on the cover and a promise of MORE SEX! MORE FUN! MORE HUNKS! JUST MORE, MORE, MORE!

Mike wanted to ask her where she got it, but he felt sick inside; he hated anything that threatened disunity. He loved all three with everything he had. Perhaps, since Anne's death, he had allowed too much to pass between them unexplored. He must talk to Jo. Trying to lighten the atmosphere, he asked Tess, a little too brightly: 'Bit of a party with the mystery man?'

'Mr Mystery was otherwise engaged. I called Liz and we went to a club.'

Silence draped uneasily over them again until Molly broke it by humming an uncertain tune to herself.

'I hope you had fun,' said Mike.

'Not really,' replied Tess. 'Not very much. Drank too much.'

Mike tried again. 'What time does your shift start?'

She looked at the clock, put her head in hands, and groaned. 'Twenty minutes.'

'I could cook you a special breakfast, Tess.' Jo twinkled with engaging malevolence. 'Greasy bacon, fatty sausages, runny egg and watery coffee.'

'You are the spawn of hell, Jo. Go to school before I tell your father about the letter I found under your pillow.'

Jo blushed scarlet, grabbed her school-bag and tugged at Mike's arm. 'Dad, what was the name of the witch who was in love with Jason and killed all those children?

'Medea.'

'Well, let's leave Medea to her breakfast.'

As they hustled out the door, Tess heard Mike say: 'What letter, Jo?'

'It's a girl thing, Dad,' his daughter replied firmly.

The traffic jam on Chalk Farm Road brought Mike to a halt behind a green Volvo full of children on the school run. The raven-haired girl inside looked twenty and obviously could not be the mother of all the four children she was driving. She was shouting at the tallest one in the back seat who was looking sulky.

The heat is getting to everyone, he thought, and decided that when he bought another car it would have air-conditioning. He grinned quietly to himself: you're getting soft, boy. Is this the same person who drove in a bust-up jeep through a war zone in Sierra Leone with the temperature over a hundred? How did I ever get so old?

Jo was in the seat beside Mike, and Molly was leaning over from the back. Mike asked, slightly nervously: 'What did you mean earlier about letting you down?'

'You remember, Dad,' chirruped Molly. 'We've got to do a biology experiment and you promised you'd help.'

A sense of relief washed over Mike. 'Of course.' It wasn't about Jane after all. He must insist that the twins go with them to Prague. It might be the making of them all as a unit.

'What about a really gory one about viruses?' Jo asked. 'What's the very, very worst one?'

'Depends what you mean. There's short, horrible ones like Ebola where you bleed like a pig or long, sneaky ones like AIDS that leave you defenceless against any bug that fancies chewing on a bit of you.'

'A virus is the smallest thing in the world, isn't it Dad?' Molly was eager to show she had remembered her lessons.

'Not quite. A virus is smaller than the bacteria that cause food poisoning and bigger than the prions that cause BSE. In fact, viruses can live in bacteria and make them sick; and proteins are parts of viruses. And some bits of stuff are halfway between bacteria and viruses. And we still don't really know about some of the microbial soup.'

'So that's clear, then, isn't it, Moll?' Jo nudged her sister.

'Virus is the Latin word for poison – which is the best way to describe your sister's current mood.' Although Mike had joshed like this with Jo on innumerable occasions, this time her face collapsed into a sulk. Shit, Mike thought. He focused his attention on Molly and explained in his gentle, persuasive tones. 'Think of the cells that make up your body as a house and viruses as squatters who can only come to life if they live in your house. They eat all your food, trash the bedroom and poison the water. Whilst they are doing that, they are creating thousands more squatters. As the pressure builds up, the dumb ones take some dynamite and blow up the house and make a run for the next one; but the clever ones spend years messing up one room at a time until it's impossible for you to rebuild. And they also build escape tunnels into other houses.'

'So if I write that little story in my exam, the teacher'll give me top marks.' Jo spat out her words.

'Oh, come off it, Jo,' said Molly irritably. 'I know what Dad's saying. Each cell has its own chemistry that viruses steal and use to make more of themselves. Then they look for another person to live in when they kill the first person. Is that it, Dad?'

'That's it, darling.'

He was surprised that Molly had broken ranks with her sister. Jo was always the leader.

'What d'you think, Jo? Is your old man of some help, after all?'

She leaned back in her seat and turned her head towards him. God, she looks like her mother, he reflected. A burning, lost sensation hit him in the stomach. Jesus, I miss you, Anne. Every fucking day. Was she wearing lipstick? He decided not to raise the issue. Oh, God, adolescence was coming like an express train. Sometimes he wished he could put his head down for ten years and wake up with Jo a woman. He pulled up outside a group of low-rise 1970s red-brick buildings that made up St Margaret's Church of England School.

Molly leant over the seat and kissed him on the cheek whilst Jo escaped into the school without even a wave. 'Ignore her dad. She's crazy about Paul Dalglish.'

'Who's Paul Dalglish?'

'It's best if you don't know.' Molly ran for the entrance as the bell rang.

CHAPTER FOURTEEN

Marie Kecman sat on the bottom deck of a red bus travelling to her job as a receptionist in a doctor's surgery near King Henry's Hospital. It was eight-thirty and the bus was full and sweltering in a morning temperature that was already in the high sixties.

Little beads of perspiration sat on people's foreheads and Marie could see a patch of sweat spreading out from under the arms of a large man in a blue shirt on the seat in front of her. It must be my stop soon, she thought. Which is it? She looked out of the window at the shops. Is that the fruit shop opposite the surgery? she asked herself. I don't recognise it.

A thin, teenage girl in a very short bottle-green dress, from which protruded burned red thighs that had caught too much sun the previous day, stared curiously at Marie. Why are you looking at me? Marie wondered. Why? 'What are you staring at?' Marie asked in what she thought was a whisper but was in fact a scream. The bus fell silent as people stared at their newspapers or into the middle distance. No one caught her eye for fear of being trapped in an embarrassing scene. They clearly felt sympathy for the girl sitting rigidly next to Marie, who was visibly shaking. Marie shuffled uncomfortably as she felt something wet between her thighs. She looked at her legs and compared them to those of her fellow passenger. The man who put his fingers in her secret place. What was his name? What? He told me I had beautiful legs. Was the seat wet when I sat down? Why is that stupid girl jumping up and running down the bus? What's she moaning about? Why am I shaking so much? What's that red patch on the floor in front of me? Why is the bus stopping? Her head whirled and she wanted to be sick.

As Marie slumped forward, her head hit the metal frame of the seat in front of her and blood poured from the cut to mingle with the dark, overflowing menstrual fluid haemorrhaging between her legs.

CHAPTER FIFTEEN

Mike looked at the clock on the wall of the clinic's reception: ten past nine. Shit, he meant to call Jack at nine and talk about the haemorrhage case. He pushed open his office door and his heart missed a beat as he saw a woman sitting behind his desk. Her head leant back against the bookshelf and her long, muscled legs and bare feet perched on top of a pile of papers.

Laura Holmes looked up at him. Her cornflower-blue eyes were as he remembered them: amused and purposeful in equal measures. 'I hear you're in trouble, Davenport, and you need a bit of help.' Her slow Montana accent drawled out the sentence and she put one hand over the other. Mike noticed that her knuckles were raw and her fingernails bitten to the quick.

'How did you know that, Holmes?'

'Elementary, my dear Davenport,' she said, and in unison they grinned in recognition of an old in-joke, a silly mark of intimacy that told him she was not angry with him. 'Tess called and said that some sneaky little bastard has alighted on these emerald shores. I was over for a conference on DNA vaccines and thought I'd drop by.' She got up, unwound her five-foot-ten frame, and came to him. They met in the middle of the small room and hugged for a long time. Her body was warm and openly welcoming and it felt good to have her back. Their last parting had been painful and debilitating. She pulled back from him, still holding on to his hands, and looked up into his face. She was a great deal more drawn than the last time they had met; but her strong cheekbones, high forehead, and mane of thick, black hair inherited from her Swedish grandmother made her look healthier than anyone who had spent four months in the Sudan should. Her lips were full and complemented a generously wide, lipstick-free mouth.

'I know. I look like shit,' she said, glancing at her faded black shorts and Nike trainers. 'But I clean up nice if you want to take a girl to dinner.'

'I'd love to. I've got a favour I want to ask you.'

As they hugged again and she kissed him on the cheek, he heard someone bang on his door and barge in.

'Mike, I've got someth—'

As the sentence stopped Mike spun round. 'Darling,' he gabbled as he saw Jane's eyes widen, 'this is Laura Holmes. I've told you all about her.'

Laura stepped back from Mike, stuck out a hand and Jane briefly clenched it before dropping her arms to her side.

'Sorry to interrupt,' Jane said to Mike. 'I didn't realise you had company.' The permafrost in her voice could have preserved the body of a T. Rex for a thousand years, Mike noted with an internal wince.

'Just going,' said Laura, sensing the atmosphere. 'I'll call you about dinner, Mike, I'll be staying at the Dorchester for a few days. I'm going to treat this poor body to the best that modern capitalism can buy before my money runs out.'

'I'll call you later,' replied Mike. At the door, conscious of Jane, they touched briefly and awkwardly, almost bumping heads in the process. As he turned back into the room, Jane's face was a mask.

'So that's Laura Holmes. I expected her to look like Ingrid Bergman the way you went on about her. I thought she had disappeared from the face of the earth on some mercy mission.'

Mike made a move to kiss her – but she edged away towards the door. 'Did you want something, darling?' he asked.

'It'll keep until dinner,' she said. 'Unless you want to cancel to meet up with your heroic friend.'

'Of course not, twit. It'll be great to see her; but you know I want to be with you.' He bent forward to kiss her on dry lips that barely responded.

As she left, Jane said: 'Don't be late tonight.'

From the bottle he kept in the samples fridge, Mike poured a half-pint of Coke into a large container and took a couple of caffeine tablets to keep him going through the day. He was wrecked. Two nights of busted sleep added to the wretched, endless heat were taking it out of him.

He punched the security code into an alphanumeric pad that allowed him access to the secure freezer unit into which he had put Palowsky's urine and blood samples before he went home the night before. They were missing. Fuck. Where were they? His mind raced as he reconstructed the previous night in his head; he had been incredibly careful, as he always was. A fug of tiredness struggled with his heightened senses. Christ almighty, I was exhausted last night, he thought, did I put them somewhere else? Did someone move them?

He put his head round the lab door next to his office. Mary Mortimer, a stubby, very determined biochemistry postgrad, was an early riser and already hard at work on a platelet analysis. 'Did you see anyone in my office this morning, Mary?'

'Nah.' Her voice was uncompromisingly Essex-girl. 'I've been here since seven and seen nobody.'

'D'you know if anyone moved some samples from the secure unit in my office?'

She looked at him, puzzlement spreading across her broad features. Mary, along with everyone else in the lab, knew the incredible precautions Mike took with anything he thought was remotely contaminated. No one was allowed to touch the samples he had labelled 'secure' without his express permission. 'No. No one's been around, Mike. Why?'

'Tell you later.' He went back to his office and phoned Jack, who was preparing for his rounds.

'How are you feeling?' asked Mike.

'Been better.'

'What time's the post-mortem on Palowsky?'

'Unless the pathologist can see the world in a grain of dust there won't be a post-mortem.'

'Don't speak in riddles,' said Mike, puzzled.

'Someone cremated Palowsky last night.'

'You're joking.'

'I don't make jokes often,' said Jack, his voice heavy from lack of sleep.

'What the fuck happened?'

'Apparently someone put on the wrong name tag and Palowsky was shipped out in the middle of the night for a ceremony that took place at Mill Hill Cemetery this morning.'

'Well, who's in the isolation room, then?' asked Mike.

'Some old guy who died last night.'

'That simply could not have happened.' Mike was emphatic.

'Believe me. Someone burned the body.'

'Shit. What a disaster. All my notes and samples have disappeared from my office. And I needed some more blood. I kept one phial in the lab. But that's not enough to work on.'

'What d'you mean, "disappeared"?' asked Jack. 'Have you lost them in that tip you call an office?'

'You know I'm always careful with samples, Jack. Someone's taken them. I'll get Security on to it immediately.'

'Jesus, Mike. There's a potential haemorrhage virus out there and you've lost the blood. I suggest you find it before someone else does.'

Mike put the phone down and it rang immediately. When he answered Susie Charles's sing-song voice responded. She was his boss's PA. 'Mike.' She gave the word two syllables. 'Mi-ike. The Head of Centre would like a word.' It was always 'Head of Centre' or HOC with Susie – never James or even Mr Graham. But Mike was always Mike. Sometimes he thought that Susie had a sixty-year-old brain in a thirty-year-old head.

'Can it wait, Susie? I've got stuff to do.'

'I think HOC said now, Mike. And I think it would be good of you to come now.'

Mike blew out a blast of air in irritation. An image popped into his head of Susie's neat, annoying little shimmies in her typing chair as she talked to him through a microphone attached to her headset. She looked like Uhura in *Star Trek* and Mike often wished he could be beamed up to another planet when he was in her presence.

'I'll be there in one second, Susie.'

'HOC will be grateful, Mike.'

Ten minutes later, Mike was still cooling his heels in Susie's office whilst James Graham took a phone call. Susie made repeated assurances that he 'will only be a teeny sec' as she sipped Earl Grey tea from her personal china cup, nibbled a chocolate Hob Nob and listened to a Cliff Richard song on the radio.

Mike tapped his fingers on his thighs, slumped back on a green sofa that had been fashionable when Terence Conran was fresh-faced, and settled to the task of working out the pathogenic permutations of a pneumonia virus that seemed to cause uncontrollable shaking and haemorrhaging. Where was that fucking blood? He tried to remember exactly what he had done with it.

He was lost in thought when, finally, the light clicked off on the mini-switchboard and Susie ushered him into Graham's office. The HOC was sitting upright in his chair, his long back straight and his shock of red hair a testimony to the strength of his Celtic ancestry. He was wearing a linen Prince of Wales-check suit from Jaeger. As a nod in the direction of the heat of the day, he was not sporting his customary waistcoat. His lips, as ever, were set in a thin frown.

'What's this I hear about a missing patient?' he asked. 'Security have been calling me since eight o'clock this morning. I don't like saying this to you, Dr Davenport, because I know you are not used to the disciplines of running a centre like this, having spent so much time with Americans in far-flung places, but your staff are not particularly well organised or disciplined.' His lined face settled into its usual craggy distaste as he talked about Mike's management skills. Graham had made it clear more than once that Mike was only hanging on to his role as Deputy Head because the World Health Organisation was insisting on it. 'You must tighten up, you know. You're not in the field now. May I suggest you go and sort out this mess with the missing cadaver? Have a report with me by tonight – including any disciplinary procedure that you recommend.'

Mike hesitated. Should he tell him about the blood? Christ, he'd better. 'I'm afraid there's another problem,' he said, stumbling over the words.

Graham sat back and let the silence draw out, waiting for Mike to confess.

Mike shuffled his feet a little. 'Someone's taken the samples from my office.'

Again his boss paused, and Mike could feel his face redden. 'Do you mean you've lost them?' said Graham eventually.

'I put them in the secure unit. I'm convinced of it.'

'But they're not there now?'

'No.'

'I suggest that you find them, Dr Davenport. Meantime, I will call Security and get them to search your lab. Your people are very careless.'

'My team are incredibly profess—'

Graham cut him off: 'I don't want excuses, Dr Davenport. Good medical science comes from patience and good practice. It would do you good to remember that. Bring me the samples and the disciplinary report.' He flicked his right hand in the direction of the door as a gesture for Mike to go, then he bent his head towards a pile of papers and started to write.

CHAPTER SIXTEEN

Tess watched Laura sip her tea. In addition to the chipped and bitten fingernails, the skin on her hands was hard and cracked. The laughter wrinkles around her eyes were slightly deeper than the last time they had met. But, God, she looked great. They were in a small kitchen-cum-sitting room in the hospital's private ward. Tess sometimes went there when she wanted to grab some peace. She and the Ward Sister were pals.

'Don't stare at me like that, sugar,' said Laura. 'I feel like an exhibit.'

'Sorry. I was just thinking how much I missed you.'

Laura put down her mug and bent over to hug Tess. 'Mutual,' she said, drawling out the word.

'So how was Mike?' Tess started to clear away the chocolate cake from the table. She had bought it from a patisserie on the way in, knowing that Laura was going to turn up.

'Can I have one more piece?' asked Laura. 'I haven't had anything as good as this since I flew into Khartoum.'

After Tess cut a large slab, Laura dolloped on two spoonfuls of double cream and tucked in with obvious relish.

'Stop stalling, Laura. What happened? Was he pleased to see you?'

Laura nodded gently. 'Seemed to be.'

'What d'you mean "seemed to"? Did he snog you?'

'Depends on your definition of snogging.' The word sounded alien to her tongue, as if she had just learned it. She smiled a little. 'No. Not by anyone's definition really. It was great to see him, though. Anyway, I think any kind of physical contact with Mike might turn into a dangerous sport if his girlfriend's face is any guide. I was lucky to get out alive, sugar.'

'God. Don't tell me Jane showed up.'

'On cue. Her girlfriend's sixth sense was working overtime.'

'She's a nightmare, Laura. Hates the kids.'

Laura sucked the spoon. 'Mike wouldn't be in love with someone like that, Tess.'

'It's not love.' Tess angrily bashed the plates and mugs into the sink. 'It's lust. Or something. Oh, I don't know. After you left, he went to pieces even more and she was kind to him. But now he seems to have recovered she's still smothering him. Even worse, she's shutting the girls out of his life.' She sluiced teabags. 'I wish you had waited round a bit longer, Laura.'

'I wish I had too, but I couldn't cope with the pain any more. I felt as if I was intruding on his grief. I don't know, I got it into my head that he would never fall in love with me.'

'He adores you, Laura.'

'Admires, maybe. Respects. Likes. But not love. He's never going to—' Her voice trailed off. 'I know it was selfish of me to go. But every day I wanted to be with him; to hold him; to touch his face. I found myself fantasising about holding hands on the beach, the whole enchilada. I felt as if my head was about to come off.' She wiped hard at the slight wetness around her eyes. 'Anyway, tell me about the girls. That was almost the hardest part. I really missed them. How's Jo's romance?'

'Don't start me on that,' Tess said, and then her beeper went.

CHAPTER SEVENTEEN

Dek Lee, Mike's PA, was listening to some hardcore thrash punk in his small, windowless cubby-hole of an office; his muscled arms were powering two drumsticks against a table. He was wearing a black T-shirt that emphasised his well-muscled body. His brown eyes glistened with the excitement of the music. When he saw Mike, he shouted: 'We played a fan-fucking-tastic gig last night. You should've come. We had four hundred old queens gagging for us. I'm telling you, we're gonna be fucking gay icons.'

When Mike punched the stop button on the recorder, Dek stopped drumming and looked displeased.

'Who issued the name tags last night for Palowsky?'

'The bleeder? I heard about that this morning. Sounded horrible.'

'It was. I asked Frances Davis to fix it.'

'What time did he turn up his toes?'

'About midnight.'

'I was in a muck sweat at midnight and hammering out our

third encore.' He battered the desk with his sticks again.

'C'mon, Dek. Hurry up. Who bagged and tagged Palowsky?'

Dek consulted his lists. 'According to this, Frances did it herself.' He swung the PC screen round and Mike saw the morgue notification form with Frances's name at the bottom.

'I've never known Frances to make a stupid clerical mistake,' he said.

'What mistake?'

'Someone put on the wrong tags and Palowsky was cremated this morning. He was in the closed coffin of a tramp who was mangled earlier that night in a road accident.'

Mike phoned Frances at home, who was shocked by the problem and assured Mike that she was very precise in her identification of Palowsky – as Mike had asked her to be. She had also definitely written on the notes that Palowsky was to be held in isolation in preparation for a morning post-mortem. Mike told her that he believed the account and not to worry. Another call established that the two porters who took the body claimed that they left it in the isolation unit as they were asked. The guard, Alan Wilkins, had seen them and signed off the delivery.

'Another fuck-up,' said Dek.

'Call Security and ask them to meet me at the Morgue,' replied Mike. 'Talk to everyone who has been in the lab since last night. Some samples have gone missing from the secure freezer. We need to find them urgently. Who else has access to the code?'

Dek checked the computer. 'Ten people have operational access.'

'Talk to each of them. I need those samples back.'

Ten minutes later Mike and Dek were standing by the door of the Morgue. A Chinese security man emerged, nodded in a friendly way and wandered off at a leisurely pace.

Winston O'Draper, the Head of Security, crunched towards them. At six foot six, he was imposing even at a distance. 'I

don't think I'll be meeting him down the club,' Dek whispered.
'Pity. I like the uniformed type.'

Mike stifled an urge to salute when O'Draper marched up to
them. He'd met many soldiers in his time on foreign assign-
ments and he knew the best way to handle them was to be
deferential and polite. 'Mr O'Draper. This is Dek Lee, my
assistant.'

'Uh huh.' O'Draper's big, ruddy face nodded at Dek.

'The nurse from my unit and the two porters who took the
body all claim that Palowsky was clearly identified when he was
brought here. Have you investigated what happened?' Mike
asked.

'I have, Dr Davenport. And I am confident that the mistake
must have been at your end. Alan Wilkins was on duty last
night; and he is very conscientious. A former Guardsman, you
see.'

O'Draper trundled into the Morgue ahead of them. The little
security cubicle was empty. 'Alan,' shouted O'Draper, 'where
are you?' His voice echoed off the tiled walls and was met by
silence. 'Strange, I spoke to him an hour ago and he agreed to
meet me here. Alan?'

A light was on in the isolation room and O'Draper led the
way in, then stopped. 'Christ, Alan. Jesus Christ. What've you
done?'

Hanging from a hook in the middle of the room, Wilkins's
bloated, naked body twisted like a flayed carcass. Mike heard
Dek retch as they saw the security guard's mutilated crotch.
His penis lay on the ground in front of him – sliced off by a
knife. On the table was an empty bottle of Scotch, a bloody
knife and a suicide note.

As they stood helplessly and stared at the wide-eyed terror on
the dead man's face and the protruding fat, blackened tongue,
Mike's pager signalled a message. Through his shock, he
registered the words. Then he said, "Shit!" and started to run.

Dek caught up with him. 'What's up?' he asked.

'Jack thinks we've got another one,' snapped Mike. He hoped Jack was wrong. If he wasn't, then it was a possibility that this thing was spreading. Jesus, that poor security guy. What made him do it?

In the post-mortem room the body of Marie Kecman lay on a table, the edges of which curved upwards to sluice the blood and guts. She had been cleaned up and Mike could see that she had once been very beautiful. His throat thickened as he recalled Anne's body, crushed from the crash, lying on a slab in a morgue. He pushed the thoughts from his head and focused on the gaping wounds of her body, which was slit open from throat to pelvis.

'She was dead when she got here. Bled out,' Jack said.

'Christ. Are you sure it's the same thing?'

'The passengers on the bus described her symptoms. They sounded similar. Her husband says she's been shaking a lot in the past few days, but he put it down to a heavy cold. Said she'd been losing her memory a lot. But,' Jack shrugged his shoulders, 'don't know.'

The two doctors watched as Fred McMasters meticulously set about the post-mortem. Fred's clever grey eyes seldom missed any detail. As Mike got closer, he noticed the smell of expensive aftershave that incongruously cut through the sharp, pungent, intestinal odours in the room. Fred wore it to remind himself that life was more important than death.

Each of the five people in the room wore a gown, mask and spectacles for protection against the fine spray of blood or brain matter. Fred talked into a microphone as he registered, weighed and probed the various organs. Mike was with him, taking samples of spleen, intestines, lymph nodes, lungs and respiratory tissue, and chilling them to minus four degrees centigrade to preserve them for analysis.

'What am I looking for, Mike?' asked Fred.

'Don't know. The trouble with haemorrhagic diseases, if that's what this is, is you can't tell from the organs what's going on. It's not like the sodding movies; the liver and spleen don't turn into mush. I'm taking some samples to ask Laura to have a look.'

'Who's Laura?'

'An old friend.'

'Ah. I remember her. The one who intervened when God gave you his time's up call. The one you bore for England about how great she is when you've had two glasses of cheap red wine.' He sliced again at some flesh. 'Ah . . . her.'

'Take that tone out of your voice,' responded Mike. 'There is no "Ah". "Ah" is definitely not on the menu.'

'Ah,' said Fred, and then a high-pitched whine bounced off the walls as the Stryker saw crunched into Marie's skull. After successfully slicing around the head, Fred levered off the cap of the cranium, cut through the outer membranes and exposed the brain, which he then extracted and put on a cutting board. They checked and weighed it before Mike carefully slivered off segments of tissue and put them in containers.

'A lot of internal bleeding,' noted Fred. 'What's she got then?'

'I wish I knew, Fred. I wish I knew. Give me a full report, will you? I'll see you later.'

As Mike and Jack walked back to the lab, Mike phoned Dek on his mobile and asked if the police had found out anything about Palowsky. Dek said they were still working on it. Palowsky appeared to have been an alias and there was no record of him with the Polish Embassy or in Immigration. Why he had an alias, no one seemed to know. There was still no news of the missing samples.

Mike gave Dek Laura's telephone number so that he could contact her and ask her to meet him in the lab. Then he turned to Jack. 'We must keep up the pressure on the police. I still can't believe Palowsky – or whatever his real name is – fell apart like that. And what was all that shaking and dementia about? And how infectious is the bloody thing? And what is it travelling in? And did he pass it to Marie Kecman?' His frustration boiled up and he said emphatically: 'We need to know where he's been. And we'd better bring in Mr Kecman and Marie's son.'

'Simi.'

'We need to test them for a virus,' said Mike and phoned Dek again to have the samples prepared for investigation.

Later that morning Mike and Laura pored over the details together in Mike's lab, while around them the team worked on the blood, tissue and brain.

'I'm worried about the shaking and the memory loss, Mike,' she said. 'The nurse who admitted Marie said she was like an nv-CJD patient in her last throes.'

'That's impossible', he replied. 'Her doctor's notes give no indication of any such symptoms.'

'Could be sporadic,' noted Laura, 'rather than new variant. And if you think of the patient Jack treated – he has symptoms closely related to CJD. D'you want me to take a look?'

He shrugged his shoulders. 'Anything's worth a try.'

Over several hours the team working on the brain decon-taminated tissue blocks from Marie's central nervous system in formic acid. Then they processed the tissue in paraffin wax and cut sections on what was effectively a small bacon-slicer. These were stained for analysis with haematoxylin and eosin dyes: the former showed up the nuclear structures blue and the latter stained the cytoplasm – the outer structure of the brain-cell – a reddy orange. Mike hovered over the team as they unhurriedly performed their task. They were used to his impatience. When they were ready they turned the samples over to Laura who disappeared into a lab.

Jack turned up with a can of Coke for Mike and a Camomile tea for himself. Beside him was Liz O'Mara.

'Hi Liz. Good to see you. Never been up here before.'

'First time I've been involved in anything like this, Mike. What d'you think it is?'

He shrugged. 'Still working on it.'

'One thing always amazes me about you Mike,' Jack said.

'What?'

'Well, contrast the discordant tip that is your office to this . . .'

Mike looked around at the precisely aligned, neat array of microscopes, cultures, phials, pens, pads and electronic organisers. 'I can't afford to miss anything. Too many people have died testing this stuff. Viruses scare the living shit out of me and I give them respect.'

Mary Mortimer, the lab assistant, came over and handed some results to Mike. 'Her white blood-cell count shows that this thing is definitely viral. And it's the same thing Palowsky had.'

Mike could see Laura at the modified Leitz microscope in the next room, examining Marie's samples. Her face was impassive, almost frozen in concentration. He went to join her, hoping she would confirm that the thing was viral. At least they had fought those before, he thought.

Green light from the screen of the Sun computer, tracing the ghostly shape of the pathogen, suffused the room as he entered. She looked up at him, her eyes momentarily unfocused.

'What've you found?' Mike asked.

'Tell you in a second.' She punched in some instructions asking the computer software to calculate the amount of the brain that was traumatised.

'Have a look,' she responded quietly. 'She had major spongiform change. In fact it's status spongiosis.'

He shook his head with a shiver, as if hit by a small electric current.

'Her neurons are all but wiped,' Laura continued. 'And the number of holes in her brain tissue makes it look like crochet. It's riddled.'

Mike peered at the cell nucleus on the screen: around it was a group of deformed, mutant proteins – these basic chemical building blocks of life, had turned against Marie Kecman's brain and devoured it.

'My god.'

'I don't know what kind of CJD variant we're talking here. But we're dealing with a major prion thing.' Laura's voice was tired but calm.

'But why the haemorrhaging and the fever and the presence of a virus?' Mike shook his head. 'I mean, Christ almighty, it sounded to me from what Jack said when he examined her that she had classic symptoms of Lassa or HFRS. Something really nasty, but at least understandable. But this . . .' His voice trailed off.

Jack arrived at his shoulder. 'What's going on?' he asked.

'Whatever she's got is throwing off mutant proteins like confetti,' Laura said.

Mike took over the keyboard and overlaid the images with those taken from other CJD cases. 'I've spent a bit of time on this stuff since Graham turned the unit into a CJD centre. This doesn't look like new variant, nor is it a sporadic form,' he noted. 'Different molecular signature.'

'I'll tell you something really weird, Mike,' said Laura, her puzzled look intensifying. 'What with the holes and the build-up of plaque on the cerebellum it looks a bit like pictures of kuru that I've seen. Certainly not a million miles away.' She turned to the PC by her side, and called up information on kuru on the Medi-Call home-page on the Web.

Liz O'Mara put up her hand and said: 'Hold on, you're losing me. What exactly's kuru? It's a kind of CJD thing isn't it?'

'How much do you know about the different forms of CJD?' Mike asked.

'Just the basics. It's caused by proteinaceous infectious particles. Prions for short.'

'Right, the normal proteins mutate for some kind of chemical reason. No one is entirely sure what happens or why; but the mutation kicks off a killer chain reaction in the brain.'

'Why are we getting viral results then?' asked Liz. 'Prions aren't viral.'

'God knows,' Mike answered. 'But even if it is prion related, it can't be kuru.'

'Kuru's that New Guinea thing, isn't it?' Liz said, peering over Laura's shoulder at the information on the screen.

'Yes,' Mike said 'It's never been seen outside of a small tribe called the Fore.' He hit the scroll button and Liz looked at some grainy black and white pictures of a Fore ritual.

'The Fore believed in some kind of ritual human cannibalism in which the brain of the dead was consumed by women and children,' said Mike. 'Somehow, somewhere down the line, it's possible that they ate the brains of someone who contracted a prion disease and it passed down the chain. The mortality rate was shocking.'

'Kuru takes years to appear,' said Jack, 'and she would have shown clinical signs of loss of co-ordination before she turned up at the hospital. And there is one fundamental difference,' he continued, 'haemorrhaging has never been associated with prion diseases.'

'So what are we dealing with?' Liz asked.

'God only knows. The terrible thing about prions is that they are insoluble. Nothing can destroy the buggers. You could bake them in a tandoori oven in hell and they'd still survive. Once they're in the brain they are always lethal.'

Laura leant back in her chair and swung gently back and forth, taking up the story from Mike. 'But the good news is that prions are not very infectious. In order to transmit disease they have to gain entrance to a new host either by inoculation or by eating infected meat. Ingestion is slow – it can take years to reach the brain from the gut. But direct inoculation into central nervous system tissue is the most reliable means of transmission.'

Mike stared at the printout of the results again. His face showed suspicion as his mind rolled around the problem.

Laura pointed to the detailed prion images on the screen and said, 'It's going to take a while to get a real fix on this. But trust me, Davenport, if it's not something like kuru then feel free to request my degrees back, 'cause clearly Harvard taught me zip. I've just got a feeling about it.'

Mike massaged his temples as he looked at the pictures. He was beginning to feel a migraine build up and needed some aspirin. Who would believe that he had a patient in London with kuru-like symptoms?

Laura stretched up in her chair, her long back arching. She began to do the sitting yoga routine Mike had seen many times. It was her way of remaining calm. He had seen her do it often when they had worked together in Bolivia, and later when she gave the girls yoga lessons.

'But how is it managing to have such a catastrophic effect so quickly?' Mike wondered aloud.

Laura bent and twisted to the side, her eyes closed. 'Think about it. We both know what happens when a patient is dying of a haemorrhagic fever.'

'Uncontrollable bleeding,' he replied, 'the blood just drains away and the virus seeks a new host.' Mike felt a shock as the memory of his own death flushed up through his thoughts like a dye in water, spreading panic as it went.

'And that's what happened to Palowsky and Marie Kecman,' she pointed out. Turning to Mike, she rolled her shoulders and said, 'Rub my neck for me sugar. The jet lag is getting to me.'

Mike could feel her supple but toned flesh beneath his fingers as he kneaded gently, oblivious to the curious eyes around him.

'Christ.' Mike nodded as he processed what she'd said. 'I see what you mean.'

'Would you two stop speaking in code,' Jack grumbled irritably.

Laura's voice was heavy with deliberation. 'What if a virus is acting like a magic bullet and somehow carrying mutant prions right into the brain? So when the virus jumps for a new host, it carries the prion disease with it.'

'But the level of febrile response from both Kecman and Palowsky suggests a level three or four virus,' Jack replied. 'These things blow up in days. Would the prions have time to replicate?'

'Good question,' replied Mike, stalking round the small room. 'But try this.' He turned to a whiteboard and quickly sketched a couple of options. 'What if the virus isn't a killer.'

'A weaker version of a haemorrhagic fever?' Jack asked.

'Yeah. If you're in healthy condition and have decent treatment you'll survive.'

'But the virus has parachuted the prions into the central nervous system and they go in for the kill,' said Laura.

'But why the explosive haemorrhagic response?' Mike asked himself and closed his eyes. 'We know that CJD patients end up in a helpless, dependent state and often die of other diseases, such as pneumonia. So what if our nasty viral bugger, having been the carrier, takes advantage of the exhausted body of the host.'

'And *bang!* Explosive exit strategy,' Laura said. 'Could be, Mike. Could be.'

'Anyway, this is all theory. We'd better find out if there's a link to Palowsky,' Mike said. 'If this thing is acting the way we've just described, well, I don't want to think what might happen.'

'Where the hell did it come from?' Jack asked.

Laura bent down and picked up her black shoulder bag. 'This little world's throwing up lots of surprises these days, babe. Someone out there might be doing a little unauthorised genetic engineering, or disturbing some eco-system somewhere, and two unconnected critters have met and married. All it needs is for the proteins of an undiscovered haemorrhagic virus to alter and find a way of passing between animals or people, and we've got ourselves a new bug.' As the others in the room digested this, she collected her stuff, ready to leave.

'Now.' She stretched her back and twisted her shoulders. 'I've had about six hours sleep in the past two days. I'm completely shot. I'm going to take a long bath with a couple of shots of tequila thrown in. Tomorrow's going to be a long day for both of us. We are gonna find ourselves a proper lab, with decent Level Four security facilities, and then we're going to find out what this little quasimodo is, and how it's hopping around.'

Mike felt queasy at the thought of a fast-acting, blood-carried CJD variant. He'd better contact the CJD surveillance unit in Edinburgh in case they'd seen anything like this.

'What are you going to tell Graham?' Jack asked Mike.

'Good question. He thinks that the whole new-variant CJD thing was a product of media hype,' Mike replied. Then he imitated his boss's accent. ' "Ten cases a year, that's all it ever was. Ten cases and we slaughtered millions of cattle. Complete madness, Dr Davenport. Complete madness." Also he thinks that the introduction of the new slaughterhouse and cattle-feed regulations have pretty much dealt with the problem. I'm pretty sure he'll think our analysis is incompetent or fanciful. He's not one for intuition.'

'Well,' Laura tapped the pictures of the prions on the screen, 'you bring him over here and introduce him to our little friends. They sure ain't candy cotton.' She swung towards the door. 'Mike, Level Four this thing. Anyone else coming in here with anything like it, and you give everyone protection. Otherwise, we've got problems. Big problems.' As she reached the door, her voice dropped a little. 'Want to join me for that drink?' It was a diffident question, positioned as a throwaway that she could disregard if the answer was negative.

Mike hesitated. 'I'd love to but . . .'

'That's all right,' Laura said quickly, cutting off his refusal. 'I'll see you tomorrow. Enjoy.'

CHAPTER EIGHTEEN

Li Danping watched as his patrician wife slowly massaged his feet. Her lush auburn hair bobbed beneath him as she rubbed on the special rejuvenating ointment flown in from a clinic in Switzerland.

It was humid outside, but his office was as cool and gentle as a spring day. He allowed flecks of concern to enter the recesses of his mind. The Company had now dispensed with almost all of the men who had contracted the disease and had gathered their blood to be stored in an underground vault in Montana as security against a rainy day.

Two batches of blood remained. Disappointingly, despite Fernandez's undoubted skills, one remained in the hands of a British doctor. And inside the warm body of an American mercenary called Andrew Samuels the virus was incubating. No one knew where Samuels was.

'Darling?' His wife's voice rattled against his ears. He looked down at her pert nose, opalescent eyes and unostentatious earrings that had cost him more than his father had earned in his long life as a waiter in a Hong Kong hotel. The Boston accent disclosed her Brahmin origins.

'Mm,' he responded unwillingly, reluctant to allow her to distract him.

She stood and reached her full five foot nine – two inches taller than him. Sarah's back was long and thin and her body followed an elegant plumbline until it reached her Calvin Klein loafers. She was wearing a simple white shirt tucked into black Dior slacks – revealing a waist that had never undergone childbirth but was extremely familiar with the inside of her personal gym. Once a month Li weighed and measured his wife before a full-length mirror in their large white bathroom. If she met his specification, he made love to her there and then, her face staring back from the glass as he took her from behind. Her obvious distaste for the position made it all the more satisfying.

'I'm very worried about Alex,' she said as she finished and wiped her hands on a thick green hand-towel.

Li smiled indulgently. 'How much does your brother need this time?' He found his continued financial support of the Brayshaws, Sarah's family, a tiresome price to pay for his wife's total obedience. The family had enjoyed power in Boston, Washington and New York for two hundred years until Sarah's father got a little too greedy in the stock market and a little too close to Li and the Company.

Sarah was part of Brayshaw's debt repayment. But with her came the family – though Li had to admit that her younger brother, Alex, was on occasion useful. Having an Under-Secretary in the State Department sometimes washed away problems. Alex had helped smooth relations with the Belizeans after the Company's Mayan escapade.

'Well,' Sarah stroked his face, but he withdrew in distaste and watched her eyes cloud with fear: she had forgotten that no gesture was welcome unless initiated by Li. She folded her hands and bowed her head slightly, not looking him in the eyes.

His heart lifted. A white woman, reeking of wealth and

privilege like the women who had ordered his father around as if he were a dog, stood before him utterly subservient.

'He needs a facility for one.' She kept her voice low and submissive.

'A million dollars?' Li snorted. 'That's a little high even for Alex.'

'He'll pay you back, darling. I promise. A few stocks have not gone as well as he thought. It's just that, you know—'

'It's just that he is a completely pathetic judge of the market.' His voice whipped her. 'Where did he get the money in the first place? I cancelled his credit.'

'He had friends, you know, kind of friends.'

'And what will his friends do if I do not extend this act of charity? Will we find dear Alex at the bottom of the harbour?'

She said nothing and waited – still and silent. Then Li spoke gently into the telephone by his side. 'Leonard, would you arrange for my brother-in-law to have credit at the bank to cover some positions on which he has gone long?'

Sarah smiled and dropped on to her knees in front of him as he had gestured. Her mouth busied itself and he was silent for fifteen seconds, then continued: 'Apparently he has some friends who may pester him a little. Would you have them contacted by a few of our colleagues and explain that he is not to be touched? And that I personally will take an interest if he even stubs his toe on the sidewalk.' He could feel Sarah's mouth around his cock and her tongue flicking hard and he blew out softly as he came. Closing his eyes, he practically whispered: 'Please come through, Leonard. I wish to discuss the situation we have about Mr Samuels.'

Sarah made as if to stand, but Li said: 'Please remain there, my dear. I am enjoying this moment of intimacy. We seldom have time for tender minutes like this.'

She remained where she was, kneeling before him, her mouth full of his sperm. Then Jacklin rapped on the door and Sarah's eyes pleaded with Li as he said, 'Come in,' in an even tone. After he offered a slight nod Sarah swallowed and stood as Jacklin glided into the room. Li noticed his employee staring at his wife in some surprise as he registered what she must have been doing. But Sarah's composure was absolute: 'Will you be joining us for *Don Giovanni* on Wednesday night?' she asked, her voice light.

'Of course, Sarah. I believe that it's a wonderful, energetic production.'

'See you there, then.' She turned to her husband and kissed him gently on both cheeks. 'Goodbye darling. Don't be late tonight.' She left, head high, back straight.

Li walked to his bookshelves to select a book to take home, slipped a first edition of Wodehouse's *Summer Lightning* from its protective wrapper, and read aloud with pleasure the opening sentences: 'Blandings Castle slept in the sunshine. Dancing little ripples of heat-mist played across its smooth lawns and stone-flagged terraces. The air was full of the lulling drone of insects.'

'Do you read Wodehouse, Leonard?'

'No', responded Jacklin, looking at Li warily, 'too frothy for me, I'm afraid.'

'Ah, so you've missed the subversion.' Li put the book on the desk beside the large folder that analysed a new gold mine in Bolivia that the Company intended to take over.

Jacklin smiled uncertainly.

Li looked him up and down. 'Wodehouse's aristocrats are weak and stupid, his middle class is venal, and his working classes are criminals. His England is a comic dystopia. Exactly as I recall the fools I had to deal with in Hong Kong.'

Jacklin nodded as if agreeing and pursed his lips a little in judicious assessment of the truth of Li's statement. Li could see the little flicks of contempt that Jacklin struggled hard to keep from his eyes.

'I have a task for you,' said Li. 'I want you to fly to England to help Mr Fernandez deal with one of our friends in the government. There is a debt the Company needs to be called in; but the debtor may be unwilling. Some of your persuasive charm may unblock the problem. I do not want any link between the Company and this virus.'

'But what about Samuels?'

Li patted him cordially on the back. 'Don't worry so much, Leonard. It'll ruin those patrician good looks. You sort out the little problem in London and by the time you have returned, I'll have fixed Samuels.' He looked slyly at the younger man. 'After all, this may be my last job before I retire.'

Jacklin stared at him for a beat longer than necessary to register that he noticed the implication. 'Consider the problem solved,' said Jacklin; then he turned and left through the double doors.

'I already consider the problem solved,' said Li.

CHAPTER NINETEEN

Despite the shimmering heat that rose scalding from the concrete ground, Simi Kecman was shivering as he waited for his social worker to pick him up and take him to the hospital for his test. He stood in a quiet corner of a scruffy green patch of grass in front of the block of flats in which he lived. Martin – his stepfather – had told him his mum had died and then thrown him out of the house with a pound to buy chips. He felt terrible, suffering with a bad cough and headache. He wanted to go home. But what was there to go home to? He could feel the tears begin again and tried to stop himself. First one drop, then another trickled down his face as his stomach felt unbelievably empty and his headache worsened. 'Mum,' he whispered to himself.

A stray football bounced over and landed at his feet; he kicked out at it in fury and it flew against sharp spikes protruding from the park fence and burst. Then his tears could not be restrained.

Alex Cosic, the boy who owned the ball, rushed over and

shouted at him: 'You'll pay for that. You'll fucking pay for that. My dad gave it to me.'

'Leave me alone.' Simi tried to walk away.

'That's twenty quid, you fucker. You better fucking give it to me or you're fucking dead.'

Simi backed off. 'I'll give it to you tomorrow.'

Alex jostled him. 'Look everyone, Simi's crying. What a fucking wimp.'

He put his face up to Simi's – who could smell his halitosis – and Simi pushed him away.

'You're a mummy's boy.'

Simi hit him on the nose with the flat of his hand and Alex yelped and jumped back.

'You're fucking crazy. Just like your mum. My dad says your mum was a tart and she died of AIDS. I'll have to take a test now. Fucking orphan.'

Simi screamed at him, jumped and grabbed Alex by his dark hair. But Alex, bigger, stronger and two years older than him, tripped up Simi and kicked him in the face: blood began to pour down Simi's face into his mouth. He could taste it.

But he refused to give up, scrambled to his feet and tried to scratch the older boy's face. The boys' bodies became entangled, each unwilling to allow the other the space to lash out with fist or boot; they both became covered in Simi's blood, which spilled over their shirts.

Michele Shepherd's long fair hair appeared above the circle of boys who were shouting and screaming their encouragement for the two combatants. 'Simi, Alex stop this at once. Both of you. Enough.' She reached in and grabbed Alex's jersey. 'You should be ashamed of yourself. The boy's mother died during the day and you are fighting with him.'

'Silly tart,' Alex shouted at Simi's social worker, who had come to fetch him.

She looked at the bloody mess that was Simi and said: 'C'mon, we're going to Casualty at once.'

Michele Shepherd's Ford Fiesta was neat and trim until Simi's blood began to leach all over the seats. The smell of Michele's expensive scent, brought back by her boyfriend Thomas from his first business trip to France, permeated the interior. But it was not enough to counter the acidic smell of Simi's urine that gathered in a pool on the carpet beneath him.

'Can't you hold it, Simi? Oh, God.'

Simi started to shake uncontrollably and blood spurted over the handkerchief Michele had given him. She handed him a box of paper tissues and tried to encourage him to use them. But by now the boy was slipping into shock. His convulsions continued and the blood spattered over the windscreen and over her.

On her mobile phone, she dialled the number of A & E and, practically sobbing, she told them she was bringing in a bleeding boy and could they be ready?

CHAPTER TWENTY

Although the humid atmosphere made Mike's shirt stick to his body like cling film, he felt as if a cold wind had blown through Graham's cramped, book-lined room as he explained his fears of a prion mutant.

Graham sat imperiously upright on his leather seat – framed on either side by gloomy, deathly, Rembrandt prints. The Head of Centre's back was straight and his eyes hard. He was looking at the electron microscope images on his desk. 'Are you seriously suggesting, Dr Davenport, on the basis of one rather vague case of an unknown prion disease – that could easily be a sporadic occurrence – and an unrelated haemorrhage case that we may be facing a prion mutation?' He shoved Mike's evidence to one side and buried it under another set of files.

Mike shuffled uncomfortably on the low, hard chair in front of Graham's battered, treacle-brown teak desk and looked at his boss. 'My intuition tells me it might be possible. And Laura Holmes is convinced.'

'I fear you may be a little overworked at the moment.

Perhaps a break would help.' Graham's voice hovered between concern and irritation.

'Let's accept', Mike's throat felt dry, as it always did when confronted with bureaucratic authority, 'that there's no connection between the two patients.'

'A connection impossible to prove because of the incompetence of your staff, I may remind you. Have you found the blood samples yet?'

Mike let the reprimand fall between them and ploughed on. 'There is still the evidence of Marie Kecman.'

'What evidence?' asked Graham.

'The prions and the haemorrhaging. Why don't you come over to the lab and have a look?'

'I can't, I have an important meeting. How long has Kecman been in this country?'

'Six years, I believe,' replied Mike.

'And how long is the incubation period for kuru or any form of CJD?'

'You know as well as I do that it could be any length of time. Months, years, decades.'

'So she could have picked it up in Bosnia. And the haemorrhaging might be another disease.'

'I've checked with her doctor and there is no evidence that she had clinical signs of any CJD-like infection. What if the haemorrhaging is the product of another mutation among prions that produces inflammatory responses? I mean, Christ, just suppose that the capsid of a haemorrhage virus got mixed up with a prion disease, or that the prions somehow mutated themselves. Who knows how it might be transmitted? It might even be in our food chain. Let's suppose—'

Graham's hand went up with the exasperation of a traffic policeman in a gridlock. ' "Let's suppose" is, as you know, Dr Davenport, my least favourite phrase. It is the last refuge of spoon-benders and astrologers. Even by your own account, this woman could not have caught an inflammatory disease from a non-inflammatory cause. You have one case, Dr Davenport. One that you know little of. I don't think I need worry over-much about wild speculation.' He swung his chair around to the side, stood and walked to the door – clearly eager to be rid of Mike. 'Besides, the Minister is making his speech soon and unnecessary public speculation on your part would not be helpful to our cause.'

'C'mon, James. You wouldn't jeopardise public health for the sake of political expediency. I think we should alert the Ministry and the WHO. I don't know what this is exactly, but if it is transmitted in food or blood, we'd better get cracking on containment.'

Graham loomed over Mike, his eyes dark and his mouth set. 'I, young man, have taken care of the public for thirty years now. I will be retiring in two years' time and I will not have my final period dogged by crazy speculations about killer bugs put about by an overexcited zealot. The reason they refused to appoint you as Head of Centre, Dr Davenport, and brought me down from Aberdeen, was your inability to monitor situations and make mature judgements.'

Graham walked to the door, pulled it open and said pointedly through tight lips: 'You've been around Americans like Miss Holmes for too long, Davenport. You're a glory hunter, what with your radio shows and newspaper quotes. Why don't you settle down to proper science and real medicine? Perhaps then I could trust you and share some of the pressures of running this Centre. Now you will speak to no one about this. Do we understand each other?'

Mike shook his head. 'No. I don't think I do understand you.'

'Goodbye, Dr Davenport.'

As Mike left, he saw Susie's face flush with pleasure at his dressing down.

Graham growled at her. 'Get me Lawrence Ellington at the Home Office.'

CHAPTER TWENTY-ONE

Shit, thought Mike, it's seven-fifteen. Kensington Place. Jane. I've got to be there at eight.

Forty minutes later he dashed into the bright, ebullient atmosphere of one of London's fashionable restaurants. Although he had never been there before, and hated posh restaurants, he knew that Jane loved it. Five minutes early, he noticed from the clock on the wall. Fantastic.

Twenty minutes later he was reduced to reading the menu once more simply to give his mind something to do. He was trying to ignore the conversation to his left between a bright-eyed man with a shock of dyed blond hair and a marine-blue shirt, and a woman in dark glasses and a straight-cut black trouser suit. He was complaining that some television actor, whose name Mike vaguely recognised, had snubbed his AIDS bash.

'But, sweetie,' she replied, 'AIDS is so eighties. Time to move on.'

Mike managed to tune them out, but the big restaurant was

too noisy with the clatter of other people trying to out-talk one another for him to phone Jane on his mobile. As he walked out, he stopped, put his hand on the table of the odd couple, still chattering as they picked at their sole with lemon grass, and said: 'Thirty million people are dying of AIDS in India and Africa as you eat. Enjoy your supper.'

Outside, people were milling around aimlessly – unwilling to go back to their stuffy houses and uncertain as to how to spend their evening. There was a curious thrum to London, as if its usual high-tensile harmonies were loosening and becoming discordant as the city tried to discover a new, lower, more relaxed register. A couple walked past him, swinging their blond four-year-old between them. The small boy smiled at Mike – a gap-toothed grin.

'Mike, how lovely,' replied Jane when she answered the phone. 'Where are you?'

'At the restaurant, of course. I've been here since five to eight.'

'Oh, you were early. Well done, darling. That must be a first for you.'

'So when will you be here?' He watched the boy plead to be lifted up in his father's arms and then grin in delight as he was hoisted on to the man's shoulders.

'Oh, a dreadful thing's happened, Mike. Something's come up at the office and I don't think I'm going to be able to come. I've been desperately trying to leave since six o'clock.'

Mike could hear the cackle of voices around her. She must be somewhere with people. Then he heard a tinkle of glasses. She was in a wine bar or a pub or a party. 'I could come and pick you up,' he replied.

'I don't think so, Mike. I've got such a lot on. And I'm really tired after staying up so late last night. I think I'll go home to bed. Do you mind? Perhaps your old friend, what's her name again? The plain girl. Ah, yes, Laura. Perhaps Laura would like to have dinner with you. Old times an' all.'

He tried to find a way of telling her he really wanted to see her without sounding patronising.

'I'm sure Laura would be pleased if you took up her invitation to buy her dinner. Did she enjoy the massage you gave her? Bye, Mike.' The phone went dead.

He tried again immediately, but she had switched her mobile off. A sad feeling gripped him as he walked into the bijou backstreets behind Notting Hill, found the car, and began the drive home. After fifteen minutes of self-recrimination about Jane, he put 'Honky Tonk Woman' on as loud as he could and allowed his mind to wander over the landscape of the disease: dipping round corners trying to take the pathogen by surprise; drifting like a cloud over featureless landscapes searching for a landmark that might point to the solution to the puzzle. He had an imaginary conversation with Anne, sharing the problem with her, as he had done so often when she had been alive. Then his phone rang. It took a few seconds for his everyday mind to resurface.

'Mike?' Laura's voice was urgent. 'Sorry to disturb your meal.'

'Don't worry about it. Jane got held up at work.'

'Ah.'

'What's up?'

'We've got another one. The woman's son. Her husband's just turned up drunk. He's got a friend with him who insists on talking to you.'

'I'll drop in on my way home.'

After he rang off, his phone buzzed again and Mike was puzzled when the flat, South London voice of the caller asked: 'Is that Dr Mike Davenport?'

'Yes. Who's calling?'

'It's Rob Fentiman from the *Sun*. You got a second to tell me about this bug that's doing the rounds?'

'How did you get my number? No, it doesn't matter. Would you please not call again?' Mike switched off his phone. Bloody journalists, he thought as he drove up the hill towards the hospital.

The scene outside the car reminded Mike of southern Spain or North Africa. Couples were strolling around with their children in tow; he could hear jazz drifting lazily down from a marquee in the park; the pub on the corner had overflowed on to the streets and gangs of people were sitting on the pavement laughing and joshing with each other.

Ten minutes later, Mike parked and joined Laura in the quiet room on the third floor where they counselled bereaved parents. She met him on the stairs. 'Sorry to drag you in, honey.'

'That's OK. How come you're back here?'

'I couldn't sleep thinking about this thing. I came back to have another look. See if I can pick up some clues about it. You know what it's like.' Her pupils looked wired; but she was clearly tired.

Mike did know. These diseases stuck to the mind like limpets, demanding solutions but hiding their mysteries as jealously as the Sphinx.

He hugged her shoulder and felt her stiffen slightly.

She moved towards the door that led into the room. 'The boy's stepfather is here. He wants to talk to you.'

Mike entered behind her. On the seat was a middle-aged man, with a fat, ruddy face beneath a cloud of long hair that was an unnatural shade of raven black. He was wearing a T-shirt and a pair of combat trousers. In his hand was a can of strong lager and on the table before him were several that he had emptied earlier.

Mike looked at Laura, who shrugged. He decided to say nothing. The man was obviously in shock.

'This is Dr Davenport', said Laura.

When the man stood, he swayed a little. A strong whiff of cigarettes, beer and BO filled the room. He put out his hand. 'Martin Kecman, Doctor. Thanks for talking to me. I've . . . It's—'

Beside him, a younger man touched his arm and said: 'It's all right, Martin. Don't worry about it. Sit down until you're ready. We can wait.'

Mike looked at the second man. He was in his late twenties, wearing an expensive-looking blue suit and had a gold ear stud.

'I'm Martin's cousin, Frank,' he explained.

Martin stared at the floor and then asked: 'Have I got it?'

Laura shook her head. 'No,' she replied, 'you've been lucky.'

'Not like my poor Marie.' He sucked down the beer again.

'So what is this thing, then?' asked Frank.

Mike sat down beside Martin; his voice was heavy. 'I'd be lying to you if I said I knew what it was or how it was transmitted.'

'So it's a mystery bug, then?'

'No. It's not a mystery. It's a form of prion disease.'

'So what's that then?'

'It's like CJD.'

'But you don't get CJD that fast. I thought it took years,' Frank said.

'It does, normally,' Mike confirmed.

'So it is a mystery then?'

'No, it's a bit like kuru. A disease unique to highlanders in New Guinea.'

'How do you catch it?' Martin's voice was tense.

Mike was reluctant to go into details. 'People picked it up when they consumed brain matter when preparing the dead for burial.'

'Whoa there,' Frank grabbed Mike's arm, 'are you telling me that there's a bug in the UK that normally exists amongst cannibals?'

'No.' Mike's voice was wary. 'I said this thing is *like* kuru in some of its features. But then so are several CJD-variant cases.'

'Is the bleeding normal?' Frank asked.

'What bleeding?'

'Come off it, Dr Davenport,' said Frank, 'Simi's social worker was covered in blood when she brought him in. She's having hysterics, poor love.'

'The blood-borne aspect of it is mysterious. I can't explain it.'

'You got another beer?' asked Martin.

'Run out, Martin,' said Frank. 'I'll go and get you some more.'

'I'll come with you.' Martin lumbered to his feet. 'I need something to eat.'

'Thanks, Dr Davenport. Thanks very much,' said Frank as they left the room.

'Nice,' noted Laura.

'Very.' Mike offered a weary smile. 'Want to come back for a bite of supper with the girls?'

She hesitated and then shook her head. 'I'd love to, but I want to do a bit of work on Simi Kecman's samples.'

Mike held her hands in his. 'Don't overdo it, Holmes. I . . . we . . . don't want you to exhaust yourself again. Come up later for a drink. Promise?'

She squeezed his hand. 'We'll see.'

'Promise.' He returned the pressure.

'I promise,' she replied and a grin tugged at the side of her lips.

Ten minutes later Mike entered his house and shouted 'Anyone interested in giving me a hug? It would be much appreciated.'

Molly rushed from the twins' study and hugged her father. 'We weren't expecting you for hours and hours.'

Jo emerged, dressed, Mike noticed in the latest girl rebel uniform of clumpy Doc Martins and ripped black jeans, and said: 'Oh, hi, Dad. I thought you were spending the night with your girlfriend.'

'My girlfriend is called Jane. And no, I'm not. Something came up.'

'I'm glad she gets as little of your time as us,' Jo retorted.

'Darling.' Mike's voice was strained. 'Play nice for a while.'

Jo shrugged and turned away again.

Molly linked her arms under her father's and tugged him in the direction of the kitchen. 'Have you eaten?' Her voice dropped to a whisper when they arrived by the fridge. 'Be sweet to her, Dad. She's just been dumped.'

'Into what?'

'Dad.' His daughter expressed her exasperation with an exaggerated blow of air and a theatrical gesture of hands on hips, elbows akimbo.

'What?'

'Not a what, a who? She's been dumped by a boy. She'll get over it. She always does.'

'What d'you mean "always"? She's twelve years old, for God's sake.'

'She's thirteen next week. She's practically a woman, you know. Or have you forgotten?'

Mike suddenly remembered an embarrassing conversation about menstruation the previous month. Tess had forced him to go and buy pads for the twins and sat all three of them down to discuss the facts of life.

'I'm still not over the fact that you can walk and talk and you start springing this stuff on me,' he grumbled, gently.

'Let me make you some scrambled eggs.' Molly took a heavy blue pot down from the shelf. 'Or there's some chilli that Tess made for supper.'

'Where is Tess?'

'In her room. She's upset about something. It's probably man trouble. I heard her crying when she was talking on the phone earlier.'

Mike pulled open the large fridge that his wife had imported from the States and extracted an open bottle of chilled South African Sauvignon. 'I'll take her up a glass of wine. Has she had something to eat?'

'No. She made the food and disappeared.'

Mike ladled some of the thick, red chilli on to a white plate and watched the juice slop to the edges; he hoped that Tess was sticking to the beef that he ordered from a farm in Scotland. Christ knew how this kuru-blood thing was jumping. It could just as easily be in meat as in anything else. As the microwave heated the food, he asked Molly: 'So, what d'you think of Jane?'

'She's not funny like mum was.'

'She is funny.'

'She's kind of sharp, rather than funny.'

Mike had silently to acknowledge the truth of that statement.

'And she doesn't really like us.'

'It's only a question of time.'

'Oh, Dad, you don't understand girls, do you? She wants you to herself. She wants to have some fun; not go to Alton Towers.'

'But you and Jo'd rather die than go to Alton Towers.'

'That's not the point. She doesn't want to be forced to do things as a family; because we're not her family. And, Dad, just think of what it'll be like in a few years when she wants to have children of her own. What will we be then?'

He hugged her. 'You'll be my girls. My darling girls. That's what you'll be.'

'We'll be grumpy, spotty teenagers with a bad attitude and a stepmother who is just waiting for us to leave for university before throwing out our clothes and books,' said Jo, slouching into the room like a thundercloud.

Molly and Mike exchanged arch glances and the microwave timer announced that Tess's supper was ready. Mike extracted it, glugged white wine into a tall tulip glass, put the meal on a tray with a plastic rose from the arrangement by the window and took it upstairs. He knocked on the door. 'Tess?' There was no response. 'All men are bastards, Tess. At least allow this one to give you a bit of supper.'

He then opened the door and Tess invited him in to her normally immaculate bedroom. Her nose was red from crying and her bed was littered with used tissues. She was curled up in a foetal position. Mike saw that her uniform was in a ball on the floor beside the large blue armchair that she retreated to when she wanted to read in peace. On the wall above the king-size bed was a UNICEF poster with a young black child staring down at them. The musky smell of scent hung lightly in the air. Beside the bed was a group of photographs showing Tess at work in Sudan when she was with the Voluntary Service Overseas. Others had the twins as babies in Tess's arms and a picture of Mike's wedding to Anne.

'What's wrong?'

'I got another one.'

'What do you mean?'

'Simi Kecman. I was on duty. I had his blood all over me.'

'Jesus Christ. I gave orders that everyone was to treat this as Level Four.'

'Graham countermanded you.'

'Bastard. What is he up to? Did you take precautions?'

'I think I'm OK,' she said. 'I made sure I had a bio-mask on me. Christ, Mike, it was disgusting.'

'Dad, there's someone on the phone for you.' Molly put her head round the door.

'Who is it?'

'A guy called Fentiman. He says he met you earlier at the hospital. Something about someone called Kecman.'

Mike was puzzled. He hadn't met Fentiman, but only had that terse conversation on his mobile. He picked up the phone and said, with irritation: 'I told you earlier I've nothing to say. Besides, I don't remember meeting you . . .' Then it dawned on him: Frank. That was sodding Fentiman.

'Look, Dr Davenport, this is an issue of public interest. You're not trying to cover something up are you?'

'Of course not. You tricked me earlier. All of that was off the record and not to be used.'

'Why not just answer my question and I can do my job? And you can get on with yours. The more you tell me, the less I'll have to make up. It's my editor; he really wants this story and he'll splash whatever I do. So you may as well help me. The dead patients were Bosnian, right?'

'Yes, Marie Kecman and her son, Simi, were Serbian.'

'According to my contacts,' said Fentiman, 'Mr Palowsky was a Serb called Uzelac.'

'What contacts? Why hasn't anyone told me?'

'Bear with me, Dr Davenport. You said kuru was a disease found among cannibals. And you know that the Serbs are rumoured to have eaten some Muslim flesh during the war as a kind of initiation ceremony.'

'Really?'

'Yeah, really. So is it possible that they could have got kuru from that?'

'Technically, yes. But—'

'Thanks, Doc.' The phone went dead.

Mike looked at Tess, who was shivering as if she was slipping into shock. 'Don't worry,' he said, 'it's a prion disease and they're incredibly hard to catch. You'll be fine.' He hugged her to him and whispered calming words. But inside his guts were churning. The fucking thing had jumped from Marie to Simi Kecman and possibly from Palowsky to Marie. Could he get Graham to believe him? They must start rounding up everyone who had been in contact with the Kecmans and Palowsky first thing in the morning.

CHAPTER TWENTY-TWO

L_i completed his meditation with a loud shout to awaken his senses from their slumber. Refreshed after an hour in deep relaxation, he turned on the CD player and allowed the internal logic of Beethoven's Pastoral Symphony to pleasure him. He was sitting in a small, glass breakfast room in his twenty-four-room Victorian house overlooking Cooper Lake at the topmost fringes of New York State. From the large plate-glass window he could see a small stream flowing under a grey-brick bridge he had built with his own hands. Beyond that the light from a crisp spring day was sparkling across the leaves of hundred-year-old trees, planted when the house was young. He felt at one with himself. This was achievement and harmony. He had made his mark on someone else's history; he had added to the world.

A soft red light pulsated from a bulb beneath the marble table on which he had placed a single white rose to aid his meditative state. No one was allowed to penetrate this room; but, even here, he could not allow the Company to be beyond his reach. The light told him that someone wanted to speak to him urgently. Everything in its time, he thought.

He poured purified water into a glass and focused on the sound as the liquid met the crystal. He sipped twice and wet his lips, then turned off the music and returned to the ancient Buddhist prayer mat on the ground. He sat listening to the sound of nightingales. The two birds were caged behind a matt-black screen at the end of the room. For two minutes Li sat, sipped water and watched the river, allowing the flow from the outside world to enter his soul. Only when he was ready did he walk quickly from the room, his bare feet pattering across the floor. A tall English butler, formerly from the English Club in Hong Kong, handed him a telephone and a note with the name of the caller. Li took both and waved away his servant. 'What is it, Fernandez?'

'Not good, I'm afraid.'

'I thought you had taken care of that particular bit of business.'

'The parcel was taken delivery of, but a doctor called Davenport has kept one of our stamps,' replied Fernandez. 'Also, it looks as if the problem has jumped. Our friend seems to have passed it to others.'

Li was silent and calculating. 'No need to be too cautious, Mr Fernandez. We have a secure line here. Can the disease be traced back to us?'

'Yes. Davenport has samples from the original donor and these could be tracked back to Belize by the WHO. If they find the resting place of the dead Mayans and take samples, they'll be able to join up the writing.'

'I would be very sad if that happened, Mr Fernandez. Very sad indeed.'

'I believe that the WHO computer system is very buggy and prone to crashing and losing data. But what else would you like me to do?' asked Fernandez.

'I have sent Jacklin to discuss this with you. He's coming on

Concorde and will be with you in a few hours.'

'But surely that isn't necessary.'

'I will tell you what is necessary, Mr Fernandez. I'm sure you would not like to undermine our long friendship by crossing me.'

'Of course not, General.'

'Jacklin will be in charge of medication from here on. And Mr Fernandez, do not call me again. I wish to know nothing more personally of this issue. All communication will be through Jacklin.'

Li cut off Fernandez and walked through to his study, a restored Victorian library, a harmony of dark wood and Chinese glass. On his desk was a small parcel. Li was irritated. His mail was always read in the breakfast room. His study was a place of reading and solitude. He opened the package in irritation. Inside was a clear plastic box containing five fingers. At first Li thought it was a sick joke. Then he noticed that on the fingers were rings he recognised: they belonged to his brother-in-law. Li wondered who had the rest of him. He looked at the box again. It was encrusted with Mayan icons. Suddenly, he knew the name of the killer.

CHAPTER TWENTY-THREE

The sound of the phone ringing crashed through Mike's slightly hungover brain. He ungummed his eyes and looked at the time – quarter to seven. It must be something urgent, he thought, and was immediately awake. 'Yes?'

'Mike?' It was Jane; she probably wanted to apologise for last night. 'Are you off your fucking head?' she hissed.

'That's a bit rough, babe.'

'Rough. Wait until the Minister gets hold of this. Let alone what Graham'll make of it. You are so fucking stupid sometimes. Can't you learn to keep your big mouth shut?'

Mike tried to work out if he was still asleep and this was a bad dream. 'Slow down. What're you talking about?'

'I'm talking about today's *Sun*.'

'What about it?'

'Let me read you the front-page headline: "CANNIBAL BUG EATING BRAINS CLAIMS TOP DOC." '

'Shit,' said Mike.

'Oh, it gets worse, let me tell you,' she said and then read out the rest of the story: ' "In an exclusive interview, top virus doc, Mike Davenport (39), told the *Sun* yesterday that a 'mystery cannibal bug is just chewing up people's brains'. Dr Davenport, Deputy Head of the London Centre for Infectious Diseases, told our reporter that: 'Serbian cannibals have got it and are passing it on.' So far, three Serbian immigrants in London, Marie Kecman (28) and her son Simi (8) and Dragoslav Uzelac (27) have caught the killer disease." '

'This is a tissue of half-truths,' he interrupted.

'Did you talk to Rob Fentiman?'

'No. Yes. Well, he pretended to be Martin Kecman's cousin. He must have paid the poor sod so he could ask me questions I wouldn't answer under any other circumstances. Jesus, can't we stop this? It must be illegal.'

'Did you answer any questions?'

'In a manner of speaking.' Mike lay back on the bed, replaying the conversation with Fentiman in his head. The creep. Through his open window, Mike felt the sun's rays heat up an already stifling room. A fat, gorged fly lazily buzzed around the light.

'There is no manner of speaking,' she snapped. 'Did you or didn't you? Christ, Mike, you'll never become Head of Centre if you keep making media gaffes like this. What've I fucking told you?'

'Don't shout at me, Jane. I don't deserve it. And I don't want to be the Head of Centre. I'm going to resign.' There was no response. 'If you want to help me,' continued Mike, 'perhaps you could suggest what I might say to the rest of the media when they catch up with me today. Look, Laura was with me when I met Fentiman. She'll verify my story.'

A silence flooded the line. Mike could tell that Jane had brought her anger under control when she said: 'You've exposed yourself on this one. Say nothing to anyone and I'll see what I can do to control the spin. And what's all this about resignation? Don't be silly. I'll call later. We'll sort this out.'

'Thanks,' he replied.

'Oh, and I'm sorry about last night, Mike. It was really difficult to escape. We must talk. See you later for a drink. Say, seven-thirty,' she signed off on a positive note.

Mike got up and brushed his teeth. His head felt wrapped in cotton wool and the mirror told him he looked like shit. He felt older this morning. As if his fortieth birthday in a month's time might actually be some kind of watershed in his life.

'Dad,' shouted Jo from downstairs, 'you're on the *Today* programme. They're making you sound like some kind of idiot.'

'Damn,' he whispered at the red-rimmed eyes in the mirror.

CHAPTER TWENTY-FOUR

In a small, stifling sandwich bar just off Brompton Road, Fernandez and Ren drank scalding coffee from mugs. The remains of his bacon and eggs congealed on Fernandez's plate.

Ren asked: 'You not going to eat that?' And when Fernandez shook his head, Ren swapped over the plates, forked the thickened yoke into his mouth and talked with his mouth full. Ren pointed at the *Sun* and its report. 'So, who's this Davenport guy?' he asked.

'He's the Deputy Head of the Centre. A clinical epidemiologist by training.'

'Yeah?'

Fernandez could see from his slightly vacant look that Ren hadn't a clue what an epidemiologist did.

'He tracks down diseases to their hosts and traces the causes and the courses of epidemics. And now, thanks to the newspapers the world thinks that Mr Uzelac got the bug in his own lovely homeland.'

Fernandez handed across a buff envelope as Ren chewed a

mouthful of limp bacon with the fat striated through it. Ren opened it and stopped chewing for a second.

'That is truly disgusting.'

Fernandez looked at it. It was a colour picture of a Muslim baby, its head burst open and the contents spilled across a Vukovar street. Two young Serbian guerrillas, their eyes as dead as the child, were grinning whilst they held the brains in their hands. One of them was Marie Kecman's first husband, the other Dragoslav Uzelac. The picture came from the Chinese Security Service.

'What's that for?' asked Ren.

'That's for the front page of the newspapers tomorrow. Davenport still has one phial of Uzelac's blood that you missed when you stole the rest.'

'Don't worry about that, man. His little freezer unit has gone into meltdown, as of,' he looked at his watch, 'an hour ago. That blood is useless.'

'Anyway,' continued Fernandez, 'for some reason he hasn't traced the disease to South America. But he could do soon, and if he does, there is a chance that it may be traced back to us. I want to lead him even further away and, even if he does claim that it comes from South America, the newspapers and the authorities will be focused on the Balkans.'

'Not bad for an old white guy.' Ren licked his lips and looked in more detail at the photograph. 'These guys are amateurs. Look at the way they're sitting there out in the open. Anyone could've picked them off.'

'Amateur killers are always the worst.' Fernandez took back the photograph, put it in the envelope, wrote Rob Fentiman's name on it and addressed it to the *Sun*. 'They don't know when to stop.' He looked at the newspaper next to Ren. It was open on page four and the sad story of the ex-army hero who killed himself the day before. Ren looked unconcerned as he glanced at the photograph of Alan in his uniform, looking proud as he received a medal from a Princess. Fernandez raised an eyebrow.

Ren shrugged and said: 'He fucked with me, man. A lesson had to be taught.' He gingerly fingered his bruised nose.

Fernandez shook his head and closed the paper. He hated dealing with emotional people.

CHAPTER TWENTY-FIVE

At nine-thirty, Mike dropped into Jill Obudo's shop. He needed a chocolate fix. 'Hi, Jill.'

'Hello, Mike.' She was looking doleful and distracted.

'What's up? Anything I can do to help?'

Her big head shook slowly from side to side like corn in the wind. 'Not unless you're strong enough to tie my Victor to the ground. He's just not the same boy since he came out from that bloody place. Anyway, you've got troubles enough of your own.' She nodded to the disappearing stack of *Sun*s on the counter. 'Seems like everyone has bought one of these today. Mr Graham came in first thing. He looked angry.'

I'll bet he did, thought Mike. He dropped in to see Dek — who had a plastic skull on his desk. When he saw Mike he pushed a button at the back of the cranium: the mouth opened in a grin and two flashing eyes popped out.

'Very funny, Dek.'

'I thought so. Having a boss on the front page of the *Current Bun* will make all the difference on the PA circuit. None of those old tarts' bosses have been anywhere other than the fourth page of the *BMJ*. Apart from, of course—'

'Robert Forester.' Mike cast his eyes to heaven.

'Old spanker himself. Caught *in flagrante* with a student nurse on the operating table by a party of Japanese surgeons.'

'Well, thank you for the comparison.'

'Dearest, his PA lived off that front page for months. Keep up the good work.'

'I've got to see Graham. Will you set it up for me? Pronto.'

'Actually, *El Creepo*'s been asking for you for twenty minutes.'

Mike went into his inner office and his heart hit the floor. Water was leaking from the security freezer: it was defrosting. He hit the keys and checked out the contents. Jesus, he'd lost his last sample from Palowsky.

'Mike,' Dek was emphatic. 'Go now.'

Graham was standing by a large sash window; the slats of the wooden venetian blind threw linear shadows into the room and seemed to slice up his long body. He said nothing as Mike entered and stood in the middle of the room. The frozen tableau seemed, to Mike, to last for ten minutes, but in fact consumed only one.

'Well, Dr Davenport. A pretty pickle. Pretty indeed.'

'Not of my doing,' replied Mike forcibly.

A soft knock at the door was followed by Susie's bird-like face. 'You have a visitor, Mr Graham.'

Crossing to the door, Graham opened it wider and said: 'Come in, Jane, come in. It's lovely to see you, as ever.'

Jane walked in. You look fantastic, thought Mike. She was wearing a crisp white shirt, a blue DKNY skirt and her bare, tanned legs ended in a pair of loafers. Despite the heat, she looked businesslike and professional.

'D'you know Jane Hume?' asked Graham.

Very few people knew of their relationship – at Jane's insistence.

'Nice to see you again,' said Mike.

'It's been such a long time,' she replied, a bit too acidly for Mike's liking. The spring thaw of this morning had obviously not lingered. She had been bombarded by press and TV looking for a comment from Mike.

'You do realise, Dr Davenport,' Graham sat on his chair and looked directly down on him, 'that the Yugoslavian Embassy has been on to the Foreign Secretary this morning demanding an apology.'

'For what?'

'For our assertion that the Serbs are cannibals.'

'I didn't say they were cannibals. Fentiman did.'

'I believe you to be a good man, Davenport, and not unintelligent. But you must learn that journalists are not interested in the welfare of the public.'

'He tricked me.'

'You should just have said no comment, Mike.' Jane's voice was professional and distant.

'I tried.'

'Not hard enough, Dr Davenport,' said Graham. 'Obviously not hard enough. Now, I'd like you to work on a press release with Miss Hume here.'

Jane took a sheet of paper from her black, leather bag and explained that she had already drafted something denying any mystery bug and apologising to the Bosnian Serbs.

'I'm not apologising for anything.' Although Mike glared at Jane for ambushing him, she held her gaze on him. 'Because I didn't do anything.'

Graham read the release, praised it, and told Mike that he insisted he sign it. When Mike again refused, Graham said: 'I may be forced to discipline you, Dr Davenport.'

Mike slapped his hand on the table and his eyes pricked with anger. Every day, nurses like Tess were having to work with viruses they barely understood. And now the potential mother-lode was opening up around them. 'Three people have died from a prion-variant disease that may be related to something in our food chain, or, even worse, is passing in blood. Give me the research support I need to work out what is going on.'

Graham shook his head. 'You have an overactive imagination, Dr Davenport. By the time I was your age, I had been running a research lab for three years. I know the need to be patient with public health issues. Otherwise, you will terrify the population. You've already lost Palowsky's blood samples; for which I must reluctantly discipline you. I think you must be much more careful.'

Mike realised he was losing his temper and therefore the argument. He brought himself under control and calmed his voice. 'James, unlike you, I have seen the worst that nature can throw at a body. I have seen pathogens that make science fiction look tame. Can't you trust my instincts? Fuck knows what is going on out there, but I suggest we find out.'

'Please don't swear in my office, Dr Davenport.' Graham walked to his desk and lifted the press release. 'Will you authorise this to go out?'

'No.'

'Well then, Miss Hume,' he turned to Jane, who was looking at Mike with a concerned expression that quickly turned to indifference when Graham caught her gaze, 'I will issue my own press release. I would like you to write it for me. It should distance the Centre, the hospital and the NHS from Dr Davenport's wild accusations.' He pulled open the door. 'Good day, Dr Davenport. If you talk to the press once more about this, consider yourself suspended. Likewise, if you spend any of the Centre's research time or capacity on this wild prion chase, you will be suspended. Do I make myself clear?'

'Perfectly.' Mike spun on his heels and left.

CHAPTER TWENTY-SIX

Jack and Tess sat by the only window of his office. It led out to a small, red-brick terrace big enough only for the few, dying pot plants that Jack still tried to coax into something resembling life. His fingers were pressing compost into the hard, dry earth around a lemon-scented geranium, and his tongue slid gently on his lower lip as he concentrated.

'Do you think Mike and Laura are bonkers on this?' asked Tess.

'Bonkers? No. Is their diagnosis perhaps wrong . . . ?' He looked into her eyes and she could see the calm pool of reflection. Then he shrugged his shoulders.

'Not enough evidence?' she asked.

'What Laura and Mike suggest is very unlikely. It's hard to see how this disease is being transmitted the way their model demands.'

Tess dipped her fingers into a jug that Jack had brought out and drizzled the water on to her throat. It trickled down her neck and on to her chest. Christ, it was a sultry day. 'I thought,' she said, 'that these new diseases could take all sorts of diversions.'

'But there is no evidence that a prion disease can become blood borne in this way. It just has never happened.' Jack tied the main spine of the plant on to a cane.

'But what if it's a black swan?' Tess's voice was thoughtful.

He looked up again, and she admired again the gentle slope of his nose and the crinkles around his eyes.

'You know,' she said, 'all swans were thought white and it was considered a logical impossibility that anything other than a white swan would be a swan at all. And then, where was it? Australia, I think. They found black swans.'

He wiped the sweat from his face, blinked his eyes twice and smiled. 'I see what you mean. You think I'm being too safe. Well, I have to be. I've made diagnostic mistakes in the past. Big ones.'

He dug hard into a plant, and Tess knew that he was thinking of the misdiagnosis of meningitis that caused the deaths of two teenagers in Kuala Lumpur, and almost led to an outbreak in the local university. He had been so ashamed that he left the country.

'I have no intention of doing so again. When Mike tells me what this is, I'll treat it. Until then, I'll not join in the speculation. There.' He stood up and retreated into the warm, soupy gloom of his office. 'That's that. They might live, after all. Although we need some rain.'

He took Tess's hands. She could feel grains of dirt and see the transfer of earth to the tips of her own fingers. He raised her from the chair on to her feet and she stood close to him. She breathed deeply, inhaling his musky smell that reminded her of sex. Slightly taller than her lover, she felt big and awkward beside him.

He leant across and touched her lips with his. 'I have something to tell you.' He took a deep breath and slowly eased out the tension he was obviously feeling. 'My mother wishes me to return home and marry the daughter of one of her friends.'

She panicked. Jack's voice was flat and unemotional. He's going to break it off. Calm down, she thought.

'She tells me she is dying, and her wish is that I should give her grandchildren.'

'I understand,' she said, her heart sinking.

'I owe my mother everything. She slaved to put me through medical school.'

Tess struggled to hold herself together.

'I've told my mother about us,' he said. 'She is not pleased.' His smile was rueful.

Tess wanted to cry but she would not do so in front of Jack. 'I understand,' she whispered, 'truly I do.'

'No, you don't,' continued Jack. 'I've paid the price for my failures. And I've given my mother everything I could. Now I will do what is good for me.'

'What's that?' she asked, her heart racing.

'I want to marry you and have children.'

'In that order?'

'Strictly,' he answered.

'Strictly when?'

'When can we start?'

'How about practising the making babies bit until we've got it down pat?' She pulled him close and down and they slid together on to the polished floor. 'I love you, Jack.' Her lips locked on his and she could see in his eyes a longing so intense and deep that it met the depths of her own being.

CHAPTER TWENTY-SEVEN

Mike crunched the gears in his car, trying to blow out some frustration as he headed to Palowsky's address in Shirlock Road, next to Hampstead Heath. Disregarding Graham's orders, Mike had spent the morning pulling out all the stops to track down the movements of Palowsky – the index patient. He bombarded the police and Immigration and invoked all sorts of obscure public health orders to force them to crank up the investigation. Graham would find out eventually, Mike thought, and then there would be hell to pay. Jane would have to write the press release explaining his resignation. He felt angry at her: she had phoned explaining that she was 'only doing her job', and that she was a professional, just like him. Their conversation had taken a downwards spiral that ended in an inconclusive, rancid silence.

Mike struggled to shake off his depression and focus on the problem at hand. It turned out that Fentiman was right. Mike was eventually told by the police that Palowsky was indeed a Bosnian Serb called Uzelac. Given Mike's anger at the story leaking to the press before he knew anything about it, the investigating inspector gave him permission to search Uzelac's rooms before anyone else, especially when Mike explained the nature of the pathogen. Mike did not want clumsy plods disturbing anything that might give him a clue as to the origins of the disease.

Fernandez sat in his Mercedes three cars behind Mike and listened to the conversation Mike was conducting with someone called Tom Grantmore at the World Health Organisation. Fernandez now had bugs operating in Mike's office, house and car. The doctor was the only one who might stumble on the truth and that could not be allowed to happen.

'Why don't we just kill him?' Ren asked from the seat beside him. He pointed two straight fingers at Mike's Volvo, cocked his thumb and mouthed: 'Boom.'

'Wonderful idea,' snapped Fernandez as he manoeuvred his big car into the slipstream of the black Metro behind Mike. 'Let's start a full-scale police investigation. That will really protect the Company. General Li will think that is a great idea. Would you like to call him with it?'

'OK. OK. Man, it was only a thought.'

'Don't think.'

'Don't talk to me like that, old man. One of these days you'll fall out of favour and I will enjoy slitting your throat. If you're nice to me now, I'll do it quickly. If not—'

'Shut up and let me listen.' Fernandez turned up the speaker and Mike's voice filled the car.

'I don't understand this pathogen, Tom. Any ideas?'

Tom's thick, dark Tennessee voice replied: 'God knows what's out there, Mike. Who had heard of Ebola until twenty years ago? Every time one of the goddam loggers rips out hunks of rainforest, or miners gouge another chunk from African soil and start a shanty town, or farmers feed chemicals or animals to each other, I wait here for the epidemic.'

'Yeah. But a CJD variant that produces inflammatory symptoms?' asked Mike rhetorically, still unable to make the symptoms add up. 'Prions don't do that. But, as Laura keeps telling me, everything is getting so fucked up these days that the best hypothesis is to test the impossible.'

'Wise girl, Laura. Who says it can't happen?'

'James Graham, and he is one of the world's experts on the subject.'

'Is that the same Graham who, in 1988, said that prion diseases would never reach significant levels in humans? And who refused to repatriate a nurse from Sierra Leone because she had Lassa fever. I had to phone the Foreign Secretary before anyone would help.'

'I take your point,' responded Mike.

'Graham's normally either too cautious or not imaginative enough,' said Tom.

'But what's the link with pneumonia?'

'Might not be one,' replied Tom. 'You know what happens when the immune system gets fucked up for whatever reason. Those little bacterial and viral bastards just slip in there and start eating whatever they can find. It's possible that your patients are picking up the pneumonia virus from being in the hospital. Nowhere worse to be with a useless immune system than a hospital: it's like a viral bouillabaisse in those places. If I get sick, I'm doing it at home.'

'Could you do a sweep for me?' asked Mike. 'And find out if anyone is reporting anything like this?'

'Will do. Send me the results and some blood and I'll have a look myself.'

'I thought you were too grand for that now that you are . . . What are you again?'

'Director of the Emerging Diseases Programme.'

'That's the one. No longer a cowboy, Tom.'

'We've all got to grow up sometime. But send me the stuff. I'm still a better scientist than you'll ever be.' Tom was the first African-American to gain top honours in Biochemistry at Harvard Medical School.

'True enough, Mr Director. True enough. See you.'

When Mike ended the conversation, Fernandez picked up the phone to Company Security and informed his senior lieutenant that they must ensure that Grantmore was to be followed and that all his calls were to be monitored. He also wanted people on the ground in Belize, just in case. If anyone else showed signs of coming down with the disease, they were to be eliminated.

'When are we going to ice Davenport, then?' asked Ren.

'When I say so,' replied Fernandez testily, feeling boxed in by the need to get Mike out of the way without drawing any attention to the Company. 'And would you stop talking as if you are in an American movie,' he grumbled.

'Man, don't tell me you don't dig Quentin. Do you know what they call a Big Mac in Paris?'

'Yes, but I prefer *filet mignon*. Now, please, leave your puerile ramblings for another occasion.' He watched with a troubled heart as Mike pulled into the street in which Uzelac had lived.

Mike noticed that many of the houses in Shirlock Road had acquired the quiet affluence of somewhere that had come up in the world. Plane trees lined the pavements and drooped shadows across Mercs, BMWs and Jeeps. A Labrador lay panting in the cool shade of one of the trees, its tongue drooling.

Pulling his sweaty shirt away from his skin, he swigged down a can of Coke he had extracted from a wine cooler below the passenger seat. The cold liquid bubbled down his throat as he looked at the house. It had grimy yellow curtains, a broken step leading into an overgrown front garden. Although it had four storeys, the owner had divided it into flats, as Mike could see from the three bells by the door. The name on the top one was Drina, another alias for Uzelac, according to the police.

Mike rang the bottom button, marked Peirce, and a hefty woman crowned by a small beehive answered him. Her pink lipstick was a little crooked and she was wearing shocking-pink ski-pants that might have looked good on someone half her age. Mike took his ID from the inside of his baggy linen jacket and showed it to her. She told him that the police had told her to expect him and that the flat he wanted was on the top floor.

She was Uzelac's landlady – Mary Peirce. In response to Mike showing her the photograph of Uzelac, she confirmed in a broad Dublin accent that he had been her tenant but that he had called himself Drina. She hadn't seen him for over a week and then the police had called to say he was dead. 'God love us, he was a good lad. Helped me often enough. Never too proud to lend a hand in the garden. And always paid on time. And in cash. I'll miss his beautiful eyes. Jesus. And he'd only been back for three weeks.' She sighed.

'Back?'

'From abroad.'

'Where abroad?'

'He'd never talk about things like that. Kept himself very quiet about his wee trips.'

The sweet smell of fried chips from Mrs Peirce's kitchen hit Mike as he stepped through the door and headed up the narrow stairs. Mrs Peirce whispered: 'Don't wake Mr Drummond on the first. He's been on the night shift and hates being wakened.'

When Mike reached the third floor, the smell of Chinese takeaway mingled with the musty atmosphere of a single man living alone. Mike opened the door, stepped in, and, with considerable surprise, was met by a spick and span room: barrack quality. There was a double bed with a bright, striped duvet. Porn magazines were stacked neatly on the pine bedside cabinet. A blue Ikea desk sat below the sash window that looked out to the back of the house. Beside the desk was a telescope trained on the bedroom opposite.

Quickly, Mike turned his attention to the desk. There were three drawers down the left-hand side and he tried each in turn – they were locked. He found a screwdriver and jemmied them open. In the top one was a sheaf of spent plane tickets made out to someone called Grabinski – presumably another alias. Why so many names?

In the bottom drawer was a small photo album. It opened with a family group – a grandmother, mother, father and three children were sitting at a large table filled with meat, bread and fruit. The smallest child was grinning on his father's lap, and applauding the person taking the photograph. Extracting the picture, Mike turned it over. An inscription read: 'Drago's sixth birthday, Osijek.'

The next group of photographs showed Uzelac in military uniform: he looked every inch the professional. A thrill of shock ran up Mike's spine when he saw that Uzelac was standing next to a much younger Marie Kecman, his arms around her as if she were his girlfriend. Were they lovers? Is this thing transmitted sexually? Mike shivered at the thought. When was the last time they had met? Jesus.

The last few pictures shocked Mike. In one a wild-eyed Uzelac, was pointing a long knife at a group of men lying dead at his feet; their throats were slashed and blood was pouring across the ground. In the last he was surrounded by four black soldiers; their gleaming faces made his seem all the more white. On the wall behind them was painted some graffiti. It was a language that Mike recognised from his time in Africa. Uzelac has been in the Congo. Probably one of a group of mercenaries. Was he anywhere near the Ebola zones? But what does that mean? Has he brought something back with him? Did he have a viral haemorrhage disease? Are the cases unrelated, after all? His head was buzzing with the problem. Haemorrhage viruses have a very short incubation period: three to eight days. Had Marie seen Uzelac in that time?

When was he in the Congo? Mike looked again at the sheaf of recent airline tickets: Guatemala, New York, Cologne. They were all dated four weeks back. But not one for London. How did he get here? Mike thought again about Guatemala. There were certainly features of the disease that were reminiscent of a

South American haemorrhagic fever, but for all his magic-bullet theories about the virus and prions, he still could not work out the connection.

He closed his eyes and again allowed himself to drift around the problem. On opening them, he saw the telescope and thought, try it the other way around. I'm looking at the problem through the wrong end. Instead of looking at the prions, I should be thinking of the haemorrhaging. It must be possible for a virus to attract proteins that mutate if they come into contact with a new life form — somewhere in the rainforest, perhaps. Somewhere like Guatemala.

He pulled open the doors of an old, brown-stained wardrobe. Inside were a half-dozen suits with fashion labels that Mike recognised from magazines, and a dozen pairs of shoes in all colours. Uzelac obviously liked to look good. Ferreting around in the pockets, Mike found credit cards made out to one of his aliases, and then his heart stood still. The man had a blood donor's card. Oh, Christ, not that, please don't let him have been giving blood.

Phoning Dek, he gave him the details and told him to get on to the Donor Service to find out the last time someone called Greg Kristof gave blood and where the batches were being stored. Mike then told Dek to have them transferred to a Level 4 location.

With Dek on the case, Mike stopped and took a deep breath. He needed to know more about this man, the index case. He looked at the half-dozen or so books on the shelf above the two-bar electric fire. Apart from a couple of Tom Clancy thrillers, there was a history of Serbia in English and then some cheaply printed books with lurid titles like *Serbia Betrayed!* and *Blood on their Hands: The Modern Ustase*. The Ustase, Mike vaguely remembered, were Croatian extremists who had been backed by the Nazis during the Second World War. He lifted the book and turned it over. On the back was the legend: 'Printed by the Friends of Bosnia's Serbs. 19 Wilkin St. Director, Brinda

Bejramovic.' When he turned the book to look at the front
cover again a photograph fluttered to the floor. Mike picked it
up and saw a very handsome woman, probably in her early
thirties, with a strong nose and high forehead, very Slavic. On
the back was written: 'For Drago. In The Struggle. Brinda.'

A noise startled him and he turned. Mrs Peirce bustled in:
'D'you want a cup of coffee, darling? I'm making one for
myself.'

'No, thanks.' He handed her the photograph.

'Have you seen her before?'

'Many times, darling. Many times. She was one of Drago's
girlfriends.' She nudged Mike in the ribs. 'Between you and me,
I think he was a bit sweet on her.'

'D'you know where I could find her?'

'No idea. I never ask questions of my gentlemen.'

Then he showed her a photograph of Marie Kecman and
asked if she had been there recently. Mrs Peirce looked hard and
shook her head. He thanked her for her help and told her under
no account must she allow anyone else into the room until he
had had it thoroughly disinfected and all bedding and furniture
had been burned. He was taking no chances.

'I thought I could give his clothes to Oxfam. He had
beautiful things. Look at this.' She indicated a cloth draped over
her arm. 'A completely gorgeous blue shirt.' She lifted it up and
Mike could see a dark stain on the chest.

'What's that?'

'Oh, it's covered in blood. He hadn't had time to do anything
about it and he asked me to take it to the cleaners' but I forgot.'

'When did he ask you?'

'About three weeks ago.'

Mike stared at it. He had a blood sample of sorts. He was
back in business. 'Get out of here, Mrs Peirce, and don't come
back in. I'm going to get someone to come quickly and bag
this. It's very dangerous. Do you understand?'

She looked scared. 'Can I get it from this?'

'No, no.' Mike soothed her. 'But just to be on the safe side, I'll ask someone to drive you to my hospital. It's in Primrose Hill, I'm afraid.'

'Oh, dear, what about Tubs?'

'Tubs?' Mike looked down and a fat, ginger tom rubbed against her leg. 'Take him with you.' Might as well test the cat, he thought, you can never tell.

He called Dek, ordered an ambulance and a clean-up team and gave careful instructions that the shirt was to be triple-bagged and taken to Laura. She would know what to do.

'Where are you going?' asked Dek.

'To a broken-hearted lover.'

'Are there any other kind?'

The offices of the Friends of Bosnia's Serbs were located in a smart, glass-fronted office block that had been gouged out of the houses in Wilkin Street in the early 1980s. Someone must have money in this outfit, Mike reflected. He was sent to the third floor and was glad to be somewhere that believed in air-conditioning. According to the radio, if it got any hotter outside, the unions were threatening to pull out workers who were not given water breaks.

The neat, tastefully grey reception area had two comfortable chairs and a glass table on which was a small pot plant. Above the plant was a poster depicting two strong hands – one clutching an Orthodox cross and the other an AK-47.

An elegant woman dressed in black jeans and an open-necked shirt came out of her office to meet him. 'Dr Davenport.' She extended a cool hand and invited him inside her room that had a beautiful Serbian wall-hanging covering one wall. 'How can I help you?' She was brisk and businesslike, and her accent was still strong. Mike could see a copy of the *Sun* on her desk and wondered why she did not immediately ask him about the article.

'I'd like to talk to you about Dragoslav Uzelac.'

'I don't believe I know anyone by that name.'

'That's curious, because he had your picture in his house. And the ambulanceman who helped him into King Henry's Hospital swears that it was you that dropped Mr Uzelac off when he was ill.' Although Mike was bluffing, he was confident that he was on the right track. He watched Bejramovic tug gently at an ear on which was a gold earring in the shape of an Orthodox cross.

'Is he dead?' she asked quietly.

'Yes.'

She fell silent and he could sense her grief begin to build. But he must press on. 'Why did you claim he was Polish and that he was called Palowsky?'

'I didn't give a name.'

'But why did he call himself Palowsky?'

'That was his name.'

'Not the one you wrote on the back of the photograph. You call him Drago.'

She looked at him and said softly: 'So I did.'

'Was there something he had to hide? Something involving you?'

'Why do you need to know any of this, Dr Davenport?'

He pulled out the photographs of the Kecmans. 'Do you know these people?' She nodded. 'They died in the most horrible way imaginable', said Mike. 'I need to know where Uzelac has been to stop the disease doing the same to others.'

'Drago was a very secretive man,' she replied.

Mike could see fear in her eyes. Do I have it? she was asking herself.

'Did he have a reason to keep secrets?' A reason like a war-crimes trial, wondered Mike.

'We all have secrets, Dr Davenport.' She stood. 'Thank you for bringing me this news. And now I have people to attend to; people who need my help.'

Mike extracted a photograph from his pocket. 'Do you have children, Ms Bejramovic? Because if you do, you'll appreciate why I want to save children like this.'

She looked at the photograph of Simi taken on his deathbed and barely flinched as she handed it back. 'Once. I had a daughter. They killed her.'

He did not ask who 'they' were: Croatians, Muslims? 'I need to know where Uzelac has been if I am to eliminate the possibility that he brought the disease into your community from abroad. For some reason, it is attacking your people first. Christ alone knows whether it is building up among others. This boy and his mother died in great pain.'

She picked up the copy of the *Sun*. 'You believe we are devils, cannibals, and you come to me for help. Why should I help you? You are a propagandist, just like everyone in the British media. Not one of you takes time to understand; to listen to the suffering of my people.'

Mike sucked his lips in against his teeth to prevent a snap reply and then, in an even tone, said: 'I might be able to save the lives of other Serb children. But only if I know what is causing this.'

Her rage spent, grief began to take its toll. 'He was so beautiful. A patriot.' Her eyes burned. 'A man dedicated to his nation.' She fell silent.

'When did he fall ill?'

'He wasn't the same when he came back from Germany. He was irritable, forgetful and drank so much that he staggered. Then, a few days ago, he started to vomit and did not stop. Then he began to shake and he had this weird stare. And he became incontinent.'

'When did the bleeding begin?'

'On the day I brought him in to the hospital. An old wound opened up and it would not staunch. By then, he couldn't remember his own name. He was running a fever and had the flu.'

'Why didn't you stay with him at the hospital?'

'We all have our reasons.'

Like distancing your organisation from an illegal alien and a war criminal? thought Mike. 'How did Uzelac get here from Germany?'

'I have no idea.'

'He didn't fly.'

'There are many ways to travel.'

'Eurostar? Bus and ferry?'

She straightened her back and said: 'You really must go. I must arrange a funeral for our fallen brother.'

'Did he talk about Guatemala?'

She glowered at him.

'Please. I must know.'

Her voice dropped to a whisper as she told Mike that when Uzelac was delirious he had said over and over again: 'I have the Spirit Death. I have the Spirit Death.'

'What did he mean?'

She shrugged her shoulders and replied: 'I think it had something to do with South America. Something he did there.'

'What? Was he a mercenary?'

'You must go now, I wish to make arrangements for a patriot's funeral.'

'Where's your car? Does it have much blood in it?'

'I've had it steam cleaned.'

Mike's heart sank. Who else had come into contact with this fucking disease? He had already impounded Simi's social worker's car and held it in festering isolation. At least Michele Shepherd's blood was currently showing no reaction to the multiple antibody tests that Mike was performing on a daily basis for her, Tess and the three other nurses involved. Simi's stepfather had disappeared and the police were hunting for him.

'Please go to King Henry's Hospital now,' Mike said to Bejramovic, 'and give me the name of the company that cleaned your car. You are all at risk.'

She sat in silence and looked at him, then nodded curtly. She had already seen what Drago called the Spirit Death destroy her man.

CHAPTER TWENTY-EIGHT

Mike phoned Tom Grantmore again and asked him to narrow down his search to Guatemala and see if he could make sense of something called the Spirit Death.

Tom replied: 'Do you know Greg Dasham?'

'Yeah. Worked closely on the big malaria outbreak in Belize a few years ago. Really funny bloke.'

'He told me recently that there was a strange rumour coming out of Belize that Ah Puch, the Mayan god of death, had decreed a great plague. No one knew what it would be but it was to be called the Spirit Death.'

'Fuck.'

'Fuck, indeed. If your guy exited from Guatemala, it's possible that he was in Belize. After all, it's next door to Guatemala.'

'You'd be looking for new variant-CJD-type behaviour allied to final exsanguination. Has anyone reported this?' asked Mike.

'Nope. Not a word. I'll ask Greg to take a drive up to the outlying Mayan villages, see if they've heard anything,' said

Grantmore. 'What else did you find from the index case?'

'His blood from three weeks ago – a week after he came back into the country.'

'How come?'

'For some reason, he cut himself and bled like a pig. I've sent it to Laura for analysis. If he got it abroad, we're on the case.'

As Fernandez listened, he realised that Mike would have to be taken out of the way – and fast. He was getting too close. Punching a number on his phone, he said: 'We need to arrange an accident for someone called Grantmore at the World Health Organisation in Geneva. I don't know the address. Get someone to do it today. As soon as possible. And make sure his computer's hard disk is wiped.'

'It'll be done,' replied Wu.

'And we need an accident at Uzelac's old place. A fire. As soon as possible.'

Beside Fernandez, Ren was nodding to an imaginary tune. 'I like it. Now we're playing rock and roll. How are we going to take out Davenport?'

'Quietly,' said Fernandez. 'Very quietly.' I am a fool, he thought to himself – not for the first time in his month-long chase of Uzelac from Guatemala to New York and from there to Cologne and on to London. I should never have tried to give the man another chance. I should've killed him when I saw him throw the girl's body into the fire.

After the final cleansing operation in the Mayan village, Fernandez had taken Uzelac to one side and told him tales of the bleeding peasants he had seen in Argentina's last outbreak of Junin virus – a hellish haemorrhagic disease transmitted in mouse urine. It wiped out people in three days and left them a bloody mess.

Fernandez automatically crossed himself at the horror of his memories and then smiled: if there is a Christian God, he thought, I will not be granted his mercy. It had been a misjudgement, he now realised, to credit the Bosnian Serb with enough intelligence to understand that Fernandez was giving him advice: instead, Uzelac had taken fright at the thought that the Spirit Death might attack him and, when Fernandez had woken the following morning, he had gone. Then Samuels, cleverest by far of the men under Fernandez's command, had sensed that the Company would not allow anyone to live with the knowledge of their actions and had disappeared into the night. Now he was the only one of the five mercenaries left alive. When Li had sent word that he wanted no witnesses, Fernandez had taken care of the rest of his men by poisoning their food: their bodies were buried under quicklime in the Belizean forest.

The Company had let it be known that the escape of Uzelac and Samuels was an error of the highest order, and, in a tense telephone call, Li had ordered Fernandez to track down Uzelac and personally ensure that his body was disposed of. The disease had been stopped in its tracks in Belize and they had just received official and backdated authority for their logging operations from the government. There must be no trace back to the Company.

'We do not want this attempt to aid our Belizean friends to be misconstrued. I don't want our friends exposed to any little political problems.' Li's gentle, probing voice continued: 'There's too much at stake for both of us, Mr Fernandez. There is your reputation for thorough preparation and delivery; of which I have ample documentation.' The threat struck home: Fernandez knew he was being told that they had enough information on him to throw him to the wolves. 'And, clearly, we would not enjoy it if we had to defend your operation in Belize to a wider court of opinion. My colleagues in the Company value their privacy, Mr Fernandez, and this mistake could be costly to us.'

CHAPTER TWENTY-NINE

Mike called Susie Charles. 'I need another appointment with James.' Surely now he had enough information to start a proper investigation of this disease.

'Let me consult the diary.'

'Now.'

Mike could see in his mind's eye Susie pretend to do something on her desk – all the time planning to offer him half an hour some time after the next summer solstice in a leap year.

'I'm afraid he's not here at the moment, Mike. If you'll just—'

He cut her off and called Dek. 'Find out where Graham is,' he said. 'I need to talk to him immediately.'

'Hi.'

'What?' replied Mike.

'I'm sure a phone call begins, "Hi, Dek".'

'I don't have time for this, Dek, for once just do what I ask.'

'Please yourself.' The phone went dead.

Mike was crawling up towards King Henry's through thick,

smoggy traffic when the phone buzzed: 'I've pulled his diary off the shared server,' said Dek. 'He's having lunch at The Reform Club with someone called Lawrence Ellington.'

'Thanks.'

'Mike?'

'Yes?'

'Don't ever snap at me again or you'll be looking for new help.'

'Sorry.'

'Keep cool, Mike.'

Mike pounded the steering wheel in frustration; he was stuck between a Rolls-Royce and an eight-wheel truck carrying furniture. He tried to turn left, but it was a one-way street. Sweat was pouring down his forehead and stinging the corners of his eyes. He spotted a tube station, abandoned the car on a double-yellow line outside and sprinted down the stairs into a swelter of bodies crammed together in a mash of uncomfortable proximity. As he was jostled, pushed, importuned and breathed over the thought that cities were simply hypermarkets for bugs was difficult to shake off. The train door opened and he boarded, trying to keep his head above the crush.

Forty minutes later he was running up the steep steps of the Reform Club in Pall Mall. He left behind the heat, smog and bustle of London and entered a quiet, cool reception area where a uniformed servant asked: 'May I help you, sir?'

Mike tried to push through. 'I urgently need to see Dr James Graham.'

The man discreetly but firmly stepped in Mike's way and prevented him going up the inner set of steps to the large room that Mike could see through the double doors. 'If you'll just wait here, sir. I'll see if he's here and wishes to speak to you.' He took down Mike's name and handed the paper to a younger man in the same uniform, who clumped up the stone steps and returned with a message that Graham would meet Mike in the library.

'Great. Let's go.'

The man handed Mike a red and blue striped tie. 'I would be grateful if you would wear this, sir.'

Mike was prepared to explode but thought better of it and did as he was told. London civilisation will fall apart if I don't wear this piece of cloth around my neck, he thought.

He passed through a large room dominated by paintings of prime ministers and Liberal grandees. A quiet crowd of mainly middle-aged men and women were sipping coffee and murmuring their small pieces of business in corners around the ground and first floors. He was then escorted to a long, book-lined library that was flooded with light from the huge windows that looked out on to the street. Underneath one of the windows in the corner, occupying a sofa and a stuffed armchair, were James Graham and Lawrence Ellington.

Graham rose and signalled Mike over. 'Not your neck of the woods, Dr Davenport. I do hope it's something important,' he said.

'It is,' replied Mike.

'How rude of me,' said Graham. 'Let me introduce you. This is Lawrence Ellington – Permanent Secretary at the Home Office. And this, Lawrence—'

'Is the young firebrand, Mike Davenport.' Mike noticed that Ellington's accent came from the top of the London caste system. Old money.

Ellington unlocked his long legs, stood and extended an arm with large, veiny but elegant hands that were puffy to the touch. His face was soft, with a buttery complexion and clear brown eyes that held Mike's gaze. He was wearing a double-breasted suit with stripes running through that would have passed as raffish in the 1970s. On his feet were brown suede shoes to add to the independent look he so carefully cultivated. The ensemble seemed odd on a man in his mid-forties. Although a civil servant, Ellington was a well-known media figure, criticised as Machiavellian by some, and as an organisational genius by others. There were even rumours that he might resign from the Service and be ennobled as a working peer in the Lords.

'You are a rising star, Dr Davenport. May I call you Mike?'

Mike noticed that he had a speech impediment that meant his 's' seemed to be produced from the side of his mouth and came out as a soft 'shhh' sound. His voice was pitched high for a man, and the words came out slowly. 'Such a pity the way the press misquoted you this morning. That's the danger of talking to unscrupulous journalists.' He sat down again and motioned Mike to the chair next to him. 'Not something you've ever been tempted by, James. Personal publicity. James has been doing excellent, really excellent work for the government for all his adult life. Never once looked for public acclaim. Have you, James?'

Graham put down his coffee cup and nodded. 'I've always thought it intrusive and something that no true scientist should cultivate. Science is best done away from such sensationalism. Coffee, Dr Davenport?'

Mike shook his head and said: 'I know the source of the mutant prion disease.'

'Really, Dr Davenport. Really. Are you still pursuing that case after my warning this morning? Now why not have some coffee and listen to Lawrence's plan to fund a major new project at the Centre?'

Mike was brisk, convinced of his theory. 'It's come in from Guatemala or Belize. It may be spreading in blood or urine, if my information is anything to go by. But we cannot rule out other modes of transmission. I've got someone examining the blood now. But this thing's taken three people out and more will follow unless we do something quickly.' He pulled out a sheaf of photographs of the people who had contracted the disease and his notes showing how each connected to the others.

'Ah, Guatemala. Or is it Belize?' Ellington offered a small, knowing smirk. 'And I thought the problem was on the other side of the world in Bosnia. By the way, did you see the apology the Foreign Secretary had to issue this morning to the Yugoslavian Ambassador? Lisa Jordan hates being humiliated. Although, I must say,' he interlaced his fingers across the bump of his belly, 'it couldn't have happened to a nicer woman. I wonder how she will respond if I now tell her the problem is apparently in Central America. What do you think, Mike?'

'Look,' Mike spoke forcefully, 'I did not say it was Yugoslavian. That was the newspapers. I just know that we have a problem and we must do something.'

A small, private smile played across Ellington's lips as if Mike had failed some exam that he didn't know he was taking. 'So, Dr Davenport . . . Mike.' Ellington stretched out his legs and crossed one ankle over the other. 'On the basis of three cases of an admittedly nasty-sounding disease, you would like to start a major public scare. Despite the fact that you have no certain idea how this is transmitted. And you have set a hare running that somehow it is like CJD. How do you think people will respond to this news? How do you think the meat industry will feel if we cause more damage to their business?'

Mike could not believe that they were responding like this. His voice raised, he said: 'I've got a really nasty bastard of a pathogen on my hands and you are talking about the fucking meat industry.'

The room fell silent as people looked around and stared at them.

'Please lower your voice, Dr Davenport, or I will be forced to ask you to leave,' hissed Graham.

'How much panic would you like to be responsible for Mike?' Ellington looked down his aquiline nose, and his big, black-framed spectacles glinted in the sunshine.

'I don't want to cause any panic,' replied Mike, struggling for control. 'But isn't a little scare better than allowing a disease to develop that we don't understand?'

Graham leaned forward on the sofa and looked as if he

wanted to throw Mike out of the window for embarrassing him in his club in front of his younger friend and benefactor.

Mike's voice wavered a little. 'This is some kind of CJD variant that is a bit like kuru – except the bugger goes through brains as if they were marshmallow. I can't tell what the variations are yet. But they are causing major inflammatory responses and bizarre haemorrhaging. And I believe the source is in Central America. Do you know how fast these fucking things can spread?'

A silence fell across the three men and they become acutely aware that the whole room was listening whilst studiously pretending to read the papers or chat about daily business.

'Tom Grantmore from the WHO is trying to find out what's going on. Aren't you going to do anything?' asked Mike, exasperated.

'Yes,' replied Ellington quietly.

'What?'

'I'm going to get more coffee.' And with that he stood and walked to the far end of the library and out into the main hall.

Graham's impassive face struggled to conceal his anger. 'Have all serum, blood, tissue and cell cultures from the so-called prion cases in my possession by close of play. Perhaps it's time for someone with longer scientific experience to take over this investigation.'

'If you are trying to cover this up,' Mike's voice resounded around the large room, 'well, you won't. Believe me.'

As Graham stared at him in astonishment and began to respond, Mike left the room, ignoring the disapproving glances of the assembled suits. He threw his borrowed tie down on the porter's counter and headed into the scalding afternoon sunshine.

CHAPTER THIRTY

Mike sat in his office, drumming his hands on the desk. He had phoned the Health Secretary, Jennifer Low, a half-dozen times. He was trying to arrange an emergency meeting of the government's Advisory Committee on Dangerous Pathogens. 'C'mon, return my call. C'mon, c'mon.' He rocked back and forth in the chair, torn between the need for action and the realisation that he had to convince the authorities that something incredibly nasty was brewing in London.

His door opened and Jane strolled in. There was a pause as they sized up one another, before the mutual assessment gave way to an awkward, bumpy kiss.

'How are you darling?' she asked.

'Been better.'

'I'm sorry about the press release.' She held his hand as they stood in the middle of the room. Mike could feel that his hands were clammy, whilst hers were cool. 'But, as you saw, I managed to make it sound as if you were misquoted by the *Sun*. The other media are turning on the *Sun* for peddling scaremongering rumours.'

Mike went back to his desk and picked up a thick sheaf of file notes and photographs. 'I'm going to see the Health Secretary later,' he said. 'She must be informed about what is going on. Graham is blocking me at every turn.'

She waited for a second before coming across and perching on the desk beside him. 'Darling,' her voice was tense, 'I wish you'd give up this obsession. It's not doing you any good with the people who matter. We've discussed many times how you must play the politics better if you are to become Head of Centre.'

He laughed a little. 'That little ambition's gone. I've pissed off Lawrence Ellington.'

'You've done what?'

'He's an odious toad.'

'He's the most powerful man in the Civil Service.'

'He's an officious, self-serving prig.'

'Look Mike, darling. Phone him up and apologise. Graham is going to go soon and you're in pole position to take over. This is just what we need to help us to get married. Your salary will go up and we'll be able to make a real go of it. Think of the number of times you've said that you'd be able to make the Centre really hum if only they'd let you. They think they can't trust you on the politics and politicians. So prove them wrong.'

He put his head back and stared at the ceiling. 'I've got to get out of this place, Jane. I can't handle viruses any more. I'm terrified.'

'Don't be silly, darling. What do you mean?'

'It happens to virus cowboys. It's a bit like riding a horse. You fall off once too often and you can't get on again. *Finito*. I'm going to resign.'

'What about us?' she asked quietly. 'Our ambitions.'

'My only ambition at the moment is to alert the bloody Health Secretary to this prion bug. Laura's—'

'Ah, the precious Laura. I thought she'd be at the bottom of this somewhere. What were you planning to do when you left here? Work with her?'

'For Christ's sake, Jane. She's one of my oldest friends.'

'She's dragging you into a mess from which your career will never recover. She's leading you by the nose and you don't seem to realise it. She wants you for herself.'

'My career's not important now. Convincing people that they have a potential catastrophe on their hands is.'

'Drop this, Mike. Or I won't be able to defend you. I don't want to hear any more about it.'

They stared at each other, both knowing that they had crossed an emotional Rubicon. The phone rang. Mike picked it up and replied: 'Be there in a minute.' He stood and said to Jane: 'That was Laura. They've got another one. Will you excuse me?'

She did not catch his eye as he left.

As Mike entered the Isolation Unit at King Henry's after another fruitless attempt to contact Jennifer Low, he saw Graham arguing with Jack. Beside the two men stood Laura, looking profoundly concerned. When Graham turned, Mike saw flecks of fear and uncertainty in his boss's eyes.

'What's happened?' asked Mike.

Laura replied: 'I've done a quick and dirty scan on this new case and it looks to me as if this sucker is travelling faster than Concorde.'

Mike's stomach ached. 'Is this a Serb?' he asked.

'Not unless you get Scottish Serbs,' said Laura, chewing at the skin at the edge of her thumbnail. She was scared. Nobody knew the incubation period for the Spirit Death. Was it a day, a month, a year?

Mike leaned back against the door and stared at the ceiling. 'So it's out in the general population,' he said.

'She lives up on Hartland Road,' Jack read from the file notes.

'That's where Marie Kecman lived. How is it travelling? Is it just blood? Could it be in the food chain?'

'Until you and I get into a Level 4 lab with the little fucker, we can't confirm what exactly we're dealing with. I can't get permission from anyone, and Uzelac's sample has been confiscated by this chump.' Laura indicated Graham.

'I don't believe you are cleared for Level 4 work in the UK, Ms Singer,' said Graham.

Laura turned, put her hands on her hips and glowered incredulously.

But Graham blanked her. 'And, as far as I understand, you, Dr Davenport, are too scared to enter a Level 4 facility. I fancy that we might have to turn this over to the Ministry.'

'Want another piece of bad news?' Jack interrupted brusquely. 'She was a prostitute. Specialised in S and M. According to the police, Mr Keeman was an avid user of the lady's services.'

Mike shook his head. 'Unbelievable. We've got a haemorrhagic disease in a woman who spends her days whipping people, drawing blood, pissing on them and playing with their shit. If this is a jumper, it's just found a pretty good way of spreading out.'

'Now, Mr Graham', said Laura. 'D'you want me to go straight to the World Health Organisation for permission to use their facilities? Shall I go direct to the media and tell them of your negligence and interference? Or d'you want to give me a suit, a virus and some peace to tell you what this fucker is? Or is that just too complicated for your little dick-brain to understand?'

Graham stared at her for thirty seconds and then hissed: 'I will see what I can do.' With that, he turned and left, hurtling down the corridor.

Part Two

THE RING OF DEATH

CHAPTER THIRTY-ONE

Alan Lipsey looked every bit as level-headed and straightforward in the flesh as he did on television. Mike noted the famous, soft, deep green, hypnotic eyes, under which a few dark shadows had been powdered away. Three deep canals of worry split his forehead; but he looked cool and in control. Mike wondered if his public face ever slipped. Lipsey's Mancunian accent had softened over the years at Cambridge and then in his time as Professor of History at King's College, London; but those who listened closely could still tell identify his origins.

On a long flight to Chad, fifteen years before, Mike had read with interest *The Cost of Freedom*, Lipsey's controversial reinterpretation of the uneasy relationship between Roosevelt and Churchill. In the book he had suggested that Roosevelt had used the Second World War mainly as a means of promoting American imperialism.

'Prime Minister?' Lawrence Ellington's voice smoothed its way towards its target.

Lipsey looked across the long, mahogany-dominated conference room at Ellington, his face passive and absorbing. 'Yes, Lawrence?'

Ellington glided around the room: 'May I suggest that we ask Dr Graham to come up with an epidemiological analysis and offer some solutions to our current dilemma?' Ellington was probing for the limits of his control over the situation.

Lipsey looked down his nose and then rubbed his neck. They had been debating this for two hours at Number Ten. 'I think that perhaps the discoverer of the problem should be charged with finding answers, don't you, Lawrence?' When he stood, Mike saw that he was much taller and thinner than he had expected.

'I don't think I have any answers, Prime Minister.' Mike pulled nervously at his right ear. The shakes were getting worse.

'Call me Alan, please. Everyone does, apart from Lawrence.'

'This is not something that I understand,' continued Mike. 'It should not exist. But, somehow, it does.' He tapped a pencil softly on the table.

Ellington again intervened: 'This is a form of CJD, Prime Minister, a type of disease with which Dr Davenport is unfamiliar. I strongly advise that we allow Professor Graham, an acknowledged world expert, to lead on this.' Ellington's cool had not deserted him throughout the past three days.

Mike had barraged him for action as the three cases became ten. The prostitute from Hartland Road had died the day before; she had been twenty-two and had two children, both of whom had antibodies for the blood virus and were showing early signs of something similar to CJD. Michele Shepherd had it, as did Brinda Bejramovic from the Friends of Bosnia's Serbs.

In frustration, Mike had camped out in the Health Secretary's office until she saw him. He had brought his case files and told Jennifer Low of his profound fears of an epidemic.

Having been summoned, Ellington, in Mike's incredulous presence, had claimed that he had activated emergency procedures as soon as he returned from the Reform Club, and miraculously had the memos to prove it.

Jennifer had told the PM, who had summoned this emergency meeting. So far there was no public panic. The press were still treating 'the cannibal plague' as a curiosity, and Jane had managed to muddy the waters for the media, who did not understand the full implications of Laura and Mike's theory about the disease. Graham's cautious briefings to the press had held sway. Until yesterday, when viral antibodies appeared in two of the nursing staff at King Henry's. This meant that, whatever this thing was, it could incubate in five days. And it was jumping fast. For the first time, Graham seemed scared.

Spending the previous night feeding data into his software to map the consequences of the spread of the disease as well as its origins, and replicating Laura's analysis, he told Mike that he had been forced to conclude that she was correct. Mutated prions had somehow become imported into a haemorrhagic virus that had previously not jumped to people. Even worse, the pathogen was probably moving in bodily fluids of all kinds — blood, urine and semen.

Now Graham sat beside a bust of Gladstone and was silent and brooding through the debate; his big eyebrows drooped towards the oak table. Finally, in his deep Scottish voice, he intervened: 'The question is, and this is the most terrifying question of all, is there an animal reservoir? If it jumped species in Central America, which it must have done to be running on rampage like this, would it jump back to a similar host in the UK? If this was a rat virus in Guatemala or Belize, would it become a rodent virus in the UK? If so, the consequences will be devastating. It will be the Black Death revisited.'

The room fell silent. Each looked at the others.

'Prion diseases are normally very difficult to catch, Prime Minister,' said Mike. 'Although this is very different, we need to organise ourselves systematically and we need to do it now. There's no more time.'

'Can it be cured?' asked Lipsey.

'Well, there are experimental treatments going on—'

'No, Alan,' interrupted Graham. 'CJD in all its forms is currently incurable.'

'But this is not simple CJD', hissed Mike. 'It's a mutant. If I'm right, and Dr Laura Singer is working on it now, the haemorrhagic virus is treatable if we can isolate the prion transformation. It can be done; but we need to work fast.'

A civil servant glided into the room, reached the Prime Minister's elbow, and spoke quietly to him. Lipsey nodded and said, 'Yes.' He took possession of something and thanked the man. 'A walk in the garden, Mike?' asked the Prime Minister. 'What d'you think?'

Around him, Mike could see the admiring faces of the politicians and civil servants. Lipsey's legendary cool was holding up.

The late afternoon sun was hot enough to blister tar on the pavement on Downing Street.

'I'd love to join you, Prime Minister,' replied Mike, 'anything to get away from the hot air in this room.'

Ellington sent a calm, but obvious flick of dislike in Mike's direction. Lipsey pulled on a pair of Calvin Klein shades, and put a little pressure into the small of Mike's back as he led him out. His voice was soft when he asked: 'Can you think of any reason why someone would bug your car?'

'What?' Mike stopped in his tracks.

The Prime Minister handed him a small listening device. 'This was found in your Volvo when you arrived. An electronic sweep is a normal precaution these days, I'm afraid. There are cheap bugs everywhere.'

'It must have been a journalist,' replied Mike.

'Possibly,' said Lipsey as he took Mike's arm and propelled him gently in the direction of the high back wall of the garden.

Outside, Mike could hear London's afternoon traffic in full

roar. The smog was getting worse and pundits on TV were talking about London turning into a new LA.

'I have taken the liberty, and I hope you don't mind, of having your house and office swept for other devices. I don't want anyone interfering with your work.' He took off his sunglasses and his animated eyes sparked and sought to establish a bond between them.

Mike was immensely flattered. 'Thank you,' he said.

'Have you spoken to anyone on the telephone recently about this disease?'

Mike thought for a second. 'Tom Grantmore at the WHO.'

'Then I suggest you call Mr Grantmore and tell him that his comments were recorded by someone, we know not whom, who wants to keep a close eye on you.'

Mike looked thoughtfully at Lipsey. A series of curious events was now connecting in his head: from the disappearance of his initial notes and samples and onwards. Was someone trying to cover this up? 'Prime Minister . . . Alan, I'm still puzzled about the index case and how he picked this up,' he said. 'He was a mercenary working in Guatemala or Belize. Which means he was working for a drugs cartel, a mining company or a logging organisation. Those are the only people who would pay that kind of money. Is it possible to get someone on to this? It would help me enormously.'

Lipsey turned and headed back towards the lights of Number Ten and the conference room in which everyone else was gathered. 'Of course. Now, I have a surprise guest for you. Let's go and meet him.'

As they re-entered the room, Mike saw a huge, bulky figure dressed in an immaculate light blue cotton suit. His large head was completely bald and a two-inch scar ran down the right hemisphere. He turned and his once elegant face looked even craggier than the last time they had met. But, unlike the last time, he looked every minute of his sixty-three years – and then some.

'I believe you know Father Andrew MacFlynn.' Ellington allowed himself a little smile, knowing that Mac, as he was called by everyone from presidents to press men, had sacked Mike a few years earlier.

Before Mike could respond, Mac answered for them both. 'Of course, Michael and I go way back. I taught the boy the little he knows. How are you, boy?' His Belfast accent was obvious under a Boston overlay acquired after twenty years in the States. His only bow in the direction of his vocation was a small silver cross pinned to his lapel, and the SJ insignia that told of his Jesuit training. He put out a hand the size of a T-bone steak and at first Mike was in two minds as to whether to shake it. Mac's failure to provide the right back-up and funding had led directly to the conditions in which Mike had caught the Machupo. And then, to make it worse, Mac had covered up the mess and switched the blame to Mike. It was only the intervention of Tom Grantmore that had stopped Mike being dropped by the WHO.

But Ellington was watching and would obviously enjoy Mike's discomfort, so he took his former friend's hand and shook it warmly. 'Mac, what brings you here? I thought you were still in Chicago.' MacFlynn was Professor Emeritus in Epidemiology at the Chicago Medical School.

'I brought him here, Mike,' the Prime Minister said as he sat down heavily, suddenly looking tired. Mike knew he had been up all night chairing a round of peace talks between the warring parties in Sierra Leone. This was now something of a specialism for a Prime Minister at the beginning of his second term, who had made such a principled stand on foreign affairs in his first.

Mike wasn't feeling too hot himself after three days practically locked in the hospital trying to work out how to analyse and treat the disease. He missed the twins and had been glad when they dropped in to see him last night.

Lipsey took a sip of iced coffee and motioned everyone to sit. Mac continued to stand as none of the chairs could accommodate his girth. Lipsey noticed immediately, sent someone off to fetch a large seat. Two burly men subsequently returned with a throne-like chair used for Helmut Kohl when he had visited Margaret Thatcher.

'Now, people,' Lipsey looked around the room, and Mike saw how his eyes scrutinised each of them, 'who will tell me how to contain this?'

Graham's voice was decisive. 'There is only one way to do that.' The sharpness of his intervention caught everyone by surprise. Graham had said little during the debate. Beside him, Jennifer Low, the Health Secretary, seemed fresh and young; her no-nonsense suit and simple make-up spoke of a woman short on time and patience. She had spent much of the day apologising to Mike for Ellington's high-handed behaviour and Graham's intransigence.

'And what brilliant way is that, Mr Graham?' Her Liverpudlian accent was unalloyed.

'We must cordon off the hospital and the surrounding areas – particularly the estate where the virus is currently active. If we quarantine the area, it will burn itself out.' Graham's voice was level and even.

Mike erupted as tiredness, anger and frustration hit him in waves. 'Are you bonkers? You're forgetting that there are people in there. Not fucking statistics.'

Graham looked pained and exasperated at Mike's interruption and, turning to Lipsey, asked: 'I believe my concern for public safety is at least as high as yours. Although I don't need to wear it on my sleeve. May I explain, Prime Minister?'

Lipsey leant forward in his chair, his eyes sharp and focused intently on Graham. His lips were pursed and tight. 'Please do,' he said and put his index finger to his mouth, where it tapped gently and rhythmically against his flesh.

Graham walked to the laptop that he had been working on throughout the afternoon and hit a button. On to a flat screen at the end of the room came a map of Chalk Farm. 'This is the area around King Henry's. And this is my model of how the CJD-variant haemorrhagic virus might spread if left unchecked.' Numbers began to march on to the screen. 'Each day,' continued Graham, 'it seems to double. As of today, we have twelve cases, tomorrow twenty-four, and by the end of the month tens of thousands of people may have succumbed. And it would have spread out from London and into the rest of the country, and from there, by ship, plane and car to the rest of the world. It's spreading only by human-to-human contact. It is not in the water supply or in the food chain.

'We must contain it within this radius.' Graham punched some keys on his computer and a model of North London appeared on the screen, with a thick red line that snaked around the outside of Primrose Hill, up Belsize Park Gardens, round to Haverstock Hill and down to Chalk Farm Road until it hits the Parkway, and then round again up Albert Road, past the zoo until it reached Primrose Hill again.

'Nonsense,' snorted Mike.

'Please, Mike, allow others to speak.' The Prime Minister's voice was gentle but authoritative. 'Father MacFlynn?'

Mac raised his body from the chair and began to pace the room. Mike was always surprised by the leonine bounce of Mac's stride. 'Michael has some experience of situations like this, I grant you,' MacFlynn looked at him. 'But I believe I've perhaps seen a wee bit more.' Mike shook his head as Mac patronised him. 'In 1976,' MacFlynn walked back and forth in front of the big screen, the cordon glowing red on the screen behind him, 'when I flew into Yambuku to help deal with the first Zairean Ebola outbreak, I thought nothing could contain it. In a matter of weeks, there were three hundred and eighteen cases and a mortality rate of eighty-eight per cent. And that was in a small, isolated area.' Mac walked behind Lipsey's chair. He paused for a second, as if recalling those days was enormously painful. Then Mike noticed that he was short of breath and a white pallor had spread across his skin. He was clearly unwell.

Extracting a King Size Rothmans from a pack in his pocket, Mac lit up — despite the explicit instructions they had all been given that no one smoked in front of the Prime Minister. He drew deep on the nicotine and then let the smoke trickle from his lips and nose, seemingly reluctant to allow any to escape. Lipsey looked as if he might say something, but then subsided as Mac continued. 'I decided to visit the other villages, thinking they would be suffering similar problems. I went in an old jeep and took an interpreter.' He sucked again on the cigarette. 'Everywhere I went there were roadblocks and sentries. We were stopped a great distance from every village and closely inspected before we were allowed to visit. Outside Yambuku, there was not one other case of Ebola. And, within weeks, Ebola in Zaire had retreated back into whatever host carried it.'

'C'mon, Mac.' Mike stood and confronted his older colleague. 'You can't be serious. You can't quarantine a modern city.'

Lipsey looked for another opinion and indicated to Philip Marber with an inclusive wave of his hand. 'Philip, this would fall to you to organise. What do you think?'

Marber, the Director of Emergency Planning at the Home Office, had said little in the meeting. Mike had met him a few times and knew him to be cautious, almost to the point of obsession. He sat absolutely still, his back straight and his hands on the table. Occasionally, he made a quick note with a black pen in a very neat hand.

Marber scribbled for a second. 'We would have to mobilise the army under the MACC rules.' Mike knew of the Military Aid to the Civilian Community orders from his futile attempts to convince the Health Service Emergency Operations group to prepare for a major blood virus outbreak. 'This would definitely qualify as a Category A problem', continued Marber. 'We would have to pay for it from the NHS budget, of course. There is no subvention for MACC mobilisation. I suggest we co-ordinate with the South-East Regional Army HQ and ask them how quickly they could be in position.'

'Tell General Treblington I want to talk to him privately,' said Lipsey, referring to the Chief of the General Staff.

'You can't do this,' said Mike. 'You don't even know precisely how it's spreading. You have no plans for it.'

'Oh, I don't know, Dr Davenport,' replied Marber frostily. 'My department and I had perfectly good plans for many years in the event of nuclear warfare. I'm sure that with Professor Graham's assistance we will be able to develop a sensible way of coping with this potential problem.'

Mike shook his head.

'Alan,' Marber looked at the Prime Minister, 'it's time to establish an Integrated Emergency Management Committee. Would you like to chair it?'

Ellington leant over and whispered something in Lipsey's ear. He nodded and Ellington said: 'No. I think this is one for the Health Secretary. Jennifer, the PM looks to you for successful integrated emergency management.'

Low looked startled as she realised that she had been put in the front line and that Ellington had placed the Prime Minister in a deniability zone. She smiled and said: 'I'll do my best, Alan.'

Lipsey thanked her and stood. 'I must go back to the peace conference. May I suggest that Mac and Dr Graham work on the model and that Dr Davenport comes up with some alternatives? We'll reconvene at midnight and make a decision. I need some answers.'

CHAPTER THIRTY-TWO

Mike was brooding on the quarantine map when his beeper sounded and offered him a message: *call Tess immediately*. Oh, Christ, she had been taking daily antibody tests that were clear so far. Be well, he prayed. He picked up the receiver of a phone on the table and looked out over the gardens of Number Ten. 'Tess?'

'Mike, I'm on my way to King Henry's. Molly is running a fever of a hundred and four and has just vomited all over her bed.' He heard noises and then Tess said: 'We're at the hospital. Come now, Mike. For Christ's sake, come now.'

Mike was momentarily stunned. Then he began to draw in shallow breaths and his body was hit by a succession of tiny shakes.

'Michael, are you all right?' Mac was beside him and taking hold of his arm.

'Molly. Jesus, Mac, Molly's got it.' He was paralysed.

'Where are they taking her, Michael? Michael! Where are they taking her?' An urgent tone entered the priest's voice.

Mike shook his head but could not speak. Mac grabbed him by his arms, and the strength of his grip jolted Mike's mind.

'King Henry's.' He started to run and realised Mac was waddling rapidly beside him.

'I'm coming with you,' said Mac.

Mike was too focused on his daughter to care whether Mac was there or not.

When they reached King Henry's, Mike noticed that the number of security guards had trebled. There were six around the entrance and not the usual guys; these were muscled and tough-looking. Regular army, Mike guessed. They tried to bar Mac's way.

'ID, sir.' A tall, muscular man put out his hand.

'He's with me,' said Mike.

'And who are you?' Underneath the black peaked cap, Mike looked into the hard, professional eyes of a soldier.

'Dr Michael Davenport.' Mike flashed his card and the guard waved them through. There were soldiers dressed in security uniforms beside one of the lifts. It had been requisitioned for access to the top floor of the hospital that had been allocated to Spirit Death patients. Mike swept past them to the next elevator, which took him to the Centre's Isolation Ward, where Jack was treating Molly.

When he reached the waiting room he saw Jo. Beside her, Tess was grim-faced and close to tears. He knelt next to them and took Jo's hand.

'Dad,' she whispered, 'she's so sick. Please help her.' A lump in Mike's throat threatened to spill over into tears. 'I'll be here, Dad. When you . . . when you—,' her lips began to tremble, as did her body. 'Papa,' she said. She had not called him that since she was eight. 'Make her better.' Her voice dropped to a soft, feather-light, sad whisper. 'Please.'

Mike did not know whether to scream his rage at God, collapse, or find some magician to cast a spell over his daughter. If she had it, it was almost certain that she would be dead in days.

'Go to her, Mike,' said Tess. And then she looked in surprise at Mac.

He walked over and tried to hug her; but she shook him off.

'If your prayers were ever any use, Mac, your god-daughter could use them now.'

'I know, Tess.' Mac's voice was empty. He had not seen Molly since the rift with Mike. And yet he offered prayers for her every day. If only God listened to an old man, to an old, tired, priest whose faith was weaker than a sapling in a hurricane.

Mike looked at the glass door into the Isolation Unit and was terrified of what he would find on the other side. He bit the inside of his lip until he chewed off a small chunk of flesh. Then he strode through, with Mac in his wake. They put on their masks and watched Jack Lim take a blood sample. Molly looked flushed and tossed and turned as if she could hardly bear to keep her flesh on the white sheet. Her hair looked as if it had been washed in puddle-water and it was matted across her forehead like seaweed.

Jack held Mike by the arms and looked into his eyes. 'We'll get her through this Mike. Someone always survives. It'll be Molly. She's young and strong.'

'Thanks Jack.' Mike's voice was thick with emotion. Have I brought this on my own daughter? How did she pick it up? Am I a carrier somehow? 'Have the antibody results come through yet?' he asked.

'No.' Jack looked worriedly at the priest. He had not realised that Mike was a Catholic.

'I'm Andrew MacFlynn,' Mac said. 'An old friend of the family. How is she?'

Jack nodded. 'I've heard a lot about you.'

'May I have a look?' Mac pointed at the notes. Jack handed them over and Mac scrutinised them, then hissed softly. 'OK. OK, I see,' he muttered, 'definitely a virus.' His big face expressed the pain that was raging through him. 'Have we tried Interferon?'

'No. I don't know what this is yet,' replied Jack. 'And until I do I'm not prescribing anything.'

'Jack, please do something,' pleaded Mike as Molly groaned loudly.

'Mike,' said Jack. 'I would give her every drug in this hospital if I thought it would do any good. But until we are sure what it is, let's wait.'

Mike sat heavily on the chair beside his daughter and held her hand. 'She's so like Anne. Don't you think, Mac?'

'The spit,' replied Mac. 'As beautiful as a mountain flower.'

As Mike closed his eyes and wept silently, he felt Mac's big hand on his shoulder.

Four hours later they were still in the room. Mike had banned Jo and Tess from entering and they remained outside as he administered the compresses and the anti-fever drugs. Molly tossed and turned, her lips cracked and dry, and she shook and shivered. She moaned for her mama and papa and Mike wanted to rip out his heart and offer it to any god to save his daughter. He wanted to stick a knife into his hand just to share her pain. Not again, he kept thinking to himself. Not after we've lost Anne. Please God, not again. He saw Tess and Jo in the observation area – a large glass window separated them from the Isolation Ward. They could see but Mike was glad they could not hear what was going on inside.

'She's dying, isn't she?' said Jo to Tess, who hugged her niece and said:

'No. She'll be fine. Just fine.'

'I'm not a fucking kid any more,' replied Jo. 'Don't patronise me.'

Tess watched as tears coursed down the girl's face. There was nothing left to say. They saw Jack saying something to Mike, then pulling back the bedclothes for them to examine Molly's body. Mike stared intently at something on Molly's back and then he put his head back and roared at the ceiling. As his body shook and he gasped for air, Jo watched her father and then broke down, screaming: 'No. Don't die, Molly.' Tess knelt to try to comfort her, but Jo was spitting and kicking. 'No. Don't go, Molly. Don't leave me.'

Mike burst into the room, laughing hysterically, and, sitting on the floor beside them, struggled to hold his sobbing daughter. His voice was exultant: 'She's got chickenpox,' he shouted into Jo's face. 'Lousy, stupid, glorious chickenpox.'

CHAPTER THIRTY-THREE

PC George Hudson gave chase to a young black man with the Community Centre's CD player tucked under his arm. He knew he would never catch up with him; too many of his wife's dinners were sitting on his stomach for him to keep up with someone as swift as Victor Obudo. And he was sure it was Victor, despite the teenager having a bright green woollen hat pulled down over his head. Few people on the estate could run at that speed. The boy should have been a real athlete instead of another druggie. He had been fine before he was sent down; running with the wrong crowd, but basically a good kid. A year in prison had hardened him, George thought sadly. He felt a little guilty; the evidence against Victor had been thin; but, as a lookout, he had been involved enough in the robbery at the local chemist's to make the sentence reasonable in George's eyes, and he had been content to be the arresting officer.

Victor clambered nimbly on to a dustbin and leaped over a wooden fence at the end of alley. George stopped and heaved in big gulps of oxygen. After a minute his heart-beat returned to normal. My Lord, it was nearly midnight and it was still hot; almost as hot as Jamaica. He wished he were sitting by the sea, sucking on a lager, rather than patrolling a London housing estate where the whites distrusted him and the blacks hated him.

He walked out of the alley and resumed his patrol. He'd talk to Jill, Victor's mum, tomorrow. She was a good woman, worked hard at the shop in the hospital, and deserved better than her violent halfwit of a boy. So much potential thrown away on crack cocaine. As he emerged on to a road that ran between two maisonettes and then up to brutal twin high-rise blocks, he saw a cherry tree in full blossom beside a filthy, yellow skip that contained the remains of someone's burned-out flat that the council was clearing out. Two small white boys – with faces masked by dirt – were searching the skip for booty.

Walking towards George, spread out across the road in a menacing row, were eight teenage black boys. In the middle, sporting a green trilby at a jaunty angle, was Victor. The two young boys took one look, jumped out in a frantic scramble, and ran for safety. Everyone gave respect to Victor's Lions of Africa gang.

George continued to walk towards them. If he showed cowardice once, he would have no authority left on the estate. He still trusted the Prime Minister's word that more money would be put into the force and that internal racism would be stamped out and more black policemen recruited and retained. When that happened, George reasoned, they'd be back in control of the street. Despite his distrust of Alan Lipsey and his greasy smile, George had voted for him.

A rhythmic rumble of noise reverberated down the road. 'Tom. Tom. Tom. Uncle Tom, Tom, Tom.'

When he reached Victor, George did not give way and the two men stood face to face. The teenager was taller than George by at least four inches and, when he grinned, George could see three gold teeth.

'Victor, how's your mum? I hear you've bought a present for her. A CD player.'

'Can't afford that, Mr Hilton. Couldn't buy a second-hand CD on my dole money. And no one's going to give me a job now, are they? Not someone with a record.'

'You should've stayed on at school, Victor. You could've become something. Someone.'

Victor stared at him and then stood to one side. As George was passing him, Victor, as if rapping, whispered: 'Tom. Tom. Uncle Tom.'

A second later, the rest joined in, stamping their feet, clapping their hands and beating sticks against the skip until the metal sounded like a warning bell. 'Tom, Tom, Uncle Tom. Tom, Tom, Uncle Tom.'

George could feel his shirt sticking to his back, but he did not look back. He turned right and headed down towards King Henry's to check up on his ten-year-old daughter Charlie, who was convalescing from an attack of bronchitis.

CHAPTER THIRTY-FOUR

The Prime Minister's eyes were rimmed with bloodshot veins. His glasses were on the table beside a copy of his book on Roosevelt and Churchill. 'I'm glad your daughter is going to get well, Mike. I was wondering how we were going to contain this without your expertise.' He licked his lips a little. 'I don't mind telling you that I'm badly torn on how to handle this. But I'm the one who'll make the decision in the end, Mike,' he said. 'In 1937, when FDR was trying to get the US to change its mind about isolationism, he made a speech in Chicago in which he made a crucial policy statement that signalled his disapproval of Germany and his willingness to help Britain. Let me read this to you, Mike: *"When an epidemic of physical disease starts to spread, the community approves and joins in the quarantine of the patients in order to protect the health of the community against the disease."'*

Lipsey closed the book and looked steadily at Mike. 'He got into deep trouble because of that speech. But he was right. We must protect the community, and, like FDR, I don't believe we have any rational alternative to quarantine. If you have any other answer, I'll think about it.'

Ellington signalled to the Prime Minister that the US President was on the phone again. This was the second time that day. The CIA had heard the rumour about the new superbug from the UK and US Immigration were talking about stopping all flights. Lipsey was trying everything to prevent this. It would be catastrophic.

Mike had been back at Number Ten from the early hours of the morning. Surrounded by the cacophony of spin doctors and civil servants from the Home Office, the Emergency Planning Division, the NHS Emergency Planning Unit milling around, making plans for the following day, Mike stared out at the night sky and felt sick and trapped. He could not believe the speed or viciousness of the prion attacks that he had witnessed that night at King Henry's.

After he had loaded Molly and Jo into an ambulance and sent them on to their grandmother's house in Cornwall, he had toured the top floor of the hospital with Jack. It was a barely contained bedlam. He saw Simi's social worker, Michele Shepherd, shaking and shivering, her fiancé by her side, staring at nothing. Alex Cosic, the boy who had attacked Simi, was coughing up blood and would be dead in hours; his parents had refused to see him. Simi's stepfather had been found in a brothel in King's Cross, and now he lay with the weird rictus smile that denoted the beginning of the last phase of the disease. Uzelac's girlfriend was weeping in a corner. That left Tess and Mrs Peirce as the only people who had come into contact with the disease who were still unscathed.

Graham had forced the medical team back into protective suits with breathing apparatus. But there were not enough to go round, and it was too hot to wear them. Most had been discarded and replaced by simple gowns and bio-masks.

Jack had tried traditional treatments, different ones on different patients. To some he gave ribavirin and Vidarabine, to others sulphated glycosaminoglycans. He was starting to throw experimental protein-inhibitor compounds at the virus, but it was hopeless. Besides, even if they could slow down the blood virus, anyone left with the prion disease would still die.

Mike's mobile phone woke him and Laura said: 'I've just heard about Molly. Nobody told me. Thank Christ she's OK.'

Mike shivered as the thought of what might have been hit him hard.

'Are you all right, sugar? D'you want me to come over there? I could be with you in an hour.'

He wanted to say yes immediately. He wanted her with him; but it was crucial that she carry on her work. 'Molly's on her way to her gran's. She'll be itchy for a few days, but there's not much of a problem. I'm OK. How've you got on?'

She had been locked in a Level 4 lab since the previous day. 'I've isolated the virus proteins from the prions. It looks a bit like some of the rat viruses you and I worked on when we were in Argentina. My instinct tells me that it's not Junin, but it's a close cousin. I've got some people trying to track down various samples from Guatemala and Belize to see if it's close to anything we can treat. Can I get some help?'

'I'll talk to Lipsey. He's promised some army or security service help in Belize. Any thoughts about vaccines?'

'I'm in touch with the guys at the Center for Disease Control in Atlanta. According to their analysis, a couple of the proteins are different from Junin – including our prion friend. So we can't use Junin treatments or vaccine. So as things stand, there's no chance in the short term,' she replied emphatically.

'Not even a DNA vaccine?' Mike was pinning a lot of hope on her specialist knowledge of the breakthrough technique that passed DNA-coated gold particles into the system to produce high immune reactions.

'Solving this could take forever, Mike. You know that. Can you come down here and help?'

''Fraid not,' he replied. 'Got problems here.'

'What kind of problems?'

'The kind you wouldn't believe.'

'Oh, God, I meant to tell you,' she said, 'Tom Grantmore's dead.'

Mike's heart sank. 'How? I spoke to him yesterday.'

'Massive heart attack.'

'But he was one of the fittest men I know.'

'It's a bastard. I loved Tom. Look, I better go, sugar,' she said. 'You look after yourself. Don't let them chew you up.'

Mike watched as the Prime Minister marched across the room to him, trailing civil servants behind him like ants. 'Come back as quickly as you can,' he said to Laura. 'There's a lot of stuff going on here that I can't talk about on the phone.' He paused. 'It'll be great to see you.'

'Bye, sugar,' she replied after a second, 'be there as soon as I can.'

Mike replaced the receiver and turned to Lipsey. 'Can we get some help for Laura Holmes? We need someone to work with the Belizean and Guatemalan governments and health agencies to track this down. There's an epidemiologist out there called Greg Dasham working with WHO. He might be on to the root of all this. The more we know the better.'

Lipsey told Ellington to give Laura whatever assistance she needed and to contact Dasham. Then he indicated to the senior figures in the room to follow him into a conference room for a briefing from Philip Marber.

Standing before a map of the zone, Marber told them that under the 'excellent chairmanship' of the Health Secretary, they believed that it was possible to quarantine the area.

'How are we going to get the people without the virus out of the quarantine areas?' asked Mike.

A silence fell on the room and Mike looked around him as the silence told him that they had no intention of allowing anyone out. Jennifer Low dropped her eyes and studied her notes.

It was left to Graham to tell the truth. 'We cannot be certain,' he said, 'who has the virus and who has not. The quarantine will be total.'

'What do you think, Mac?' asked Lipsey, eager for support.

'I've been thinking it over, Alan. Mike might be right, after all. The model I was talking about is fine for little villages in a vast country. It won't hold for the concentrated areas of a modern city. What I said before was wishful thinking.'

As Mike smiled his thanks at Mac, sour looks passed across the faces of most of the other people in the room, who, Mike saw, clearly wanted Mac to sanction their views.

'Besides, there are vast civil rights implications.' Jennifer Low's voice was wavering a little with stress as she spoke. 'Aren't there, Alan?'

Lipsey walked around the table and placed his hand on hers. 'Thank you for reminding me of that, Jennifer. Here's the struggle going on in my mind: is it better that one man die or a hundred?'

Low flushed slightly. 'One.'

'And, therefore, is it reasonable to allow one to suffer to preserve one hundred?'

'Yes, but—' A crimson wash appeared around Low's throat as she found it difficult to see a way round Lipsey's logic.

'I'm afraid morality is composed of "yes, buts,"' the Prime Minister's face looked lined and worried. 'And politics is made up of "but, yesses". There is always doubt, but someone must make a decision.'

'What will we tell Parliament?' asked Low.

Ellington leant across, touched Lipsey's arm lightly, and intervened. 'It would be impossible to recall Parliament from recess in time,' he said, 'and we don't want to cause unnecessary panic as a result of political grandstanding by some of our less balanced parliamentary brethren. I've checked and under the revised Emergency Provisions Act you have the right to act in consultation with the Privy Council.'

Lipsey looked thoughtfully at the Health Secretary: 'We must move quickly in the public interest, Jennifer. Parliament would restrict our ability to act and increase the fatality rate.' He turned to Ellington. 'Thank you, Lawrence, would you arrange the Privy Council meeting for two hours' time?'

As Marber began to explain the ways in which he intended to handle the public order problem, Mike interrupted. 'We need to set up triage centres. A battery of tests will tell us within a reasonable level of certainty whether people have been exposed to or are incubating the virus. People who have this will exhibit clinical signs pretty quickly. There's been a recently developed multiple antibodies test for haemorrhagic viruses that will tell us definitely who is carrying the viral part of the disease. EEG analysis will throw up any sporadic CJD-like abnormality.'

'It's too risky,' said Graham. 'None of these tests is reliable. And as Dr Davenport well knows, EEG is no test for kuru or new variant CJD. And all that a negative antibody result will tell you is that someone doesn't have the disease currently. But they may be incubating it.'

'If we do nothing, we may be consigning everyone inside the zone to this disease. We don't need to do that,' said Mike. 'We can save tens of thousands if we are brave enough to do so. We can eliminate ninety per cent of the risk.'

'It's a risk not worth taking, Prime Minister,' said Graham decisively.

Marber intervened. 'Dr Davenport is on to something. We need to offer hope to those inside to prevent mass disturbance. I think we should do this. We can still isolate smaller groups outside the main zone.'

Lipsey looked into the middle distance and then nodded. Marber passed some notes to the civil servant beside him who phoned some instructions through to the modelling specialists in Emergency Planning to set up half a dozen mobile testing centres in churches and schools on the outer rim of the cordon.

'What are we going to do about the other patients in King Henry's?' asked Mike. 'The ones without the disease.'

'Can we evacuate to another hospital?' asked Lipsey.

'Yes, of course, Alan,' said Marber. 'However, we must keep those who have been exposed to the virus inside the zone.'

'What about the hospital staff to treat them?' asked Mike.

The Prime Minister said: 'We'll have to ask for volunteers from King Henry's. I don't want to expose anyone else to this.'

Mike fell silent as Marber clicked a few bullet points on to the screen, overlaying the map of the zone. 'I plan to let it be known this morning', he said, 'that a new terrorist group is at work in London – environmentalists, perhaps. And that they have planted bombs around the roads identified by Professor Graham. That will offer the perfect excuse to close the area down and send the media off on the wrong track long enough to complete the cordon.'

Mike blew out hard; he could feel the pain in his gut as he knew what was coming. 'And what of those who have the Spirit Death, and those who will contract it during the quarantine period?' he asked.

'We will treat them, Dr Davenport,' replied Marber.

'Whatever the mobile medical team needs,' said Lipsey with feeling, 'they'll have. Medicine, food, accommodation, whatever resource we have at our disposal.'

'But they must stay within the cordon once they have entered,' said Marber.

Ellington opened a buff folder in front of him and consulted his notes. 'There's something else, Prime Minister.'

Lipsey turned and Mike could see his eyes were flat and prepared; he was unbelievably calm.

Ellington continued: 'We must recall anyone from the area who has travelled abroad in the past few days.'

Mike could swear he saw Lipsey wince a little as the realisation that he would have to contact his counterparts around the world and tell them that Britain might be releasing a plague on the earth. How long could and should he withhold the information? If it could be contained, he would be better not initiating a worldwide scare.

Ellington closed the folder with a quiet slap, stood elegantly and slipped the file from the desk under his arm in one fluid movement. 'Passport Control is checking the address of every British citizen who left in the past few days. We'll track down all the people who may have been in touch with the disease.'

'How many do you estimate?' asked Lipsey.

'Not many, I would think. A dozen at most have left the country. We are tracking a family down who left for California and two nurses from the hospital who are in New York. Apart from that, there's a group of teenagers in Germany for a soccer match. We've contacted the Embassy, who will arrange for them to be sectioned off discreetly until we can test them.'

'Are we sure we have covered everyone, Lawrence?' asked Lipsey.

'I hope so, Prime Minister. The ferries could be a problem. Security is a bit lax there on both sides of the Channel. Someone might've slipped through.'

'Make sure no one has,' said Lipsey. 'Who's controlling the media?'

'I've set up an emergency team to co-ordinate our message. If you don't mind, I'll chair it,' replied Ellington.

'Who's been running it so far?'

Ellington consulted his notes. 'Someone called Jane Hume.'

'Keep her involved. She's done a terrific job. Keep the buggers as far away from the true story as you can. We don't want mass hysteria. I will not have this country turned into a pariah. We must act quickly and decisively to kill this thing. No one is to know. Especially not the Americans, or God forbid, the Chinese. What's happening about the Chinese PM?'

'He intends to cut short his visit because of some internal dissent,' said Ellington. 'And, talking about internal dissent,' he turned to Marber, 'what are we going to do about the communication problem?'

Marber showed them a model of the cell and satellite phone systems operating out of the London area. 'We've instructed the companies to refuse to accept calls from phones located inside the zone. The satellite systems' computers are refusing to up-link the signals.'

Ellington asked: 'Is that completely secure? What about police and ambulance communication devices? Or CBs?'

'All land-based reception can either be jammed or ignored. I think we're OK. No one will be able to contact the media until we are ready.'

'Perhaps we should shut down the ferries and airports until we have this thing under control,' said Graham, poring over a model of the spread of the disease that showed it engulfing the world in a hundred days.

Walking to the computer, Lipsey pushed the OFF button and the image disappeared abruptly from the screen. 'Let's stay with what we know. And what we know is that no one outside the hospital and the immediate area has contracted the disease. Let's get going, people. No more talk. I want action.' He put his arms around Mike's shoulders. 'May we speak alone?'

The others in the room busied themselves with tasks. It was going to be a long night.

Outside, in the warmth of the early morning air, Mike could hear the sound of a solitary aeroplane heading off to its destination; its lights sliced through the dark sky. Lipsey was silent as they walked around the garden. A civil servant appeared with a tray on which were two large Scotches. 'Will you join me?' Lipsey took the glasses and handed one to Mike.

'I don't normally,' replied Mike, 'but I will.'

He tipped the liquid to his lips and the sweet smell of the Black Label swam into his system, quickly followed by a slight sense that the edge had been taken off his tension. Lipsey stood quietly and Mike was aware that he was waiting for the right moment to speak.

'I was listening to what you were saying. We need someone inside the quarantine zone who will supervise the treatment of the patients and the research programme. It's what Marber and his boys call the Bronze Team: the tactical specialists on the ground who know what they're doing. You're the best man to do this, Mike. We need you.'

Mike's insides turned a somersault as he anticipated both the question and his refusal. He did not want to appear a coward in front of Lipsey.

'I think I can help you out there, Alan.' Mac's big voice broke between their silence. 'I'm ready, able and willing.'

They turned and Mike noted again how old Mac had become; lava lines of wrinkles marked out his forehead and flowed back from his eyes until they almost met his ears. His chest, previously muscled and strong from manual labour, seemed to sag down against his shirt.

'Thank you for the offer, Mac.' The Prime Minister's voice was warm. 'But you know as well as me that I cannot accept it.'

'Of course you can. Someone like me should die in harness. I'm no more use to God than a can of cat meat. So why not allow me a wee bit of purpose as I hobble towards oblivion. Mike here has two kids who love him. I've not even got a mangy dog.'

Mike watched Lipsey smile and look at Mac with soft eyes. 'A pretty speech, Father, but what if you break down again? Who would then lead?'

'What's wrong with you, Mac?' asked Mike.

The priest screwed up his face, turned and stomped back to the house. The Prime Minister watched him go, shook his head and sipped on his whisky.

'What's wrong with him?' asked Mike after a few seconds.

'Cancer of the stomach. He's in remission; but it could come back at any time.'

Mike shook his head. Mac was the last person he thought would have stomach problems. He'd seen the priest eat everything under the sun – from maggots to armadillos – and thrive on it without even a mild case of diarrhoea. Now to have stomach cancer seemed perverse of the God that Mac believed in.

'Will you do it, Mike? Will you lead the mobile medical team?'

Ten minutes later Mike sat on a hard chair in a darkened room and tried to prevent the bile rising any further from his gut. He was sweating and could feel rivulets trickling down his back. He had turned the Prime Minister down flat, without a second's hesitation. He knew he would be useless inside the cordon, packed in with the virus, knowing what it could do to him, what it would be like to live out his nightmare once more. No, he could not do it. It was impossible. Unacceptable. Graham could fucking do it; if he had listened to Mike this might not be happening.

Lipsey looked pained when Mike refused and had piled on the moral pressure. But when Mike held out, Lipsey expressed his 'disappointment but not disapproval' and asked Mike who else might lead the team. Mike, again, would not answer. He had no intention of sending people into a death zone from which few might return. He put his head into his hands. I do not owe anyone my death. I do not.

'Mikey.' He looked up and saw Mac's huge body framed by light from the large sash window. The priest had used the pet name he had for Mike before their relationship had fallen apart.

'I'm sorry to hear about the cancer,' said Mike.

Mac leant against the wall and took a drag from a Rothmans. 'Not half as sorry as I am.'

Mike saw how greedily he sucked in the smoke, almost in defiance of his illness. 'What am I going to do, Mac?'

'In what sense?'

'Lipsey is pressuring me to go into the quarantine zone.'

'Tell him to go fuck himself. Let him go inside the zone if he's so fucking concerned.'

A smile threatened to break out on Mike's lips. Just like Mac to say exactly the thing that Mike felt. When Mac resorted to swearing, it was normally to make a point: a baroque exaggeration of his emotions.

'Anyway, I've told the little turd that I can't see why he needs the second division when he's got a premier league player here.' Mac's Belfast accent became thicker as his emotions intensified.

'I wish you had protected me as well before, Mac. We might not have gone through the crap of the last few years.'

Mac took another fierce drag on his cigarette.

'When I was lying in the clinic,' Mike's voice was tight, 'aching with fever after Laura saved me, I wanted you to suffer the way I had. I recalled every petty act of jealousy on your part, every put-down, every miserable night when you dragged me out drinking in some backstreet hovel because you could not sleep again, every brothel that I had to go and find you in. I grew to hate you, Mac. You abandoned me.'

The priest had an anguished but faraway look in his eyes. His fag was down to the filters so he pulled another from the pack and lit it from the dying light of the previous one. Again, he drew deep. 'I had gone mad,' he said in a whisper. 'I'd been told about the cancer.' He turned away from Mike, as if he were incapable of telling this story, the tale of his betrayal of his best friend, face to face. 'And I did my own prognosis. I thought I had less than six months.'

Mike could see the priest's shoulders heave. He might be crying, thought Mike. But he made no move to touch him. Whatever place Mac was in, he wanted to be there.

'You were my pride, Mikey. I thought you were invincible.'

'You did not give me protection, Mac. I didn't have enough drugs or equipment.'

'Don't you think I know that?'

'Why, Mac?'

'They were trying to replace me with you. They said you

were more . . . what was the word? Modern, that was it, "modern" in your approach. I wanted to show them I could lead a team that was faster, leaner and more capable than anyone else's. I wanted to fight them and the cancer. They were going to dump me after twenty years.'

'You almost killed me.' Mike shook his head. 'I was working eighteen-hour days with only four people to help me deal with one of the worst Machupo outbreaks of the decade.'

'They thought you were some kind of wonderkid,' said Mac. 'I kept telling them that you were too impulsive and too nice to play in the big leagues. I was trying to protect you. You weren't ready.'

Mike's voice was gentle; he had worked out his anger with Mac a long time ago. 'I knew that, Mac. They had already approached me to take over from you and I declined. I had no intention of replacing you. Besides, it would have involved living in the US and I didn't want to uproot the kids.'

Mac turned back towards him. He had regained control of himself, but Mike could see the wet of his tears on his jowls. 'Laura told me,' the priest said. 'Nine months ago.'

'So why didn't you call? You didn't even send me a letter when Anne died.'

Mac sat on an armchair across from Mike and leant forward. 'God is merciful, Mike. But I don't think I'll receive much mercy. I've got that stupid Belfast pride. The stuff that makes people kill each other for centuries – even unto the sixth generation. I'm a stupid, wilful old man.'

Mike leaned over and patted his hand.

'But there was more, Mike. I was ashamed of myself. Complete and total. I', he rubbed Mike's hand and gulped in long breaths, 'had a kind of breakdown.' His voice trembled. 'Took to the bottle a wee bit. Broke a crucifix on an altar and pissed in the chalice. The full Graham Greene.' He rubbed his finger down the side of his nose. 'When Anne died I was in a clinic – as our Yank pals call it. I was drying out and being pumped full of limp-lettuce therapy. When I found out, it was too late, and it was just another thing to add to my guilt.'

The grandfather clock in the corner of the room chimed three. Outside the door, in the offices of Number Ten, Mike could hear people making preparations to drop the cordon across Primrose Hill in three hours' time. Army units were moving into place and the police were erecting roadblocks through the night.

The phone rang and Mike picked it up. 'Yes?'

It was Dek. 'Jack's got it.'

CHAPTER THIRTY-FIVE

Tess was sitting next to Jack when Mike arrived. Her face was drained white beneath her blue cap and her emotions were strung out. But she was outwardly calm and she held Jack's hand as gently as a dog carrying an egg. She was wearing proper barrier-protection clothing.

Jack's eyes were open and Mike could see that terror had burrowed deep into his soul. He knew what he would feel in the same circumstances. They had both witnessed the rapid five-day descent into the gibbering, pitiful creatures that patients had become before the last moment when the virus exploded through the body's apertures to find another host. The virus was confused. It shouldn't have been in people and did not know the protocols. Mike guessed that the link with the prion disease had sent the virus's RNA into a flat spin as it tried to realign its identity.

'Can you speak?' Mike asked his friend.

As a white tongue protruded through Jack's cracked lips, he tried to form a word and Tess leaned over to give him a drink of water.

'What happened?' asked Mike.

Tess's eyes were large with emotion above the bio-mask she was wearing. 'Jack treated a little girl a few days ago,' she said. 'The child was thrashing around in the last stages of the disease and she bit through his glove and nicked his hand. She was bleeding from the gums, but Jack checked immediately and could not see any cuts. He thought he had managed to escape any contamination.'

Mike closed his eyelids and contemplated again the enormity of his friend's condition and what was happening in the streets of London. No one was immune: young or old, rich or poor. The plague machine was beginning its random selection.

Jack beckoned him in close and Mike strained to hear him whisper: 'Don't desert the people. They need you. Promise me.'

Mike shook his head. 'I can't do it. I'll be no good in there. I've got some kind of post-traumatic stress disorder as a result of the Machupo attack. It could flare up at any time and I might collapse.'

'Please?' asked Jack again.

A mute shake of Mike's head produced a spasm in Jack. Tess tugged at her brother's arm and pulled him across to a corner. 'What's wrong with you? He's dying, for Christ's sake. Tell him anything. Make him feel good.'

'I can't, Tess. I can't.'

'If you ever loved me, do this. He's done everything a man can do. Fucking hell, Mike. Grow up, grow up.' She hit Mike on the face and began to weep. As Mike hugged her tight she gulped air and struggled to bring herself back under control. 'He wants me to kill him,' said Tess faintly.

Mike saw a syringe on the locker beside the bed. Tess disengaged from his arms and they stared at one another, aware of their responsibilities to preserve life and of the brilliance and dignity of the man dying in front of them.

Mike had never in his life conducted euthanasia. He believed in fighting to the end. He would now be dead if Laura had decided to let him go two years before in Bolivia.

'Don't do it, Tess,' replied Mike urgently. 'There's always a chance. You know that. Jack's strong, he's got real willpower. He'll survive. Someone has to.'

She turned, looked longingly at Jack's brown, pained eyes as he slowly shook his head in two small movements, and recalled his plea when he sensed that he had contracted the disease. She had made her vows to her lover. That took precedence over anything she had promised to the state. 'We decided to get married yesterday,' she said as she took Mike's hand. 'I was longing to tell you; but nobody would let me know where you were, and then Molly got ill and I forgot to say anything, and then you were gone.' A tear meandered down the side of her nose and dripped on to the floor.

'Jesus Christ.' Mike kissed his sister on the head.

She leant back into his body and looked into his eyes. 'I've asked Mac to come in a few minutes. He's going to marry us. Will you be a witness?'

Mike hugged his sister tight and nodded. He returned to Jack's bedside, sat on the bed, took his friend's hand and made his promise. 'Whatever it takes, I'll be there. I'll fight this thing.'

A knock at the door signalled the presence of two people: Mac and Laura Holmes. Mac was carrying a missal and the host; one for the wedding and the other for extreme unction.

Quietly Laura came over and hugged Tess, who clung to the tall, rangy figure with her long dark hair scraped back from her strong, Nordic face. Laura stroked Tess's hair.

Mac asked quietly: 'Shall we begin?'

The wedding march consisted of the beeps and whirring of the machines that were keeping Jack alive and his wedding ring was borrowed from Mike's finger, but Jack and Tess were so clearly in love that it ripped Mike apart. Laura stood beside him and held his gloved hand tightly.

When Mac pronounced them husband and wife, Tess wanted

to howl her rage at God and her love for Jack. The others prepared to leave to allow them privacy. 'No,' said Tess, urgently. 'The last rites. He wants them.'

Mac looked at her uncertainly.

'Just do it, Mac. Jack believes in your God and it'll give him comfort. Don't pretend that you have religious scruples, not at this stage in your life. Show some humanity.'

Mac looked at her, his face the shape of a deflating balloon, and began to utter the incantations of a Catholic's preparations to meet God in a state of grace. The three others stood round the bed to witness the passing over. Mac's blessings and entreaties rose over the sounds of army lorries outside moving barriers and troops into place. When the priest finished Tess thanked him gently and asked everyone to leave. Mike looked at the syringe by the bed and at his sister. She did not catch his eye as he left.

When the door closed, she pulled an armchair across in front of it and then wedged the handle. She did not want to be disturbed on her honeymoon. She took off her face-mask and gently kissed her new husband on the lips. She was prepared for any risk in order to ease his transition from this world to the next. His eyes lightened, and slowly and painfully he forced out three words: 'I adore you.'

Taking the syringe, she lay beside him on the bed and sang. All she could think of was the Beatles' lullaby: 'Golden slumbers fill your eyes/Smiles awake you when you rise/Sleep, little darling, do not cry and I will sing a lullaby.'

He turned his head to watch her and then moved his fingers to meet hers. Then he touched the syringe. This was their pre-arranged signal; worked out that afternoon.

'I want to come with you.' She shuddered as the tears piled from her eyes.

Panic filled Jack's face and he looked desperate to speak but couldn't. He motioned that he needed a drink and she filled his mouth with a little liquid. 'No. I forbid you,' he whispered.

'I don't want to live without you, Jack. It's not fucking fair.'

He shook his head and forced another word: 'Please,' he pleaded.

She huddled beside him and again kissed him, risking all to be one with him. Then she took the syringe and tenderly inserted it into a muscle. She put her head on Jack's chest, listening as his heart stopped beating. Tears flowed on to his skin.

CHAPTER THIRTY-SIX

Ren looked out of the window at the top of the four-storey house they were renting and noted another armoured personnel carrier roll down Primrose Hill Road. He checked it out through his binoculars.

'That's the fourth APC since five o'clock. These guys have got some fucking gig on. And', he turned to Fernandez, 'it's the SAS playing soldier out there.'

Fernandez was fiddling with the knobs on the miniature reception equipment, sweeping for a signal from Mike's house. They had heard nothing now since his daughter was taken to hospital. Also, Mike had been inaccessible for three days, either locked in the hospital or, more worryingly, being ferried around in police cars.

Although nothing that suggested that Mike had found the location of the disease in Belize had fed back to the Company through their contacts in the British security services, Fernandez was still under orders from Li to kill him. The Company had already dealt with the WHO man, Tom Grantmore, who had been killed on the day that Mike had called him. Grantmore was drugged to make it look as if he had suffered a massive heart attack. A similar end would be suitable for Davenport.

All of the details of Uzelac's passage from Guatemala had been erased – along with every scrap of paper in Uzelac's flat, destroyed in a fire. At least when Jacklin finally turned up most of the problems would be dealt with. Fernandez was angry that Li had felt it necessary to send one of his boys from H.Q. over to take charge of the operation. He should've killed Davenport earlier. It would have made life easier.

Fernandez had wanted to kill Davenport at his home: it would have been simple and quiet. But Davenport spent all his time at the hospital and the presence of the new guards had made it impossible. He had had to adopt a higher-risk strategy.

Fernandez had been surprised by the media reports that the Spirit Death had been contained and was causing few deaths. This did not correspond with what he had seen in Belize. Either the government was lying or the high-quality medicine at King Henry's had found a cure. But, the disease was still high profile and profile was the last thing that his masters could tolerate. As far as they were concerned, secrecy was the key to good government – secrecy allied to overwhelming brute force.

Wu Shuo stood and his massive frame cast a shadow across the room. His flat, implacable Mongolian features addressed Fernandez thoughtfully and he placed a hand on the Argentinian's shoulder. 'I want this done today, Mr Fernandez. We have waited too long. The Prime Minister arrives today and we don't want any embarrassment.'

'Too fucking right, man,' Ren rocked back and forth, spraying imaginary bullets at the APC stopping on the street below that was spilling out soldiers. 'What are these guys up to? I'm going down to have a look.'

'I'll come with you,' said Fernandez.

Ren went to the front door, pulled it open and stepped back in surprise.

'Fuck, man. What's that?'

Fernandez came to his side. 'Who? is the question. Not what?'

A body was propped between the frame of the door. A metal pole had been driven through the rib cage and the corpse was wedged upright. A noose around the neck was connected to a hook on the lintel. The face was hidden by a Mayan mask depicting, noted Fernandez, Ah Puch, the god of death. He flinched a little when he saw that the face underneath was bashed in and the tongue cut out. Both wrists had been slashed and the blood, spilled down the expensively cut cotton trousers, had dried hard. The carcass was beginning to smell and the cloud of flies that covered the wounds rose as one when Fernandez moved the body. 'I think we should bring Mr Jacklin inside,' he said. 'And then call the Company for waste disposal. Then I must talk to General Li.'

CHAPTER THIRTY-SEVEN

'What are these soldiers doing?' George Hudson was on the phone to his Sergeant, Tom Fleming. George had just returned home from the hospital, where he had been denied access to his daughter, Jasmine, on the grounds that she was sleeping off the drugs. She would be allowed out in the morning, George was told by a nervous-looking young nurse. She looked as if she had been crying. Beside her had been two tough-looking security guards that he had not seen on his last visit there. Must be staffing up.

'Some problem with the Chinese Prime Minister who is turning up today,' replied Fleming. 'Some deranged environmental pressure group is threatening to bomb the procession. He's giving London Zoo another panda. The greenies think it's not much payback for ripping out the bamboo forests and killing off most of his pals and sending their dicks to Hong Kong as aphrodisiacs.'

George looked out of his window on the top floor of his house on Regent's Park Road and saw the extent of the roadblocks that were being thrown up. 'Seems a bit over the top, Tom. How far are they taking it?' Fleming described the hot spots where roadblocks were being established and George blew out a whistle. 'My lord, that's a big area to contain. Don't they know any more about the possible attack than that?'

'When they find out, they'll tell us, George. Get some sleep and by the time you wake up things'll be back to normal.'

'Cheers, Tom. See you later at the station.' George turned back into his living room and sipped on a welcome cup of tea, into which he glooped honey.

'You put any more of that sweet stuff in your tea and you're gonna be too fat to catch a tortoise, let alone one of those young boys running you ragged.'

George looked up and smiled as Lucille, his wife of twenty years, came from the bedroom. Her short legs and full body were encased in a yellow T-shirt that snagged on her thighs. Her face was round with big eyes that could turn from adoration to suspicion in the space of a second.

She came over, leant down and kissed him on the lips, and he could taste her stale, sleepy breath and the faint echoes of the perfume that he had bought for her thirty-seventh birthday the previous year. He patted the bulge that contained his eight-month-old son.

'How was the little man in the night?'

'Kicking like a centre-forward.' She rubbed the lower part of her belly ruefully and asked: 'Did you drop by to see Jasmine?'

'Yeah, but she was sleeping,' he said. 'We can go this afternoon.'

Two small, querulous voices came tumbling into the room. 'No, you can't,' one cried. 'Dad, Dad, he wants to play with my football. Ow. He pulled my hair, Mum.'

Wynton and Miles, their two boys aged seven and six, respectively, opened their day as they intended to continue. George loved the noise.

CHAPTER THIRTY-EIGHT

Mike watched the helicopter pictures on a bank of monitors. He was in the 'gold' control room at which all strategic decisions were to be taken. The tactical team was code-named 'silver' and the operational boys 'bronze'.

'Gold' had commandeered the large rotunda of a building at the edge of the quarantine zone about a mile and a half from King Henry's. Mike observed a burgeoning bureaucracy springing up around the Senior Co-ordinating Group. Jennifer Low was sitting on a black plastic chair, sipping coffee from a polystyrene cup. Her eyes were flat and she looked pale and tense. She caught his eye and offered an uncertain smile.

The viewing room was on the top floor of the three-storey brick building. It was dark and only a few lights were allowed to breach the gloom. Beside Mike stood Lipsey, Ellington and Mac. Little by little, street by street, Chalk Farm and Primrose Hill were being sealed off. Traffic jams were building up on Regent's Park and Elsworthy roads. Mike could see cars being turned back and bemused pedestrians on both sides of the barriers crowding around soldiers asking questions.

The cameras on the top of the army's armoured personnel carriers homed in on the many faces before them. Children were laughing and cheering and Mike could see that even the adults were obviously looking forward to a doleful phone call to their boss followed by a day in the garden, the pub or the park.

On the local radio station, the DJ was saying: 'And for all you people in the Regent's Park area, there's a burst water main spilling out all over the place. The police recommend that you stay home for a few hours. Catch a few extras zees on them. No one's getting in or out for a while. Oh, and that was the good news, folks. The bad news is that the Northern Line has had a bomb threat at Mornington Crescent and a derailed train on the West Hampstead Line has snarled that up. Bummer. Here's something to cheer you up, the Hollies and "The Air that I Breathe".'

The media message was the same across all platforms. Jane Hume and the government's Information Agency were doing their job very effectively. The story was sexy and they were releasing tidbits every hour to keep the machine fed. They were preparing for the impact of the total news blackout for the area that would be initiated that afternoon. RAF helicopters would be patrolling the area in a few minutes to prevent any news helicopters from overflying the zone. Flight paths were being diverted for all commercial airlines.

Mike listened to an intelligence colonel issuing a string of commands to troops who were blocking off every possible exit from the zone. One after another, tunnels, roads, railway lines, even helipads were being closed down and made secure. Lessons learned in Northern Ireland and the Balkans were being applied with maximum efficiency. Soldiers were unrolling ten-foot-high razor wire down the banks of the railway lines leading into Euston.

Mac put his big hands on the table and watched the images of bemused commuters and determined soldiers on the bank of monitors. 'This won't hold them for long. It's going to be obvious in a matter of hours that the poor buggers aren't going to get in or out, and then the questions will begin.'

The Prime Minister, standing behind them, said softly to Mike: 'Have you made up your mind once and for all?'

Mike looked at him, the fingers of his right hand tingling with tension.

Jack's death had strung him out. He hated the fucking virus. It was ripping through the immediate area, taking out lives as if they mattered less than that of a butterfly. But could he cope?

'I know about your problem, Dr Davenport,' continued Lipsey, 'but you are a brave man. Do you think that there might be a chemical solution to the challenges facing you?'

'What do you mean?' asked Mike.

'Have you tried beta blockers?'

'What?' Mike shook his head in confusion.

'For your nerves. I use them myself on some occasions. They calm me down.'

Mike turned to face him, his face red. 'Prime Minister, I know what these viruses can do and now one of my best friends has died. I think that I'll need a little more than prescription drugs to enable me to lock myself in a quarantine zone.'

Lipsey scrutinised the eight screens. 'There are tens of thousands of people in there who may die unless we help them. You are one of the few people in Britain to have treated cases like this. You owe it to your country and to these people to give succour, Mike. I will give you every help you require: drugs, people, ambulances.'

'Will you give us control over the army?' asked Mac.

'The army, unfortunately, must be allowed to stay outside and protect the rest of London; but you will have many able policemen on the inside. They'll maintain order,' replied Ellington.

'Do the police know what is going on?' Mike could not disguise the venom in his voice when talking to a man he considered soulless.

Ellington's eyes did not look at all phased. 'I don't think that would be advisable. Do you? We wouldn't like to cause a riot, now, would we? We need the police force in there to contain any potential disturbances. We'll tell them what's happening in time and then issue them with protection.'

'You are a piece of work, Ellington. You don't care about those people, do you?'

Ellington, dripping with scorn, replied: 'On the contrary, Dr Davenport. Unlike you, I'm doing my job. Which is to do everything in my power to prevent a mass outbreak of a disease that may be sweeping through those people', he pointed at the screen, 'as a result of negligence on the part of you and your research team at King Henry's.'

'You bastard, Ellington.'

Mac caught Mike's right arm as he spotted it twitching to punch out Ellington.

'There was nothing I could do about this,' hissed Mike. 'I tried to warn you. But you and your friend Graham ignored me.'

The Prime Minister's voice was clipped. 'I don't care about blame now. I want answers. Now stop squabbling, all of you. Try to help.'

A silence fell between them and Mike regained his self-control. 'Is there any more information coming out of Belize?' he asked.

'Lawrence?' Lipsey looked at his, by now, right-hand man.

Ellington opened the folder in his hand and consulted the information. 'Sadly, Dr Dasham, the WHO epidemiologist, died in a car crash yesterday and there is no evidence on either his computer or those of Dr Grantmore about something called the Spirit Death. The Belizean authorities assure us that they have no such disease and that the only sad event of recent months was an assault on several Mayan villages by Guatemalan drug smugglers.'

'But Tom assured me—' Mike was bemused. What's going on

here: the samples in his office going missing, Tom's heart attack, Dasham's death? 'Was there any unusual activity in the area. Logging or so forth,' he asked. 'That might have triggered something.'

'Get someone to look into it,' Lipsey ordered Ellington. 'Now, Mike, what are you going to do?'

Mike stared at Ellington and at the Prime Minister, then he walked into the corridor, found a quiet spot and breathed deeply, forcing himself to be calm. The bile would not leave his throat. What am I going to do? He closed his eyes and decided to call the twins. In a small room with windows looking across Regent's Park he could see a tube station where crowds were gathering. Trains were stopping four stations north of Hampstead on the Northern Line and at Euston to the south.

When he reached his mother-in-law on the phone she told him that, although the hundreds of spots were driving her mad, Molly was fine and her temperature was dropping back to a hundred. A half-smile played across Mike's lips at the thought that a former killer like chickenpox was now a minor childhood ailment; so much so that parents took their kids to homes where children had it in order to get it out of the way early. There will be no one looking for Spirit Death parties, he thought grimly.

Jo picked up the other extension. 'Dad, when are you coming down?'

'I'm not sure I can be there for a while, darling.'

'Molly needs you. Can't you drop whatever you're doing and come to see her?'

'Jo, I'm in trouble.' He tried to sound calm, but instead was sepulchral.

'What's up, Dad?' Jo's voice was tight.

'D'you remember the story about Ulysses?' he asked.

'Yeah. Why?'

'D'you remember what you said? That he should keep his promises, no matter the consequences to his family.'

Her reply was cautious. 'It was only a story, Dad. And I didn't mean it. Family always comes first.'

'Let me explain why I have to keep my promise to someone and why I won't see you for a while.' He was shuddering from top to toe as he made his decision to go in with the Spirit Death. 'There's a nasty bug going around,' he said, 'and I promised Jack I would treat it. I'm going to be gone for a few days.'

'Don't do it, Dad. For once, think of us.'

'I am thinking of you, darling. When you grow up, you would be disgusted with me if I did not do everything in my power to help people. I could not live with myself if you thought I was a selfish coward.'

'I'd never think that, Dad, you know that. Whatever it is you're going to do, don't. Be with us, please be with us.'

'You know, I've been struggling to think what your mum would've wanted. It's easy to con yourself with memories. But, despite the fear and worry that I would never come home, we always both agreed that I had to go into a situation if I was needed and they asked. Well, I am needed and they have asked. I love you, darling. Look after Molly for me and stay as far away from London as you can. I promise you with everything in me I will see you soon.' He hit the OFF button on the phone and looked out of the window at the crowd around the tube station as it began to sway with anger.

When he entered the main control room Jane was with the Prime Minister. Her eyes were wide with adrenaline as she listened to him outlining the media strategy. She was nodding rapidly.

Turning to leave, she saw Mike and hesitated, then Ellington said: 'Jane, may I speak to you for a second?' She held Mike's gaze for a moment and then turned away to join her new boss.

Mike walked downstairs sadly and out into the blinding sunlight. Jennifer Low stood outside, staring at a group of five-year-olds snaking off in parallel lines, each child holding another's hand. They were dressed smartly in uniform. As

Jennifer tugged on a cigarette, Mike could see that her hands were shaking.

'How are you doing?' he asked.

'Been better,' she replied. 'Not every day I'm held responsible for imprisoning thousands of people.'

'Not your call, Jennifer.'

'Yeah, I know.' She exhaled the smoke forcefully. 'Collective responsibility and all that. I'm a good corporate citizen.'

He could see her eyes glisten a little.

'So why do I feel like shit? Did you know I was a nurse before I got into politics? A staff nurse in Liverpool.' Her voice was small and seemed to drift with her thoughts.

'Do you want to talk?' he asked.

'I haven't smoked one of these in years,' she said as she stubbed out the cigarette. 'Bummed it from Mac.' She walked back up the stairs. 'Duty calls,' she replied. 'We've both got jobs to do, Dr Davenport.' As she disappeared, Mike heard her say: 'Only doing my duty.'

CHAPTER THIRTY-NINE

Li was in the back of his discreet Lincoln limousine, protected within his cocoon of bullet-proof glass and strengthened metal. Beside him, his wife Sarah, her elegant legs crossed and covered by black D&G slacks, concentrated on a biography of John Keats.

They were rolling towards a small, upstate airport and a chopper that would take them to New York City and the Company's tall, white office tower. Sarah's brother's funeral was that day, the rest of his body having turned up in the harbour. On his torso was carved a Mayan death symbol. Despite their efforts, Li's people could not track down the killer. And now Jacklin was gone too, with similar marks on his body. Samuels had been thorough.

Li was tense about the situation in London, particularly with the visit of his friend, Chung Fuhe, the Chinese Prime Minister. Li had promised Chung that the 'little accident' would not cause him any embarrassment on his trip. Chung had made it clear that he did not want any connection to be made between the Company, the PLA and the British virus. Li had recommended that Chung meet Lipsey outside London, but at the last minute Chung had decided to suffer from a diplomatic version of the flu and not turn up at all.

Li looked out on the steam rising from the road as the sun sucked the rain back from the earth. It gave him pleasure to reflect on the endless flow of the world. Today's problems made more sense to him when awash on a sea of universals. He was talking to Fernandez on the phone. 'Who killed our friend?' he asked.

'Who knew he was coming?' enquired Fernandez.

'I did, as did Mr Jacklin's assistant, Julia, who arranged the tickets; but I can assure you she is an innocent in this.' One of Li's assistants had assured him of this truth after ten hours of violent interrogation. 'Darling,' he turned to Sarah, 'would you take some flowers to Julia West, the poor girl is feeling a little nervous after the events of the past few days? I believe she's at home after an unfortunate fall.' He spoke into the phone again. 'Apart from Julia, me and you,' he said to Fernandez, 'no one else knew.'

'The Mayan reference is very disconcerting,' commented Fernandez. 'The action must have been carried out by someone who knows about the Central American story. If not Samuels, then someone else with that knowledge.' Fernandez sounded tired to Li, who wondered if he was up to the job. Perhaps it was time to replace him with a younger man.

'And who might that be?' asked Li.

'Someone inside?' Li listened as Fernandez stated the obvious. Many would like to see him fall and blame an unknown assassin; but information on the Spirit Death was highly restricted and few knew of it.

'And why would they have decided to trouble Mr Jacklin?'

'To draw attention to my incompetence,' said Fernandez heavily, 'and therefore to implicate you.'

As the car stopped, Li opened the darkened windows and

allowed the sunshine to pour across his face. 'A strong argument, Mr Fernandez, but no one other than Samuels and Jacklin knew enough to add the elements together.' The sun felt good to Li as it licked at his cheek. A fresh breeze ruffled the tops of the trees surrounding the small airport as he watched a yellow chopper lift and tilt towards the rippling lake at the end of the runway. A male voice called out his name and he turned his head to see his pilot running across the tarmac. Peter Lyall's long, blond hair flowed behind him as he sped towards the car.

'What's so urgent, Peter?' Li asked when the pilot reached him.

'I was told that you had to have this immediately.'

'And who told you that?'

'Someone at your office?'

'Can you remember who that was?'

'Mr Jacklin,' said the pilot. 'I recognised his voice.'

'Ah, Mr Jacklin. Thank you, Peter. Would you take the package and stand over by the helicopter? Sarah and I will be with you in a few minutes.'

Li rapped on the window that divided him from his Vietnamese driver, Chris Chi.

'Chris, would you pass your expert eye over the parcel carried by Peter. And if it is safe, would you bring it back to me?'

Chi's brown eyes were sharp and alert as he nodded. As Li told Fernandez of the curious turn of events, he watched Chris scanning the packet for explosives. When he was satisfied that all was well, Chris returned with it in his hand. Standing beside the car, he unwrapped the richly patterned red paper and revealed a carved wooden box. Li recognised some Mayan symbolism in the carving.

'Open it, Chris, if you will.'

There was a silver key on the side that Chris turned and the casket opened with a soft puff. Chris looked at it, surprise briefly registering in his eyes, and turned it towards Li. Inside was a heart; a human heart.

'Was Mr Jacklin's body intact when you found it, Mr Fernandez?'

'His heart had been cut out.'

'It has just been returned.'

'What?'

'I believe we have Mr Jacklin's heart with us.'

Chris closed the box again and showed Li the lid.

'And whoever the sender was, he has also given us the message that Ah Puch has taken his revenge.'

'It must be Samuels then,' said Fernandez. 'Only he knew that we were surrounded by images of Ah Puch when we conducted the cleansing operation.'

'I'm surprised he has survived,' said Li, 'if the disease is as virulent as you make out. I think it's time we increased our vigilance about Mr Samuels. He may be inside your quarantine zone if he delivered Mr Jacklin's body to you yesterday morning. Alex Brayshaw was killed yesterday. It's just possible that Samuels made both hits, or had an associate conduct the business for him. He may want money and will therefore contact us. I suggest that you find him and arrange for his termination. If he is in the States, I will find him.

'However, he may just lie low and wait out the epidemic,' continued Li. 'Ask Mr Ren to look around and see if Mr Samuels is anywhere to be found. He will stand out from the crowd.'

'What shall I do about Davenport?'

'Is he close to identifying the Belize route?'

'Probably. He has people working on it.'

'We must prevent this information emerging. I will personally take responsibility for the British and Belizeans. And perhaps he might be accident prone. We'll talk later.' Li closed the connection and told Chris to send the casket to the Company's lab for analysis. Then he turned his attention to his wife and saw that her face was frozen and immobile as she resolutely read her romantic biography. She heard only those things she wanted to.

'What is your favourite line from Keats?' he asked, touching the cover of the book.

Her smile always intrigued him – crooked and imperfect, but at the same time suggesting a sensuality that she would never allow herself to feel.

Her voice was flat, with no hint, that he could detect, of irony as she picked through the last stanza of Keats's *To Sleep* like a metronome:

> 'Save me from curious conscience, that still lords
> Its strength for darkness, burrowing like a mole;
> Turn the key deftly in the oiled wards,
> And seal the hushed casket of my soul.'

'Will you miss your brother, my dear?' he asked.

She stared out into the daylight and he noticed her eyes were hard and angry. Li had caught Brayshaw hitting Sarah across the face when drunk after a New Year's party a few years before. He wondered if that was the only time.

'Of course,' she replied dully. 'Of course I shall.'

CHAPTER FORTY

DI Joe McCormick watched in amazement as the young captain in front of him implacably refused to explain any more about the roadblocks or to allow him to leave through the cordon of barbed wire and APCs at the bottom of Euston Road. 'Look,' said Joe. 'I've got a murder inquiry to deal with and I don't have all day.' He was on the small side for a policeman and had to look up at the six-foot-three SAS man. Joe's face was saggy and lined; he had the pallor of a man too used to the inside of smoky bars and the bottom of whisky glasses. This irritated him beyond measure: he had been teetotal since throwing up all over his dad when he was seventeen. At the time, his father was passed out on the ground as a result of a three-day bender. When Joe woke up, he vowed he would never touch another drop. And he never had.

A small cigarillo was burning in his right hand. Joe allowed himself five a day – no more, not even under extreme stress. But he could not get through the day without them. And his favourite shop was on the other side of the armoured car. The soldier shrugged and turned back towards his men, who were wearing masks and protective gear.

This was weird, thought Joe. He took a step towards the Captain and took his shoulder. 'Don't be rude,' he said to the younger man. 'Now, excuse me, I must get on.' Joe strode purposefully onwards until he heard a harsh, clipped order: 'Stop him.'

Joe was surrounded by four men who grabbed him, put him in an armlock and forced him back to the other side of the cordon. His arm hurt like buggery and he struck out with his right foot. One of the soldiers, a lad of no more than eighteen, stuck the butt of his rifle into Joe's stomach. Joe collapsed on to the ground, crying out in a mixture of pain and surprise. Then he was dragged for ten metres by the shoulders and deposited on the pavement. Around him were shocked commuters who sat in their cars, staring at the scene before them. But no one moved to help.

'Don't fucking try that again, or it'll be your balls next time.' The soldier who had winded him looked down at him and Joe could see contempt in his eyes.

Furious and humiliated, Joe lashed out and caught the lad on the shins. Within seconds, blows were raining down on him from three sides and he was bleeding profusely from his head. Blood flowed into his eyes and he curled up in a ball to prevent damage to his ribs and lungs as the kicks pummelled him. When he was about to pass out, he heard ambulances edging their way between the four armoured cars that were strung across the street.

The lead vehicle was an army crash ambulance with advanced trauma life-support capacity. It stopped, and Mike jumped down and screamed at the soldiers, who shrugged and retreated back behind the barriers. 'Help me get him up,' he shouted to Laura in the back of the ambulance. Between them, they managed to help Joe into the back of the vehicle.

Whilst Mike stitched his wounds, Joe noticed that the

doctor was wearing a green safety mask. 'What's going on?' he asked.

'You'll find out soon enough,' replied Mike. 'I'm taking you to the clinic until your concussion is out of the way.'

He got back into the front and drove them to the old AIDS building. It was low slung, on two floors, with a flat roof. Someone had once had the bright idea of painting it white but after a year of disuse the paint was peeling off and, here and there, Mike could see a broken window. He stopped the van and got out.

'Good choice, Mikey,' boomed Mac from the passenger seat. 'What was the other option? A doss house?'

CHAPTER FORTY-ONE

Victor Obudo was edgy. He hadn't scored for a day. But the CD he'd nicked had dropped twenty quid into his lap. Lying on the sofa, he dialled the pager of his dealer on his mobile phone. No signal. He was irritated. He needed his stuff. He'd picked up the habit when he was inside and now it gnawed at him – another present from the machine. Fucking police fitting me up, he grumbled as he searched round the flat to see if he had stashed anything for a rainy day.

His mum called out from her bedroom at the end of the thin corridor in their small flat. 'I'm not feeling too good. Get me something from the chemist. And would you phone the hospital and tell them I'm not coming in today?'

'What do you want, Mum? There's some aspirin in the kitchen. I'll get you that.'

'Thanks, honey.'

He phoned again. Still no signal. There had never been a problem before with it. His frustration mounted.

'Victor, please, I need some water.'

'OK. OK, Mum. I'll be through in a second and then I'll fetch what you need. Want a cup of tea?'

Again he called. Again no signal. He threw the phone at the wall in fury; it hit solidly, then fell to the ground where the detached battery looked up at him like a stranded beetle.

'Victor? What's going on? I'm not feeling too good, darling. I'm kinda shivering. I need something, Victor.'

You and me both, thought Victor. You and me both. 'Coming, Mum,' he said and walked towards her bedroom.

CHAPTER FORTY-TWO

It was nearly lunchtime before Mike had settled himself and his small team. Joe was sitting in the dusty office in a daze at the news that Mike had imparted to him. He tried to phone his boss at Scotland Yard, but there was no signal.

'They've cut off all the telephones. The land-line exchanges are not transferring calls and the mobile companies have jammed the signals from their cells.' As she spoke, Laura looked at the bruising around Joe's head. 'They don't want anyone spreading this story before they're ready to deal with it.'

'I just don't believe it.' Joe shook his head slowly. 'You can't create a quarantine zone. Not in this day and age. How can they cut off mobiles?'

'Not difficult with terrestrial,' said Mac, 'but if they're cutting off the satellites, that will be another thing altogether.'

'Thanks for everything, Doctor, but I'm leaving,' said Joe and headed for the double doors at the end of the empty twelve-bed ward.

As he reached them, Mac asked: 'Where d'you think you're going?'

'I'm going home to pick up a few things and then I'm taking a little holiday somewhere warm and isolated,' replied Joe.

Mac began to unpack bandages and anti-virus drugs. 'I don't think you will be somehow. They've been told to shoot anyone who tries to break out.'

Joe laughed. 'Come off it, this is Britain. No one does that kind of thing.'

Mac looked him up and down and in his thickest Belfast accent said: 'And how many people did English soldiers shoot in Ireland?'

'That was different. That was terrorism. This is our own people.'

'From now until this crisis is over,' Mac returned to his unpacking, 'your body is a form of terrorist bomb as far as this government is concerned. They will kill you.'

Joe reflected on the beating he had just received and considered that perhaps the fat priest was on to something. 'I'm going to the local nick to see what's going on,' he said.

'You do that,' said Mac.

Laura had gone off in search of Mike, who was leaning against a wall in a corridor, his face white and sweat glistening on his skin. He was hyperventilating; his eyes, in a fixed stare, were focused on the wall.

'What's wrong with you?' Laura asked fearfully.

'I can't do it,' he said between clenched teeth. 'I've got to get out of here.' Laura forced him to sit down and put his head between his knees to prevent him from fainting. She stroked his right hand. 'We're all terrified. You would be mad not to be.'

'But I've lost it. I can't walk out there or treat anyone. I've just lost it.'

'What d'you mean?' Her voice was low and husky.

'Since Anne died, I've been unable to go into a Level 4 lab. And now I'm living in one. My nerves are fucked.'

She lifted his head and said: 'No one will keep you here
against your will. If you want to leave, all you have to do is call
Lipsey.'

Mike opened his hand and showed her a bottle of beta
blockers. 'What d'you think?' he asked.

'I think that the Mike Davenport I know doesn't need pills.
What time do you have to make the broadcast?'

He looked at his watch. It was almost midday. 'In two
minutes.'

'You'll be fine, sugar, just fine.' She held his hand as he
groaned, then let the sound turn to a growl and finally a
howling, tumbling scream that filled the dingy corridor with
its filthy walls and ripped posters that urged people to 'USE A
CONDOM – SAVE A LIFE'. She hugged him and he held on tight
for a few seconds. Her eyes were bright as she looked up at him.
'C'mon. Let's do it,' she said.

They walked to the reception area where a PC was set up
with a specially installed fast network line that would allow
him to talk via streamed video to the staff at King Henry's, who
were being held in isolation at a secure former mental hospital
in Hampstead.

Mike sat beside the computer, adjusted the camera next to it
and turned it on. Immediately, his image was conveyed to
closed rooms filled with doctors and nurses. He pushed the
RETURN key on the keyboard and saw miniature images of each
group of people on his screen. He clicked on a close up of Liz
O'Mara, the Irish doctor whom Tess liked so much, and the first
person to treat a Spirit Death patient. He needed to make the
pitch intimate and aim it at one person if he was to have an
impact on them all.

Liz's face was white and freckled. Her face bore the usual
exhaustion of a Senior House Officer, but there was an intensity
to her eyes Mike had not seen before. He remembered looking
in the mirror the first time he had spent a week in a fever zone.
Her eyes carried the same haunted look and the same fear that

the next time it would be her. Can I really expect these people to come in here, he thought? But then, if I don't, what hope will anyone have inside the quarantine?

He began to speak. 'I know that you are shocked by the news from Primrose Hill.'

Liz nodded a little, and her eyes darted from side to side, gauging the response of the people around her.

'We are under siege from a virus that we barely understand. So far, we have lost six nurses and, earlier tonight, Jack Lim died. I cannot promise you that you will be one hundred per cent safe in here. I cannot promise you anything other than total support and commitment from me; total vigilance and caution about your safety; and the gratitude of every member of this community. I believe that we have methods that will protect every member of the medical team here. We just need to be careful. All diseases can be contained.'

Hooded and uncertain, Liz's eyes showed that he was not getting through. He did not want anyone in the quarantine zone who did not appreciate the risks involved, but he needed some brave people.

'I have two daughters,' said Mike. He punched up an image of Jo and Molly and broadcast it to the people watching. 'I want to return to them. I want to see them grow and marry. I want grandchildren. But I cannot leave the people inside this quarantine zone without medical care. We are in a war with this virus. And we can and will win. I've been with Ebola in Zaire and Machupo in Bolivia. I've seen this evil and I've seen how, by the will of nurses and doctors and the people, we can defeat it.' He paused for three beats. 'I beg you. Join me.'

The strain on Liz's face was immense and he could clearly see a struggle going on in her mind. He had to believe he was getting through to her and the others.

'If you don't come, there will only be three of us in here. All three of us have experienced similar situations in the past. We are convinced that we will leave here alive and well. But we need your help. If you leave us alone, we will surely die, because we will be exhausted and make mistakes.' He brooded on Liz's eyes as she shook her head. She wasn't coming. Shit. She wasn't coming. 'I can say no more to you. Search your conscience. Think of how you will feel in a month's time if you ignore this plea. Each man and woman has his or her limit. But we can only be true to ourselves if we surpass those limits. The Prime Minister will address you in a few minutes. The barrier will close in two hours' time. Whatever decision you make, you will live with it for the rest of your life. Thank you for listening to me.'

When he had finished, he was drained and his forehead was glistening with sweat. Laura placed her hands on his shoulders, bent in close and muttered her approval: 'I'm proud of you.'

Mike was breathing heavily, as if coming to the end of a six-mile run. He sucked on a bottle of Coke and tried desperately to reconstruct his speech. Was it good enough? Was I persuasive? Should I have sold it more? Oh, Christ almighty, why am I here?

CHAPTER FORTY-THREE

Fernandez watched as Ren berated a young, belligerent soldier standing guard in front of an APC whilst his colleagues were unrolling razor wire across the road. It was obvious that something major was happening. But what? He did not believe the nonsense about bombs. They had now driven or walked in a large circle seeking a way into Central London. At every major exit road, APCs were parked two hundred metres behind waves of razor wire. In front of each barrier were a half-dozen soldiers in green hazard suits, masks dangling on their chests as if expecting a gas attack. Fernandez guessed with sinking heart that they were being quarantined. The last time he had seen a protective suit like that, he had been wearing it in Belize.

Fernandez stepped into the argument and tugged on Ren's arm. 'I think we should go home.'

'I'm going nowhere, man. We've got business in town.' As Ren pushed the soldier on the chest, a look passed between the four men surrounding him.

'Just move back, if you don't mind. It's for your own good,

sir,' the Lieutenant said in a measured voice. 'I strongly recommend that you listen to your friend's advice and return home.'

'Fuck you,' growled Ren.

One of the soldiers pushed him back and Ren lashed out with his boot. Fernandez was conscious suddenly that the men around him were prepared to fire the plastic bullets in their guns. These were hardened, unsentimental soldiers, one of whom put the muzzle of his gun into Ren's chest, saying: 'I don't think you understand me, Chink, this is your last chance to turn around.'

Ren smiled. His pupils were reduced to pinpricks and he put his palms up in front of his chest. 'Sure, man. Sure. Whatever. Sorry to trouble you.' He turned nimbly and walked towards a block of garages that overlooked a filthy alleyway.

'Where are you going?' asked Fernandez, trying to catch up with Ren.

'Go home, old man. I've got things to do.'

'Don't be stupid, Ren. We've still to take care of Davenport and get rid of Jacklin's body. Then we'll find a way out of here.'

'Sure, sure.' Ren broke into a trot, then a sprint and dis- appeared behind a large furniture-removal van. When Fernandez reached the vehicle, Ren had slipped into an alley- way. As Fernandez waited in the sunshine, a hazy, empty, pregnant moment enveloped him. Then he heard four rapid-fire shots. Looking back at the roadblock, he saw that the soldier who had called Ren a 'Chink' had collapsed in a bloody heap. All around in the houses and flats people poked their heads out of their windows and looked in astonishment at the soldiers surrounding their fallen comrade.

A hush fell. After seconds of silence a teenage boy ran down the road in the direction of the platoon. In the confusion, one of the soldiers spotted him pulling something from his pocket as he charged at them. He shouted: 'Halt. Stop.' But the boy continued to run. A series of orders poured from the Lieutenant.

'He's got a gun,' someone shouted, and one of the soldiers fired: the boy tumbled backwards as the plastic bullet crashed against his skull.

Again silence descended on the scene. It lasted one second, then two, and by the third the soldiers, in a clatter of organised noise, retreated back behind the wire. From the alleyway, a thin, middle-aged man hurtled out shouting: 'Brian. For fuck's sake, Brian. What are you doing?' His voice was filled with fear as he knelt and cradled the dead boy in his arms.

As the Lieutenant trained his binoculars on the scene, he observed the smashed eye and face, and the toy gun by the boy's side. The father stood, raised his fist in the direction of the soldiers and cursed them. A crowd formed around the father and son and a wail rose from the boy's mother.

The Lieutenant phoned his Captain and asked for permission to go in and retrieve the lad.

'Hold your line,' the reply came back. 'I repeat. Hold your line.'

Fernandez waited for Ren by the furniture van and watched a crowd of fifteen teenagers gather, with a young black man operating as a ringleader. The first stones began to hail down on the soldiers. A few seconds later, Fernandez felt a touch on his shoulder. He turned, and Ren, with a smile wider than the Yangtze, said: 'That'll teach the arrogant fucks.'

Fernandez shook his head. 'Let's leave,' he said, 'before this place erupts.'

'Too late.' Ren grinned as the first petrol bomb exploded against the APC.

CHAPTER FORTY-FOUR

'No one's coming, I've blown it.' Mike sat in the passenger seat of a twelve-seat minibus beside Laura, who leant on the steering wheel and concentrated on the one hundred metres between them and the armoured personnel carriers behind the razor wire. Mac was driving an army coach fitted with stretchers and had parked behind them. They had asked Lipsey for army drivers as back-up, but had been refused. It was operationally vital, Ellington had argued, that the army had complete focus on their most important job: protecting the rest of the UK.

'Be patient, sugar. They'll come. I know it.'

They waited at the bottom of a long alley between two office blocks that was to serve as an artery rendezvous point between the bronze and silver teams. It reminded Mike a little of movies about handovers in Berlin before the wall came down. A single line between the wire, broad enough only for one person, led down towards them.

It was five minutes from the deadline. Not one volunteer had

joined them and there seemed to be no activity at the other end
of the alley.

'I was useless,' said Mike as he stared morosely at uncollected
garbage behind a fruit and vegetable shop. A high, sweet,
rotten smell of decaying produce filled the air.

'You were brilliant.' Laura was emphatic as she looked at
him. 'If they don't come, they're cowards. But they will. I know
they will.' Her voice was filled with hard hope.

Mike looked at the clock on the dashboard in front of him.
'Four minutes and counting.'

'They'll be here.' She nodded and started to hum a country
and western song that Mike didn't recognise, but that he
assumed came from Tammy Wynette or one of the other sisters
of doomed love that Laura played at full blast. He watched the
clock tick on mercilessly — seconds thudding into receding
seconds. Then, suddenly, it was over. Two o'clock. Nobody.
Not one. Mike's spirit sank.

There was a thick, emotional silence in the bus.

'What do we do now?' he asked Laura.

'I have no idea. No idea.' She shook her head, unwilling to
believe in the cowardice of her own profession. She had seen so
much bravery in Africa and South America; so many doctors
and nurses putting themselves into dark holes of pain and
despair.

Mike touched her hand. 'I'm sure I can still get you out of
here.'

She smiled at him, leant over and kissed his cheek. 'What?
And miss the chance to save your life a second time?'

Mike could see the fear in her eyes; she knew as well as he did
what they were letting themselves in for. 'I've an idea,' he said.

'What? A quick African immigration policy for medical staff
with guts?' asked Laura.

'No. There must be . . . what? . . . at least a half-dozen GPs
and doctors inside the cordon. Must be. Let's try them. And
how many nurses? Dozens.'

She looked thoughtfully at him. 'True.' She nodded. 'But how do we contact them?'

'I'll ask Lipsey. He'll find a way. Come on. Let's get back.'

As they fired up the engine, Mac swayed towards them. 'Where d'you think you're going, boy?' he asked.

'It's over, Mac,' replied Mike. 'We'll have to do this ourselves.'

'Are you mad?'

'You can leave if you want, Mac. But I'm staying.'

'Oooh,' Mac's voice dripped with what Mike perceived to be amused sarcasm, 'brave boy.'

'I take it that you know something I don't,' said Mike, detecting the signs of superior knowledge on Mac's part.

'Oh, I know simple things. Very simple things. Like', he reached inside the minibus and picked up the man-portable communication phone that the army had given to Mike before he entered the zone, 'turning on the phone when people are trying to get in touch with you.' He handed the phone to Mike. 'They contacted me because you were unobtainable.'

As Mike flushed to the roots of his hair, he heard a voice say: 'Davenport. It's Ellington. Where've you been? We've been trying to call you for twenty minutes.'

'Sorry,' mumbled Mike, 'technical problem.'

Ellington got straight to the point. 'We have a group of volunteers here. About ten. Is that enough?'

'No. But it'll have to do. I'm sure I can recruit others inside the zone.'

'I've vetted them,' said Ellington, 'and chosen the people with the least to lose and with no families on the outside. I don't want anyone crawling all over us trying to get them out. Each of them has signed a disclaimer absolving you of any responsibility for their death.'

Laura whispered angrily: 'What a bastard.'

Mike was thinking of a stronger epithet.

'I take it the government is indemnified,' said Mac to the speaker phone.

'Of course.' Ellington sounded offended that anyone would think that he could have missed such an obvious detail.

'Send them in, then, boy,' announced Mac. 'Send them in before we all die of boredom.'

Ahead of them, a flurry of soldiers created a parting in the wire at the top of the alley, and a tall, woman swayed through and bounced against one of the soldiers, who held her arms to steady her. She pushed him away and staggered towards them.

'You'll recognise this person, I suspect,' said Ellington.

Mike peered at the outline of the strong legs, straight back and short hair. 'Christ,' hissed Laura softly at his side. 'It's Tess.'

'And she's as pissed as a Dominican friar on a Saturday night,' noted Mac.

Mike jumped from the seat and ran towards his sister, who was retching against a wall. As he reached her, she looked up, shielding her eyes from the sun. Her sunglasses were on the baking tarmac at her feet. Her face was a mess of tear-stained make-up, snot and vomit.

'Need a used nurse?' she asked. 'Only one careful owner.'

When Mike folded her in his arms and pulled her head towards his shoulder, she rubbed her face against his chest like a tired baby.

'Go home, Tess,' he pleaded. 'Please, go. Look after the twins. They need one of us.'

'They need both of us, big brother. And there is nowhere else I can be but here.' As she pulled herself away and looked into Mike's eyes, he could see a drunk's manic determination; then suddenly her face dissolved again. 'I know I'm smashed, Mike; but I'll be sober by nighttime. If you send me back out into the world, I'll be a drunk for ever. Please, Mike.' She clung to him. 'Please.'

As they hugged, Laura said: 'She's a big girl, Mike. Let her make her own decisions.' Then she led Tess to the minibus and laid her down on one of the stretchers.

As a thin line of six people walked down the alley towards

them, Mac came up to Mike's side and proclaimed loudly: 'Jesus Christ, they've sent us the halt and the blind. What do they think we are? A therapy centre?' He raised an eyebrow. 'You've got that persuasive touch, Mike. A leader of men. You should've let me do the speech. They needed a bit of Belfast emotion.'

Mike stepped towards the first person – a middle-aged woman wearing a smart, linen suit and a wide-brimmed hat trimmed with ribbon. She offered her hand from her wheelchair and said: 'Good to see you again, Mike. Although the circumstances are a tad odd.' Her voice was light but brittle.

'Just a tad.' Mike leant down to kiss her fingers, and replied. 'Good to see you, Daisy. I wasn't expecting a Nobel laureate.'

'I was in the territory. I just hope that jallopy', Daisy Wooldridge waved in the direction of the minibus, 'has decent disabled access. Otherwise I'll complain to the disability lobby about lack of access to a plague zone. I've as much basic human right to kill myself on some quixotic suicide mission as any able-bodied chump. And', she nodded in Mac's direction, 'I'm not going in anything driven by the fat priest; we'll probably overbalance.'

'Laughing in the face of adversity again, Daisy.' Mac walked behind her wheelchair. 'Let me just take you to the minibus.'

Daisy snorted and pushed a lever on the arm of the chair and shot away from them both as the electrically-powered wheels sped over the ground.

Mac turned to Mike, who shrugged. 'I dunno why she's here,' said Mike, 'but Christ, she was the best molecular biologist in Europe before the MS and her retirement. If she's up to it, she's welcome. Laura needs someone to help her with the research.'

'She was an irascible old bag when I first met her twenty years ago, and she is still one now,' said Mac emphatically. 'Just keep her out of my way.'

Mike looked at the line of volunteers and smiling grimly at him was Liz O'Mara. He closed his eyes as he realised it was his words that brought her into a death zone. Then he smiled as Dek marched towards him, his big-muscled arms swinging loosely by his sides. When he reached Mike the smell of marijuana on his hair was unmistakable. 'Thanks, Dek.' Mike was close to tears as he saw his friend. 'I was hoping you'd come.'

'I'd do anything to get on the front cover of the *Current Bun*, you know me. Good publicity for the band. We'll be number one by the time I get out of here. I just hope it's not a posthumous single for yours truly.'

The soldiers began to close the top of the alley and Mike was startled to see a woman wearing blue jeans and a red shirt pushing angrily at the army's Forward Control Point Commander, who was restraining her with one hand and was holding into the telephone with the other. She took the phone forcibly and spoke angrily into the mouthpiece; then she gave it back to the soldier and stomped down the alley towards Mike as the cordon was sealed behind her.

Jennifer Low's hair shone in the sun; her back was straight and her eyes clear when she put out her hand to shake Mike's. 'Couldn't do it. Collective responsibility my arse. This is wrong and I won't be part of it. That smug bastard Ellington finally got to me. I poured a pint of milk over his head.'

Mike's eyes opened with pleasure at the thought.

'I told you I used to be a nurse. A bloody good one at that. So I won't be a complete waste of space.' She linked her arm under his. 'Now, let's get cracking,' she said.

CHAPTER FORTY-FIVE

Tess Davenport woke from a drunken sleep that had plunged her into deep, turbulent nightmares. She felt terrible: everything hurt and she could barely remember the time since Jack's death. Vaguely, she could recall demanding to see Mike, and flashes of horrible memories jumped out at her in a fragmented jumble of images. Fuck it, she thought, today is another day.

Her tongue was furred like the inside of a kettle and she licked around the roof of her mouth, searching for moisture. Although desperate to go to the loo, she could not face moving. Someone is bound to give me a lecture, she thought. Better to stay in bed. Or, rather, not bed. She felt the floor around her. Where on earth am I?

She ungummed an unwilling eye and discovered she was lying on a tiled floor covered by a white hospital blanket. Looking up, she saw that she was in a cubicle in a reception centre. On the walls were AIDS posters filled with dire warnings and hopeful images. A quick flash of memory told her she had passed out in Mac's arms as they entered the clinic and had told everyone she wanted to sleep on the floor. They must have taken her at her word. She groaned and turned over in the knowledge that she would feel better in the morning. She closed her eyes, fighting the nausea, and pulled the sheet over her head.

CHAPTER FORTY-SIX

Victor Obudo was feeling sorted. He'd tracked down his dealer and the effects of his purchase had wired him. 'Let's burn the fuckers out, man,' he shouted. 'Fucking sickos,' he roared as he pointed at the clinic, protected behind a wire fence and steel double gates. 'If we get rid of them, the power'll let us out of here.' I've been locked in once before, Victor was raging inside, and I'm fucked if they'll do it to me again.

Around Victor was a gang of forty teenage boys of all races – black, Asian and white. They had been inside the cordon for fifteen hours. And another stifling night where even the most relaxed people found sleep impossible had sent them pouring out into the street looking for trouble.

Word had spread fast when the first six Spirit Death cases were admitted to Mike's clinic. It was hard to disguise the twisting, retching bodies of the patients. Soon, with the government's announcement of the quarantine, people in the surrounding houses were putting two and two together about the clinic.

Someone in the gang had produced a radio and they listened to the news announcer: 'The Prime Minister assures everyone living in the Primrose Hill area that the government is doing everything in its power to normalise the situation. There is no danger to people who take the right precautions.'

'Yeah, right, man,' said Victor, 'why aren't you fucking here, then? Tcha.' He made a circle with his thumb and index finger and produced a dismissive air wank.

' "The problem will be rectified within days," said Jane Hume, the government's official spokeswoman. Meanwhile, residents should stay at home until it's their turn to go to the testing centres that will open first thing in the morning. The Chief Commissioner of the Metropolitan Police, Sir Charles Carter, appealed earlier for calm.'

As the granular Yorkshire tones of Carter growled at them from the radio, Victor spat on the ground and then sucked his teeth against his gums, producing a snake-like sound. 'Dick-head,' he snapped.

Victor was leading one the gangs that had spontaneously formed after the soldiers had shot the boy. Around the perimeters, as close to the barbed-wire barricades as the soldiers' water cannon would allow, they had set alight cars. The lights burned in the sky and the smell of smouldering rubber and sounds of breaking glass permeated the area. Bottles of beer, wine and spirits – looted as soon as night fell – were drunk and then hurled at the clinic.

Victor jumped on to the roof of a sleek, black Mercedes and addressed the gang beneath him. He was wearing a blood-red cotton shirt that dropped open and revealed his slim, muscled torso. On the left of his chest was a large yellow tattoo of a lion. Extremely loose fitting, well-cut black trousers and expensive two-tone leather shoes completed his uniform. In the heat and anger of the moment teenagers had melted and merged with their enemies: a half-dozen skinheads and twenty other white guys and girls in grungy black jeans formed up with Victor's

Lions of Africa: 'They think we got to stay here and rot until they say so.' Victor pointed at the radio. 'But I don't think so.' He emphasised every word. 'The power'll listen only to one thing.' He held up a Molotov cocktail. 'Only one thing.' He raised the other hand in a clenched fist. 'What do you think?' He shouted the question.

'Fucking right.' A dozen ragged voices punched into the night air.

Victor again kicked out his words, this time in a rhythm: 'Fuck the power,' he chanted, stomping on the car. 'Fuck the power.'

This time hands responded in a stiff-arm salute and repeated his rap.

'Let's see what you fuckers are made of. Are you hard enough?' He jumped down and they fanned out behind him in a phalanx. Victor got behind the wheel of the Mercedes, stolen earlier from outside a house at the back of Primrose Hill, took a tape from his pocket and inserted it into the stereo. A deep rumble of bass that almost lifted the car from the ground was followed by the crash of drums and a beautiful, high-pitched African voice singing of freedom. Victor revved the car for thirty seconds, feeling his adrenaline mix with the drug cocktail. This was living. Fucking living. He smashed his right fist into his left palm and slammed on the accelerator. The car hurtled forward like a battering ram.

Twenty seconds later, when the gates of Mike's clinic were smashed and helpless on their hinges, Victor emerged from behind the wheel to triumphant cheers. Someone handed him a bottle of rum, from which he took two swigs, before he leaped on top of the wrecked car, the lights of which illuminated the peeling blue paint of the double front doors of the clinic and the large plate-glass window of the reception area.

The full moon – red and shimmering mysteriously in the smog and haze – hovered above the clinic as Victor lit the taper of his Molotov cocktail, arched his back and lobbed the bottle, which burst through a window and erupted in a flood of flames. The grimy curtains caught fire and shrivelled like a moth's wings in a candle flame.

Tess Davenport woke screaming when the sound of the petrol bomb hit her before she felt the heat. As she opened the cubicle door, a wave of flames flowed towards her. She saw lights through the double doors that led into the clinic and scrambled across the floor on her hands and knees, working on pure instinct. But there was no way through: the fire illuminated then consumed the AIDS posters on the walls, and began to melt the plastic chairs dotted around the reception area, sending spumes of noxious smoke into the air. The sprinklers that should have been dousing the flames were unresponsive. The heat and overpowering smell of burning plastic beat her back against the wall and panic threatened to overwhelm her.

The clinic's doors opened and a tremor of cold air hit Tess from the outside world. Two people made their way towards her, wet sheets wrapped around their heads and air-masks covering their faces. Tess tried to make her way to them but the smoke filled her lungs and she almost passed out. Trying to beat down the buzz in her head, she felt hands grab her under the arms and drag her across the floor. Then another bomb hit, followed by hails of rocks that clattered and bounced against her head and arms.

She and her rescuers lay there stunned as the fire licked at their clothes. Then they recovered and were moving across the floor again towards the light on the other side of the doors. When they burst through Tess sucked fresh air into lungs that felt seared and painful. Through her shock, she was aware of Mac issuing orders to take her to a ward for treatment for burns and shock. Looking across, she saw Mike and Laura lying against the corridor wall, tears streaming down their soot-blackened faces and hair. 'You look like shit,' she said and passed out.

'Thanks yourself.' Mike's smile at his sister was quickly extinguished as he heard people smashing the roof with hammers. He turned to Mac. 'Organise fire extinguishers. I saw three or four in the corridors. And there are buckets in the cleaner's cupboard. Bring them.'

'It'll be like pissing to put out the fires of hell,' said Mac. 'Let's evacuate and find somewhere else a bit more isolated.'

'No.' Mike was adamant. 'I'll not let this scum force us out of here. We're making a stand. If we run, we might as well condemn our patients to death.'

'OK, OK,' grumbled Mac. 'I was only making a point.' He indicated Dek and one of the volunteers: Linda Wu, a rake-thin, anxious-looking Chinese nurse, whose slender limbs disguised her physical strength. Mike knew nothing about her other than that she had come, she said, out of Christian duty. 'C'mon, Dek, Linda,' ordered Mac, 'John Wayne here thinks we can put out the fires on our ownio.'

As the three moved off, Laura found two fire blankets and she and Mike held them against the doors, which were beginning to catch fire. A handful of the others passed buckets hand over hand to douse the wood and the blankets. Plaster crashed from the ceiling to the floor. Then the atrium windows smashed in just behind them. Another petrol bomb rained down through the gap but Mike managed to smother it before it ignited. 'Got to get rid of those bastards on the roof,' he shouted.

'Oh, God, now he thinks he's Spiderman,' said Mac as he returned with another extinguisher and held it ready to blast the door.

'Give me that,' ordered Mike. 'I can think of better uses for it.'

'Get your own.'

'Don't be obstinate, Mac.'

'That's rich, coming from a man who hasn't listened to a word I've bloody said for days. Have the thing, then.'

Mike took the canister, ran up two flights of stairs to the

second floor and found the fire exit on to the flat roof. He pushed open the door and looked out into the bright night sky, made hazy by the many fires from the quarantine zone and the clinic below. He could see three teenage boys hammering on the concrete roof with sledge-hammers. Jumping out, Mike turned on the fire extinguisher and ran towards them. The attack surprised and disoriented them and two ran for the side of the building and jumped down on to the roof of the van that had enabled them to climb up in the first place. But one stood his ground, and with the illumination from the moon, the street lights and the fires, Mike recognised him. It was Victor Obudo. His mother had shown Mike her son's photograph many times.

'Victor?'

The teenager registered this curious phenomenon of someone who knew him with a slight nod of his head. 'Yeah?'

Mike turned off the extinguisher and edged slowly across the roof. 'Why are you doing this?'

'You've got fucking crips in there. Get rid of them and we're out of here.'

'Are you mad? D'you know how many people might catch this disease before it burns itself out?' asked Mike. He and Victor were within a metre of each other and Mike could see that a kind of manic energy was pouring through the boy. 'Attacking this clinic only means that it's impossible for anyone to be treated. Do you understand that? Do you? It could be you down there.'

'Not me. I'm not gonna get the crips' disease.' He spread his arms wide and exposed his chest to the night sky. 'I'm a fucking warrior.'

Mike didn't see the knife as it flashed towards him, but instinct swept him backwards and it only caught a nick on the top of his arm. He slipped down on to one knee in shock and tried to edge away as Victor's boot caught him in the gut, winding him. After two more kicks, Mike could think about little other than survival as he rolled into a ball.

Victor knelt down towards him and Mike could smell the rum on his breath. 'Get the fuck out of here,' said Victor. 'Or next time I won't be so gentle.'

As daylight surfaced bright and hot, Mike surveyed the scene outside the clinic. The road was strewn with ripped-out railings, rocks, broken bottles and fragments of cars that had rammed the building. Here and there he could spot syringes that had nothing to do with treatment and everything to do with addiction.

Beside him was DI Joe McCormick, the policeman he had helped the previous morning.

'Good neighbours you have here.' McCormick nodded at the blackened walls of the reception area and the blown-out windows of the three wards on the side of the clinic.

'I'd like to be charitable,' said Mike, 'but if I could get my hands on them I'd de-bollock the lot.'

'Might be difficult with the ladies,' McCormick smiled.

'Whatever.' Mike shrugged. 'They're mad, these people. No,' he rubbed his hands down his cheeks, 'that's not true. They're scared.'

'Don't go soft on me, Doctor. They're what they seem — thugs, in or out of a quarantine zone.'

Mrs Peirce, Uzelac's Irish landlady, bustled over. She was wearing a lilac cat-suit and balancing a tray of coffee cups.

'Cheeky bastard.' She laughed at one of the firemen who made a remark about her bottom. 'What would your boyfriend say?' This elicited a cheer from the man's otherwise bedraggled and grim colleagues. She handed Mike a scalding styrofoam cup, which he took gratefully. She had turned up first thing in the morning offering her services. 'I feel a wee bit responsible, son,' she had told Mike, 'and I want to help. Besides, the kids don't need me now.'

She looked at McCormick's burning cigarillo and said: 'Not

good for your health, lovely; you should give them up.'

'What? And being here is like a health farm?' McCormick waved at the clinic, sending a shower of ash in the direction of the building.

'Don't be sarcastic, son. This is God's challenge to Mike and me. Isn't it Mike?'

'Sure is, Mrs Peirce.' Mike popped a couple of beta blockers into his mouth and chased them down with the coffee.

As Mrs Peirce swayed back into the crowd on heels more suited to the Locarno dance floor of 1955, Mike and McCormick walked towards the building, passing two fire-tenders and milling firemen and policemen. Although the fire had been brought under control hours before, all of them were wearing masks and respirators despite Mike's assurances that they would be safe. Dark myths about the disease were already at large inside the cordon.

'Thanks for helping me last night,' Mike said to McCormick. 'We phoned the police a couple of times; but they seemed to be unavoidably delayed.'

'They're royally pissed off.' McCormick blew out the smoke from his cigarillo and wondered whether to take up cigarettes again. He needed real comfort. 'They feel betrayed, used and angry. If they and their families are not allowed out by tonight, they're going on strike. We're not some kind of disease fodder.'

Mike was appalled. 'Look. I know that this is bad for all of us, but surely you can't leave people behind in this mess. I need volunteers to help us.'

They stood on what was left of the porch and McCormick surveyed the water damage and the huge black streaks of smoke on the brickwork. 'No one is going to volunteer. They are all too scared.' He waved his arms to take in the scene. 'How are you going to carry on with all this damage?'

'We're OK. There's a back entrance and enough space for a hundred patients. We've converted the gym and offices upstairs to sleeping accommodation for the volunteers.'

'How many?'

'About twelve.'

'That enough?'

Mike shrugged. 'It's what I've got.'

'How many sick now?' McCormick's voice was slow and appraising.

'Come and see.'

McCormick drew away. 'Not today, Doctor. I'm—'

Mike fiercely took his arm and held it despite the policeman's attempt to unlink. 'There are ten people in there. I reckon eight will be dead before evening. I have no idea how many more will be here tomorrow and the day after that. And I have no idea how long it will take for this thing to burn out.'

McCormick managed to prise off Mike's fingers. 'All the more reason for the men and women with families to get out of here,' he said.

Mike felt drained beyond belief, and yet he knew he would be even more tired before this was over. 'Of course, you're right,' he said wearily. 'Of course they must leave. I'll have to see if I can organise something else.' He turned and walked away, but McCormick's voice called him back.

'I don't have any family, Dr Davenport. I'll be back here later. Looks as if you need a little bit of help around here.'

As he watched McCormick slouch away, Mike's spirit suddenly soared like a bird on an unexpected thermal.

CHAPTER FORTY-SEVEN

George Hudson was praying as he stared at his daughter's twisted, impassive face: praying to a God in which he had ceased to believe many years before. His beautiful, delicate, soft Jasmine had wanted to be a dancer and after he and Lucille had scrimped to give her ballet lessons, he had been unbearably proud when he took her to class for the first time. She had looked like an African princess among all those pale, timid white girls. Her back had been erect and her head high; her almond eyes had surveyed everyone as if she knew that she would soar higher, spin faster and feel the dance better than anyone else in the room. And now her body was contorted and her spirit broken. That wasn't Jasmine staring back at him. Not *his* Jasmine.

A hand was placed on his shoulder and Mike said to him: 'I promise she won't suffer.'

George sat in silence, his big hands, hard from time spent digging in his allotment, sat folded one across the other on his lap. He was covered in a gown from head to foot and on his face was a mask. Although he wanted to hug his dying child, he had been told firmly by Tess that such an action would endanger not only himself but the rest of his family.

'Have you been tested yet?' asked Mike.

George shook his head, as if by being mute he might contain his pain. If he spoke, he knew he would break.

'Would you like me to do it here?'

Again George did not respond. Mike watched as Jasmine began to shake violently and he knew the spumes of blood would follow soon.

'Please go, Mr Hudson. I don't believe you will want to see this.'

George grabbed Mike's arm and hissed: 'I'm not leaving.'

Mike spoke urgently: 'Please. Hold the good memories in your mind. Remember her life, not her death.'

George looked at Mike and stood, his eyes burning, his pupils retreating into a small point of darkness. He stood quickly and Mike, sensing the other man was going to lash out, held up his hand in self-protection. George stopped and his head dropped on to his chest. Then he marched passed Mike to the door. 'When shall I come back?' he asked.

'It won't be long,' said Mike, preparing for the final turmoil of Jasmine's death.

Mac opened the door and accompanied George out into the corridor, then returned to the Death Room, as they now called the small, light, single-person ward. They had to ensure that the explosion of blood that marked the final phase of the disease was contained and quickly disposed of.

A Mozart concerto was pouring quietly but sweetly from a cassette player by Jasmine's bed. Mike had music playing everywhere in the hospital to remind everyone of joy and liberation.

'I'd rather die to the sound of Alfred Brendel than so-called life-saving machines,' he told Mac.

'Let me die to the sound of sweet music,' Mac muttered to himself.

'What did you say?' asked Mike.

'I said the music'll drown out the screams.'

Mike saw him turn to Jasmine and make the sign of the cross. He watched the calm, careful eyes of Linda Wu. She had barely slept since arriving, but then who had? There were now thirty dead bodies to be incinerated at the Council's garbage dump. Despite Joe McCormick's best efforts, and his own increasingly urgent pleas to the outside authorities, Mike could not find enough people from the emergency services to act as undertakers. He had been told that the army was refusing to order its men in and no one was prepared to volunteer for such an obvious suicide mission. Fear ruled. At first, it was all Mac could do to convince the pathetic local Anglican priest to offer some kind of spiritual solace to the bereaved; those, that is, who wished to see the bodies or be near the dead.

But Mike tried to focus on the many acts of small heroism: Mary Peirce and her endless watery cups of coffee; a young nursery school-teacher had turned up on the doorstep volunteering to do the laundry; a pharmacist who had offered his shop for making drugs; and two GPs who had turned themselves into a triage unit – willing to check out any case that turned up. Jennifer Low was pouring herself into everything. Sleeping fewer hours than anyone else, chasing and harrying everyone into organising supply raids on local stores for bedding, towels and whatever else they needed. She and Joe made a formidable logistical team.

'Thar she blows,' said Mac as they watched Jasmine's body go into spasm and throw out spumes of blood.

Two hours later what was left of Jasmine Hudson was in a thick, blue body-bag sitting in a quiet, room with dimmed lights that dulled the horror. George looked at her sweet face, destroyed and racked by pain. Then he pulled the zip up and the bag closed over his love. The main emotion George Hudson felt was fear for the rest of his family. Jasmine was gone; but who else had it? Had Jasmine passed it on before the accident?

Had she picked it up in hospital? Suddenly, he had to get out of there. An engorged panic hit his throat and he found that he wanted to be among the living. He did not look at Jasmine as he hurried from the room and the clinic.

At home, the boys were sitting happily in front of a cartoon on the TV and Lucille was drinking coffee from a green mug. Her face had sagged and her eyes were red from weeping. She did not rise to greet him, fearful of his news. Hugging her arms around her body, she turned away and then locked her right leg over her left until there was little of her body left unguarded. When George touched her, she flinched and shrugged him off.

'She's, she's—' he began.

'No. Don't tell me, don't tell me how she is,' Lucille responded curtly. 'You took her to that hospital. I told you she was fine and that a visit to the doctor was all she needed, but you insisted. Jasmine deserves the best you said. And look now. Look. You've killed her. You've killed my baby.' Her eyes were hard as she glared at him.

He tried to hold her but she shrugged him off. By now, the boys had turned to look at them, open-mouthed and wide-eyed with bemused emotions.

'Please, darling. We've got to get to a testing station. It's our time. We've got to get out of here.' As George put his hand on her shoulder, she glanced up at him and spat in his face. He closed his eyes, and with big tears pouring down his fat cheeks, he sat heavily on the floor, heaves of emotion rising in his chest.

The boys looked on transfixed. Then, in a scared voice, Miles asked: 'Mum, why is Dad crying?'

Lucille fell on to the floor beside George, who had his head buried in to his knees and was rocking back and forth. She cradled his back. 'I'm sorry,' she sobbed. 'I'm sorry. I can't bear it. I can't bear it. I want her back. I want Jasmine back.'

'Where's Jasmine gone?' asked Miles. 'Can we go see her?'

CHAPTER FORTY-EIGHT

'Is there anything I can do to help? My test is tomorrow, but I feel helpless and I'd like to make a contribution before I go.'

Mike surveyed the elegant, grey-haired man who was talking to him. The guy's face was tough but calm and he looked as if he could handle himself.

'Do you have a medical background?' Mike asked.

'I'm afraid not. But I believe from your colleague,' he nodded in the direction of Joe McCormick who had taken responsibility for transport, 'that you need ambulance drivers. I'd certainly be happy to help with that. I used to drive in the army.'

Linda Wu walked across the reception area and Mike was puzzled as a flash of recognition passed between her and the stranger and Linda hurried on, her head down. Before he could ask the man how he knew Linda, Mike was distracted by someone calling his name. Daisy Wooldridge barged into the room in her wheelchair. 'We've got a problem. Come now.'

'What kind of problem?'

'Scale of one to ten?' she asked.

He nodded.

'Eleven.' She spun the chair like a racecar driver and took off in the direction of the makeshift lab that she and Laura had established, leaving Mike to follow.

Mike turned to the man and said: 'Glad to have you with us . . . Mr?'

'Jones,' he said, 'Lou Jones.'

'I'm sure Joe there will tell you how we are set up. I'm afraid it's all a bit primitive and we're running out of diesel, although the government has promised us some more. They are talking about a late night helicopter dump of supplies. We need more now, though.'

'I'll see what I can do to help,' Jones replied.

The lab was rigged in what used to be the massage room. Mike smiled at the noise coming from a CD player: a high-pitched echo of whale music from a disc that Daisy had found. It did little to lessen the effect of the overwhelming stench of dead and living animals that clung to the room. Laura had requisitioned a dozen rabbits, cats and rats and they had been experimenting with different ways of isolating the prions and separating the virus. They had also been picking up dead rats and other animals from inside the zone to see if any changes in the virus might be detected. Furthermore, blood from a sample of patients was taken every hour to track the development of the virus.

Laura turned the music down. She was grim and troubled; worry lines tugged at the corners of her mouth and her face was white from exhaustion.

'What's wrong?' asked Mike.

'I don't know. Bad feeling, I suppose. I think that there's a chance that it's mutating again.'

'What? How?'

'If our results are correct, it might have jumped back into the rodent population.'

She pointed at some rats they had trapped a few days before

in the cellar of the clinic. 'They've got it,' she said.

'Fuck.' Mike's face collapsed at the news. He felt that someone had punched him in the gut. 'If it's in the rat population, then it'll be out of the zone by now and in the general population.'

'But so far they don't have the characteristic prion mutation,' continued Laura.

'What? You mean the rodent version has managed to fight the prion mutation?'

'Looks like it.'

'But whatever they do have,' said Daisy, 'if it's like Lassa or Junin, it'll be transmitted in rodent urine to the human population. So frying pans and fires.' She scooted across to the PC and showed Mike the vector model that explained the means by which the disease could spread. The variation was minor. It was recognisably the same virus; but the prion effect wasn't there.

'But,' he asked, 'is the prion latent and will it emerge later?' Mike was bemused as he peered at the results intently, praying that the mutation was less virulent.

'Your guess is as good as mine,' said Daisy. 'If the prion is suppressed in the rats but reappears in humans then there isn't much hope of containing this inside the zone.'

Mike slumped back against the wall. Had the past three days been for nothing?

'I'm sorry, Mike.' Laura stood by him, reached up and touched his masked face with her gloved hand. 'The good news, if such it is, is that it's proving one of my theories correct. Namely, that the virus is reasserting its normal RNA. It is possible to fight this thing. We just need the resources.'

'So,' said Daisy, cautiously, 'here's what we're thinking.' She drew pictures on the white wall with a blue marker pen. 'As far as we can see, the progress of the virus is triphasic. It enters the bloodstream and for a few days it operates perfectly normally as a Level Three haemorrhage pathogen. Then, somewhere around day three or four, it carries the mutant proteins into the brain where they trigger fast-acting CJD. Over the next four to ten days spongiosis rapidly attacks the central nervous system, and then in the last twelve to twenty-four hours the virus attacks the weakened host with the painful results we see all around us.' She paused and thought for a second, then returned to her drawing. 'Laura and I have been working on a theory. If we can bind a chemical to the normal proteins in the virus and prevent it mutating, we can catch it in phase one and treat the attenuated haemorrhagic fever with drugs that we know work against it.'

'Basically, we heal the virus and not the patient,' said Laura. 'We know that the virus is not a killer and that we can probably treat it.'

Daisy scooted back from the wall and waved her arms at the illustration: 'If we can prevent it reaching the second phase, the patient will survive. And, if I am right, a version of one of the current vaccines may be developed quickly to prevent mass outbreak.'

'What do we need?' asked Mike.

Laura replied: 'Three things will help. Serum from someone who has contracted the disease and survived. If we have that, we can save people in the first phase. So start praying. Second, we want to find a way of binding compounds to the virus. Let's get people working on that. And third, there are some experimental CJD drugs that no one has tested on humans. I think it's time, don't you?'

Mike walked down the short corridor to the office in which he had set up camp. They had run out of wards and he could see half a dozen patients lining the increasingly stifling corridors. Tess, Liz O'Mara, Jennifer Low, Linda Wu and Dek Lee were rushing from one person to the next, doing their best to calm the terrified and comfort the dying. The smell of blood and vomit was overpowering. They were running out of the will to cope. Liz had haunted eyes that dug into Mike's soul. She was terrified, standing beside a fragile young mother-to-be who was beginning to rock and shake. Her face was milk-white with dark, bruised rings around her eyes. Her husband was pacing outside the clinic.

'She's going into labour,' shouted Liz. 'Oh, my God, no.'

Tess and Linda Wu ran across. 'Liz,' shouted Tess. 'Help me move her into one of the single rooms.'

Liz was rooted, her mouth open. 'No,' she said. 'No.'

Mike joined them. 'Please, Liz, you're the only one with recent gynae experience. We need your help.'

Liz turned and started to walk away until she bounced into Mac and stood still.

'For Christ's sake, girl, remember your oath. C'mon now.' He spun her round and marched her in front of him.

'What can we give her?' asked Tess.

'Can anyone do an epidural on her?' said Linda Wu frantically.

'No,' ordered Mike. 'We've no needles.'

'What good are we, then?' groaned Liz. 'What fucking good are we?'

'It's too late,' said Tess, her gloved fingers inside the woman. 'She's fully dilated and I can feel the baby's head.'

The woman's body heaved and pushed a half-dozen times and then a flood of blood poured over the white sheets on the bed, followed by something that was once a foetus but was now a hollow and deflated mess of skin, intestines and faeces. The mother's back arched and blood spumed from her as she shuddered into death. A gloomy silence descended on the room, then Mac said: 'I'll go and tell her husband.'

Tess found a winding sheet and covered the tiny figure; then she lifted it and took it to the makeshift morgue. She was weeping.

As Linda pulled a sheet over the mother, Mike said: 'Let's seal off this room.'

'I'll clean it, Dr Davenport,' replied Linda. 'We need the space.'

Mike looked at the blood on the walls, the floor and Linda's clothes and said: 'No, leave this one. It'll take till next week to sort. Go and look after the living.'

'You mean the almost dead.' Liz walked quickly past him.

Inside Mike's office, the curtains were closed against the relentless heat. On the floor was a sleeping bag and on the desk a clutter of chocolate-bar wrappers and plastic trays containing the remains of the Pot Noodles that he survived on. As he looked at the mess, he remembered that he had to talk to Joe McCormick about establishing an effective food-supply line. Ellington had promised a relief convoy from the army; but it had not arrived, despite repeated assurances.

Mike ripped open a bar of Galaxy and took a second to enjoy the sweet, cloying sensation against the roof of his mouth. Then he sat down at his laptop and dialled a special number that linked him via satellite to the PM. All the telephone land-lines were still cut off, as were those of the terrestrial mobile-phone companies. Mike could see from the television news that the government was still operating a total news blackout on pictures from the zone. And the previous night he had been pleased to hear Jane Hume saying that the government's well-resourced medical task force in the area was coping admirably with the few deaths that they had so far witnessed. The Chief Medical Officer had assured the world that the virus was under control and it would only be a matter of a few days before the situation returned to normal.

Jennifer Low sat down beside him as Mike's screen flared and his video conference call with Lipsey began. Flanking the Prime Minister on a round table were Ellington and Jane Hume. Ellington's face was impassive and sleek. Jane looked electrified with excitement; she shuffled around on her chair.

'Mike,' Lipsey's big voice sounded tinny and tamed through the laptop's speaker. 'I have Lawrence and Jane with me.'

'Congratulations on your promotion, Jane,' said Mike.

'Thanks Mike,' she purred. 'How are you? I'm very proud of you. And I'm longing to see you.'

'I'm tired,' said Mike, and rubbed his face.

'Soon be over,' noted Lipsey.

'Will it?' Mike sounded surprised.

'So I am informed by Mr Graham. Apparently the stream of patients has slowed to six or so today.'

How did he know that? wondered Mike. Do they have surveillance cameras?

'Only because our ambulances have run out of fuel and we can't collect anyone,' replied Mike. 'There are dead people uncollected on the street. Which means that there are hundreds more dying inside their houses. When are you going to resupply us?'

Ellington intervened. 'The army thinks it is a suboptimal time to enter the quarantine area. They are being fire-bombed and believe that any attempt to reach you would be counter-productive.'

Jennifer interrupted: 'Hang on, Alan. You promised Mike when he came in here that you would get him everything he needed. Don't back out on him or there'll be hell to pay when we come out of here.'

Lipsey ignored his Health Secretary and spoke directly to Mike. 'I shall meet all my promises, Dr Davenport. Is there anything urgent that you need?'

'Yes. I want access to experimental CJD drugs that are being developed by the drug companies. Can you arrange that? And we are closer to understanding the disease. If we send out the data, will you organise people to work on it? We'll be doing some final work over here and we'll have it with you by tomorrow.'

'There will be a helicopter drop as soon as we can get it there. Now, is there anything else?'

'There's a problem.' Mike's voice was hesitant.

'I said you'd be supplied in good time, Dr Davenport. You must take me at my word.' Lipsey's voice was strained. 'You are a hero and I'll not let you down.'

'Yeah right,' muttered Jennifer.

'No I don't mean your lack of help is a problem. Although it is,' replied Mike. 'There's a possibility that the prion disease and the virus are mutating again.'

'What does that mean?' asked Lipsey, his face looking startled.

'It may have found a niche among the rat population.' Mike watched their faces in turn as the shock of his statement registered. He'd just told them that they were facing the equivalent of the bubonic plague. 'But this is only a theory. Neither Laura nor Daisy is certain. They've just found something worrying among some rats in the clinic. We don't know what's going on. If we could find out more about the origins of the virus, it would help. Have you tracked it down to Belize? If it was a rodent virus, then we can isolate it and perhaps adapt one of the existing vaccines.'

Ellington interrupted: 'We have no further knowledge of the origins.'

'Well get some. We need to know.'

'How is the new mutation transmitted?' enquired Lipsey in a calm voice.

'In dried urine.'

'Are rats the only problem?' asked Ellington.

'What do you mean?'

'Dogs, rabbits, cats. Will it jump to them?'

'I think it unlikely. I've never seen a rat virus jump species.'

'It found a way to us.' Lipsey's voice was thoughtful. 'Might it spread to others?'

'Oh, Christ, I don't know,' muttered Mike. 'I don't think so.'

Ellington intervened: 'What do you suggest we do about it?'

A voice to the side of Ellington, belonging to Graham, said: 'You must use poison.'

Mike shook his head in irritation. 'Come off it. How many rats are inside the quarantine zone? A hundred thousand? And who's going to lay the stuff? Where will I get that much support in here? They're trying to burn me out as it is.'

'And,' said Ellington, thoughtfully, 'as soon as this possibility is assimilated by the population, we will have unprecedented civil unrest.'

'The answer is to cover the area from the air,' said Graham.

'What are you talking about?' asked Mike, afraid of the answer.

Graham came into picture, looking older and unshaven. He put a map of the zone on the table and started to draw around it in felt pen. 'We can dump bromethalin pellets in sacks in all of the tunnels running under the inner cordon and on obvious exit roads and lanes.'

'But that's an acute toxin.' Mike was appalled. 'You'll kill every animal in here. Not to speak of what this will do to any human being who might pick it up. Are you mad? God knows how many people you might kill.'

Ellington interrupted: 'James is quite correctly pointing out the logic of our situation. We cannot allow this to pass into the general population.'

'I don't even know if the experimental results will hold,' said Mike. 'We need more evidence before we act. I beg you to find the virus in Belize. Prime Minister, you promised me your support. Don't do anything hastily. There are too many lives at stake.' He watched Lipsey lick his lower lip for a microsecond.

'I must protect our people.'

'I thought we were your people,' said Mike.

Lipsey nodded abstractedly, then stood up and walked away. A second later Mike was staring at a blank screen. He looked around the room, feeling small and inward-directed. What should he tell the team? Is it time to leave? Can we leave? He ejected the disk from the laptop that had recorded the conference. He and the team wanted to make sure that history knew the truth: they had harrowing pictures of the last few days that even the most hardened audience might find hard to take.

'Bastard.' Jennifer's voice was cracking with anger.

'He's a fucking bastard. I always knew it, but I tried to ignore it in the interests of the party. He's toast when I get out of here. Fucking toast.'

Alan Lipsey stood at a long window looking across at the media circus that had camped on Horse Guards Parade. Ellington was by his side, his hands behind his back.

'The Americans are talking about closing their ports and airports to British citizens, or to anyone who has come through the Britain en route. Unless we demonstrate that we have this under control by midnight tonight we will be cut off from the States.' Ellington's voice was monotone as he relayed this information.

'I know,' said Lipsey, 'the President called.'

'The French and Germans are fuelling the flames and asking for bans on British exports on the Continent,' continued Ellington. 'And the French have closed the Tunnel.'

'The bastards will ruin us.' Lipsey's voice was hard. 'What are the Chinese saying?'

'They're giving us absolute and total support on the basis of our mutual understanding about the Belize situation.'

'Will they help us isolate the virus?' asked Lipsey.

'They are imposing maximum distance between themselves and the Company that started all this. They are claiming that the PLA hierarchy sold the Company years ago. And I'm sure they have the documents to prove it. The Chinese will remain broadly helpful diplomatically at the UN; but that's the extent of their liability as far as they're concerned.'

His face set hard, Lipsey's eyes narrowed. 'We must explain to them that the price is higher than they have paid. I want absolute support against the Europeans and access to any Spirit Death blood they hold for research purposes. I take it we have kept the evidence of the bugs that can be traced back to their people.'

Ellington pursed his lips. 'They claim not to have any sera. But I'll see what I can do.'

'Have the Foreign Secretary inform the Chinese that I may feel the need to expose an atrocity in Belize,' said Lipsey. 'After all, we have a long-standing relationship with that country and I would not be at all surprised if I received a delegation of Belizeans asking about a violation of their civil rights.'

As Lipsey watched the police ushering back a crowd of protesters comprising the families and friends of people locked in the zone, he asked in exasperation: 'Doesn't anyone understand I'm doing this to save them? What would they have me do?'

'The people seldom understand, Prime Minister.'

'Where are we putting those who pass the antibodies test?'

'We have requisitioned a dozen remote holiday camps and caravan sites in Yorkshire, Humberside, Ayrshire and Cornwall,' responded Ellington. 'I've arranged for lots of lovely television pictures of happy children playing on the beach at the government's expense. The ones who are coming out now we are keeping in secure accommodation. I'm afraid in their trauma they might inadvertently say something that could spark a crisis.'

'How long does Graham suggest we keep them there?' enquired Lipsey.

'A month or so, just to be certain. Besides, we cannot afford any dilution of the message of hope that we have engendered.'

'Anyone showing signs yet?' Lipsey's voice was tired and thick with emotion.

Ellington shook his head.

'What do we do about this new development?' asked Lipsey.

'Two things.' Ellington was decisive. 'You must contact the RAF immediately and have them prepare transport helicopters to drop poison into the quarantine area.'

Lipsey looked at him and shook his head. 'I made a promise to help Mike Davenport and I intend to keep it.'

'You cannot afford the luxury of promises, sir. You have responsibilities.'

They stood together in silence for a minute. Lipsey was lost in thought as he watched the protesters marching in a ragged line two hundred yards away. Then he nodded his head once; his eyes looked at the floor rather than at the calm, impassive man at his side.

'Good decision, Alan,' said Ellington briskly, using the Prime Minister's preferred form of address for the first time ever. 'And we must enact the emergency evacuation procedures for the Royal Family and senior members of the cabinet. I would suggest that we put water between us and the disease. Who knows how quickly this might spread when it escapes the zone.'

'Don't you mean "if"?'

Ellington's tone was hard as he said: 'There will be no holding this if it gets out. We will need to wipe out the rat population of England. Tens of thousands of our citizens will die, if not millions.'

'What would our public position be if we were to leave London?' asked Lipsey. 'If they think we running from a sinking ship, we'll lose all credibility, and probably start a panic.'

'I suggest at the very least a well-deserved holiday at Balmoral for HRH and an overseas visit, perhaps Canada, for the heir to the throne.'

'And the cabinet?'

'Perhaps the whole cabinet need not be told. I suggest you need a three-day task-force symposium on disease control. We can fly in an American professor to validate the exercise. Once there, we can assess the situation. You cannot put the government at risk, Alan. I believe the Isle of Man has a fine conference centre.' Another silence enveloped them, then Ellington mused: 'In 1665, sixty-nine thousand people died of the plague. In 1667 that dropped to thirty-five. In the intervening year the City burned down, including the wharves in Thames Street in which the rats flourished. Fire is the great cleanser.'

Lipsey walked towards a grand mahogany door and said: 'I have no idea what you're talking about.'

Mike was typing at his computer, re-assessing Laura's data. He longed for an Internet connection to the Center for Disease Control in Atlanta; but Ellington would not allow any open lines between the zone and the outside world. Christ, I'm tired, he thought. Gradually his fingers stopped typing and his head dropped on to his chest. Small whines emerged from his lips as he fell into a deep sleep.

Louis Fernandez had finished walking the wards. He had promised Li to have one last go at finding Samuels. Davenport's people had impressed him as he carried out his fruitless search. They were fools, throwing themselves into the salvation of people who would inevitably die. But they were brave fools.

Needing to gain access to the files to see if Samuels had ever been there, Fernandez was checking each room. He looked through the windows of the Level 4 lab and saw Laura and Daisy working feverishly as they tried to track the mutation. Knowing enough about viruses, he gave the scientists a wide berth. As he wandered down the dark corridor, surrounded by groans and screams, he was taken aback a little when Linda Wu stopped him. She was dishevelled, and her gown was covered in blood.

'Hold on,' she said, and signalled him into a small changing room. They had rigged up some UV and a double-bagging system for the gowns. Linda stepped from her clothes; they had long given up on any form of vanity or privacy. Her thin, naked body was beautiful. After she had bagged her cast-offs and pulled on another green gown, she said: 'Thanks for helping out.'

'Someone has to,' he replied.

'I know you from somewhere,' she said.

'Hardly likely. I've lived in Cornwall all my life. I was only here visiting friends and I got trapped. That's why it's taken me so long to get a form for the testing centre.'

'Can I get you a drink of water?' she asked.

'Thanks.'

She handed it to him, and then asked: 'How is Ren these days? I haven't seen him since he used to hang out with my brother a year ago.'

'He's f—' Putting the cup on a white table, he tutted, then struck Linda with the flat of his hand. She tumbled back, hit her head against the wall and passed out.

Fernandez tied her hands and blocked her mouth with tape. Then he locked her in the cupboard while he decided on the best way to dispose of her. A straightforward cut to the throat, he thought. No point in prolonging this.

'Christ, Daisy, can't you get yourself a cup of water.' The door burst open and Mac's frame filled the door.

'Who are you?' he asked.

'Jeremy Philomen,' said Fernandez.

'And what are you?'

'I'm a doctor. I thought I might be able to help out.'

Mac sized him up. 'You certainly can.' He pointed in the direction of the reception. 'There are half a dozen people down there with everything from the cold to the clap. They all think they're going to gloop blood all over the place at any moment. Fancy a spot of triage?'

Fernandez smiled and agreed to help. But, when he left the changing room he turned left, in the direction of the room he had seen Davenport enter earlier. The doctor was sound asleep when Fernandez put his head around the door. Perfect, thought Fernandez. He locked the door, not wanting any fat priests to interrupt him this time. Then he checked out the file on the laptop's screen that Mike had been working on. The team had traced the epidemiology of Spirit Death back to the little rat that first produced it. Fernandez quickly wiped the file, and then browsed in the patient register, searching under name, then ethnicity, then blood type. There was no evidence of Samuels.

Mike snuffled and said: 'Go to bed, Jo; stop being a pest.'

Fernandez stared at him and felt the long, jagged blade in his pocket. Time to go, Dr Davenport, he thought. Beside the computer, he saw a picture of Mike with the twins. The girls had their arms entwined around their father and all three were in the act of tumbling back into a swimming pool. Fernandez turned it face down. He had grown to admire Davenport. The man had the kind of courage he possessed and the values that he had once espoused, before the dirty war exposed them for the sham they were.

'Jo, you'll not wear make-up.'

Fernandez placed the blade near Mike's throat. He owed Davenport an easy death – one long slice, followed by two quick punches to the heart. The man would feel little pain. He looked at Mike's face: it had aged five years in a week; no longer pretty, but much stronger. Do it now, he urged himself. He drew the blade across Mike's neck, then folded it quickly in two, put it back into his pocket and left the room as a bustle of noise told him that they had found the Chinese nurse.

CHAPTER FORTY-NINE

George Hudson stood in line, waiting his turn to see the doctor and have his blood checked for viral antibodies. He had already been subjected to EEG and other tests. If he tested positive, as several hundred had already, he would be escorted by the army to one of Mike's ambulances by soldiers, and taken to hospital. If he refused, he would simply be told to go home.

This he had been told in a matter-of-fact manner by an army nurse whose face seemed bruised by the brutality of what she had witnessed in these last five days. George looked around him at the others in the line. Each had the same slump-shouldered gait as they shuffled forward towards the ten doctors at the end of the school assembly hall.

Eight such test centres had been set up on the perimeter of the cordon. They were surrounded by razor-wire and army trucks. The doctors wore red full-body plastic suits, as did the soldiers guarding them. At the back of the hospital was a decontamination tent in which they were pounded with chemicals as if they were coming from a Level 4 lab.

There was only one exit from the room, as far as George could see. A single door that opened out to freedom. He prayed fervently that he and his family would be allowed out.

George recognised Gladys Tremlett, a seventy-year-old former school-teacher, who stood weeping quietly. He tried to give her a smile of encouragement, but her eyes remained fixed on the floor, where a puddle of urine had formed around her feet.

A commotion shocked him from his thoughts. He heard a muffled scream from somewhere and then he was certain he heard the ululating wail of a child. A shiver ran through everyone in the room as each sensed the fear in the other. But they did not look around, or catch an eye, or acknowledge the possibility that someone had failed the test and was being sent back into the zone. They clutched hope to them as if it were a scared baby.

George felt a flush of shame through his body and he reached out and put his hand on Miles' black hair. His son, subdued by his mother's stern warnings, reached up to touch his father's arm and then stepped up to the red line painted on the floor that marked the last stage of the waiting area.

'Next.' A young, male doctor of around thirty-five ordered him over with a wave.

Miles looked up at his father, uncertainly.

'C'mon. Hurry up,' the doctor's voice sounded frayed and tired and his voice was amplified by a microphone inside his plastic helmet. 'There's a hundred people behind you.'

'Hey, enough of that,' George ordered, 'he's only a kid.'

A soldier standing by the side of the doctor stirred, but the man held him in check with a shake of his head.

'Sorry,' he said. 'It's been a long day. D'you want the tests?' he asked.

George stared at him, breathless. This man held freedom in his white hands. He bent down and whispered to Miles, 'Be a brave boy.' Miles shuffled forwards and the doctor took a pin and pricked blood from his thumb, transferring it to a slide that he slipped under a microscope. He was looking for the flare of glowing green that would tell him whether the child had the viral antibodies. Each person had already been subjected to a battery of other examinations that were being collated on computers round the building. From a machine beside the doctor slid out a computer bar-code.

After a minute or so of agony, the doctor looked up again, put the code on a white card with Miles' name on it and handed it to his boy. Then he repeated the procedure with George.

They were ushered by two soldiers through the door at the back and suddenly they were in a tunnel of green canvas. He could see Lucille and Wynton. Miles ran to his mother and grabbed her round the legs.

'Forward, please.' A soldier nudged George in the back. 'Keep moving, please. There are lots of people behind you.'

They shuffled forward to a checkpoint where the tunnel diverged into two paths. Soldiers there took each person's card and ran it through a scanning console. They were then funnelling people down the tunnels ahead, where they disappeared through plastic flaps.

George asked if he could stay with Miles and Lucille clung to Wynton before a soldier apologetically parted them. He explained that each person had to go through a chemical shower as a last precaution against the virus. The boy was weeping and George asked again if he could accompany his son.

'Sorry, mate.' The Belfast accent of the soldier sounded sympathetic, 'it's impossible. Our orders are that everyone does it separately. You'll see him on the other side.'

George, his stomach churning, urged his son forward. A minute later, he followed, past the machine that read the bar-code on the card and through the flaps. He found himself in a shower room. He took off his clothes and was pummelled by jets of fluid in the small cubicle. Then he left on the other side and found himself in a long, thin room, like the inside of a trailer. Along the wall was a bench covered in track-suits, and a pile of trainers cluttered up one corner. As George pulled on some clothes he heard a commotion coming from behind the door. He looked through and saw a half-dozen soldiers surrounding Lucille, who was shouting at one of the impassive men. When she saw George, she turned to him, her eyes wild.

'They won't tell me where Wynton is. Have you got Miles?' her terrorised voice rose a notch when she saw George was on his own. 'We're not leaving without our boys,' she screamed at the captain in charge of the detail.

'Calm down,' he ordered. 'Your boys are fine. We'll look after them.'

'No. No. If they've got it, I want to be with them. I don't want to leave.'

George put his arms round her. 'She's right, we're not going without them. Please let us back into the zone.'

'I'm afraid you don't understand,' the captain's voice was level, unemotional and unaccented. 'Your boys are clean. You two, I'm afraid, have the disease and we must ask you for your own safety to return to Dr Davenport's clinic where you will be offered the best treatment available.'

There was an awful silence as Lucille stiffened in his arms and George gasped for breath.

'I want my boys,' she moaned and slid to the ground, 'I want them.' She scrabbled across and reached out to the captain. 'Please give them back to me. Please.'

The man took a step back. 'It's for the best.' He consulted an electronic organiser to check her name against her picture. 'Mrs Hudson. We'll do everything in our power to assist you in achieving a full recovery and then you will be reunited with your children. Come on, now. You don't want them back in the zone, now, do you?'

She spat at him and in one, quick movement leapt at his face, clawing at the plastic and trying to pull off the hood. George desperately tried to pull her away before the inevitable happened and she was beaten by the other men coming rapidly towards them.

'Leave her, leave her. I've got her.' But Lucille's strength surprised him and she clung on until a white riot stick caught her across the back and she gasped in pain. George grabbed the attacker round the middle and pulled with all his strength until he was slammed back against the wall by two other men and felt the flash of agony as a rifle butt caught him in the guts and a stick rammed his temple.

When he came to, George was lying on a bed in what seemed to be an ambulance. Beside him, Lucille had her hands tied to a hook next to her and her legs were bound to the metal frame of the bed.

George edged himself on to his elbow and whispered urgently, 'Are you all right, Lucille? Did they hurt you?'

She muttered something under her breath and stared dully in front of her. George recognised the effects of heavy tranquillisers. Sweet Jesus, what's wrong with these people? he wondered. Where has their humanity gone?

The inside of the ambulance was pitch dark and from the front, the driver's cabin, George could see flickers of ultra-violet light. Whoever was driving them was taking no chances. Then the doors at the back opened suddenly and sunshine flooded in, blinding him. He heard a voice he recognised; it was one of the nurses who had treated Jasmine.

'My god, what have they done to you?' Tess Davenport gasped her words. 'What have they done?'

CHAPTER FIFTY

Mike was listening to the Stones bumping and grinding out the opening chords of 'Satisfaction' on the stereo as Joe McCormick drove him in his grubby BMW estate that smelled vaguely of fish – the product of Joe's great passion for angling. This was almost the strangest sensation of all, Mike reflected, as he caught himself humming the music. He was shocked that his mind could still engage with something as trivial as a pop song. There was a normal world to return to. 'Outside', as the team increasingly called the rest of London, was real. It was a world of croissants and cappuccino, of bookshops and music performances, of well-stocked hospitals and pharmacies, of people who smiled. The DJ on the radio giggled at some joke sent in by a listener and dedicated his next song to 'the guys and dolls in Primrose Hill; get well soon'.

Mike switched off the radio and looked out the window at the devastation caused by four nights of rioting. Half a dozen houses were burned out in the estate near to King Henry's; windows were blackened and doors were hanging crazily on hinges. Spray-painted in lurid red across two of the buildings was the word CRIP, the slang name that had come to signify those with the disease. Mike hoped the people inside had not died in the flames. But, then again, perhaps that was preferable to the explosive pain of the Spirit Death. He crushed this thought as pathetic and unworthy of the effort being put in by his team.

'What did Linda say about that guy who knocked her out?' asked Mike.

'That he was friends with an unsavoury bloke who hung out with her brother, who works for some Chinese logging company. Apparently, he had a reputation for violence.'

'What on earth was he doing with us?'

'Laura thinks that he must have had something to do with the logging company in Belize.'

'Ellington claimed earlier there was no evidence about such a company. But then he only lies when he opens his mouth. I'll tell Lipsey next time we talk. They might be able to do something about it at last. But I suppose there was no harm done, other than poor Linda's sore mouth, and my copy of the epidemiology report going missing.'

At the corner of the street, the little grocery shop owned by Gupta Singh had been looted: around the broken front window, with its ragged special offers signs, were burst packets of tea and sugar and smashed bottles of ketchup and coffee. A perfect breeding ground for rats, Mike thought gloomily.

'Is this where she lives?' asked Joe, as they pulled into a road dwarfed by two high rise blocks. Here and there in the flats were pock marks of burned-out windows from which smoke drifted in a desultory way into the bright, innocent-blue sky. The streets were deserted and the rubbish, uncollected for almost a week, was piled high in the streets where the residents had tipped it out of the windows.

As Mike and Joe opened the car doors, the cloying smell hit

them. Joe covered his nose with a handkerchief and Mike looked on in disgust at the carcass of a dead tabby cat that had been ripped in two. On each of its legs was a piece of string; presumably someone's idea of kicks was to rend it limb from limb. Its body was now a home for maggots.

'D'you think this is going to work?', asked Joe. 'Does Mrs Obudo have much control over her son?'

Mike shrugged. 'I have no idea. I doubt it. But you never can tell; he may be soppy about his old mum. Anyway, it's worth a try. We can't face another night of these attacks and Victor is the ringleader.'

Jill Obudo's flat was six flights up and by the time they reached it Joe was puffing.

'Got to give up those cigarillos. They'll be the death of you.' Mike punched him playfully on the arm.

'Thanks, Doc. I'll think about it when I'm sixty.'

As they moved along the walkway, they could see Outside clearly. The streets of London were closed off for a mile back from the quarantine zone and the roads were empty apart from troops patrolling and army vehicles shuttling wire and barriers. The razor cordon was now ten feet high and the sun glinted from it as it snaked around the zone.

Mike knocked on the door and called for Jill: 'It's Mike. I need to talk to you.' Curtains twitched in the houses of either side, and further up the corridor someone quickly opened and closed their door. Jill did not answer.

Mike peered through the letter box and saw Jill's body on the ground. She was shaking and shivering. Her face had blown up like a pumpkin and was badly bruised from whatever fall she had taken.

'Christ, she's got it.' Mike spat out his words quietly.

'Jill, can you hear me? Can you open the door?'

She groaned and tried to crawl in their direction but quickly stopped as the convulsions hit her again.

'Go downstairs and fetch the kit. Get masks and gloves for

both of us and bring my bag. I'll need to sedate her before we get her out of here.'

As Joe sped off, Mike put his shoulder to the door but it did not budge. He kicked as hard as he could. Still no joy. He picked up the remains of a bottle of whisky that was lying beside the railing and carefully smashed the side window. Stretching in, he tried to reach the lock, but it was tantalisingly just out of reach. After thirty seconds Joe returned, his face ruddy with exertion.

'Stick to the doctoring,' he wheezed, 'and leave forced entry to the pros.' He swung at the lock with the heavy hammer he had brought with him from the car and smashed his way in.

Jill was thrashing around and Joe made to grab her.

'No,' ordered Mike. 'Protection.'

They gloved up and Mike searched in his bag for a sedative. He administered it and slowly Jill's body relaxed. As they bent down to lift her, they were shocked by a snarl coming from the bedroom. 'Leave her, you cunts, leave her. She's not got it.'

Mike looked up and saw Victor sitting on the floor, his eyes sparking with whatever uppers he had stuffed down himself and his arms wrapped around his legs. His chin was on his knees as he watched them. Beside his leg, Mike could see what he took to be some kind of automatic gun. Its snub nose was pointing directly at him.

'She's sick, Victor. We've got new medicines that might work. Why don't you help me get her to a clinic?'

Victor pursed his lips, shook his head, and dropped his right hand on to the weapon. 'No. You get me a proper doctor. She's not got your thing. I'm taking us out of here. Breaking out of this fucking situation. Tonight.'

'You'll be dead before you reach the wire, Victor,' said Joe. 'They're not playing games out there.'

'Can't hold two hundred of us, man. Some of us'll get through.'

'Yeah, sure,' said Joe. 'You ever heard of Bosnia or Belfast?

Well,' he nodded in the direction of Outside, 'those guys out there have seen it all. They'll obey whatever orders they've been given. And they've been told to shoot to kill. I know, believe me.'

'Who are you?'

'A policeman who has had the thankless responsibility of telling his men that their own colleagues would shoot them if they set one foot outside the zone without their blood being cleared through one of the TCs.'

'Weak, man. You're all weak. We're lions. Warriors. We'll get out. And she's coming with me.'

Jill began to groan and she gripped hard on Mike's hand. Mike had no idea what stage she had reached and began to worry that she might succumb to the febrile, explosive moment here. 'She's going to the clinic. It's her only chance,' he said.

As he tried to lift her, he was pushed back against the wall by Victor, whose face had become distorted with rage. Mike felt the cold metal of the gun against his forehead. 'You touch her again and I'll leave your white brains on the wall. You leave her, hear me? Leave her.'

Mike felt his limbs go weak, his heartbeat surge and sweat suddenly pour down his torso. 'She's going to die unless I do something,' he replied.

'She's not going into your clinic. That's where she'll die.'

'I'm taking her,' insisted Mike.

'I'm getting sick of you. I think I'll kill you anyway.'

Mike could see Victor putting pressure on the trigger. He peered into Victor's eyes; they were pinpricks of madness. Victor's mouth opened wide and he said: 'I'm a fucking warrior.' He pulled the trigger.

Mike collapsed on to the ground.

'I always leave an empty chamber in the clip.' Victor smirked, 'As a little frightener.'

He knelt down beside Mike on the floor and a crack of bone signalled Joe's boot catching the teenager square in the face.

The gun clattered across the floor and Victor, blood pouring from his nose, slithered across to reach it. But Joe kicked him in the groin and he doubled up in agony. Joe reached for the gun but Victor uncoiled and sank his teeth into Joe's cheek. As the policeman recoiled, Victor grabbed the weapon. He aimed at Mike and fired but caught his mother on the arm. She grunted, her body span and blood spattered on to the walls. Victor stared in horror, dropped the gun and shouted: 'Mum. Jesus, Mum.'

He tried to reach her, but Mike grabbed him in a bear hug. 'Don't touch her,' he shouted. 'Her blood is highly infectious.'

Victor struggled and almost broke Mike's grip.

'Mike,' said Joe.

As Mike turned, Joe brought the butt of the gun down on Victor's head with full force. The teenager slumped unconscious against Mike's body. Jill's blood was seeping towards them. 'Let's get her back to the hospital,' said Mike. 'And be careful. Very careful.'

CHAPTER FIFTY-ONE

Fernandez walked through the streets as a muggy dusk smothered its way across the city and the zone began its nightly descent into anarchy. He felt good. Letting Davenport live was just about the best thing he had done for thirty years. He moved quickly, but at an even pace, aware that any sign of tension, any wrong look, could trigger an attack from the gangs that were forming, fighting, fissuring and reforming through each night. In his pocket he carried his blade – enough to blind anyone who had the misfortune to try to take him on in close combat; but nothing was proof against bullets, as he knew better than most. And guns were now commonplace at night after ram-raids on gunsmiths'.

There had been no sign of Samuels at the clinic or in the computer records, which made his vendetta all the more mysterious. He didn't seem to be in the zone or have the disease. And Fernandez strongly doubted that his bitterness was caused by a love for the Mayans.

Across the road, he saw a couple holding hands. The woman

must have been in her early twenties and his heart lifted when
he looked at her. He had witnessed so much death and smelled
such foul stenches throughout the day at the hospital, to see
such beauty was a joy. Fernandez envied her partner, who held
her tight to him.

He heard a noise and looked up. A gang of about twenty
white boys, probably thirteen or fourteen years old, sauntered
towards him. They looked drunk and dangerous.

'What are we gonna do?' they chanted. 'Kill the crips, kill
the crips.' At each mention of the word 'kill' they punched the
air with their right hands. They were carrying baseball bats,
cricket stumps and, Fernandez noted with alarm, one of them,
tall and skinny, had a sword.

They walked straight at him and he edged off the pavement
and on to the road to avoid contact. As four of the boys stepped
into his path, Fernandez put his hand inside his pocket and
gripped the stubby handle of the knife. It felt comfortable and
calmed him; these boys had gone mad and had more drugs
inside their bodies than was in the local pharmacy. In fact, most
of their stash had been looted from the local pharmacy.

The leader of the boys shouted: 'Street fuck.' They descended
like a pack of wolves on the girl across the street, and she backed
against the wall, cursing and spitting at them. Her lover was on
the ground, being kicked in the face. The lad with the sword
stepped forward and, as he held it at the girl's throat, she
stopped screaming and began to whimper: 'Don't.' The boy,
with a mad, broken face, grinned and said: 'You'll like it, slag.
You all do.'

He pulled up her pink T-shirt and exposed her right breast.
The gang were shouting, 'Street fuck, street fuck,' 'Go for it
Gasser.' 'Give it to her up the shitter,' someone shouted, and
laughter erupted.

Fernandez emerged fast at the edge of the group. He did
everything at top speed, knowing that any uncertainty could
result in his death. But he was damned if this girl, who had

given him his one moment of joy in the day, would be ripped apart by these thugs. With one move, he grabbed the boy's hair, pulled up his head and cut a three-inch slice down his right cheek. Then he took the sword and held it to the lad's throat. 'Anyone want a piece?' he asked in a flat London accent he'd learned from British mercenaries. 'Anyone want a fucking piece?' He spat at them and pressed the blade into the flesh around the boy's Adam's apple.

The gang looked at each other and then at him, assessing, sensing, operating as the pack they had become. If one had challenged, the rest would have followed. But Fernandez knew he had the leader in his arms and the rest lacked someone to organise and make coherent their collective will. He half thought of cutting the boy's throat and making a run for it, but the risk was too high.

One of the boys commanded: 'Let Gasser go and we'll bugger off.'

'Gasser stays with me until you've gone. Then I'll free him. Tell them, Gasser. Time to go home.'

As Gasser nodded, Fernandez could feel the boy's tension, anger and humiliation. He sensed their disappointment in their leader's capitulation; but Fernandez admired him for it. The kid knew that he would have a strong chance of revenge – if not against Fernandez, then against some other poor bastard who would cross his path that night.

One of the boys broke the semicircle and turned back in the direction of the road. He was followed with a kind of loose discipline by the rest. A few shouted at Fernandez: 'We'll fucking kill you when we get you. We'll cut off your balls.'

They marched away and then were gone around the corner. Fernandez spoke quietly to the girl who was frozen against the wall. 'Go. Now. Before they come back.'

She looked at him, uncomprehending.

'What's your name?' asked Fernandez.

A second later, she answered in a voice that barely rose above a whisper. 'Sandra.'

'What do you do for a living, Sandra?'

'I'm a nursery-school teacher.'

Fernandez leant in until his face was visible to the boy he held and said: 'Hear that, Gasser? That slag is a nursery-school teacher. Do you remember nursery school? Remember how nice they were to you? Some milk, a biscuit, wiped your nose, sent you home to Mum with a smile on your face. And you were going to rape her. Make you feel good?'

Gasser was silent.

'I didn't hear your apology,' said Fernandez and tightened his grip on the boy's hair.

'Sorry,' croaked Gasser.

'Now get on your knees and kiss the ground at her feet.'

'Fuck off.'

'Listen, son, I've killed nicer men than you. I suggest you do what I say.'

By now, Sandra's boyfriend was on his feet and staggering over to them. He reached Sandra and folded her into his arms; Fernandez sensed that she was reluctant to be touched, and would remain so for a long time.

'Down.' Fernandez put his foot into the back of Gasser's knee joint. As the boy sank to the ground, he felt the steel of the sword on the back of his neck. 'You know how to kiss,' said Fernandez. 'You just purse your lips. Now do it.'

As Gasser put his face to Sandra's feet, she caught Fernandez by surprise by kicking the boy full in the face and gave her rescuer a triumphant grin. She raised a hand in thanks and he nodded at her; her eyes were deep and translucent and he wished he'd met her late at night in a bar in Soho when he was twenty years younger.

As Sandra and her boyfriend ran to the street corner and then on to home, Fernandez knelt down and said to Gasser: 'Civilisation is a thin veneer, boy. It's best that you try to stay inside it.' The boy craned up his head and spat at Fernandez.

'Let me give you a little lesson, son', said Fernandez as he brought the sword down on Gasser's thumb, severing it. 'When you go to war, you must be prepared to die.'

He stood and left the screaming boy writhing on the road. As he walked away, two old women who had come on to the balcony of their house to witness what was going on applauded him. He gave them a courteous bow.

A few minutes later when he arrived at the house, Ren was at the window, nodding. His face was half shaded by the light from the low lamp below the window. Fernandez's heart sank. He wanted to be on his own and he had to deal with this psychopath. Ren was obviously listening to some bloody rock music, Fernandez thought as he watched his colleague's mind-less nodding. Sure enough, when he entered the house, music hammered at him full blast. He sighed and entered the kitchen, where he took out the last dregs of a bottle of chilled Chablis. It had been a long time since he had had a drink, but he felt that he deserved it after a day among the death scenes at the clinic.

The wine sat sweetly on his lips and he thought of going to bed, but the racket of the music was too much to bear and he walked upstairs shouting: 'Ren. Will you stop that noise.' Fernandez walked into the room and stopped abruptly. He put the wine on the mantel-piece and calmed himself as he assessed the situation. Ren continued to nod at him, suspended on a noose hanging from a beam on the ceiling. His mouth gaped open and his eyes bulged. On the table, laid out neatly, were the bloody stubs of Ren's teeth; someone had clearly tortured him. The green rug below the body was stained with dried urine and faeces.

Although the stench in the room made Fernandez's stomach flip, he moved closer to the body to study the pattern of slash marks on the skin of Ren's thin, bony chest. Calmly, he drew the curtains and turned on the main light. The shape crystallised immediately – a crude approximation of Ah Puch looked back at him.

But Ren had not been in Belize. Whoever had killed him was looking for me, he reflected. As he looked at the bloodied pliers and the sliced body, Fernandez knew immediately who had done the deed. Samuels had boasted that when he was involved in covert CIA operations he had often used the extraction method on cocaine smugglers.

Fernandez turned off the light, walked to his bedroom and packed a bag with some clothes and his satellite phone. He tried to call Wu but there was no reply. Having found a litre of petrol in the shed at the back of the house, Fernandez returned and doused Ren's body. It swung gently back and forth. He set fire to a dish cloth, dangled it away from him, then flipped it on to the corpse. It caught immediately and Fernandez watched briefly from the door as Ah Puch's image began to blister and pop. He turned, walked downstairs and fled into the warm, noisy night.

CHAPTER FIFTY-TWO

Laura and Mike sat on a formerly elegant two-seat sofa on the roof of the clinic. They had dragged it up there from the old games room that now housed their children's ward. Their tape recorder was playing a sweet dreamy, Van Morrison tune about growing up. They sipped tequila in the companionable silence on which Laura had insisted until she asked: 'D'you remember that furlough on Lake Titicaca?'

He offered her a warm smile.

'When we both nearly made fools of ourselves?' she continued.

'We were very drunk,' he suggested as mitigation.

'Not that drunk to stop before it got out of hand,' she replied softly. She clasped her hands together and looked out at the flames consuming a church spire in the distance.

As Mike poured them both another shot, the conspiratorial silence that fell on them was tinged with guilt.

'How's it been since Anne died?'

'Bloody awful for the first six months. The twins pulled me

through. I needed to survive for them. And your help was crucial?' He held his palms towards his face and scrutinised them. They were steady. 'And then I lost my nerve big time. Couldn't touch a petri dish with a space suit on.' He started to laugh.

'What are you laughing at?' she asked anxiously.

Mike tried to stifle his giggles but his body heaved with convulsions.

'If you don't tell me what's so funny I'll pour this bottle of tequila over your head.'

'It's just,' he shook his head in wonderment, 'two weeks ago I needed therapy just to get me into the bloody office in the morning and now I'm living in the middle of a hot zone, up to my arms in blood that is more virulent than anything else on earth. And here I am drinking and listening to Van the Man.' He stood up as the Irish voice smoothed into another lyrical tune. 'Care to dance?' He offered his hands.

Laura looked up at him and replied: 'As I recall, you have two left feet.'

He pulled her up and in close to his chest; her body was tense and she felt stiff and unfamiliar in his arms. As they shuffled around in a gentle circle, she pulled her head away from his and looked into his eyes.

'Don't hurt me, Mike. Not after all this time. Not with what I feel for you. It would destroy me.' She dropped her face into the space between his shoulder and his neck.

Mike moved his hand up to cradle her hair. 'I won't hurt you,' he whispered. 'Ever.'

They danced on, impervious to the noise of rioting, unheeding of the fires burning, disregarding the deaths around them. They sought from each other some sense of security and unity, a bond that would hold them together when this was all over. They were fearful of the first kiss, scared of their memories and of the future promises that their lips would seal. Then he felt her mouth on his; softly at first and then urgent. He felt dizzy with tension as he slipped her hand into his. She clenched hard and he longed to forget where he was and what had happened in the past days.

She pushed him backwards on to the sofa, and still kissing him hard, pulled down her trousers and shucked them on to the tarmac. His penis was bulging against the front of his clothes and she sprung it free and erect. She sat on top of him, still silent, but looking at him with eyes that were full of love. Then she lowered herself slowly on to him. He almost came immediately, but forced himself to slow down as her groans reached him above the noise of the riot below. She moved ever more quickly until he could no longer stop himself. 'Come now, Mike,' she groaned. 'Now.' Her back arched, she bit her lower lip and let out a long hiss of satisfaction that echoed the release that he felt himself.

A few seconds later, she draped her body across his and kissed his chest.

Locked in that moment, they were not aware of the first Molotov cocktail until it struck the metal heating duct at the edge of the roof and spilled its fire towards them.

'Christ almighty.' Mike exploded with anger. 'Here they come again.'

A hail of bricks followed and windows began to shatter. 'Burn the crips, burn the crips,' the chants rumbled and roared.

Joe McCormick was on the roof a minute later with a fire extinguisher, quickly followed by Tess and Dek carrying buckets and fire blankets. Seconds later, another figure rushed past Mike and stood on the parapet that faced on to the road. Silhouetted against the fire, Victor Obudo raised his gun into the sky and fired three rapid bursts. A silence followed: a deep, confused, uncertain moment as the crowd below identified Victor as the gunman.

He bellowed: 'These people are under my protection. My personal protection.' He brandished his weapon and sent a crackle of bullets just above the heads of the gang that sent them running for cover. His grin turned quickly to fury as someone let fly with a rock and caught him a glancing blow on the arm. This was followed by a bullet that ricocheted off the wall beneath him. He dropped back from the ledge and took cover beside Mike.

'There are no leaders now, Victor. Only mobs,' said Mike.

Victor stood again and fired into the crowd. Mike heard a loud, piercing scream and then a torrent of curses.

'There are still warriors, man.' Victor's eyes were sparking.

'Stop it, Victor,' ordered Mike. 'You'll make it worse.'

'They're not getting my mum.'

'Well go downstairs and protect your mother. You're not doing any good here.'

Another Molotov cocktail smashed on the parapet and a loud cheer erupted. Mike looked out and saw the wave of people following two cars that were revving up to launch another attack. Christ, what are they going to do? They'll going to burn us to the ground.

The sound of the cars was drowned out by the thwucking of helicopters. There was a line of five snaking across the sky in single-file formation. At the edge of the cordon, the aircraft broke ranks and headed for different quarters of the zone. One came directly at them and hovered above the crowd, before dropping a large bag that burst open and spilled its contents into the gardens in front of the clinic.

'Joe, have you got the binoculars?' asked Mike urgently. When Joe handed them over, Mike walked to the edge of the roof and scrutinised the scene. 'Christ, they're not even giving me time,' hissed Mike. 'They're dropping rat toxins.' He saw a teenager smearing another with the foul-smelling cake in which bromethelin was encased. The boy would be very sick by morning, and he'd probably lose his eyesight.

The helicopters were equipped with water cannon, which they turned on the hostile crowd around the clinic, drenching them. The shock seemed to dispirit rather than incense the gang and they began to drift away.

By daybreak, Mike thought as he watched them go, the zone will be covered in dying dogs and cats and the rats will have retreated to the sewers and tunnels. He ran downstairs two at a time until he reached his office where he grabbed his mobile phone. The Downing Street switchboard operator told him that Lipsey was unavailable. Mike tried the personal number that the Prime Minister had given him as hot line to be used in emergencies. 'That line is no longer available,' an electronic voice recited. It had been disabled. Mike stared out of the window at the departing helicopter, and the scale of the betrayal raged in his heart. He dropped his head on to the table as a wave of exhaustion hit him.

'Mikey.' Mike looked up at the sound of Mac's voice. 'I've a present for you.'

'What?'

'A miracle.'

'What kind of miracle?' asked Mike.

'There's only one kind of miracle. The one in which you choose to believe. Otherwise it's dumb luck. Come and see.'

As Mike walked into the ward with Mac, Laura and Tess stood in wonderment around Jill Obudo's bed as she smiled back at them. Her brown eyes were warm and calm and she held on to Victor's hand as tightly as she could. Laura was holding a phial of blood drawn from Jill a few minutes before. 'We got ourselves a serum, sugar,' she said.

'You're joking.'

'Nope. This lady's antibodies have just stormed the gates of hell and,' she held up the blood, 'come back to tell the tale.'

'Hello, Dr Davenport,' said Jill sleepily. 'Thank you for saving me and looking after my boy.' Victor stared into the middle distance. Mike reflected that Jill would remember nothing of the past two days, but her son would forever carry the guilt of almost killing her.

'How are you feeling?' Mike touched her bandaged arm.

'Still a little sore. Just a little bit.'

'Mike, you'd better call the army and get Jill out of here,' said Mac. 'Her blood is our best defence.'

Mike took Laura to one side. 'Has she entered the prion phase of the disease?'

'I'm praying that she hasn't. She seems fine. No obvious signs of the second phase.'

'Why has she survived?'

'Who knows? And at the moment I don't care. We might be able to use the antibodies in her blood to treat those in phase one and the experimental drugs to treat those in phase two.'

'How much of her blood can we safely take?' asked Mike.

'Not much, she's in a pretty weak state.'

'Enough to treat one person,' said Mike. He turned to Mac and Tess. 'The canteen. Staff meeting.'

A few minutes later, the team sat on cheap plastic chairs or leaned against the wall. Despite the red eyes, sallow skin, moral and mental exhaustion, each had survived this far. Linda handed Mrs Peirce a cup of Earl Grey in a chipped mug, and Mike watched the older woman mouthing a silent thanks. Mac split a cigarette in half and shared it with Joe, who lit up the two butts, and both men drew smoke long and thankfully into their lungs. Tess had an arm around Liz and was whispering soothing words in her ear. Dek was drumming gently on the table and giggling conspiratorially with Laura. Jennifer Low sat quietly by herself. Mike knew she was stunned and disgusted by the behaviour of the government. A half-dozen others, who had joined them in their week there, clustered around as well.

'Jill Obudo has survived,' said Mike.

Silence. Then Jennifer asked: 'What do you mean?'

'I mean she's come through it. She's on the mend.'

'Yessss!' Dek punched the air.

'It seems that her immune system is the first to resist. We have Jill's plasma. Enough, perhaps, to treat one other person who contracts phase one of the Spirit Death.'

A small blip of hope spread round the room.

'We have a choice,' said Mike. 'A big choice. And not one I'm prepared to take alone. This has to be a democratic decision.' He surveyed them one by one. 'We cannot do this by majority vote either. It has to be unanimous. One dissenting voice will carry the day. Each of you deserves that.' A few faces began to look puzzled and a restless stir ran through the group. 'We can either give this to one of our patients now and hope that it works. Or', he spoke softly, 'we can hold on to it until one of us gets it.' Their attention was intensely fixed on him. 'I want to get Jill out of here and into a hospital Outside as soon as I can. And we can't take any more of her blood. So what we have is it, unless and until someone else recovers. There are two ways to do the vote: a secret ballot', he pointed to a dozen pens on the table, 'or with a show of hands. Does anyone have a preference?'

'A secret ballot,' replied Mac. 'Everyone is entitled to consult their conscience in private.'

The others nodded in agreement.

'Just to be clear, though,' said Daisy, shifting her weight in her chair, 'I believe that we should give it immediately to Lucille Hudson, who is carrying a baby. We have the chance of saving two lives.'

'D'you know the meaning of the word secret, you old bag, or would you like me to give you a dictionary?' Mac sounded stern, but the room by now knew the double act for what it was worth.

'Dark things hide in secret places.' She smiled at Mac. 'There, you know my vote. The rest of you get on with your furtive scribbling.'

Mike handed out the pens and paper and said: 'Write "keep" or "use" on the pieces of paper and put them on this fruit bowl.'

A minute later, the paper slips of fate filled the bowl. Mike picked up the first. 'Use.' Then the second. 'Use.' Third, fourth and fifth. 'Use.' Then Mike paused as he opened the sixth. Then with a heavy voice he said: 'Keep.' He laid it to one side, ignoring the sound of weeping coming from Liz. 'It's not me,' she cried, 'not me. I promise you, I voted to use it. I promise.'

Tess hugged her tight. 'Of course you did,' she said softly.

The next voted to use the serum, as did the next two; but the final two were marked 'keep': Mike looked at the two piles and stood up. 'The three people who voted "keep" are entitled to the use of this blood. They have shown by their courage in being here that they are dedicated and therefore their consciences are clear and they should not be judged.'

Daisy sped forward until she was next to Mike, then span round on her back wheels and landed with a thump. 'Bollocks,' she exclaimed. 'You may as well know.' She held up her hand and showed a large gash down the side of her thumb. 'I've got it. I sliced through my glove yesterday when I was doing an experiment. I've probably got more of the sodding thing in my bloodstream than I've got blood. I demand that those of you who voted "keep" retract. As the person with the disease I renounce my rights to the anti-serum.'

Mac said gently: 'It's not yours to give, love. The serum belongs to the group. And the group must decide.'

Daisy was shaking with anger and tears began to well in her eyes. 'I know what you're thinking. I'm a spinster cripple who is going to die in a few years anyway. That's why my word doesn't count. Let me tell you something: I love my life and I want to live as long as I can. But there is a chance of bringing a baby alive out of this charnel house. A new life. Please reconsider your votes. Please, Mike, let's have a second ballot.' She started to cry and Mac leant down to kiss her on the cheek.

'You're a mad old bastard, aren't you? C'mon, I'll take you for a walk. I've a wee stash of Bushmill's in my bag. We could both do with it. Let's leave the young people to settle this.' As he pushed her out, she was still sobbing. 'By the way,' he looked at Mike, 'I voted "use" as well.'

The rest of the group exchanged glances and looked to Mike for guidance.

'Let's try again, Mike,' said Joe. 'I want to change my vote to "use".' His face reddened and he coughed.

'Good man,' Dek said, 'righteous decision.'

They ran through the process again. When Mike found the only vote for keeping the serum, he cursed silently. He got to his feet and tapped his fingers gently on the table. 'Fuck it. I've changed my mind. Democracy wins by thirteen votes to one. Whoever voted "keep" can leave the clinic with my blessing. That'll make it unanimous.' He walked quickly to the door, issuing orders for Tess to hook up the blood whilst he talked to George Hudson.

Laura followed him out. 'What if I had been the one who voted "keep"?'

'I wouldn't want to marry you any more.'

'Who says I'd have you?'

Mike turned in full view of the rest of the gang and kissed her long and hard. She returned it with such ferocity that Mike was knocked back against the wall.

The others applauded. As Tess walked past them, she said: 'At last.'

CHAPTER FIFTY-THREE

As the first of the Spirit Death anti-serum flowed through the veins of Lucille Hudson and into her unborn child, men in black biosuits with air-filters and face-masks flitted around the buildings at the centre of the zone. The soldiers had been told that all the inhabitants left inside the cordon were dying or dead from the virus, and, trained for germ warfare, they were taking no chances.

Operation Pepys was known only to three people. Nothing was written down, no orders were officially given or received, the soldiers were not doing what they were doing. History would record only that gangs of hooligans had started a series of fires that raged uncontrolled through the streets of the zone, burning all who could not move. In the dark the men who did not officially exist worked hard piling inflammatory material and incendiary devices in a precisely defined, mathematically accurate circle, increasing the possibility of a contained fire-storm. By two in the morning they had retreated as quietly as they had come, leaving behind the conditions for the conflagration that Ellington and Graham had convinced the Prime Minister would ensure that Britain would be spared the disease. The storm was due to erupt at dawn.

Mike, sitting in the armchair beside George Hudson, kept nodding off. He was running out of juice. Tess asked: 'Shall I check on her?'

It was five hours since the serum had been administered. Mike nodded, wide awake now that the acid test was coming. Tess inserted the thermometer in the sleeping woman's rectum and waited. Beside him, Mike could hear George's laboured breathing. He had tried to keep him away from his wife; but there was no way that George would agree. He was showing no signs of the disease and it was always possible he would be lucky, so Mike had given in.

Tess looked at the gauge, pursed her lips, took out another thermometer and did it again. Mike was by her side as the indicator climbed into the fever zone. Then it stopped. Her temperature was down by five degrees. A tingle of excitement ran all the way down his legs; they might have a fightback on their hands.

'I think she's going to be OK, George,' he said. 'I honestly do. I feel it in my bones. Her temperature's back under control.'

George's rheumy eyes filled with tears. He bowed his head in a dignified thanks and then turned to look at his wife.

Mike rushed into the makeshift lab, with its skinned, dissected rats, its knives and blades, its autoclave and electron-microscope. He clapped his hands, danced Laura around the small room, desperate to kiss her but unable to do so because of the masks they both wore, then pushed a laughing Daisy out of the lab in her wheelchair. 'We've done it.' He pulled off his mask and took Daisy out into the open air. The gangs had gone and a silence had replaced them, punctuated only by the sound of helicopters and the distant rumble of music.

Laura and Mac came out to join them. Laura and Mike removed their masks and kissed before Mac elbowed his way between them and gave Mike a bear-hug.

'Well done, Mikey. Well done, boy.' He coughed and spluttered as his overenthusiasm got the better of him.

'Why don't you give up smoking, you fat fool?' asked Daisy.

'I'd rather die,' retorted Mac.

'Actually, I've never smoked,' she replied. 'D'you mind if I try one?'

Mac handed her a cigarette and said: 'Just the one, don't want it to be habit forming, do we now? Not when there's that lovely serum building up inside Mrs Hudson, all ready to pay you back for your generosity?'

Daisy wheeled herself to look up at the moon that shimmered at the corona. 'I don't know what you mean.'

'We can use her blood to produce serum for you, you old trout,' said Mac. 'We should hook you up now. The quicker you get it the better.'

'And why do you think I've got the disease?' she enquired. Mike, Laura and Mac stared at her. She lurched up the disabled-access slope and said: 'Some people need help to find the good in themselves, that's all.' As she went back into the clinic, the others spontaneously burst out laughing.

Mike's mobile phone interrupted them.

'This must be Lipsey,' he said. 'I'm glad at least he has the balls to call.'

'Mike, it's Jane.' Her voice was a hoarse whisper. 'Get out of there now.'

'What?'

'You must get out. They're going to do something dreadful. I don't know what it is. But I'm being asked to prepare a press release expressing their disgust at hooliganism inside the zone, and their sadness at so many deaths. You must leave.'

'I can't. We've got fifty patients and a serum that works. Tell them I have a recovered patient in here and I need to get her out. Tell them that Daisy and Laura are on the brink of developing a vaccine.'

'They won't listen to me, Mike. I'm just a mouthpiece.'

'Alert the media. Tell the world what's going on.'

'No one would believe me, darling.' Her voice caught a little. 'Not after the misinformation . . . lies . . . I've been feeding them for a week. Please go, Mike. You've got to be out by dawn.' She closed the connection. Mike explained to the others what was going on. 'I'm going to talk to Victor. He might be able to help.'

Victor was dozing by his mother – his head on the counterpane – when Mike and Mac nudged him awake, invited him into the corridor and asked him for the best vantage point to see Outside.

'Top of the flats.'

'Would you come with me?'

'I don't want to leave Mum.'

'If you don't help me, few of us will see tomorrow, including Jill.'

Victor looked at him, sizing him up. 'C'mon then. Tool up.' Mike's quizzical look was met with an exasperated sigh by Victor. 'A knife, man. You need proper equipment if you go out there.'

'Oh, you mean like this.' Mike pulled a razor-sharp autopsy knife that would slice skin as if it was air.

Victor smiled. 'Wicked. Does that have a friend?'

Mac wheezed and said: 'Let me come with you. I want to find out what's going on.'

'No way lardy is coming.' Victor shook his head. 'It's bad out there. We'll have to move quickly.'

'Look, laddie, I was facing down the Mau Mau when you were a wee piccaninny,' Mac growled.

'What's a piccaninny?' Victor asked Mike.

'You don't want to know. Sorry, Mac. There's plenty to do here.'

Mac shuffled, off growling that he was twice as fit as any young bastard and that he'd show them.

*

The streets beyond the clinic were empty. Here and there a sudden move showed that some people were still around. But Mike guessed that most of those who passed the test were Outside by now. A week was time enough to have completed the programme.

The flames from houses that been torched the previous day still smouldered and sent out flickering shadows of moving animals. The corpses of dozens of cats and dogs who had keeled over under the impact of the poison littered the streets. Rats and mice had eaten away at some of them, exposing brains and intestines. The rats themselves would by dying by their thousands in warm, dark holes, their urine drying and sending the virus out into the tunnels and drains. Mike prayed that people had not gone into hiding in the tube; they would be replacing one slow death with a more painful one if the poison reached them.

Mike was appalled to see the cadavers of two people who had died of the Sprit Death, simply lying out in the open. A small white child of four or five, abandoned by his parents, lay dead in the garden of an immaculate semi-detached house. His head rested in a neat flower bed of red gardenias that echoed the dark, almost black, blood that had dried around his mouth, eyes, nose and yellow Mickey Mouse T-shirt. His eyes stared up at the indifferent sky. In the street opposite an otherwise healthy-looking and fit woman in her forties was propped in a sitting position against a bus shelter. Between her legs was dried blood. Something had chewed off her right hand and she was decomposing rapidly, the sweet smell mingling with that of soot, fire and smog in a witches' brew.

The block of flats in which Victor had lived was wrecked. Broken chairs, sofas and tables were scattered across the front court, where they had been thrown from windows. Many colours of glass glinted like a shattered mosaic. Somewhere close by a dog howled a painful cry of impending death.

Inside the entrance to the block in a shaft of light, they saw a young Asian girl bent over on her hands on her knees, her small breasts exposed and her eyes staring at them. She could have been no more than thirteen. Behind her, a fat white man in his thirties was fucking her. On the ground in front of her was a bag filled with glue, and next to that an empty bottle of cider.

'Mr Everest,' shouted Victor. 'Jesus, what the fuck are you doing?'

The man shuddered as he came.

'That's the headmaster at the St Saviour's School,' Victor said to Mike. He stepped forward and swung the butt of his gun into Everest's face. Blood spurted from the man's nose as he fell and smashed the back of his head against the wall. 'No call for that man. You got to have some standards,' Victor said to the unconscious teacher. Then he picked up the grubby green shirt and put it around the girl's shoulders. 'C'mon, Daljit. Come with us. I'll look after you.' She took his hand and was led to the first flight of stairs. 'Her brother must be dead,' said Victor. 'No way he'd let her stay here to face that kind of shit. No way. He was righteous.'

A lot of righteous people have found that fear conquers all, thought Mike, but said nothing.

Ten minutes later they reached the roof. Mike produced a set of binoculars and scanned the moon-illuminated horizon. The army had demolished houses at the extremity of the outer cordon, crudely bulldozing them to create a wasteland. The aviary at London Zoo had been flattened and earthworks had been erected around the edges of the long, snaking wall. Soldiers were dumping white poison across the no-man's land that had been created. They would not allow a living creature across.

Then something else caught his eye: it looked as if practically the whole of the London Fire Brigade was lined up around the zone. Suddenly, he knew what they were going to do. 'There's not many ways to stop a disease in its tracks,' he said to Victor.

'One way is quarantine, which they've already tried. But keeping us closed in here will be useless if the virus jumps to the animals. They've tried dropping poison to deal with the rats, but they need nature's and mankind's final defence. Fire.' He waved his hand in the direction of the engines in the distance. 'They're going to burn the rats. The animals will head for the tunnels and sewers where they will be gassed or poisoned.'

'Fuck, man, what about us?' growled Victor.

'We are the "price they have to pay". I can just hear Ellington saying those very words.'

'What are we going to do?'

'Do you know anywhere safe?' asked Mike. 'Anywhere you have hidden out when you were a kid or where the gang hung out? We need to get underground.'

'What about the tube?'

'No, they'll gas it for the rats. We need somewhere sealed off.'

'I'll find something.'

'Quickly.' Mike ushered him away. 'Do it quickly.'

Mike took Daljit back to the clinic and administered a morning-after pill that he had scavenged from the family-planning clinic along the way. If they survived this, he did not want the kid suffering another calamity. He passed the girl over to Linda, who clucked over her, offered a chocolate biscuit and escorted the traumatised child to a quiet room on the top floor.

Mike summoned the rest of the group and told them the problem. There was a stunned, silent disbelief that their own government would do this to them. Eventually, Daisy said: 'They can't.'

'They will. It was inevitable,' responded Mac. 'It's an unfolding logic. Once they took the first step to set up the zone, they dehumanised the inhabitants. Now we're not people, we're a problem, a statistic. We've fallen inside the kind of political calculation that assesses the benefit of blowing up military facilities in Iraq and killing the surrounding citizens. It's a well-trodden path. So let's not be too surprised.'

'You sure Victor won't just do a runner?' interrupted Joe.

'He won't. I'm convinced of it.' Mike shook his head forcibly, then said: 'Mac's right. We've just been fed into an epidemiological model and been found to be disposable. But the one thing they can't calculate is how these statistics will behave. We've got hearts to resist and minds to find the means. They will not kill us. We must remain alive as witnesses, a reminder to the nation of what they were prepared to do.'

'Brave words, Mike,' replied Joe. 'But what exactly are we going to do?'

'Survive.'

'What are we going to do about the patients?' asked Tess.

'How many could take a journey? And how many will die tonight?' Mike was urgent in his questioning.

'We've fifty-five left,' said Liz O'Mara in a tiny, trance-like voice. 'I reckon twenty-two will die or would not able to travel. That leaves you with thirty-three.'

'How much transport can you rustle up?' Mike asked Joe.

'We don't have much petrol, so we can't travel more than a mile. But we've got three ambulances, the two minibuses, my estate and a couple of cars that were donated by people who went Outside. That should just about do it, if the walking wounded can sit up.'

'What about the rest of the patients?' asked Tess.

A silence descended on them.

'We only have two options. One is to leave them to burn to death. The second—' He paused and looked at the ground hesitantly. Then he raised his head. 'I've never believed in euthanasia but we can ease these people out painlessly. I cannot see that we have any moral alternative. Does anyone disagree?'

Mac shook his head. 'I can't do what you ask, Mikey. Life is life and it's not ours to take.'

'Your choice,' replied Mike gently. 'Everyone must follow their conscience.'

'Leave the dying ones here, Mikey,' replied Mac. 'I'll stay behind and look after them; it's over for me anyway. I'll tend them and we'll take our chances.'

'No.' Mike was adamant. 'You can do little for them now. And I will not let them die in an unnecessarily painful way.'

'It's murder, Mikey.'

'I used to think that, Father,' said Linda. 'But no more. I've seen enough pain now. I want some of these people to go as quietly as they can. There is no alternative.'

Mac's eyes surveyed the room, realising that he was outnumbered.

'Each do as you will,' Mike said. 'But let's move quickly. I want to be ready to move in half an hour.'

As the doctors and nurses quietly prepared to administer a painless death, Joe, Mac and George Hudson helped the dazed and sedated patients to the minibuses. Those who could not walk were carried on stretchers to the army bus that Mac had first driven into the zone what seemed like a year ago. Jill Obudo and Lucille Hudson were propped up in the back of Joe's estate. Dek, on Mike's instructions, filmed the evacuation on a digital camera.

When he had finished, he found Mike looking around the ward at the five people he had killed by his own hand. He had fought for them against the odds of nature but could not protect them from the overwhelming odds of man. He wept great sobs of painful hatred for himself for doing this and for the world for forcing him into it. Dek took his hand and they stood in silence for a few minutes, the din of helicopters racing overhead beating against their ears.

'There was nothing else you could do,' said Dek.

Mike walked into his study to pick up the rest of the disks that had documented life in the zone. The lights fizzled, then failed as the electricity was cut off. All essential services were now gone. In the moonlight, he searched beside his PC and found what he was looking for. As he turned to go, he stopped in shock. Someone was sitting on a hard-backed chair by the window, the moon casting a cold light across her ravaged face.

'What are you doing, Liz?' he asked. 'C'mon. It's time to go.' He tried not to stare at the needle pointed at her vein, or at the plunger ready to send the drugs that would end her life in minutes into her blood-stream.

'I don't want to return to the Outside. I've seen too much.'

Mike knelt on the floor beside her and looked up into her eyes. A prick of blood sat on the point of the needle. She had a hard, angry look, in contrast with the earlier fatalism. She clearly meant what she said. 'I wish I could join you,' he replied in a flat, straightforward tone. 'I asked you to come and join me and you, alone of all the doctors in King Henry's, made the toughest decision of your life. I brought you in here and I have not given you the support you deserve, for which I apologise from the bottom of my soul.'

She watched him warily. 'You thought I was pathetic,' she said. 'And I was.'

Mike shook his head. 'You were the bravest because you were the most terrified. Look at us, for God's sake, we're hardly the Magnificent Seven: Mac's nearly dead, Daisy too; Laura's a virus junky, as am I; Linda Wu's a religious maniac; Jennifer is in a personal hell; and Tess . . . well, Tess lost herself when Jack died.' He settled into a more comfortable position on the floor by her feet. 'You're the brave one. You're a normal doctor. And yet you had the guts to come.'

'I hate them.'

'Who? The government?' he asked.

'The crips.'

'Why?'

'They showed me how pathetic I am; how useless we are. I want to believe in something and I thought that medicine was it. Now what?' she asked. 'I've just killed five people. What do I have to believe in?'

The sound of cars revving up outside told Mike that Victor had returned with a hiding place, but he fixed his eyes clearly on Liz, willing her back. What could he offer? Compassion? Affection? Respect? 'You must want what I want,' he said.

'What?' she asked hesitantly.

'Revenge.' He showed her the disks. 'There's enough here to blow this stinking government sky high. I want to live to see that. Dig deep into yourself and tell me that you don't want to see those bastards on the Outside suffer.'

She closed her eyes, listening to her internal voice. Her finger momentarily tightened on the syringe, then she looked at Mike and smiled. He was fearful that it was a prelude to her suicide but, slowly, she lowered the needle.

'Revenge is a kind of wild justice,' he said.

The ragged convoy was ready and waiting on the street in front of the clinic. Mike surveyed the battered line of broken-down vehicles and their bust-up occupants and a smile played on his lips. Then his phone buzzed.

'Davenport? It's Ellington. I'm instructed by the PM to offer some of you a safe escort from the zone.'

'What about the patients we are treating?' asked Mike.

'That's impossible, and you know it. We've already paid an enormous political price to contain this disease. We haven't gone through that just so that you can reintroduce it to London. The offer is only to those of your team who do not have the virus.'

'Call me back in a minute,' said Mike, 'I want to talk to the guys.'

They crowded round.

'Well?' asked Joe.

'They're going to let us out,' replied Mike.

'Yeah,' said Dek and he and Victor smacked each other's hands.

'Provided we leave the patients behind.'

A cold anger fell over the group; Mike could see it in every eye.

'Anyone who wants to go can leave. Anyone?'

'Fuck 'em,' said Liz O'Mara. Everyone stared at her. 'And the horse they rode in on,' she continued.

'Righteous,' said Victor as a chorus of approval sang out around the group. 'Let's go.'

Mike turned off his phone and threw it high and looping into the clinic's garden, where it landed in the wreckage of a white Volvo. 'Let the bastards sweat out their betrayal. Let's move.'

'Don't you want to know where we're going first, John Wayne?' asked Mac. 'Before you say "Wagons Ho".'

Mike grinned, asked Victor where they were headed and then said to Mac: 'C'mon, fat man, Belsize Park station awaits us. Assuming, that is, that you can fit your bulk into a car.'

'Don't worry about me, son.'

It was four-thirty when they set off slowly through the burned-out landscape. They had an hour before the sun rose to make it down to the old Second World War air-raid shelter before all hell broke loose on the surface.

'How long can we last?' Mike asked Joe.

'We've enough water for about three days, which is a day and a half more than the food supplies. After this trip, there's no more petrol. And the painkillers will be gone by close of play tomorrow, so don't plan on having a headache.'

'They won't come in to clean up this place for two or three days, will they?' asked Mike.

'If that. They'll be controlling the fire round the perimeter. And then they'll make sure the pest-control boys have their time in the tunnels and sewers. They won't get to us for days. But what then?'

'We've got to save these people, Joe. I've got an offer Lipsey will not be able to refuse.'

'Suicide?'

'Don't be sarcastic. I get enough of that from Mac. No, we've got serum and a possible vaccine. Laura and Daisy are a long way down the track because they were using human beings rather than monkeys. They know exactly how the disease progresses, and with good facilities they could develop a DNA vaccine for it.' Mike peered into the gloom and then at the clock in the car. 'Half an hour to go.'

He closed his eyes in tiredness, an act that saved his eyesight when the windscreen caved in under the impact of a lump of masonry thrown from the roof of a house. As Mike jumped from the car six feral, wild-eyed teenagers, four girls and two boys, made a run towards them. The sight was made more bizarre by the fact that they were wearing the highest-quality suits and dresses and their looted shoes would have cost them a month's wages before the quarantine. Their elegance was in sharp contrast to the wild gunfire coming from them and spraying the minibuses.

Victor leapt from the vehicle containing his mother and screamed to the driver: 'Move on, move on.' He knelt and fired at the kids, who scattered in shock and then ran behind the hulk of a bus. Victor followed.

Mike said urgently: 'Go, Joe. Get out of here. I'll meet you up there.' He pointed up the five hundred yards to the tube station and the shelter. Then he extracted a scalpel from his bag and ran to join Victor.

'This isn't the place for you,' Victor hissed when Mike reached him. 'Go back. They need you.' Laura and George Hudson, who was carrying a machete, joined them.

'You'll need help,' said Mike.

Victor held his right arm up and they stood still. He looked around the edge of the bus. The kids had disappeared. 'Shit,' he muttered, and then he, too, slipped away. The air was still enough for a second to hear the wail of fire engines coming from Outside. Then the sound of gunfire was followed by a body tumbling in among them from the top of the bus. Mike looked up and saw Victor clambering across the roof; his face was grim. The kid on the ground was probably sixteen. Mike knelt to see if he could find a pulse but the boy was dead. Three bullets had penetrated his brain.

'I hate this,' said Mike. 'It's mad. We're killing people to save people.'

'No madder than any other war,' replied George Hudson. 'These kids want to kill us. We've no other choice but to defend ourselves.'

Victor ran around the bus. 'Got another one,' he grunted. He stumbled forward, a six-inch blade protruding from his side.

'Little fucker sliced me, Mike. Can you believe it? Cunt.'

Mike felt the wound. It was deep and blood was pumping from it. He pulled off his shirt and tried to staunch the flow but it was hopeless. The wound had penetrated through Victor's ribs and was causing traumatic internal bleeding. Victor shivered in Mike's arms and died a second later. Mike closed the teenager's eyes and cradled his head. A rush of sound over his head caught him off balance and he fell back from Victor's body. From above him a teenager girl with peroxide hair and bright red lipstick tumbled backwards with her belly ripped from side to side. George stood back in disgust at his own handiwork. 'Had to be done,' he said.

Mike saw that the girl had a long, jagged blade in her hand.

'She was just about to kill you. These kids must be taking every drug left in the zone.' He bent down to pick up Victor.

'What are you doing?' asked Laura.

'Taking the boy back to his mother.'

'Leave him,' she ordered. 'He's dead.'

'His mother saved Lucille's life. She deserves to see her son.' George tried to haul Victor's body on to his shoulders, but staggered under the weight.

Laura hit him on the face with the flat of her palm. 'How many more of those kids are out there?' she hissed. 'We've got no time to wait for you to carry the boy. Put him down, and let's get out of here,' said Laura. 'I've had enough of death; let's see if we can do something about life. Lucille needs you.'

George closed his eyes, knelt and slid Victor from his back, his shirt now covered in the teenager's blood. As the body slumped to the ground George touched his face and said: 'Thanks, son.'

The sun was beginning to rise as they jogged up Belsize Park Road. Not much time, thought Mike. A few minutes later a glorious, red, bloated orb framed the little group as they struggled to escape into the underground system. Tess was escorting Jill Obudo to the stairs when she saw the shirtless Mike and bloodied George. She controlled her fear in front of Mrs Obudo.

'Is my Victor, OK?' Jill asked Mike anxiously.

'You've got a great lad, there,' replied Mike, 'a real warrior. He's holding the line further down the road. He's found another hiding place and—'

Tears welled in Jill's eyes and Mike could tell immediately that she knew her son was dead. He averted his gaze as she nodded and descended into a crooning misery. 'Hurry,' he shouted to Dek and Joe. 'These bastards will be punctual.'

With an almighty roar, the Screen on the Hill cinema, an elegant building two hundred metres from the station, erupted as a series of incendiary bombs lit it up from the inside. The fire leapt from the roof and mingled with the morning rays of sunshine.

'The bastards are early,' exclaimed Joe. As they picked up the last patient, they heard explosions rumbling across the zone like thunder and they saw shoots of blue and red fire outshine the dawn.

'Avenge, O Lord, thy slaughtered saints,' prayed Mac.

'Amen to that,' said Mike. 'Come on, let's get out of here.'

CHAPTER FIFTY-FOUR

Fire began to roll over the tops of houses and down the elegant streets, sucking oxygen into itself, internalising energy and releasing it in huge explosive attacks on the next buildings. The sound of collapsing houses and factories was all pervasive. It drowned out the death cries of Spirit Death sufferers shaking in beds, spuming their lives on to sweat-encrusted sheets; it overwhelmed the howls of dogs and the scuttle of rats; it obliterated the ticking of clocks, the music from radios and the words from abandoned televisions.

The incendiary explosives were placed next to the newspaper shop inside King Henry's Hospital. As daylight seeped across the ragged carpet floor, it was met by three massive explosions that took out three storeys and then, floor by floor, the fire flowed through antenatal rooms and geriatric wards until it reached the corpses on the Spirit Death ward. Jack Lim's decaying body lay propped up in bed where Tess had been forced to leave it; his face melted in the heat and his flesh blistered until the white bones pushed through. In the rooms beyond the flames claimed the other victims of the disease; cleaning and purifying, destroying and purging.

The flat in which Jill and Victor Obudo had struggled to live was consumed in minutes. Jill's oak table that she had polished endlessly first warped, then twisted and became ash. House by house, room by room, memories were devoured. Photographs of families dissolved, medals won for bravery in world wars, for swimming in the Olympics or for the multiplicity of everyday achievements bent and burned as if their existence had no consequence.

The AIDS clinic in which Mike and the others had struggled hard to achieve salvation was transformed into a crematorium for the virus. The rats that had prowled among the dead burned as they ran for the exit. Those that escaped down into poisoned drains met a slower and more painful death.

Black, acrid smoke gathered in the street, merged and mingled, twisted into thick shapes. Above the zone, the smoke occupied the dry dawn sky, massing and dominating, propelled upwards by the fire-storm below.

Lipsey and Ellington watched on television as Operation Pepys delivered on its promise. By afternoon the cleansing would be complete.

CHAPTER FIFTY-FIVE

The smell on the stairs at Belsize Park station was of decomposing animals, and some humans, as Mike noted from the three corpses on the way down. They found the door that led away from the tube station and into the long-disused approach to the deep bomb shelter. Electricity ran from the station's own emergency generator that Joe had found and started. The low-wattage bulbs shed a watery yellow light. God knows how long the power will survive, thought Mike.

It took them twenty minutes of careful manoeuvring, trying to avoid bumping the patients on stretchers, calming those who had raging fears. The sound of Daisy cursing whoever was carrying her ricocheted up towards them, as well as her commands to look after her wheelchair. This was followed by Mac's boomed instructions that she should 'belt up before she wakes the dead'.

When they reached the bottom and pushed through the rusted door, they saw row on row of filthy metal bunks dating from the Second World War and held in readiness for the third.

It had fallen into disrepair in the mid-nineties, but was still serviceable. Musty air-shafts let in fresh air, or what passed for freshness forty metres underground. But at least they were secure whilst the fires raged above and the poison surged through the tunnels.

Tess organised the disposition of the patients whilst Liz checked everyone out. She took her time, holding people's hands, whispering in their ears, putting her face close to theirs and gently trying to soothe people who might die at any time. Jill Obudo and Lucille Hudson were given beds and surrounded with sheets to offer some basic protection.

Mike put a grimy sheet on the ground and found a bag for a pillow. He lay down gingerly, his body aching with a bone-weary tiredness. He'd been surviving on four hours' sleep a night for a week. Laura snuggled up next to him, curling her body close and resting her head on his arm. He wanted to tell her he loved her but before the words formed on his lips he was asleep.

'Mike.' It was Liz; her voice was tense but controlled. 'Lucille's in labour.'

'Mm,' said Mike sleepily. 'Get her to a ward and phone for a midwife.'

'Little bit difficult, that,' replied Liz.

The sound of a rat scuttling along the wall woke Mike with a start. Jesus, of course, he was dreaming of Outside. He hauled himself on to one elbow and heard the moans of the Spirit Death patients that echoed around the shelter like cries.

'What if it's like the last girl? What if the baby's got it?' Liz was anxious.

'What's Lucille's temperature?' asked Mike as he got to his feet and took a swig of water, letting it refresh his mouth.

'Thirty-eight-point-five.'

'Not disastrous.'

A scream filled the cavernous shelter and they ran to Lucille. She was on her feet, her legs splayed and her body in a half crouch. Beneath her was a pool of blood and amniotic fluid. George was holding on to her arms and she leant into him.

'You can do it,' Tess was saying. 'Remember the exercises. Help her, George.'

Tess said: 'I can feel the head.'

'I'm scared,' moaned Lucille.

'You'll be fine,' said Liz.

'How the fuck do you know?' groaned Lucille as another contraction hit her.

'Push,' instructed Tess. The baby's head crowned. 'Big push. He's coming.'

A minute later the baby was inched out until, with a rush, it was in Tess's arms. She quickly checked for haemorrhaging, but saw with relief that the boy was fine. He was not breathing, so Tess held him up, gave him an old-fashioned smack on the bottom and was rewarded with a lusty yell. She hadn't realised she was crying until that moment.

Liz helped Lucille as the placenta plopped on to the ground. Then she and Tess laid the mother back on to a cushion composed of blankets and a clean sheet and put the baby on her belly. Laura asked Lucille if she could take a sample of the baby's blood, but Lucille turned her head away and began to shiver with cold and shock. George held out his son's arm and Laura took the sample to be tested for phase-one Spirit Death antibodies. It seemed as if each of them was investing their whole self in the health of the baby. Everyone moved quietly, trying to tend the dying whilst hoping for the new life.

Mike held Laura's hand as they watched the test results. Then they returned to the parents. Lucille seemed unable to touch her child, while George stroked her hair and whispered that he loved her and that the baby was beautiful.

Laura knelt down to look in Lucille's eyes. 'He's clear. You've got a healthy baby boy.'

A whoop went up from Dek, followed by a rumble of cheers from those patients who were conscious. Liz smiled for a second then pulled Mike away. 'Frances Robertson is about to crash,' she said. 'I've prepared a separate area as far from the baby as possible.'

Two hours later Mike looked at his watch. It was morning again. They had been in the shelter for twenty-four hours. It was time to go. He gathered the team together in the middle of the room, knowing that this would be the last time they would be together. There was a ripe smell from each unwashed body; all the men were unshaven and everyone's hair was matted. He could tell a few were dispirited and had retreated inside themselves, depression clogging their minds like flu. Some sat cross-legged, others stood and tapped their feet, a few lay flat and looked into the gloom of the tunnel. The electricity had failed an hour before.

'OK. It's over,' he said gently. 'We've come a long way and I've got to get us out of here. We've run out of testing kit; we used the last of it on the baby, and none of us know whether we've got the disease. And we can't take any serum from Lucille. So here is my suggestion: Laura and I go up top and make a run for Outside. I'll contact the Prime Minister and negotiate a way out for us.'

'What if he says no?' asked Joe. 'He's cut us down so far. What if he captures you and leaves us here to rot?'

'That's why Laura is coming. She knows, at least theoretically, how a vaccine may be made. It might take months or years but, at the moment, the details are in her head and nowhere else. They need us.' He looked at each of them in turn. 'Anyone who wants to come is welcome. I reckon it will be pretty inhospitable up there and that people still need you here. What do you think?'

Mac shuffled to Mike and pulled him close. 'Good luck to you, Mikey. Spit in Lipsey's eye for me.' He hauled himself over to Lucille, where he sat clucking at the baby that his parents had named Victor.

Daisy wheeled herself towards Laura and took her hand.

'Have you remembered everything I told you?'

'Yes, Mother.'

Dek gave a surprised Mike a lascivious kiss on the lips. Everyone around them grinned and Dek said: 'I've always wanted to do that, loosen up those heterosexual stays.'

One by one, they said their goodbyes until only Joe and Jennifer remained. 'I want to come with you,' said Joe. 'I feel useless down here, nothing more than a spare pair of hands. Besides, I'm dying for a cigar.'

Mike nodded.

Jennifer said: 'I'm coming out too. It's time the world knew what Alan Lipsey has condemned these people to. And a former member of his cabinet is the best person to tell them.'

The group of four set off down the long, crepuscular shelter, passing the shaking and grunting patients for whom any salvation would be too late, but knowing that they were also leaving twenty people who could be nursed back to health if they got out in time.

When they reached the end of the corridor they heard a curious, high-pitched noise outside. The smell hit them first as they slowly cracked opened the door: it was a mixture of poisonous gas and dead rats. Mike signalled them to put on their masks and use what was left of their meagre independent oxygen supply. He had expected something like this.

He stepped out into the landing, his feet landed on something soft that moved. Not stopping to think, he took two steps forward and waited for the others to join him before pulling the door firmly closed. When his eyes adjusted to the dark, he saw the carnage around him. The stairs were thick with rodent bodies, their eyes gleaming red and many with their tails tied together as, in their panic, they had become inseparably entwined. Although the noise was drowned out by the rush of oxygen in their helmets, Mike could almost feel the sonic vibrations as hundreds of rats squealed a lament.

He signalled Joe, Laura and Jennifer forward, kicking

animals from the stairs and making slow progress to street level. In their madness some of the rats leapt for him, scratching and biting at his clothes. His stomach heaved with fear. When he turned to check on the others he saw that Joe had fallen and was surrounded by rats, some biting at his air-hose. Christ, if he loses that and sucks in the urine-filled air, he'll have the new strain of the virus, thought Mike as he rushed to help, almost toppling over himself in his haste. Dozens of rats were leaping across Joe. Mike and Laura swiped first at the ones around his face before hauling him to his feet. As Joe screamed inside his helmet, Mike quickly checked him over. The suit was shredded. They must get upstairs quickly.

Minutes later, they were in the station, hauling back the gates and stepping out into what used to be Belsize Park. They ripped off the masks and breathed in the acrid morning air.

The sight staggered Mike. It was like pictures from the Blitz. No, he thought, not the Blitz: it was like Dresden after the fire-storm caused by the Allied bombing. Whoever had planned this had done it brilliantly.

The cinema across the road was a burning stump of a building, and a row of white stucco houses that once changed hands for millions of pounds was a smouldering ruin.

'Some insurance claim,' noted Joe.

Laura ran her hand through her tangled hair and looked staggered.

Jennifer hugged her arms around her body. 'You can see all the way to Primrose Hill,' she said as her eye traced across the cracked, jagged wreckage of the street to the world of London beyond.

'Not much left of King Henry's.' Mike pointed at the wreckage of the hospital. 'But Outside looks fine.' In the middle distance they could see the Telecom Tower and beyond that Centre-Point on Oxford Street. A long army helicopter rose above the horizon and headed towards them.

'So what's the plan?' asked Joe.

'There's no way we'll be able to cross open ground,' said Mike. 'We'd be spotted a mile off. So there's only one way to go.' He nodded at the door from which they had just exited. 'Back the way we came.'

'Uh.' Joe shook his head. 'No, no. You are not getting me back in there.'

'What are you,' asked Mike, 'a man or a mouse?'

'I could grow to hate you, Davenport,' said Joe.

'By the end of today, you'll have to join the queue. Is your suit OK?' Joe checked and nodded. Mike span round, plugged himself back into the oxygen and headed down the stairs into the tube system that led to Euston station and Outside.

When they reached the tracks, Mike went to the southbound platform and closed his eyes when he saw the makeshift cardboard homes under which a dozen people, probably crips, had tried to hide from the terror they were facing above ground. They were white faced, and flecks of foam had dried on their mouths as they died from the poison that had been pumped through the tunnels. He jumped down on to the line and began to stride towards the other world at the end of the tunnel.

As expected, there were more horrors every step of the way. The tube was an open sewer of death. Mike grew angrier and more determined but then suddenly noticed that something was wrong: the hissing in his mask had stopped and he looked down at his gauge: he'd run out of air. Was the poison entirely gone or diluted sufficiently to allow him to breathe? He knew it had been a risk to come this way; but if he'd gone along the top, they'd have been spotted before they reached Belsize Park Road. The helicopters were only one part of a huge surveillance operation in the zone.

He signalled Laura across to him and checked her supply. She had another twenty minutes left. Mike had made sure that she had the fullest tank. She pinched the air supply to hear what he was saying.

'I'm going to take off my mask. I think I'll be OK, but if

anything happens to me, you must get out of here and make sure the vaccine is made. They'd be fools to think that the Spirit Death is going to disappear. It jumped once and it'll do it again. Just like Ebola.'

He recoiled with disgust at the intensity of the smell when he slipped off his helmet and replaced it with a simple bio-mask from his pocket. It had protected him from Spirit Death thus far, and he hoped that it would cope with whatever poisons were in the tunnel.

They edged forward once more and reached the light of Camden Town station. The colourful posters advertising holidays in Greece – 'A BIT OF HEAVEN' – and underwear – 'SAY HI! GUYS' – mocked them, as did the young family of four huddled in death below the chocolate machine, which was smashed and empty. The remains of a chocolate bar was in the hands of the youngest girl, who looked as if she had been seven or eight.

As they passed through the station and on down the line, they entered the most dangerous zone. Mike saw the scorched corpses of animals, including foxes, that the army had burned – presumably with flame-throwers – at Mornington Crescent, the station that was the front line between the zone and Outside.

Mike heard voices ahead and stopped. The group flattened their backs against the curved tunnel wall, ignoring the bodies piled up around them. A powerful light shone across them as someone swung a torch around among the corpses. Mike moved forward cautiously, the others following him in single file. As they rounded a bend, they could see inside the station. Soldiers were milling around, drinking tea from plastic containers; some were laughing. A radio banged out a song from the charts and the man closest to them was clapping his hands in time to the tune. Mike silently indicated that they were to go under the train that was parked in the station. He went first, grateful that the last carriage protruded a little into the tunnel. Crawling on his belly across the burned skins of the rats, he swung himself underneath the chassis, carefully keeping away from the live rail.

Laura began a slow crab-crawl towards him. Through the gap between the train and the platform, Mike could see the boots of the soldiers sauntering around above. Don't look down, he prayed. Don't look back. Laura reached him and waited while Joe followed them. The song on the radio ended and Mike heard a rustle of activity and then a commanding voice asking what the fucking hell everyone thought they were up to. 'Is this a tea party? Get down there and check for fucking rats and crips.'

Feet rattled on to the train above Mike's head and suddenly a light flooded the tunnel, illuminating Joe. His shadow filled the wall before he dropped to his knees and fired Victor's gun at the lamp, which smashed and plunged the tunnel back into blackness.

'Fucking hell. What the fuck was that?' shouted the commanding voice.

Jennifer was with Mike and Laura a second later, followed by Joe, who was breathing heavily. As the soldiers cautiously made their way into the tunnel, shining torches to where the bullet had come from, Mike and the others were slowly crawling on their bellies to the front of the train. Mike emerged first, stood gingerly and, seeing nothing in front of him, signalled for the others to join him. As they clung to the wall – creeping away into the cover of darkness – they were caught in the train's headlights that had been turned on by the driver as he prepared to drive to Euston. For a second, he could not believe his eyes: four people in spacesuits. Then he shouted: 'Look out! Crips.'

'Stop,' shouted one of the soldiers. 'Immediately.'

Joe let loose a volley to cover them, and they ran with bullets following them down into the darkness, ricocheting deafeningly from walls and sleepers.

'Christ, we'll never make it,' said Joe as he watched the soldiers jumping down into the mouth of the tunnel.

The commanding officer gave an order: 'Into the train. We'll catch them at the other end. Now.'

A clatter of boots was followed by the whining sound of the train firing up its engine.

'Fuck,' whispered Mike.

The group flattened themselves into shallow crevasses in the tunnel walls. As the engine hurtled past them, its light blinding, Mike could feel the wind from the speeding carriages as it threatened to suck him under the wheels. His heart was pounding, and when he looked across at his companions, pressed against the wall, fear was etched deep into their eyes. The train whistled past and they could hear the brakes squeal as it stopped at Euston station. Half a dozen torches pierced the gloom as soldiers ran back along the tracks and sought them out. Mike looked up and saw a maintenance shaft that ran above the tunnel and probably all the way to the next station.

'I'm going to talk to them,' said Jennifer, taking off her mask, 'help them to see sense.'

'No. They'll kill you.' Mike held on to her.

'I'm a cabinet minister, Mike. They won't harm me. Let me negotiate with them. I'm from Liverpool. I could sell sand to the Arabs.' She shook him off and walked down the tunnel, her long hair waving behind her. 'Listen to me,' she shouted. 'I'm Jennifer Low. I need to talk to Alan Lipsey urgently. Please will you take me to him?'

'I'm the Prince of Fucking Wales,' a voice responded, 'just back off and wait for an ambulance to pick you up.'

'I'm not ill,' she persisted and continued to walk towards them.

'Everyone left in the zone's a crip and our orders are to shoot anyone who tries to escape. Now, I'm being kind to you. Go back.'

'I'm coming through and you will give me a phone and establish a link with the Prime Minister.'

'Stop, now,' shouted the soldier.

Mike could see that her back was straight and she walked with confidence, then her body jerked back in mid-air as the first bullet hit; followed by a second that took off half her skull.

'Bastards,' shouted Joe and opened fire.

They heard a thud and saw a soldier spin and tumble away as Joe's bullets caught him. Joe then retreated back up the tunnel as the rest of the squad opened fire. Mike grabbed Laura and scuttled up the metal ladder to the maintenance balcony.

Joe continued to fire, but this time the response came from behind him; he was in a crouch in the middle of the track, firing left and right, buying the others time. Laura tugged at Mike's suit and began to crawl along the walkway.

Then all was quiet. They turned and watched the soldiers slowly converging on Joe's body. Then keeping as quiet as they possibly could, they reached the roof of the train. Suddenly, a commotion broke out down the tunnel and he saw Joe making a run for it. All the soldiers were chasing him and it was safe to drop down from the walkway. They slipped down a ladder to the ground, then scaled the platform and entered the first carriage of the train. A shout behind them told Mike that they had been seen, and they began to run through the train, followed by four soldiers who had run up from the tunnel. They were running as fast as they could, a carriage ahead of their pursuers. All the doors closed, and they were stuck. They turned and in shock and frustration realised that it was almost over. The soldiers were on them, guns pointed their throats.

Mike pulled something quickly from his trouser pocket. It was a phial of blood. His arm was trembling with exhaustion and anger. 'Stop,' he screamed. 'Just stop.'

The soldiers looked at one another, clearly confused. What was he holding? Mike held the glass tube up like a grenade.

'This blood is filled with the virus. Any of you make a move towards us and you get it in the face. You'll be dead by nighttime.'

The man with the commanding voice turned out to be a sergeant. He entered the carriage and grinned at Mike. 'What do you think this is, pal,' he said in a broad Glaswegian accent,

'Indiana Jones? Just put it down before we shoot you.'

'Like you killed all the others,' said Laura.

'I don't know what you mean, miss. Nor do I know where you came from. I've my orders not to allow anyone through from these tunnels and it's my duty to carry out those orders to the best of my ability.'

'I need to see the Prime Minister,' said Mike. 'Please take me.'

'It's a long journey to the Isle of Man. So why don't you just give me the blood and we'll see what we can do?'

The sergeant walked arrogantly towards him, protected by the battery of guns. Mike hated him with everything that was in his body, soul and spirit. He flicked the top off the phial and threw the contents in the man's face. Immediately it began to sting the Sergeant's eyes and he started to scream, fell back against one of the seats and from there collapsed to his knees.

Mike opened another small flask of blood and shouted: 'He's dying now. He's got the virus. If you stay here, it'll spread to you in minutes. We don't give a fuck, because we've got it already.' He raised the glass in the air and threw it to the ground, where it exploded among the men, splashing their uniforms. They ran through the open doorway and into the station.

'That was a good trick,' said Laura as they ran for the exit staircase to the far end of the platform. 'How did you manage instant virus attack?'

'I had a feeling that the old blood trick wouldn't work, so I mixed in some acid and red dye.'

'Sometimes I worry that our kids are going to inherit your weirdness,' she said as they took the stairs two at a time and found themselves in an empty Euston station. It was a mess of food wrappers, newspapers, bags and cases that seemed to have been abandoned in a rush. He saw the headline in *Time* – 'London, The New Plague'. No wonder Euston was a ghost station.

The date on the announcement board was that of two days before. Christ knew what was happening in the rest of the city. Mike felt in the pouch at the side of his suit and produced a phone card, found a phone booth and dialled the Center for Disease Control in Atlanta.

He got a ringing tone and then a beautifully modulated Georgian voice asked if she could help him. Mike dropped the phone in amazement. It worked. He'd come up from hell and found that the phones were working.

'Get a move on,' urged Laura.

Mike asked for the Head of the Center, an old acquaintance of his called Frank Denton.

'Jesus, Mike. What's going on over there?' asked Denton, after a perfunctory introduction.

'I need to get Laura out of Britain and into safe hands. She knows how to develop the vaccine; but she needs a lot of help. I don't trust anyone in this country. Will you get on to the US Embassy and send a car. We'll wait outside the Institute of Education. It's just behind Gower Street.'

'There's only a skeleton staff in the US Embassy, but I'll do what I can.'

'Oh yeah . . . I need some temporary sanctuary as well. Can you arrange that?'

'You kidding?'

'Yeah,' said Mike, 'I suppose I am.'

They walked hand in hand out of Euston. It was a glorious day, a slight wind was gusting and rain clouds were beginning to pile up in the sky for the first time in six weeks. Mike had forgotten what rain felt like and was surprised when the first fat drop fell on his face. A few minutes later they were standing behind a concrete pillar in the Institute as the clouds released a flood of rain across the empty, parched city. They held hands and let the rain batter them, wiping away grime and sweat, and then pulled off their spacesuits and allowed the water to penetrate through their shorts and T-shirts. Streams ran down the sides of their faces, into their eyes, on to their bare feet. The drew it into themselves like a lover.

An American Embassy Cadillac pulled up and, cautiously, from behind the pillar, Mike and Laura studied it. Someone finally emerged after two minutes and scanned the area. He had a large golf umbrella from St Andrews. Putting it down, he got back in the car and waited.

'Let's go,' said Mike to Laura. They skirted around the vehicle, approaching it quickly, and Laura jumped in the back. Mike was about to join her when, mirrored in the window, he saw an army personnel carrier on the other corner. It edged forward and Mike screamed to Laura: 'Run.' But it was too late: the doors locked and the tyres screamed as the car sped off. Mike watched helplessly as Laura beat the driver on the face, then ran after it, but bullets whipped across the street in front of him. He veered away and doubled back towards the Institute in a low, stumbling run. The APC's doors opened and six soldiers jumped down and took off after him.

At the rear of the concrete building, Mike saw an abandoned mountain bike, jumped on and set off into Goodge Street. He looked back and saw two police cars speeding after him. The rain battered his face until he could not see. He skidded round a corner and on towards Tottenham Court Road. The police cars skidded to a stop, and the soldiers who were yomping towards him yelled: 'Stop. Immediately.' Yeah, right, thought Mike. Stop and we'll shoot. Fuck you.

When he reached Tottenham Court Road, the police had almost caught up with him, but he crossed the road and headed over a scrubby little park that led down to Charlotte Street. As he turned the corner, an unmarked Rover took up the chase, clipping his back wheel and sending him hurtling towards the plate-glass window of a television station. Mike skidded to a halt, span away as a bullet took out the glass and spilled shards over him, and pedalled furiously for Soho until the car came alongside and shot the front tyre out from under him. He tumbled forward and lay on the ground as the Rover's door opened. A tall, cadaverous man in a baggy brown suit stepped out and held a gun to Mike's head.

'I wouldn't if I were you,' said Mike, pushing the barrel away. 'You never know where I've been.'

The rain mingled with the blood from Mike's nose and dripped on to the ground, where it was quickly sluiced into the gutter. Like tiny, spiralling islands, it disappeared down a drain.

A police van pulled up. 'In.' The man signalled, the back-door opened and Mike was pushed inside. When he took a seat, a grille separating the front from the rear was pulled back. 'Nice to see you again, Davenport,' said Ellington before turning and managing a small, grave smile.

Mike put his head against the cool metal of the van and two policemen in masks got in on either side him.

Mike entertained himself by singing 'Piggies' from the Beatles' *White Album* very loudly:

> 'In their eyes there's something lacking,
> What they need's a damn good thwacking.
> Dum, dum, dum.'

He banged on the floor with his feet in time to the music, oblivious to the stares from the two policemen. The van stopped and he was hustled into a police station in Soho and down into a mirror-walled interview room. A doctor in a spacesuit entered and took a blood sample. Mike presumed that they wanted to ensure that he was clean before they did anything.

He looked at the mirror and said to the people he knew were behind it: 'Any chance of a pizza? Pepperoni if you've got it. Oh, and an ice-cold diet Coke would be to die for.'

Half an hour later, one of the policemen entered. He was in an ordinary uniform. Mike did not show his relief that he was negative for Spirit Death antibodies. He wouldn't give the bastards the satisfaction. Grounds, the name on the policeman's badge, put down a gooey-looking microwaved four seasons pizza and a warm can of Lilt.

'Pizza Express shut then?' asked Mike. Grounds turned and left in silence. Mike put the horrible mess into his mouth and chewed, enjoying the small pleasures afforded by the moment. Ellington entered with two plain-clothes men. They sat behind the table on which Mike had perched his food.

'Delicious, this. After seven days of living on cup-a-soups and Pot Noodles.'

'What do you want, Davenport?'

'Where's Laura?'

Ellington leant back and pursed his lips.

'Don't bother with good cop, bad cop.' Mike bit down again into the pizza, scooping melted cheese into his mouth with his fingers. He swallowed. 'I've seen the movie. Laura knows about the vaccine and I stashed the serum before you picked me up. Oh, and it should be said, I have recordings of every conversation that Lipsey and you have had with me. Furthermore, I filmed everything that happened in the zone.'

Ellington opened a pack of cigarettes, slipped one out with elegant fingers, and put it between his lips.

'I didn't know you smoked, Ellington.'

'You know . . . what with this and that . . . the odd cigarette', he waved it in the air, 'doesn't seem so much of a problem. And you know how much I like to solve problems. And you, my dear Davenport, are a problem. What are we to do with you?'

Mike shook the can of Lilt a little and opened it in the direction of the policeman who had put the gun to his head. The liquid splattered over his chain-store suit. Mike smiled at his own childishness. But he felt secure; they needed him. 'I have a very small price,' he said. 'My team are still treating maybe twenty people. Given that we now have a serum that we can use, and a possible vaccine, I want to bring them out and look after them somewhere properly: a decent hospital.'

'And if we don't?'

'The disks are in an envelope inside a post box. Tomorrow they will be on their way to the BBC, ITN, CNN, SKY News . . . Oh, and I thought, that the French would like a copy, along with Iraq and Iran. I wonder how the Foreign Secretary's moral foreign policy stance would look if the world knew that we slaughtered our own citizens?'

Ellington stood, walked around the table, pushed the pizza to the floor with a disdainful shove and put his hand on Mike's shoulder. 'See, the thing is, Davenport, we've already issued your obituary. It was prepared lovingly and tearfully by the delightful Jane. She is a pretty girl. I don't know why you threw her back in the pond. Still, one man's loss is another man's et cetera, et cetera.'

Poor Jane, thought Mike.

'So no one is expecting the second coming, which I see you intend in your new Christ-like state of purified grace.'

'Purified by fire, as you might say,' responded Mike. 'I want to talk to the organ grinder. So, if you wouldn't mind.'

Ellington shook his head. 'The PM knows nothing of this.'

'Right.' Mike stretched the word. 'Just get on with it, Ellington; you wouldn't take a piss without Lipsey holding your dick. You will not contain Spirit Death. It's out there and will come back. You need a vaccine and Laura and I know how to produce it.'

Ellington signalled to the two men behind the desk. They took off their coats and the one Mike sprayed with Lilt smashed him across the face. The other kicked him in the guts.

'Stop it, now,' ordered a voice. Lipsey walked in and said to the two men: 'I'll deal with this.' Lipsey lifted Mike to his feet.

Mike's nose-bleed had opened up again and he was spreading blood around as if his nostrils were a soda fountain. Lipsey handed him a tissue and Mike held the white paper to his nose.

'I'll accept your proposal, Mike. On one condition.'

'What's that?'

'That you do a press conference with me supporting the government's position and saying that we did everything in our power to help. You do that and you can have your hospital, and I'll arrange transport out.' He turned to Ellington. 'Where are Mike's people?'

'In an old bomb shelter in Belsize Park. The ground's a bit unstable around there, I think. Could be a cave in.'

'Shut up, Ellington,' said Lipsey. 'I asked for geography, not a threat. In fact, why don't you go and set up the media for me? You are so good at that.'

Ellington stared at him. 'If that's what you wish, Prime Minister. Assuming, that is, that Dr Davenport wishes to appear.'

Mike looked from one to the other, his stomach churning with hatred, and nodded his acceptance.

'Good man,' said Lipsey. 'I knew you were rational. We did do everything in the public interest, you know. Now,' he clapped Mike on the shoulder, 'you get yourself cleaned up. I'll send a nice clean suit and tie down and I'll see you in Downing Street in an hour.'

'I want Laura there.'

'Of course, you must have her. She's a very strong-willed girl and would be nowhere else but at your side.'

'And I want evidence that my people are free before I speak.'

'Easily done, Mike,' said Lipsey. 'Arrange it, Ellington.'

'Oh, and I want a mobile that works. I want to tell my kids that I've survived.'

Lipsey looked at him and handed over his own. 'Tell them I'm very proud of their father,' he said.

An hour later, Mike had showered and was standing in the Prime Minister's cosy private study on the first floor of Number Ten. A small mahogany desk, a round table, with chairs for half a dozen, an espresso coffee machine and a bust of John Stuart Mill gave the room an almost suburban normalcy. The only items that stood out were the large late Matisse depicting a primitive rite of spring and the flat, wide-screen television set on the wall on which Mike was watching helicopter pictures of Tess and the others emerging one by one from the tube station. Laura held his hand and bit lightly on her lip as they counted them all through.

'Look!' Mike pointed at a limping figure and a grin split from one ear to the other. 'There's Joe. How the hell did he manage that?'

'And there's Dek,' said Laura, with relief.

Jane entered and told them that the media were gathered. She met Mike's eye with a steady gaze as if to say, 'I was only doing my job.'

'Ready?' Lipsey pointed to the garden, where a scrum of reporters and cameras was ready to record and scribble.

The Prime Minister stood up and spoke for ten minutes about the heroism of Mike and his staff; and of the impossible choices imposed on the government by the dreadful disease; of how Mike had always had their absolute support; and of how they had supplied him as best they could.

As he spoke, the vans containing the survivors pulled up at a major teaching hospital in West London. The drivers were surprised to see news trucks waiting for them. They had been told that this was a private journey. When they halted at the security gates, the rear doors of the vans burst open and Tess, Liz, Mac, Linda and Dek emerged to tell their story.

At the press conference, the Chief Political Correspondent from the BBC held a DVD player and said: 'Prime Minister, are these your words?' As Lipsey's conversation with Mike, telling him that he was prepared to kill hundreds of people, floated on the afternoon breeze, Mike turned to Laura and whispered: 'Dek made one last copy. I told him to get it to the media somehow. I guess he succeeded.'

Laura held his hand and leant in to kiss him. 'You are a bitter and twisted bastard, Davenport.'

'Somebody has to be,' he replied.

CHAPTER FIFTY-SIX

'A satisfactory diversion, Mr Fernandez, wouldn't you say?' Li and Fernandez sat in Li's office and watched Alan Lipsey at the press conference in London as the Prime Minister initiated an immediate investigation into 'whichever misguided person launched these unprovoked attacks on the people of London'.

'I can't believe that anyone now will care about the disappearance of a handful of Mayans. Or, with our friends in the Belizean armed forces being so effective in covering our position, that anyone will find out anything. And if they do, they'll put it down to some unfortunate quirk of nature.'

Fernandez sat straight-backed in the chair, with his hands folded in his lap. His journey through the zone had been unnerving, even for a seasoned veteran like himself. He had seen sights worse even than the dirty war against the communists in the seventies. After his escape, he had left the country on a diplomatic flight via the Chinese Embassy. It was one of the perks of the Company's links with the Chinese People's Liberation Army.

'The Company is reviving its operations in Belize. We have now been granted an extensive licence, provided first we exterminate the forest rat that caused the little glitch of nature in the first place.' Li sipped a cup of herbal tea from a delicate Meissen cup with a blue glaze, and, for the first time in weeks, allowed himself to relax.

'What about Samuels?' asked Fernandez.

'He must be dead, surely? If he was in the quarantine zone.'

'I escaped . . .' Fernandez walked to the edge of window and looked out over the harbour. 'And what if he's loose in New York somewhere?'

Li approached him and touched his back. 'Mr Fernandez, are you are losing your grip on reality? How could he have been in London and New York at the same time?'

Fernandez pursed his lips and brushed away Li's hand.

'Now,' said Li, 'I have an assignment for you in Hong Kong. Why don't you go home and pack?'

Fernandez walked into Li's private elevator that would take him down to the street; he was feeling light-headed, but put it down to jet lag and the events of the past two weeks. A sneeze began to tickle his throat and mucus began to spill from his nose. God, he thought, not a cold after all this. As he stepped from the elevator into the dark cavern of the car park, there was a sudden rush of noise and someone was holding him by the throat in a vice-like grip. His neck was about to be snapped. 'Samuels? Let me explain,' he croaked, then said and thought nothing more as he sank lifeless to the ground.

Wu Shuo stepped back and signalled to two Company security men to dispose of the body. It was a shame about Fernandez. He'd liked the man but he had brought shame on the Company. Wu Shuo nodded in satisfaction at a job almost complete. He had dispatched Ren with great pain as the man had deserved, but Wu was pleased that Fernandez was allowed to die quickly.

Later that night, Li and Sarah arrived at their home in the

Hamptons. It was an imposing mansion with Gothic pretensions, built as a wedding present for a Guggenheim in the forties. Li could meditate best there.

'My darling,' he said, as he sat in a loose white suit in his glass conservatory, 'will you wash my feet for me? You do it so well.'

He watched Sarah return, her own feet bare, and her elegant hands holding a black water basin. She washed him, and then with large, white towels, patted him dry. He thanked her and asked to be left alone. Taking off his shirt, he assumed the lotus position and began to focus in his mind's eye on the unfolding of a white rose from its outer petal to its inner core. As he reached deep into himself, he felt someone grab his arm, before another person plunged a needle into his vein. Looking up in shock, he saw two men wearing spacesuits. The one who was carrying a hypodermic syringe was Wu. Then he passed out.

The two assailants waited for a few seconds, then walked from the room, closed the door and sealed it with strong tape. Once that was done, the smaller of the two turned off her oxygen and removed her mask. She flicked a switch and inside the room white metal grilles descended over the windows and sealed in Li as the Spirit Death virus coursed through his veins.

Sarah Li shook her hair free and Wu offered her a bow. 'The Company is grateful for your support,' he said, pleased that he had managed to eliminate all those who had brought shame on the Company and the PLA by their mishandling of the Belize fiasco, including Sarah's own treacherous brother who had threatened the Chinese government with blackmail. Sarah had hated her sibling for his weakness and for his role in convincing her father to sell her into slavery with Li. But she had always been afraid of him and his rages. Now she was free: of Li's hatred, of her brother's venal uselessness, of her own fear.

She returned Wu's gesture, went to the bedroom, stripped off her suit and put it into a rough canvas bag that was to be collected and disposed of. Then she showered, stepped into a navy-blue Christian Dior dress, and called down for her bags to be collected by the chauffeur.

Sitting in the back of the car as it turned out of the gate, she looked back at the conservatory and savoured the long, slow, agonising death of her husband.

CHAPTER FIFTY-SEVEN

Alan Lipsey shifted uncomfortably on the low-slung green sofa and offered up his face to the make-up woman. The bags under his eyes were marked and puffy. He was finding it difficult to sleep, and was resorting to pills that made him feel hungover in the morning. Still, he reflected, whatever gets you through the night.

A thick-set woman with highlighted auburn hair, thin, disapproving lips, and cautious brown eyes sat opposite him on a large chair. Periodically she tugged at the hem of her skirt, as if unconsciously she knew that it was too short. Alan had known Mary Hartley twenty years previously, when she'd been a bloody good investigative journalist, but the last ten years she had been plying her trade on daytime TV, and now was the star of *Mary Live!*, a phenomenally popular show. The format, a 'caring' zoo show, had distressed individuals pouring their hearts out to psychiatrists and counsellors with the studio audience voting on what treatment they should receive (at the TV company's expense for the first thousand pounds).

Lipsey had heard rumours that Mary was hitting the bottle heavily, depressed at her lack of prime-time success and the younger aspirants to her throne coming up on cable stations. She had pleaded with Alan to come on the show to discuss the Spirit Death crisis. Jane Hume, whom he had appointed as his new personal press officer after her success in burying Ellington, had talked him into it. Lipsey was worried that it was tacky, but Jane had explained that it was safest place to 'unburden his emotional baggage'. He had to steer clear of the piranhas in news and current affairs. Lipsey's brief from Jane was that he was a man like any other, who suffered like any other, and that the public no longer wanted supermen running the country. They needed to understand, forgive and applaud Lipsey for his bravery and courage in defending the country from the Spirit Death. She said: 'Don't be afraid to cry Alan. If you feel like it, that is. Don't fake anything.'

Lipsey watched himself on the monitor. He had not cried since his father died forty years ago. He grimaced a little as he saw his picture. He had aged ten years in the past four months. He wasn't eating enough, he realised – his face was too thin and starchy. Perhaps a week in the sun would do him a power of good. He had been invited by the US President to Camp David for a week's R & R. Not before time.

Mary took the cigarette from between her lips. She was the only person allowed to smoke on set. Thick lipstick clung to the butt and he watched, queasily, as she picked a piece of tobacco from her tongue. She listened to something in her ear-piece and nodded thoughtfully and then glanced down at the notes on her pad.

Lipsey was not worried about Mary. She was notorious for her patsy questions and Jane had vetted everything in advance. He worked through in his mind the permutations of answers and the modulations of his voice. He had to be very careful to express exactly the emotion he felt at the thought of so many deaths in Camden and his disgust and total abhorrence at the

revelation that the army, on Ellington's orders, had torched
Camden. Ellington's suicide the previous week was still
rippling through political circles and Jane was firefighting the
ridiculous notion that Lipsey had driven Ellington to it.
Ellington was mad – it was as simple as that. Couldn't cope
with being frozen out of power. Typical bloody theatricals,
though, blowing his fucking brains out in front of the statue of
Churchill in Parliament Square.

The floor-man cued in the music and Lipsey quickly sat up
and looked smart, relaxed but quietly passionate. The short,
romantic theme music faded and the studio audience applauded
as Mary walked towards them and up a flight of stairs. She held
on to the hand of a teenage girl with short-cropped black hair
and big eyes that were filled with excitement at being on TV.
The girl had been in the zone for the first few days.

'Today. In a very, very, special *Mary Live!*, we are privileged
to have the Prime Minister, Alan Lipsey, with us to talk us
about the very human pressures of the recent problems in
Camden. Please welcome – Alan Lipsey!'

The audience applauded and Mary trotted down the stairs
and across to sit on the chair opposite Lipsey.

'Prime Minister,' she began.

'Please, call me Alan.'

She smiled as if he had offered a privilege unknown since
Christ offered Peter the keys to the kingdom of God.

'Alan, tell us what it felt like to . . .' She seemed lost for
words. Where's she going? Lipsey wondered. This was not what
they agreed. '– to have suffered so much these past few months.'

Lipsey relaxed. He put his hands together as if in prayer and
then briefly touched his forefingers to his lips. 'My suffering is
completely insignificant compared to those who died so
tragically as a result of this terrible, terrible plague. It is those
people I feel for.'

'I understand that Alan. I know how you feel for people.' Her
voice was low and throaty; the product of cigarettes and a

thousand hours of TV trauma. 'But what I would like to know is how it felt for you throughout this crisis. What were *you* feeling?'

'It was the worst experience of my life.' Lipsey noticed a slight trembling in his hand. The image of a boy hovered in his mind. The child was lying in the street beside his mother; her body was shaking as the disease claimed her. The boy was weeping. Lipsey had seen the pictures from a helicopter camera. He had to steel himself to reject his instinct that he should send in a snatch unit to bring the boy out.

It was the image of the boy's wretched face that he saw each night before he went to bed. Lipsey's face looked wretched to the watching nation, ragged and drawn. He was a soul in struggle. He paused and after a fraction of a second, his eyes filled with water. The director was screaming at the cameraman to get in close. The room was still, electrified by the sight of the PM's emotion.

'There was a priest during the black plague,' he said. 'He ran a small parish in an isolated community in Yorkshire when the plague broke out. He persuaded everyone in the village to stay and wait it out. Many of them died. Women, children. But no one left. They sacrificed themselves for the greater good. That's what I felt like during our plague.'

He swept his eyes across the audience – they had their arms collectively wrapped around him, caring for him. Loving him for his emotion and his strength.

Mary smiled sweetly. 'The difference, of course, Alan, was that you were not in Camden. You were outside.'

Where was she coming from? Lipsey thought. She slipped that one in.

'Yes. Well, I desperately wanted to go in. But it was, you know—' he gestured, 'impossible.'

'But not impossible to send in Dr Mike Davenport. Nor to desert him and the patients he was attending.'

He felt a trickle of sweat on his back. 'As is well known, I did everything in my power to give every form of aid and assistance to Dr Davenport. He has acknowledged that in public.'

'Only under duress. I have a personal statement from Dr Davenport if you would like to look at the monitor.'

Davenport's face was relaxed but serious as he denounced Lipsey in a two-minute statement to camera.

At the end, after a pause loaded with tension, Mary turned to Lipsey and asked:

'Do you have an answer, Prime Minister, to these allegations?'

Bitch. She's trying to build her career off the back of this. Lipsey cursed his own weakness for needing to come on the programme to explain himself. Why did he listen to Jane?

'As I said earlier, Mary.' He kept his voice easy. 'I was faced with an impossible set of choices. I could not allow the plague into the rest of London. I had to make the kind of trade-offs that you would have made in my situation. I had to protect the majority of people in London and the rest of the country.' He thought for a second, then said, 'My conscience is clear.' He immediately regretted the words.

Mary stood and walked to the audience. 'I know you are a remarkable man, Prime Minister. Able to compartmentalise. I'm impressed that with so many deaths laid at your door your conscience is, as you say, clear. Let's go to the studio audience.'

She bent down next to a black woman. Her face stared sternly at Lipsey.

Mary took her hand and looked into the camera; her face filled with humanity and warmth — she called it her Every-woman look. 'This is Lucille Hudson. She escaped from Camden with Dr Davenport. She almost lost her child. Why don't you tell us about it Lucille?'

Lipsey caught a glimpse of the clock high on the studio wall. Another twenty minutes to go. Shit, shit, shit. He smiled back at Lucille and prepared his reply. He was in for the fight of his life.

CHAPTER FIFTY-EIGHT

Tess hugged her legs to her chest and looked out from the porch of the holiday home at the sight of Molly and Jo walking on either side of Laura. All three were spattered with mud from their walk along the rain-soaked coast. The late morning air was fresh on her skin and a light wind washed her face. She could smell the chicken that Mike was preparing for lunch and was nursing a glass of Chablis. Mike's eyes were closed and he was leaning against a post. 'Jo seems much happier,' said Tess.

'Apparently she met a boy down from London who shares her new-found interest in poetry,' replied Mike lazily. He opened his eyes and saw Molly jump on to Laura's back and both of them collapse into the mud. Jo was roaring her laughter at the sight of them caked head to foot, until Molly reached up and dragged her sister into the mire.

A drizzle of rain pattered against the roof of the porch and sparkled in the surrounding sunshine. 'Anne would've approved of Laura, Mike,' said Tess.

'I think I'd better run a hot bath.' Mike's voice drifted

lazily in the air as his fiancée and daughters hurtled full tilt towards the house. He could hear their laughter as he walked upstairs.

EPILOGUE

In a dingy basement room in the Bronx, a rat gnawed at the face of a man who had been dead for three weeks. The room stank of his blood, his faeces, his urine and his intestines. The walls were stained, as was the floor. Beside the bed on which lay the corpse was a photograph of two friends standing at a bar in Buenos Aires; their arms were linked and each had a smile for the other. These had been happier days for Paul Samuels and Louis Fernandez. The days before the Spirit Death. The rat's eyes sparkled in the dark as it ran for fresh meat.

EPILOGUE

Exclusive extract from the new novel by David Docherty

THE KILLING JAR

Published in Autumn 2001
by Simon & Schuster

CHAPTER ONE

As screams filled the midnight air, Harry Yeats sprinted to the dam wall and peered into the reservoir below. Pulling out his binoculars he focused on a black, seal-like creature floating among the reeds. It flipped over and moonlight illuminated a pale human face, gaping windpipe, and terrified eyes.

'Jesus Christ.'

Douglas, his Border collie, began barking fiercely as an outboard motor roared down by the river. Cursing softly, Harry dropped to the ground and scrambled around in his green rucksack. 'Where is it?' He tipped up the bag and a clatter of lenses and cameras fell onto the walkway. Finally, he found the gun. Jumping on top of the two-metre-wide wall, he steadied himself then released the flare. It exploded above the Doon, flooding it with light.

From a small boat, a figure dressed in black threw something high into the air. As it tumbled and swirled, Harry snapped half a dozen flash shots. The orange glow was fading as he ran to the round security turret at the far right of the Doon

Platinum Dam. It was squat and forbidding.

He shouted at the top of his voice. 'Turn on the searchlight!'

A long, startled face appeared at the door.

'What's going on?' Eric Gilchrist, Head of Security for the Doon complex, grabbed Harry's arm. The dog snarled and Eric took a step back.

'Douglas.' The collie was immediately controlled by Harry's voice. 'Dead guy in the water, Eric.' He raced up the external stairs to the turreted roof, Eric and three other bulky, uniformed men trailing in his wake.

'There. Down there.' Harry pointed and one of the men swung the beam in the direction of his arm, picking out the body as it swayed in the waves.

Harry trained the zoom of his Olympus C-3060 Pro on the figure.

'Trying to make a bit of money on the side?' The security guard's broad North County accent was filled with sarcasm. 'A few shots for the *Sun*?'

Harry ignored him and focused on the dead face. 'Christ Almighty,' he whispered. 'It's Sally Carter.'

'The teacher from The Ark?' Eric peered through binoculars. 'Why was she diving here at this time of night?'

'C'mon. Let's get down.' As Harry led the way, an explosion reverberated around the hills.

CHAPTER TWO

Harry yawned as he drove out of the main entrance of the Doon complex. It had been a long night filled with interrogation and activity. He and the local police knew one another well, initially from the ten years he had spent photographing and studying the wildlife around the Doon River, then with more friction through the four years Harry had been one of the co-ordinators of DREAD – Doon Residents against the Dam. Since the dam opened three years before, the mutual suspicion between Harry and the officers had softened, but DI Frommer, the first detective on the scene, was still suspicious of his reason for being on the dam.

Harry had to explain in great detail that he had permission from the dam's security force to take photographs of a family of wild mink for a newspaper piece. Eventually, they woke a very grumpy picture editor at two in the morning to confirm the story. Then Frommer had demanded the memory stick on which Harry had recorded the digital pictures. At their request, Harry had used a PC at the mine to download and analyse images which revealed that the item thrown into the river had been a sword. At dawn, police divers went in search of the murder weapon, but they stood little chance in the fast-flowing Doon.

He stopped at the top of the hill and looked back at the Platinum Mine and its dam. The scene laid out below him reminded him of a Bosch painting: gouged caterpillar tracks, gigantic eight-wheeled trucks moving God knows what to God knows where, hundreds of yellow- and red-hatted workers scurrying around restlessly, then heading down into the five-mile-long mother-lode of platinum. In the bright sunshine, the dam was grey-black, colossal, fat with rock-fill and earth and filled with water containing tailings – the thick poisonous slurry of crushed rock and chemicals left over from the mining process.

To the right of the complex lay the remains of an old slate mine, a mile-wide and hundred-metres-deep crater that looked like a moonscape. Its buildings were derelict and old tools rusted in the ground. McLean International Mining, the owners of the Doon set-up, had exhausted the slate after fifty years of exploitation.

Leaving behind the noise and dust of the hundred-acre complex of administration blocks, canteens, car parks and Visitor Centre, he headed down a steep, twisting road that had recently been widened at the expense of hedgerows on either side and into the mining town of Doonside.

A few years before the discovery of platinum, the main street had been the preserve of three thrift shops, a general store that sold everything in small amounts, a cut-price pawnbroker, a tiny independent bookmakers which seemed permanently filled with small men smoking cheap cigarettes, and a pub with bricked-up windows. One by one each gave way to renovation by major chains (the pub and the bookies), or were bought and transformed. The Co-op became an up-market Indian restaurant, and the thrift shops were turned into a mobile phone centre and Internet café, an electronic goods store and a bistro. But each of these enterprises were dwarfed by the new shopping centre Harry passed on the outskirts of the town.

Alongside this was a new estate designed to house 600 families attracted into the area by the success of the mine. Fred Cunningham, the farmer who sold the land, had retired to Florida on the proceeds. Harry did not grudge Fred his good fortune; the poor old bugger had scraped a living from unforgiving ground for half a century. The sheep industry had gone the way of slate and he was on his last legs when McLean International turned up with a large cheque and guaranteed planning permission.

It was with relief that half a mile out of Doonside, Harry turned off the dual carriageway onto a narrow, single-track road that led into the 90,000 acres of forest, rivers, wildlife and scattered farming communities of the Doon Nature Reserve. This valley had been his home for three years as a full-time wildlife photographer and before that he and his family had spent every holiday walking and riding in the district. His house was a mill cottage near the Doon River estuary. The dam, which sat at the side of the 200-hundred-metre-high valley just outside the Reserve, could be glimpsed from Harry's bedroom.

As he bowled along, loving the way the brilliant sunlight illuminated the yellow gorse, the primroses and the beech trees that bent over the road to form canopies through which shadows floated on wild flowers, he turned on the local radio station and listened to a phone-in.

'How could anyone complain about a mine here? North County has had mining for five hundred years. These protesters are daft. There are thousands of jobs at stake.' The female voice was local and complaining about the annual demonstration that commemorated the opening of the dam.

'You simply don't understand.' This voice certainly wasn't North County. Posh, south-east, Harry thought. 'This mine is unnecessary. It takes ten tons of rock to extract an ounce of platinum and the chemicals left behind will poison the water for generations. And it's incredibly dangerous.'

'This was a North County decision for North County people. We had a – watchamacallit? – referendum in all the parish councils and we supported the dam. This is our land.' The woman's voice was filled with angry desperation.

'This was a capitalist decision for short-sighted people,' retorted the protester.

'Thanks for that grrrreat deebate,'growled the DJ. 'And now for Ike and Tina and that "River Deep and Mountain High".'

**SIMON &
SCHUSTER**

DEVIANT WAYS

Chris Mooney

A master killer calling himself the Sandman is out for
revenge in the USA. He's slaughtering not just one
person but whole families and complete neighbour-
hoods, unleashing devastating explosions nationwide,
and watching the horror unfold on a sophisticated
network of surveillance cameras. No one knows why
he is committing his crimes.

But Jack Casey – ex-FBI profiler and now cop in a posh
Boston suburb – knows this: the Sandman wants him
in the middle of the case, and wants him to suffer . . .
even more than when a psychopath's unspeakable
crime shattered his own life. Jack's lover knows
nothing of this shocking past, but the Sandman has
found him and his cutting-edge electronic devices are
silently monitoring Jack's every move.

Possible motivations for the Sandman's crimes come
gradually to light, and Jack begins to wonder if the evil
he is fighting emanated from his own side of the law . . .

ISBN 0 7432 9230
PRICE £10.00

POCKET
B O O K S

DEVIL'S CODE

John Sandford

'I'm into something a little weird here. I don't want to
worry you, but if anything unusual should happen, get
in touch with Kidd, okay?'

When the writer of this letter dies suddenly, allegedly
burglarising a software company, his sister turns to
Kidd – artist, cuomputer whiz and professional
criminal – to find out what really happened.

Before long, Kidd and his sometime partner/lover,
LuEllen, are up to their necks in trouble . . . the sort of
trouble that leads to flowers on a grave. Computer
hackers, scientists and crooked businessmen all play
their parts as Kidd gets ever closer to discovering the
truth behind his friend's death.

ISBN 0 7434 15574
PRICE £5.99

POCKET
B O O K S

THE GIRLS HE ADORED

Jonathan Nasaw

The man in the prison cells calls himself Max. He
admits to killing the cop who found him sitting in a car
beside the still-warm body of a disembowelled young
woman, but he claims to be suffering from DID, the
multiple-personality disorder that is a common alibi
for the worst criminals. Assigned to assess the truth of
Max's defence is strawberry blonde psychiatrist Irene
Cogan. When Max masterminds his bloody escape
from prison and kidnaps Irene – he agrees to undergo a
course of therapy, during which Irene is introduced to
a succession of his alters – his alternative personalities.
To her alarm, it seems that one of them has a distinctly
unhealthy penchant for strawberry blondes.

And it looks like it will be up to FBI Special Agent E. L.
Pender, who has been on Max's trail for over a decade,
to find them before Irene discovers exactly what that
penchant entails . . .

ISBN 0 7432 09710
PRICE £10.00

POCKET
BOOKS

TRUE JUSTICE

Robert K. Tanenbaum

The nightmare begins with the discovery of a newborn
baby, apparently murdered and then casually
discarded with the city's refuse. Butch Karp, chief
assistant DA for New York County, is ordered to
prosecute the baby's fifteen-year old Hispanic mother
by his boss, listening to public outcry.

Meanwhile, Butch's wife, Marlene Ciampi, has
returned to practising law after spending time as a
private investigator. Her first case, in a small Delaware
town, is to defend the middle class teenage mother of
another dead baby, found in a motel dumpster. The
girl claims it was stillborn, but the infant's father is
singing a different tune, under pressure from an
ambitious DA.

On different sides of an incendiary national debate,
Butch and Marlene suddenly find their own teenage
daughter, Lucy, at the centre of a horrifying crime . . .

ISBN 0 7434 0393 2
PRICE £5.99

POCKET
B O O K S

This book and other **Pocket** titles are available from your book shop or can be ordered direct from the publisher.

☐ 0 7437 1557 4   **The Devil's Code**   *John Sandford*   £5.99

☐ 0 7432 0971 0   **The Girls He Adored**   *Jonathan Nasaw*   £10.00

☐ 07434 0393 2   **True Justice**   *Robert K. Tanenbaum*   £5.99

☐ 0 7432 0923 0   **Deviant Ways**   *Chris Mooney*   £10.00

Please send cheque or postal order for the value of the book, free postage and packing within the UK; OVERSEAS Including Republic of Ireland £1 per book.
OR: Please debit this amount from my:

VISA/ACCESS/MASTERCARD ....
CARD NO...
EXPIRY DATE...
AMOUNT £...
NAME..
ADDRESS...
....
SIGNATURE..

Send orders to:
SIMON & SCHUSTER CASH SALES
PO Box 29, Douglas, Isle of Man, IM99 1BQ
Tel: 01624 836000, Fax 01624 670923
http://www.bookpost.co.uk or
e-mail: bookshop@enterprise.net for details
Please allow 28 days for delivery.
Prices and availability subject to change without notice.